I SAW
THE
SKY
CATCH
FIRE

Also by T. Obinkaram Echewa

THE LAND'S LORD

THE CRIPPLED DANCER

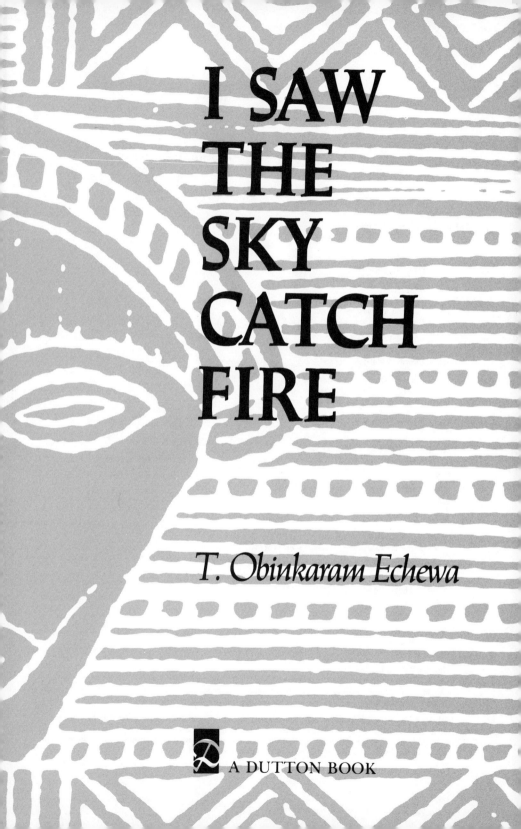

I SAW
THE
SKY
CATCH
FIRE

T. Obinkaram Echewa

A DUTTON BOOK

DUTTON
Published by the Penguin Group
Penguin Books USA Inc., 375 Hudson Street,
New York, New York 10014, U.S.A.
Penguin Books Ltd, 27 Wrights Lane,
London W8 5TZ, England
Penguin Books Australia Ltd, Ringwood,
Victoria, Australia
Penguin Books Canada Ltd, 10 Alcorn Avenue,
Toronto, Ontario, Canada M4V 3B2
Penguin Books (N.Z.) Ltd, 182–190 Wairau Road,
Auckland 10, New Zealand

Penguin Books Ltd, Registered Offices:
Harmondsworth, Middlesex, England

First published by Dutton, an imprint of New American Library,
a division of Penguin Books USA Inc.
Distributed in Canada by McClelland & Stewart Inc.

First Printing, January, 1992
10 9 8 7 6 5 4 3 2 1

 REGISTERED TRADEMARK—MARCA REGISTRADA

LIBRARY OF CONGRESS CATALOGING IN PUBLICATION DATA:

Echewa, T. Obinkaram.
    I saw the sky catch fire / T. Obinkaram Echewa.
        p.   cm.
    ISBN 0-525-93398-0
    1. Women—Nigeria—History—Fiction. I. Title.
PR9387.9.E27I2   1992
823—dc20   91-20294
                                                      CIP

Printed in the United States of America
Set in Garamond #3
Designed by Leonard Telesca

PUBLISHER'S NOTE
This is a work of fiction. Names, characters, places, and incidents either are the product of the author's imagination or are used fictitiously, and any resemblance to actual persons, living or dead, events, or locales is entirely coincidental.

—To my grandmothers:
Otolahu Nwamkpa and
Nwanyi-Enwegh-Nluma Olenga

—To my mother:
Ojiugo Ejama-Nma

—To my daughters:
Chinyere Ojiugo and
Olenga W'Amara
With affection

Contents

PART
ONE

1

Women's Wars

NNE-NNE WAS IN A STATE THAT night before I left home. *Amuma-Muo*, it sounded like, but the feast of Ngwu, the spirit that possesses people in our area, was long past, and besides I had never known Nne-nne to be possessed before. Was she drunk? I weighed that possibility but discarded it. My send-off had featured a lot of drink, and throughout the day she had imbibed steadily—tossing shot glasses of *eti-eti* into her throat, tilting her head back like a drinking hen, shutting her eyes fiercely, and making horrible faces as the sharp vapors of the gin wafted into her nostrils—or had clicked my grandfather's carved horn with every guest who stretched out a tumbler or drinking gourd toward her, and had obliged everyone who invited her to toss a joint libation to the spirit of one ancestor or another.

Land, have a drink!

Ancestors, have a drink!

Ikputu nwanyi, have a handshake!

Noble woman, in whose cap God has put an eagle feather, give me your five!

Ndichie, here's a libation to you before I drink mine! By the time the last of our guests departed, Nne-nne's eyes were a palm-nut red, and her voice barely an audible rasp. But, in the end, I concluded that she was not drunk.

As my send-off began to wind down, and some of the guests began to say their farewells, I had imagined that Nne-nne and I were going to have a tender parting conversation, since I would be leaving early the next morning for Agalaba Uzo, from where I would proceed to Lagos and the United States, after a few days with Stella and W'Or-ima. However, what actually took place was a strange monologue, half recited and half sung, as if Nne-nne had a recording device inside her or had recently learned ventriloquy. And while I was splayed across a chair, too tired to think deeply but too intrigued to fall asleep, she sat tireless on a low kitchen stool. Her legs were thrust out straight in front of her, left leg on top of right leg, toes wiggling like large, dark worms, hands thrust into the folds of her wrapper between her thighs, back straight, head high, head scarf askance like a jaunty cap. While her face played out a dissolving repertoire of emotions ranging from gaiety to somberness, words and stories tumbled out of her mouth in quick and nimble parade. As was her habit, she had lowered the lamp's wick to conserve kerosene, and the light around us was a hazy brown. Beyond the room through the open door, a thick darkness was being rinsed by a slow rain.

The excitement I felt at being about to go overseas was displaced from the center of my consciousness by the concern I felt for Nne-nne. I could even say that I had dreaded this moment alone with her, and many times during the day my heart had suddenly throbbed and then ebbed at the thought of it. For while Nne-nne did not appear sad, I felt sad listening to her heroic chant. More than that, my heart was being squeezed by a vague fear prompted by the superstition that when old people talk the way Nne-nne was talking tonight it was because they sensed their own impending deaths and wished to sow their memories in the wind before death forever sealed them. God forbid! I shuddered and shrank away from the thought of Nne-nne's possible death, but then listened attentively to her to detect any stray phrases that would corroborate my fears. I did not want Nne-nne to die. If she died, I would have no other choice but to come home and keep our compound open. Having her alive was the only reason— excuse really—that allowed me to consider leaving home. I was now the only surviving male in my direct line of people, and while I was gone I needed her to keep the weeds in check and the fire burning in the compound. True, I had just married Stella. True also that Stella had recently given birth to my daughter, W'Orima. However, Stella and W'Orima were new attachments, not yet fully grafted to my life. Nne-nne, on the other hand, had always been there and was now the only living attachment to all of my past.

Another concern of mine was that, young or old, recently grafted or eternally attached, Nne-nne, Stella, and W'Orima were all women, and I was abandoning the custody of my ancestral compound to women. How inexorable my travel to the United States was, how well or poorly Nne-nne could look after the compound and herself, in the end, did not really matter. The simple fact was that I was abandoning our collective past for what I thought was my inevitable personal future.

But Nne-nne insisted that she could look after both the compound and herself. "I am a woman, yes," she was now saying, "and I am old, yes, but I am also *awtu aligh-li!* No limp or half-erect penis will ever find its way into me!"

I could feel my brows lift with surprise and my lips pull apart in an unbelieving smile, as Nne-nne's language staggered me. Before tonight, I had never heard her allow herself the liberties many of the old women often took with coarse language. For example, the ceremonies following the birth of a new baby were usually bawdy free-for-alls of language and gesture, as the women simulated intercourse, pregnancy, and birth, while doing their famous Crotch Dance. But I had never seen Nne-nne participate.

Yet, in all of this, my strongest sense of that night was of something eerily fateful and transcendent, like a deathbed confession. My mind kept stretching beyond the room, far beyond Nne-nne and me, and into the boundlessness of space and time, which I sensed in the darkness and the rain beyond the half-open door. I felt like someone in a séance, surrounded by the darkness and the rain, the occasional titter of bush babies in the raffia palm trees outside, the buzz and erratic flight of moths and other insects, which I dared not kill because, as Nne-nne used to tell me when I was little, those insects could be carrying the spirits of ancestors. And in the middle of it all, Nne-nne's voice.

Nne-nne's testimony was not about herself, though, but about Oha Ndom, the Solidarity of Women.

"A woman is the hen of this world," she said. "You know how the children's song goes:

> Grandmother's hen
> Laid seven eggs
> One for the fox
> One for the wolf
> One for the cat
> One for the dog
> One for the market man
> One for the medicine man
> And only the last one for Grandmother herself.

"Ajuziogu, my son, is that not so true? Is not every woman, in one way or another, the hen of that song? Am I not it?" She dabbed tears off the corners of her eyes. "How many children did I conceive and deliver? Have I not lost all of them to one form of death or another, so that none will be around to bury me when I close my eyes for good? Your father was my last surviving son. And then, at the end of it all, I had to bury your grandfather six months ago. If it were not for you now, my son's son, how would anyone know that I have been to the well and come back with some water?" She drew a long breath and proceeded to reverse herself. "But I am not complaining," she said. "No, I am not complaining. As the saying goes, I may be sleepy but I am not yet dead! The proverb also says that God, who created the itch, also created fingernails. I just have to keep scratching.

"You see, a woman suffers patiently, privately, and long. Men brag about their feats and their sorrows, and often you will see them sitting by roadside logs swapping kola nuts and tobacco snuff or standing in clusters around the *gadaga* of someone whose raffia tree is running wine, and saying that women moan and groan and recite their sorrows in song, while men grunt and bury their sorrows in their hearts. Not so, I tell you. What makes a man groan will draw only a sigh from a woman.

"A man is the cock of this world, I tell you. A woman is the hen. A cock crows haughtily. A hen clucks quietly. A cock mounts a hen, flaps his wings in rapture, falls off, and then struts away, having done what he takes to be his life's work. The men even have a proverb that says: 'After I have penetrated a woman and left my seed in her, if she does not become pregnant, she alone knows why not!' But it is the hen that carries the eggs, lays them, sits on them, hatches them, and scratches the garden for her chicks. And when there is a hawk in the tree, who opens her wings to hide the baby chicks? And after the hawk has flown away, with or without one of the chicks in his claws, who then comes out of his hiding place and squawks longest and loudest? Is it not the cock?

"Yes, Ajuziogu, my son, men and women are like their organs. A woman's is mostly private, tucked away like a secret purse between her legs, with little to give away how big or deep it really is. A man's, on the other hand, hangs loosely and swings freely about for all to see. At the sight of a woman, it swells with pride and longing and waves mightily about. But once inside a woman, it thumps a few times, loses its seed, and soon collapses. A few years into old age, and men have to offer sacrifices and pour libations for their erections. Their prides no longer swell as strongly or rise as loftily, and if they manage to find their way into a woman, they are quickly humbled and soon withdraw.

"A woman endures. A man is like the froth on top of the soup, foam on top of the pot of palm wine. A woman, though, is the soup, the *ugara* wine that lies coiled up like a snake at the bottom of the pot. Like palm wine, a woman gets stronger with age. The woman in a woman comes out as she gets older. So, my son, do not worry about me. Whatever has not got the best of me up till this point has no chance at all of getting me now. . . .

"Is it not a wonder, though, about this rain tonight, that it held off until your ceremony was over? Whether it was Agbara and his rain stones or God himself in heaven who did it, I am very thankful that everything turned out so well, that so many people came and the whole ceremony was grand. But this rain now falling reminds me of a time long, long ago, when I was a young bride, and a woman rainmaker from near Eketa Igbodo destroyed the rain stones of all the rainmakers around here. The woman's name was W'Obiara. A widow named Ufo-Aku was having an *ihie-ede* ceremony, but her husband's brother, who had inherited her as wife from her dead husband, was envious of the ceremony because Ufo-Aku was a headstrong widow. He paid the rainmakers to draw down a deluge on her feast.

"But Ufo-Aku was another *awtu aligh-li*. By hearsay, she heard of

W'Obiara and sent to fetch her. When W'Obiara arrived, the men scoffed. Who had ever heard of a woman rainmaker? they asked. Soon enough, they heard about W'Obiara.

"On the final day of Ufo-Aku's ceremony, on the day she was supposed to parade through the market and receive gifts from people, the sky turned the color of indigo from the rain clouds. W'Obiara raced through the village, holding a young palm frond in her left hand and a straw fan in her right hand. She was a little woman bare to her waist but wearing two layers of loincloth that she tied *isi-ngidingi,* to show that this was war. She trotted from compound to compound, and in every compound she entered, she challenged the men in a retort of justification. She recited the countless ways in which men mistreat women, and at the end of her recitation she demanded that any man present dispute the truth of what she was saying. 'Answer me,' she screamed, 'if you have an answer!' But no man had an answer for her, and in celebration of her victory, she did a little dance and waved the palm frond around and fanned the air with her straw fan.

"When Ufo-Aku's parade through the market was about to begin, W'Obiara lit a big fire on a corner of the market clearing and heaped green leaves on it, so that the smoke swelled. She sang and danced around the fire. Many people who would not have come to the market that day because of the threatening rain came out to see her. Most brought cocoyam and banana leaves to shelter themselves from what they believed was surely going to be a downpour. Some even said they had come to see the rain put out this noisy woman's fire.

" 'Tell me,' W'Obiara asked bystanders, 'what is the name of the rainmaker who lives that way?'

" 'Njoku,' someone volunteered.

" 'Njoku *di'm,*' she chanted. 'What do you have against me? How have I ever wronged you? Have you ever asked me for anything, and I refused you? *Anything?* Why then have you planted rain stones in the ground? Why do you want to spoil a widow's feast? Njoku, answer me, if you have an answer. If not, then let the gods be the judge between you and me. If you do not have an answer, then let the sun shine.'

"W'Obiara repeated her mock queries of every rainmaker whose name was mentioned. She stalked around the market clearing in the longest strides she could get out of her short legs, like a warrior daring anyone to challenge her to a joust, brandishing her fan and palm frond like a war machete and shield. At one point she reached into the folds of her loincloth and took out a small gourd filled with *onunu*. As she sprinkled the black powder over the fire, the smoke turned red. Onlookers marveled. It had been threatening to rain, but so far no rain had fallen. Ufo-Aku's ceremony neared its climax. She and a trail of followers were slowly approaching the market accompanied by songs and dancing. W'Obiara, dancing more furiously, invited the women standing around to join her. But none would for fear of their husbands. She begged them to bring her twigs for her fire, but only a few of the bolder or older ones obliged.

" 'I am a woman!' W'Obiara shouted. 'Only and merely a woman, with a slit between her legs, which in response to a man's entry goes *taka-taka-taka*. Wife to my husband until he died, even though he treated me like a squatting log. I did not kill him. He was my only husband, but I was not his only wife. Five other women were wife to him. Before I was married, my mother and my aunts taught me songs to sing to him while he was inside me, to assure him that I appreciated his prowess and his art. I kept my hips supple for him and could match his every thrust. All his life long, I gasped and whispered and moaned for him: Husband of great power and prowess. Slayer of a hundred enemy warriors. Filling me with joy from the surging strength of his groin! I always did my duty. He did not always do his.'

" 'But I am not here to boast,' W'Obiara said, 'or even to speak about my misfortunes. I am here to drive away the rain. To beg the clouds to disperse. To invite the sun to return. I am asking the sky to catch fire. Catch fire, sky, please catch fire! Sun, be my lover! Stop hiding behind those clouds and come and shine on me, and I will give myself to you any way you want me. Sun, please shine on a widow's feast! Clouds, please go away! Shake, trees, shake! Shake the clouds away! Blow, winds, blow! Blow the clouds away!'

"W'Obiara whirled in a way that made everyone marvel that there was so much vitality in such a small and old woman. Lightning flashed and crackled. Thunder growled and rumbled. Every tree in the market clearing began shaking in unison with W'Obiara. If a tree was not shaking enough, W'Obiara waved her fan at it, and at once that tree began shaking with the others. Soon the sky began to lighten. It did not rain until much later that night, and by then Ufo-Aku's ceremony was over. Just like tonight.

"Ndom!" Nne-nne said. "Another name for a woman is *pagha-pagha-yeghe-yeghe.* One by one men marry us, impregnate us, and husband us. But together as Oha Ndom, we are fiercer than the first windstorm of the rainy season. Fiercer than the Imo River in flood!

"When the White man came and took over our land, what did the men do? They fought here and there, heaved high and ho with threats of what they were getting ready to do, held long talks under the big trees and in the end handed over the land and all of us to him. Near the road junction at Icheku, the White man hanged five men, including one *mbichiri-ezi,* Uka-Umunna, for beheading a slave during the burial ceremony for their father. One slave! One *osu* was beheaded as a tribute to a dead man, and on his account the White man hanged five men, all of them *dialas.*

"Bravery—at the burial ceremonies for a man, the other men hold long ceremonies of braggadocio before the *ese* drummers, talking about ancient bravery, as if there is nothing to be brave about in the present. Who around here has recently killed even one enemy warrior? Who is the lion killer for this generation? How many men nowadays go into the marshes near the river and come back with so much as a dead monkey?"

I could feel my face tightening, since many of the things Nne-nne was now saying made me think of my grandfather. Was she talking about him and his failures? Nna-nna had been a smallish man given to bragging about old-time bravery, a man whose wings (proverbially) and leg (literally) had been broken by misfortune—a prison term resulting from his kinsmen having betrayed him to the police for making "illicit" gin. In my grandfather's lifelong battles against the injustices of his relatives, he had been a nerve-grating complainer, while Nne-nne had been the feisty fighter. I could recall on one occasion, one of the witching trials to which my grandfather was subject, Nne-nne had pulled up her loincloth and turned her naked buttocks up into the faces of the men's assembly, and dared them to do their worst with her! The men were so astounded that they did not know what to do to Nne-nne. Needless to say, in the end, they avenged themselves on my grandfather.

In any event, right now I was feeling a tinge of loyalty for my gender, and for a spell that made me much more awake and attentive to what Nne-nne was saying.

Nne-nne continued: "You heard of the Enyimba War at Agalaba Uzo ten years ago, which started because a White man shot six men to death for refusing to dig coal for him at Elugwu. The men were imitating Ndom then, but how long did they last? One week and no more. But the Women's War lasted for months. Yes, Ndom was like bush fire in the dry season. Ndom put down babies, market baskets, farm baskets, weeding hoes, and pounding pestles. Doused their cooking stands with water and asked their husbands to fend for themselves and feed the babies. Ndom tied their loincloths in *isi-ngidingi,* girdled wreaths around their waists, unplaited their hair, painted their faces with indigo and charcoal and circled their eyes with ash, let out war whoops, and went to war!

"Heartless Munchi soldiers came from Ugwu Awusa. Black men as you have never seen black before, blacker than midnight, with scars on their faces as if all of them had been scratched by bush cats. *Onuru vuru, anugh zia* soldiers, who were said to be willing to kill their own mothers if their headman told them. But Ndom was not afraid. Ndom said, *'Kama ji si, nku gwuu!'* Like the *ihere* fly in the proverb, Ndom said: 'Rather than shame one of us, kill all of us!' At Achara Imo near Ahiaba, Ndom dug hidden pits in the road and the lorries carrying the Munchi soldiers fell in. At Mboko and Umu Oba, Ndom cut the message wires that ran along the trian tracks. At Mbawsi and Ogwe, Ndom set fire to the letter houses.

"Nwa-D.C. [District Commissioner] thought he could buy peace with Ndom by handing over the chieftaincy caps of all the Yellow Cap Chiefs that were the cause of the trouble. Ndom took the caps but continued fighting. The White man thought he could buy peace with Ndom by putting Chief Njoku Alaribe of Ikputu Ala in prison. Ndom set the prison on fire, freed the prisoners, sat on the head warder, and captured Chief Alaribe. The White man took Ugbala hostage. Ndom took the White woman hostage!

"*Ala hentu!*

"The earth heaved! The earth heaved and heaved again in many places at once!

"But I have to finish the story of Ufo-Aku. Her husband's brother, now her own so-called husband, was even more angry with her after the success of her ceremony. He beat her badly on that night of her joy and nearly put out one of her eyes. But even that was not the end of it. From that day of the feast, all the men of the compound began pecking at her and looking around for things to accuse her of. When they began to say that she was a thief, she went to Obizi and brought back the fearsome juju, Ala Obizi, and placed it before her accusers and asked them to swear on it that any of them had ever so much as seen her take a second look at something that did not belong to her. The whole village was in an uproar. When Ala Obizi is called out to right a wrong, it is *gburu bara uru, gburu bara okpukpu!* [a double-edged knife!] and it does not stop at the one evil for which it was called out. So as the priest of the juju set him up by the market clearing and tinkled his *ogele*, half the men in the village left home or hid in their houses. None dared come close to the all-searching eye of Ala Obizi. Not one person would swear.

"But then Ala Obizi is not a juju to trifle with. It does not come out and go back into its hut for nothing. When the men refused to swear to the truth of their accusations against Ufo-Aku, omens of its displeasure were soon visible in that compound, and the men were forced to make costly sacrifices to placate its roused spirit. And all of that made them even more angry with Ufo-Aku.

"In the end, witchery was what they got her for. Was Ufo-Aku a witch? Am I a man? Anyway, Ufo-Aku did not realize that a plot had been laid against her. On the night the conspiracy unfolded, she was returning from a visit to another village when darkness overtook her. It was deep into the night, but the night was light because of a full moon. By Ama Ukwu Umu Ojima, near a trail that joined the two branches of Ojima, Ojima-Ukwu and Ojima-Nta, a man was sitting on a branch that overhung the road. As Ufo-Aku walked past, the man emptied a calabash of indigo sap on her. Terrified, she began screaming, but her screams only brought out the other conspirators, who were hiding in the nearby bushes. They tore off her clothes and dragged her naked to a witching judgment. Now, you know witching judgments are not supposed to be held at night. These men said they had found Ufo-Aku dancing naked in the middle of the night in the face of the full moon—something only witches do. They swore falsely before everything they claimed to hold sacred and cited as proof the fact that her whole body had turned black. But is not black what the skin turns when it is covered with indigo dye? Were not their own hands black from the same dye?"

At this point, Nne-nne paused, one of the few times she paused during that remarkable night. I watched her push out of her chair and twist her neck one way and then the other. She noticed that I was watching her and smiled. And then she began shuffling around the room shaking various pots that had held palm wine earlier in the day. When she found one with some wine still left in it, she tilted it over my grandfather's old drinking horn and made a face as the dregs of now sour palm wine tumbled into the horn.

As she sat down again, I asked her, "So, what happened to Ufo-Aku in the end?"

"What happened to her?" Nne-nne chuckled, shaking her head. "She left town."

"They killed her?"

"Ajuziogu, have you never wondered why so many people in this town and in all the other towns around here are named Egbulefu or Ehilegbu or Umunnakwe? Is it not because innocent blood is often shed, and quite often a man's relatives will not let him take a drink of cold water, which his gods have given him, and afterward hang up his cup in peace? On your radio thing, when they speak in our language, I have heard voices say from Elugwu and Elegosi that the White man is to blame for all that is bad among our people. But you have heard me say, as you used to hear your grandfather say when he was alive, that there is plenty that is wrong with this land that did not start with the White man. And now that they are saying that the White man is about to leave, you will see, the evil will not leave with him.

"You see, Ufo-Aku was a soft woman, a gentle woman, who had not chosen to grow the bristles of *uvuvu,* the stinging caterpillar. And because among her own people back in her maiden village there was no man of substance among her relatives, no brother with a strong enough eye to stare evil down, her people consented to accept a cow in compensation."

"A cow for a human being?"

"Yes," Nne-nne replied with another chuckle. "Only they never received the cow they were promised. You see, they received promise of a cow and were given a ram to hold on to until the cow could be bought from Afara. They killed the ram and ate it and that was all they ever got." She now broke into a full laugh, a tired laugh she did not seem to have the breath to sustain, and which, in the end, turned into a yawn. "I see your brows lifting in wonder," she commented. "Life around here is all trickery, Ajuziogu. Every village you can name owes every other village a return trick from somewhere in the past. That is the way it has always been—a tricky man dies, a tricky man buries him, as the proverb says. In the old days, the death of Ufo-Aku would have been cause for vengeance and revengeance, leading perhaps to war. Not for the great value anyone puts on a woman's life but for the loss of face that would befall Ufo-Aku's people if their sister went unavenged. But nowadays, everyone is at the risk of the White man's law, and anyone who kills, whether in vengeance or village war, is tried for murder.

"A ram's head for a woman's head." She shook her head and chuckled without mirth. "A woman is truly a hen. Every part of her body is demanded as sacrifice to one juju or another. No, less than a hen. A woman is nothing. Yet, a woman is everything! If a man is high like a tower, a woman is deep like a well! If a man is a mountain, a woman is the ocean! A woman is like a god! A woman's crotch is a juju shrine before which men always kneel and worship. It is their door into this world. That is why we always sing the Crotch Song whenever a baby is born. As a reminder. And in my time, Ajuziogu, I have seen many an infant enter the world covered with more than mucus. A woman trying to push out the baby loses her bowels on him! But you take that same infant and wash him, suckle him, and feed him, and in the end he grows up to be a man. Yet, men say, *Nwanyi abugh ihie!* A woman is nothing!"

As she continued speaking, images of the village women doing the *Ohie N'Ole?* dance filled my mind—women of all ages, miming intercourse and pregnancy and childbirth, standing wide-legged, rocking on their heels, throwing their hands into the air and slapping their crotches in unison, as they jointly answered the lead singer's question: Where do they all come from?

Ohie n'ikpu! was their answer.

> Tall men?
> From the woman's crotch!
> Short men?
> From the woman's crotch!
> Hunters and warriors?
> From the woman's crotch!
> Chiefs and court clerks?

From the woman's crotch!
Even the White man?
From the woman's crotch!

"But I am glad, Ajuziogu, that you are my grandson," Nne-nne was now saying. "That you are a man. The way things are arranged in this world today, a man fares much better than a woman. A man is the part of the tree that grows above the ground and bathes in the sunshine. The part that wears the flowers and the glory. A woman is the roots, buried deep in the muck and manure. You see, Ajuziogu, if you were a girl," she paused and took a deep breath, perhaps noticing what must have been a change of expression on my face. "If you were a girl, a woman, there are things I would tell you that you would recognize because they would ring an immediate bell in your heart, things only a woman knows. . . .

"Is it not an irony, though," she said, changing tone and speed, "that your own first child should be a girl? You wanted a boy. I wanted a boy for you and for this family, which needs to be reseeded. The word on your grandfather's lips as he lay dying was *boy*. This family needs a boy, for you are now the only one left to carry on. But we get a girl. That is all right, though. A girl is all right. I have named her W'Orima because of that special birthmark she has between her brows. That is a mark of her destiny. She will probably have your good head and her mother's good face and all the good luck that the Equalizing Hand of God owes to this family for all the grief and evil we have suffered. I know that."

Her chuckle heightened my attention. I squeezed my eyelids tightly together to get the sleep out of them, then opened them wide.

"In the months since your grandfather died," Nne-nne continued, "do you know who has been flouncing in front of me? Uhuaba. Can you imagine? Uhuaba, who has not had a good change of loincloth in two years. You saw him here today at your ceremony stalking around as if he and I shared a secret. I suppose because he is a man and I am a woman I should welcome his overtures. But, Ajuziogu, were it not for politeness I would have laughed. I did laugh inside me. I thanked Uhuaba for recognizing that I was probably in need of things only a man could provide. But I did not say what was really on my mind, which was '*Okoro otu nkpuru amuh, ke muna-gi, k'oleke!*' [Feckless man with only one nut in his testicle sac, whither you and

I!] If Uhuaba felt like a rooster, he should have gone before some other hen to spread his wings and do his dance. This hen surely is never going to squat low for him. Your grandfather left a few pieces of fertile land, which I am now of course holding in your name, to keep your relatives from trying to snatch them. I have all the money I need to buy this and that. And I can crush a head of tobacco in less than half a day and make enough profit from the snuff to help Uhuaba buy a new loincloth. But a man is entitled to a man's privileges.

"It is a lonely life for me, though, now that your grandfather is not here. Often I wish there were more people around, my children and grandchildren surrounding me in a big, noisy compound. I long to hear many different human voices of all ages. But Death has taken everyone but you and me, Ajuziogu. And now, of course, there is W'Orima. I thank God that our vine is sprouting a new life. Yet, when I am by myself on days when it rains *eghu erigh, okuko atugh,* or late at night when it drums on the roof, I curl up under a cover and listen to voices from long ago, your father and the rest of my children, your mother. It has been a long life, full of unexpected turns and memories I cannot even begin to recount. Your grandfather is more than a voice. I feel his presence. His smell is still trapped in his clothes and in various nooks of this house. Sometimes I think I see him off the tail of my eye, but when I turn he is not there. A few times I have found myself talking to him as if he were in the next room; then I catch myself and goose pimples cover my body.

"But all that is no reason for you to be concerned about me. As I say, for every itch there is a fingernail. There is a destination I must go to. I promised your grandfather on his deathbed that as long as I live not a single day will pass when cooking smoke does not rise from my kitchen and trail into the sky as a sign that life continues on this compound. That will be my daily sacrifice to his memory. And to the memory of everyone else who is buried on this compound. That is why I have never left here overnight since he died. That is why when you invited me to come and stay for a week at your place at Agalaba Uzo I had to say no. I will keep this compound open until you finish traveling and return to take it over—this *ama nwanyi,* as the rest of the kindred despisingly call us. I will keep your grandfather's house standing, keep the weeds from overrunning this scar that we have carved out in the face of the bush, have the fences mended and the roofs thatched. Someday—soon, I hope—I will hand it over to you and consider my life's work completed. I used to think it would be this year, but with this new journey you have won, this new thing you have achieved, I can wait awhile longer. If your wife and daughter can stay with me, so much the better. Their company will break my solitude.

"But do not worry at all, Ajuziogu. As I always say, I may be sleepy but I am not yet dead. What we have before us is not sunset or evening but sunrise and morning. You are a rising star, Ajuziogu, and of all the people who were here when you were born, I am the only one to see you come to full light. When I think of how you were born and survived, I am certain that you came into this world to do something special, which you have not yet done. In the last few months, since you won this journey to America, I have often thought of the wonder of your birth, how the doctor cut open your mother's womb with a knife and took you out. No one had ever before heard of such a thing. I not only heard about it, I saw it. People came from far and near to see you.

"If you had not come here to stay, a cough which you caught as a baby would have killed you. You got it from the breast of a woman at Abayi where I took you to be suckled. Your own mother was too sick in the hospital to nurse you. While she was there, I took you to various women who had babies about your age, and whose milk was flowing. In this one case, the woman picked you up, just to hold you, and before she had a chance to tell me that her child had the cough, you had grabbed her breast and started nursing from it. And then after you caught the cough, I could not take you to the other women for fear you would give it to their babies. That womans' baby from whom you caught the cough died. You lived. . . ."

I can recall that at this point I rose from my chair, kicked off my shoes, and stretched, rising on my toes and raising my hands like an athlete signifying victory. I remember looking down on Nne-nne and smiling and her smiling back at me, her lips stretching slowly to expose her tobacco-stained teeth and dark gums. She was more spirit than flesh. Her face had become thinner with age and the unadmitted grief of losing her husband; the furrows on her brows were deeper; her eyes were sunk deeper into her skull; the veins were more visible on her neck. Her little flaps of breast, about which she often bragged as having suckled a tribe of children, were marked mainly by their hardened, dark nipples. Her arms were straight and thin and showed no bulge of fat or muscle; the fingers that she tried to interlock with one another were gnarled out of shape with rheumatism. It was difficult to imagine where the fight would come from, which she had a habit of promising to any man or spirit that would dare to affront her or seek to deter her from the work she felt she had to complete before her light dimmed.

As I stood stretching and twisting the kinks out of my joints, she stood up in front of me and then took my hands and swung them playfully from side to side, grinning from ear to ear, and looking me over as if she wished I were smaller, so she could pick me up in her arms. Then she said:

"This America to which you are going, is it the same as London?"

My brows lifted with surprise, and then I smiled. I had never heard her say London before and I wondered where she had heard the name. Probably radio. "No, it is different," I replied.

"But it is the same White man's country?"

"No, it is different. Well, it is a White man's country too, but a different part of it."

"And all of them are still in this world of human beings?"

"Yes."

"And the only way you can go there is by aeroplane?"

"You can also go there by steamer, but that takes a very long time."

"Well," she said, heaving her head from side to side in pure delight, "I never thought I would ever fly in an aeroplane or travel to London, but here I am with my boxes packed and about to set out in the morning. You know, as long as you are going I feel as if I am going. My own flesh and blood, son of my son, is flying in an aeroplane to White man's country. Who says I am not lucky? Who says that life has not been kind to me? . . ."

She let go of my hands and walked into her bedroom. While she was gone, an assortment of thoughts crowded and clouded my mind. I felt like someone being swept forward by a flooded river and had the intense wish somehow to escape from the current, find a foothold somewhere and from there to chart my own course, speed, and direction. No way. I was surrounded by a sea of inevitables, and nothing was left up to me. My going off to the United States was inevitable. So was leaving Nne-nne, Stella, and W'Orima behind. So were my misgivings and my sadness over the whole thing.

Then there was a sense of annoyance that Nne-nne had kindled in me because of the various things she was saying about men. I was a man, and therefore the things she said about men, she said about me, even though she sought to draw me aside and award me an exemption as her grandson. I was a man, yes, but *her* man, her grandson. Even so, that was a gratuitous concession, for there were things, portions of her heart, that she admitted she would share later with my wife and daughter but could not share with me—because I was a man. Beyond all that, there was the fact that my present predicament condemned me. If Nne-nne was saying that men were truant to their duties, then I was clearly being truant to my duty by leaving her as custodian of my ancestral compound. Her willingness or even eagerness to stand proxy for me offered only the skimpiest solace.

In addition, I was also my grandfather's grandson, ready to mount a *manly* defense on his behalf and on behalf of my gender. Yes, what Nne-nne said about all men she said on behalf of Ndom, but I also realized that the history that most directly informed her soliloquy was her own, and therefore the man she inveighed most directly against was my grandfather. Yes, Nna-nna had been an ineffectual man, much larger and stronger and braver in his own heart and imagination than in actuality and physical manifestation, promising in his youth but then waylaid by the conspiracy of his relatives and other misfortunes, and thereafter having his wings broken and his mouth full of stories of what might have been, stories of good old days filled with virtue and high-mindedness.

Nevertheless, beyond these feelings, I was intrigued to hear Nne-nne talk. Throughout my life, at least for that part of it during which I had been aware of her and Nna-nna as my grandparents, she had tended to be the silent one, smiling and exhaling and exploding grunts from deep within her chest in lieu of speaking, while my grandfather had given frequent vent to the "things buried in his heart." But there was no mistaking the robustness of Nne-nne's spirit, even in the past when she had chosen to be reticent. I knew from experience that between my grandfather and her, she had been the fiercer warrior, apt to hurl herself at the enemy with abandon and defiance.

Women, I thought. At the daily market or the water pump at Agalaba Uzo, where I had lived in the two years since leaving school, fiesty young women would often hurl themselves at a man twice their size, exclaiming: "Kill me! Kill me right now! You will never prosper in life unless you kill me! And after you kill me, you have to swallow me! And after you swallow me, you have to digest me! And that is when you will choke to death on my remains, because you will never be able to get rid of my remains! So, go ahead and kill me!"

Emerging from her bedroom, Nne-nne dangled before me a small piece of cloth tied into a knot. Sitting down and putting her knees together to make a platform, she gingerly untied the knot to reveal a smaller, older yellow piece of fabric, in the center of which were a strand of hair and a single pearl. "This," she said, touching the fabric with the tip of her finger, "came from the dress of the White woman. This is her hair, and this pearl came from her necklace. We cut off her hair and darkened her skin with indigo and gave her wrappers like ours, so she would not stand out so much.

"Six of us were assigned to guard her. Three actually stayed with her. The others hid in the bushes around us to act as messengers and lookouts and let us know if someone was approaching. We sent messages with whistles and birdcalls. The sound of *ahia* meant soldier. A hiss meant a delegate from Ndom had brought us a message. The sound of a swallow meant a local farmer. At night we all huddled together and slept in turns. When the early morning partridges sounded their first alarms, we woke up and one of us ran to a designated spot to receive instructions from Ndom on what we were supposed to do that day. . . ."

I marveled at the verve with which Nne-nne told her story. As she spoke, the war seemed to come alive in her face and in her eyes, and even beyond that, her attention seemed to be turned inward as if she were reading the words from a screen somewhere in her mind.

"We had many songs," she said. "Ndom fought the war with many songs, but one of the favorites was the one that went:

> If I die from the White man's gun,
> If one of his police or *kotima* shoots me,
> Ndom should not put itself at risk avenging me.
> If they merely lock me up in their prison,
> Ndom should not put itself at risk rescuing me.
> All I ask from Ndom is a decent burial.

But the answer to this was

No! No! No!
Where one is shot all of us will be shot.
When one dies, all of Ndom dies.
Where one is buried, all of Ndom is buried!
Ndom is one!
Undivided!
United!
Ije ka nma n'ogbara! [Travel is best in large company!]"

Nne-nne continued talking. Past midnight I went to the door to exchange the stale wine vapors that filled my lungs for a breath of fresh night air. I stood in the doorway for several minutes staring into the darkness and allowing my imagination to roam across our village and all the nearby villages, as I had traversed them during all of my early life, and then across the entire country, and then across the oceans to America where I would be in about a week. I was surprised that I had not yet outgrown the fear of looking up into the night sky. When I was a child, Nne-nne and others used to tell me that the stars that filled the skies at night stood for people's souls and that shooting stars were the souls of dead people departing for the Great Beyond. So looking up into the night sky and seeing a shooting star was like seeing a person die, and I had always been afraid of that. Tonight, however, there was nothing I could have seen if I had dared to look. Thick clouds obscured the skies.

I tried to expand my imagination beyond America, to encompass what I felt was the universe out there, flung far and wide and high above the clouds from which the rains were pelting the ground, vast expanses of nothingness and fullness stretching light years away in every direction, a universe so vast that every spot in it, even the little house where Nne-nne and I were, could, for all practical purposes, be its center. I had an urge to yell into that darkness, to let go a long ululating howl. I remembered that when my grandfather was alive, he had a habit I used to think of as strange—howling, as I wanted to howl, into the night, or discharging his flintlock gun noisily into the darkness. I now understood why he had done it. It was to make a mark in this big void, like a ship blowing its whistle in the fog, to signal our existence in this vast emptiness.

I suddenly felt very sad. I suddenly did not want to go to America and leave Nne-nne by herself. Her long incantation of previous battles was intended to reassure me (and herself?) of her mettle and courage. She was willing to go on fighting, but wasn't it time that she retired honorably and left the battles to me? In vowing to fight and win, she was asserting her own resolve as a person, but by the same token condemning us, her menfolk, who had left her no choice. Me, particularly, since I was the only one left. The men who founded our compound and who used to live in it had all died and abandoned her and me—an old woman and a mere child of yesterday, as she used to say—and now I was leaving her to go thousands of miles away. What choice did she have, except to fight? And that, she implied, was the reason Ndom went to war in 1929.

When I turned around from the door and sat down again, Nne-nne was telling the story of Nwanyi-Uguru, the Harmattan Woman. "It is from Nwanyi-Uguru that we got the saying *Akpobiri-akpobiri churu Amapu oso!* [The slanted machete sent the whole village of Amapu on the run—and it all came from one woman's kitchen!] Everyone called Nwanyi-Uguru a thief, and it is true that she and her children stole things. But mostly it was things they needed to eat, because she was an abandoned widow. Abandoned because she was ugly. "Ugly," Nne-nne repeated so strongly that I could feel myself smiling. "Some faces are bad, but Nwanyi-Uguru had a particularly unpleasant face. It was not her fault. That was the way her *chi* had made her. In addition, her teeth had fallen out and her hair grew in patches, and her skin was covered with white blotches. Yet, no woman is ever so ugly that a man cannot be found who is prepared to be kind to her long enough to get between her legs and make her pregnant. So, Nwanyi-Uguru was the mother of six men.

"You have heard her story. A man one day falsely accused her of stealing and without verifying the fact took a whip to her. When her children heard of it, each grabbed a machete, and the six of them together ran from compound to compound, looking for her whipper. In whatever compound they ran to, the inhabitants, both men and women, fled in terror, not daring to stand and bandy words with six angry men with gleaming machetes. Six men, all out of one woman's kitchen, drove out the whole village of Amapu!"

Then, Nne-nne said, referring to my tie, "Why do you 'book people' wear that cloth rope around your necks, as if you are trying to strangle yourselves?"

"I do not know," I chuckled in reply. "It is just something you wear."

"When you reach America, I imagine you will be wearing things like that all the time. I notice you are not taking too many of your clothes."

"A tie helps keep off the cold," I said. "America is a cold country. In one of their seasons, it becomes so cold that water turns into ice."

"Great God in heaven. You will write me and send me photos?"

"At least once every month."

"Ajuziogu," she said suddenly and solemnly, "there is one promise you must make me. If I die before you return, if death comes for me and asks me a question I cannot answer, I will leave enough money for a coffin and select my own burial cloths, so that anyone around can give me a decent first burial. But there is one promise you must make me. That you will give me a proper second burial, call a feast for four days, and give my people at Umu-Awah a good-sized cow. Will you do that for me? And let the gunshots boom in my name for four whole days? And let the *ukom* drummers drum that time?"

"Nothing will happen to you, Nne-nne," I replied. "You will be right here when I return."

"I plan to be," she said, trying to force a chuckle, "but if I am not, then do as I say. Of course, this is something your father should have done, but there is no one else left now but you. So you will do it. I know you will."

I drew in a long breath and tried to formulate an answer, but before I could come up with one, she had, to my relief, resumed talking about the war.

I had heard most of these stories before, in parts and pieces and from different sources. They were part of the general lore of the villages. I had heard many versions of the story of Elizabeth Ashby-Jones, the Englishwoman who had been traveling around observing "native women" when the war broke out in 1929, and how the women of Ikputu Ala, where she was at the time, had kidnapped her. But Nne-nne had never before revealed the full extent of her participation in guarding the famous hostage, nor given any hints that she had souvenirs from that enterprise. Even at that, it was years later, after my return from the States, that I discovered about a dozen handwritten pages out of Mrs. Ashby-Jones's notebook among her things.

Looking back on that strange night, I can only guess at Nne-nne's motives in telling all of these stories together. I do remember clearly, though, that she told them without hitch or seam, and they all seemed to cohere naturally. Oyoyo's story was perhaps intended to show the solidarity of Ndom, their collective sighing and spitting at something that brought dishonor to women. On the other hand, Ahunze's story revealed the singular resolve of which a woman's heart is capable. And of course she figured in the start of the war because of her relationship with Akpa-Ego, who was the actual spark that ignited the conflagration. In the case of Ugbala, well, Ugbala was Ugbala, a woman for all seasons, *Kwasara akwasara, guzoro eguzoro, no n'ala acho nma!* [High in the sky, big on the surface, deep in the ground!]. All these stories were an account of the assorted pressures building up in the earth, of the coughs and the hiccups emitted by the Land to relieve some of that pressure before the final upheaval.

Ndom!
Iyi omimi! [Deep river!]
Imponderable!
Incredible!
Impossible!

2

Why Women Go to War

"ALA HENTU!" NNE-NNE SAID. "THE EARTH heaved. But before it heaved, it shivered and sneezed many times. And showed many signs. But no one saw the signs, or could read them." She gave instances:

In one of the villages that made up the town of Usotuma, a small village called Okporo Obasi, it had been the custom of many decades for the women to sweep the market clearing early in the morning every eighth day. Otolahu, treasurer of the Women's Solidarity, usually sounded the *ekwe* after supper the night before to remind everyone. But rarely did anyone forget—this had been custom for such a long time—and furthermore, the village's eighth-day market, Eke Obasi, was in session later in the afternoon. Other parts of this custom were that two or three times during the season the women weeded the main footpaths that led to the junction where the market was situated, and at the end of the final weeding of the season, the men and the children joined the women in cleaning up the entire village. Every compound was swept, every roof rethatched, every wall and floor rubbed down with fresh clay. The men repaired the market stalls and pruned the trees, so that dead branches would not fall on market goers during windstorms. The village's juju, Obasi, had his hut and shrine at the corner of the market cleaned and festooned with palm leaves and flowered wreaths.

When all this had been done, there was a big feast, Emume Ahia Obasi, the Obasi Market Feast. A delegation of men went to Afara and returned with a big, humped cow, which the men ceremonially presented to the women, proverbially to "take the sweeping broom from their hands." Friends and neighbors from nearby villages were invited. Daughters of Okporo Obasi who were married in other villages came home for the feast accompanied by their husbands and their children, each bearing a jug of wine and assorted gifts for the home people. The feast lasted for up to four days and culminated in a huge, colorful parade of wives and daughters through the market.

That had always been the custom for as far back as anyone could remember—until the year after the taxes came. That year there was no cow. No cow because there was no money to buy it. The men had totally exhausted the contents of their treasury to pay their taxes for that year, and instead of a delegation to Afara, they had sent a delegation to the Women's Solidarity to explain their embarrassment. The women grunted heavily. Their faces fell. "Mmmh, all right," they said. Of course, there had been rumors for weeks that what did happen eventually was in fact possible. Of course, everyone knew that the men had been under pressure for months to find money to pay their taxes. Even so, the women had hoped against hope that their men would somehow find a way to do them proud, that through some heroic effort, through some dint of resourcefulness that would bring a smile to their faces when they heard about it, their men would find a way to continue the tradition. A good excuse for failing was never quite as good as succeeding in spite of difficulty. They were disappointed and the tradition was indeed broken.

There was a feast, but it was flat like palm wine without *ntche*. The excitement of anticipating the return of the men sent to Afara, the ceremonies associated with watching, discussing, tethering, trussing, killing, and skinning, was not to be had. Ditto for all the ceremonies, big and small, associated with making a sausage out of the stomach and the intestines, the little quarrels that always arose about what special groups should get what special parts of the meat. In the absence of the common cow, people made do with group goats and individual chickens. On the whole, that year's feast was not very festive.

The following year was even worse. Not only did the men not have the money to buy a cow from Afara, they sent a delegation to the Women's Solidarity seeking to borrow money to help pay their taxes.

The women refused.

The men were consterned but initially good-humored. However, as the deadline neared for paying their taxes, they lost all sense of humor and talked sternly to their wives.

Still, the women said, "No!"

At length, however, divisions arose within the Women's Solidarity. Some advocated lending the money to the men. These asked: "What kind of feast could we possibly have if our husbands and the fathers of our children are in the White man's jail?" Still, a majority of the women said no. The money in the treasury was theirs to keep. The men should find another way to pay their taxes. Throughout the year, they had scrimped and collected cowries, which had turned into manilas, then farthings and halfpennies and pennies, and finally into shillings and pounds. Before each year's festival, they paid most of this money to a tailor or seamstress who made a new outfit for every woman in the village, so that during the market parade at the height of the festival, they all came out dressed alike, singing and laughing and teasing and bantering with one another, complimenting one another on how good they looked in their clothes, discussing how good this year's design was compared with the designs of previous years:

"*Ikodiya*," one woman called gaily to another in mock astonishment.

"*Oweyi!*" the other jauntily replied.

"Could that be you that I see?"

"Yes, it is me you see. Have I not always told you that there was nothing wrong with me that could not be cured by a good bath and a new set of clothes? Don't we all look good?"

"*Ozugwo!* You look as colorful as a royal python!"

"*Arirah!* With your *uhie*, you look as colorful as *arirah*."

"*Ibara!*"

"Yes, *ureh!*"

"Yes, *amara*."

What would they be left with, a majority of the women asked, if they were forced to give up this one highlight of their collective year?

For their part, too, the men were not altogether united. Some of them thought it was demeaning to manhood to seek to borrow or seize the women's money. Others thought it was far wiser to lose a little face with their own wives than to go to jail for not paying their taxes. Yet, even those who were for getting the money from the women in whatever way possible recognized that something was amiss with this state of affairs—something that should have been straight was crooked; something that should have been erect was leaning.

Seeming to relent, the women asked if the men wanted to borrow the money or to have it given to them.

"Borrow, of course," the men said, jointly snickering and winking at one another. The money belonged to their own wives, and hence was really money they were borrowing from themselves. If it was a debt, it was "payable when able."

In the end, a diehard group among the women said no. Then hearing a rumor that the men were planning to do something untoward, a small group of women devised a plan to send the money in their treasury out of town for safekeeping. Ugbala was the person with whom they decided to entrust their strongbox. The collection box had two locks. Otolahu, the treasurer, held the box. Nwanyi-b'Uka held one key. Imoria held the second key. These three women were delegated to take the box to Ugbala.

The men got wind of the plan and in response organized a raiding party. Several men jumped on the delegation as it was about to leave the village and took both the box and the keys. The three delegates woke up the whole village with their screaming. They had recognized their assailants and demanded for them the type of treatment usually accorded to thieves. The women massed in the marketplace and with a united voice said, *"Emegh-eme!"* [Something unspeakable!] They flung their market and farm baskets, their head ties and loincloths, on the ground and said that this was an abominiton of a type they had never seen or heard of before. The men met later in another corner of the market and voted to tell the women not to make such a ruckus, lest the people of the neighboring villages hear of it and shame them.

In the end, to calm the women, whose excitement rose over the days, the men agreed to consider the money a loan. "We will pay you back quickly," they promised the women, "and put back the smile on your faces." But no, they would not sign an agreement with their own wives showing that they had borrowed the sum. Their words ought to suffice as an instrument of trust between them and their own wives.

Needless to say there was not much of a festival that year. There was no cow, and no money in the women's treasury for new outfits. Some women suggested that they wear the previous year's outfits. "No!" was the general response. Then someone else suggested covering their faces with indigo, and to this everyone said "Hey-ey-ey!" That was a uniform everyone could afford, and it fit their mood perfectly. They had a dispirited and mournful parade, one that people talked about for months, improvising their own drumming because the men refused to drum for them.

Nne-nne said, "A woman suffers long. A woman is like a pot that at long last boils over and drowns the fire that is making it boil. Ndom went to war," she said, "because the proverb says that if the main debtor cannot pay the debt then the person who stood surety for him has to pay it. With a grunt, mmmh!, deep in her heart, a woman understands a man. But a woman does not want to go on forever understanding that her husband cannot any longer get his penis to rise, or at least to twitch a little once in a while. That is a manner of speaking. For a time, a woman is willing to understand that the hunt may be difficult, that animals in the forest may be nimble and hard to track, that some of them in fact may be dangerous, but she does not want to understand forever that her husband comes home every day empty-handed from the hunt. A husband has to win sometimes, track and kill some game animals sometimes, overcome someone or something sometimes, be a hero sometimes, so that when his wife lies beside or beneath him, she can feel associated with strength and victory, rather than weakness and defeat, so that when he leaves his seed in her, she can feel that she has been implanted with strong, virile seed and not *afiri-kpoto*, and if perchance she becomes pregnant, she will be the mother of robust and stouthearted children, not of cowards and weaklings. No woman wants to be married to *okpokoro futa, na nri eghela!*" [a hapless oaf].

"When the War started," Nne-nne said, "the women of Okporo Obasi were in the forefront of it."

Nne-nne continued: "In another village named Umu Okere in Ikputu Ala, a man named Uru-Akpa was too ill to pay his taxes. 'Let his son pay for him,' someone who did not like him suggested in the village assembly. 'Otherwise the whole village will have to make up the difference.'

" 'Yes,' the whole assembly agreed. 'Let Oso-ndu [the son] pay for his father.' "

Oso-ndu, a struggling young man, was exhausted from having to pay his own tax. No matter. His kin and fellow villagers said: "Pay." The White man did not hear "Please, *biko,*" when it came to taxes. He did not listen to "Have mercy because I am sick." No. Government was like an implacable juju demanding sacrifice. It was sacrifice or your life. And if the juju took your life, it made the same offer to your next of kin beginning with your sons. Yes, Government was like a juju.

Uru-Akpa gnashed his teeth and wept from his sick bed when he heard what his fellow villagers had said. "Let them take me to prison if they want someone to take to prison," he said.

They would not do that. The court messengers would not arrest a sick man. What would they do with him? Carry him and his sickbed into the lockup? To do so would almost be like sacrificing a sick animal to a juju.

Teary-eyed, Oso-ndu's mother went to women's assembly with a plea. *"Ndom ibem,"* she said. "My only son is about to go to prison because he is unable to pay his father's tax. My heart is grieved. I am ready to do anything necessary to stave off this evil thing that has camped at my door. I am ready to strip myself naked or even to go to prison myself, if that is necessary. I have only one piece of cloth worth folding and bringing out for you to look at. Here it is. Hold it in pawn for me against the ten shillings you will lend me. I shall redeem it in six weeks or you can do whatever you like with me."

The women of the village lent her the money but would not keep her cloth. "What will you cover yourself with when you travel?" they asked. "Will you go to the market naked?"

"Tax! Tax! Tax!" Nne-Nne said, sighing and shaking her head. "Nowadays no one seems to mind the tax much, but in those days it was like trying to put a leash around the neck of a young goat for the first time. Before the tax came, the times of the year were reckoned from the Feast of Mgbara Ala—so many weeks before the Feast of Mgbara Ala, so many weeks after the Feast of Mgbara Ala. But after the tax came, it became the most important event of the year, such that if you asked a man, 'What time of the year is it?' he was apt to reply, 'It's three weeks before tax time,' or 'It's four weeks after tax time.' Tax was so fearsome the first year it came that it killed Ahu-Ekwe, the chief priest of Mgbara Ala. Early in the morning on the day after paying his tax, Ahu-Ekwe got up to go to the latrine and was ambushed by the Spirit of Mgbara Ala. Later, it came to light that he had used money that someone had given him for a sacrifice to Mgbara Ala to pay his taxes. Ahu-Ekwe never recovered and left eight widows.

"You may ask," Nne-nne continued, "where were the men when the women were at war?" The same question, she explained, had been asked by the White man at the end of the war. Where were the men when their wives were parading around with machetes and pestles, with war wreaths around their heads and loins? Why did not the men quell their wives? Or why did they not join their wives at the war, or ask them to step aside so that men could do what men are supposed to do?

The answer, she said in response to her own questions, was that the men were nowhere. They were there but not there, in a manner of speaking. Their hearts were not in their chests anymore, or they were beating ever so feebly. Their pricks were limp with fatigue, their testicle sacs empty. "You know how sometimes you are in the bush looking for snails," she said. "You move aside rotting leaves and you come upon a shell that makes your eyes bulge with delight it is so big. However, as you pick it up, its weightlessness makes your heart sink in despair. It is empty. My tongue hesitates to utter it, but in many ways our men were almost like that. They were like soldier ants that had been scattered by a broom and hence lost their formations and lines of march. You know, when soldier ants are in their formations, next to and on top of one another, they flow and surge like a river. Scatter them with a broom, and what you get is a crowd of giddy little animals sniffing around with their feelers for their fellows and their purpose. They are themselves only when they are in formation. Our men had become like that," Nne-nne said. "It was as if a man was sleeping with his wife, when suddenly there was a noise of a burglar breaking into their house in the middle of the night, and the husband, who should have been the wakeful and watchful one, was snoring and snoring and nothing could rouse him, and in the end, the wife had no choice but to get up and try to fend off the burglar by herself.

"When the White man came, the world truly did a somersault. Top became bottom, and bottom rose to the top. The scum also rose to the top from the bottom of the river. The froth you see is not made up of bubbles of aroma, as on flavorful soup or delicious palm wine, but bubbles of stench as on top of a pot of fermenting cassava. . . .

"At first, the White man bought slaves and left. He did not stay. Then a few stayed in places like Opopo and Boni and Kalagbari. No one then seemed to mind the White man much. He bought things that we had no use for and brought other things for sale such as cloth, beads, soap, and kerosene. Ajuziogu, the hospital where you were born had electric lights. Now, at home we have these hurricane lanterns. In the old days, we used to soak a wick in coconut oil and use it for a lamp. On her return from the market, a woman could walk a mile and visit two or three compounds before she found a neighbor with a going fire from which she could then borrow an ember and take it home to start her own fire. Nowadays, we spray kerosene on wood and strike a match.

"The White man had magic, which mesmerized our men. When the White man wanted slaves, our men left whatever else they were doing and began to hunt slaves to sell to him. They kidnapped strangers and children, women and weaklings, and sold them. They banded together and made wars and conducted raids for slaves. Then, one day, the White man said: 'No more slaves! Slaving is now against the law.' So slaving came to be against the law, and the people who had made it their life's work were left without a livelihood. Now the White man said: 'Palm oil!' Again all the men went into palm oil. The palm fruit that used to rot on the trees suddenly became very valuable. Our people became a palm oil people, spending most of their time harvesting the fruit, extracting the oil, cracking the kernels. For a woman, palm kernels fed her family, put crayfish in her soup, enabled her to buy a head of vegetables in the evening market, or a block of salt, or a handful of pepper. If a man wanted to buy a good hoe, a good machete, a bicycle, or a loincloth for himself or his wife, palm oil paid for it. Palm oil is what your father sold to get the money with which he paid the bride price for your mother. Palm oil built your schoolhouse and paid your school fees month by month. The coin we use, even today, the *sini,* has the palm tree on one face and the head of the Queen of England on the other face. When all of our lives had become pawned to the palm fruit, the White man could control our lives by yo-yoing the prices up and down. When the prices were good, our soups were filled with meat and fish and we could buy an extra length of cloth for ourselves. When the prices were down, we ate *okpoko* and *ngbugbu* and the loincloths we bought years before rotted on our waists.

"In response to all of this," Nne-nne explained, "our men became downcast and dispirited without knowing why. They became sullen and melancholy. I know all this from personal experience in the case of your grandfather. When a man like him is seized in front of his wives and children by a force he cannot overcome or bargain with and is carried away by it against his will, screaming and flailing helplessly, as your grandfather was when the *kotimas* came to take him to jail, he does not recover in a lifetime from the morale that ebbs from his chest at that moment. His wives and children, before whom his impotency has been exposed, never forget the moment.

"So, Ndom went to war to avenge the men. Or perhaps to rekindle the courage the men had lost. And that is not the first time something like that has happened. There is a legend among the people of Ama-Achara, for example, about a woman called Mgba-Afor, whose husband was killed during a war between two neighboring villages. The story goes that Mgba-Afor's husband was killed in battle, and her husband's people were fleeing in defeat. But then Mgba-Afor said if her husband could no longer fight because he was dead, and his people would no longer fight because their hearts were faint, then she would fight! She took up her husband's shield, spear, and war machete to carry on the fight in her husband's place. On seeing her, the fleeing men of her husband's village turned around and found new courage, continued the battle, and in the end won it.

"And do you know how Ndom found out we were to be counted? When word came down from the D.O., the chiefs summoned not the women but the men to tell them to tell their wives. The chiefs seemed to know that summoning the women would have been like walking into a beehive.

" 'Tax,' we all said on first hearing about the counting.

" 'No,' the men said on the strength of what the chiefs had told them.

" 'What then if not tax?' Ndom wanted to know.

"The men opened their hands in bewilderment. They did not know.

Who knew why the White man wanted certain things? All they knew was that there was supposed to be a count."

Ndom!

Nne-nne went on and on. Her stories festered in my heart as I watched her eyes narrow and then widen, her face open and then stitch together in wrinkles. Recalling some of the history I had learned in school, I began thinking of our people's first contacts with Europeans: Mungo Park and Richard Lander, Major Clapperton and William Baikie, Mary Slessor and the Church Missionary Society. And of course, Lord Hogarth, Governor General and famous conqueror and pacifier of the emirs and sultans of the North, otherwise also known as the creator of our modern state. He it was who promulgated the idea that there ought to be uniformity among the various regions of the country, and therefore since the people of the northern provinces had chiefs, the intractable and difficult-to-govern tribes of the southeast ought to have Warrant Chiefs appointed for them, and since the northerners paid a head tax, the people of south ought to do the same. Furthermore, Lord Hogarth argued forcefully, unless native treasuries were established, and these chiefs learned how to collect and spend money, how could they ever learn to govern themselves in a modern, scientific way?

But to tax them, Hogarth said, you first have to count them.

And who became chiefs? According to Nne-nne, mostly people who had theft or another form of dishonesty in their nature, but whose dishonest inclinations had been kept in check by the rigid traditions of society. Such people welcomed the White man and his liberties. And after they became chiefs, they stole in broad daylight and called what they did by other names. They saw left and called it right, and saw right and called it left. People like our own present chief, Orji, who was often rumored to have been once a cohort or a fence for Harmattan, the most notorious thief our area had ever seen. Harmattan was the one who used to boast that the reason people locked their houses was mosquitoes, not him, as he could get into any house he desired. Yet Orji became a chief.

For the White man, Nne-nne said, "outstanding" seemed to have meant "tall." All the Warrant Chiefs were tall young men who stood like banana trees growing luxuriantly in an old cesspit, huge stems and broad leaves but no fruit. Elders and men of real substance tended to be quiet and coy. Scrawny, not brawny. At the *amala* assembly, they spoke last not first, softly and not loudly, and their special talent was the ability to weave a consensus among those present, to link the past with the present and the present with the future. Warriors warred but tended to die young, exhorters and harranguers sooner or later lost their voices, but deliberators were like the slow drizzle that watered the farm much more thoroughly than the sudden but brief cloudburst, for only through *akatiko* did the well-preserved snake become *iwi agwo*.

Our people had no chiefs before the White man came. The White man could not abide such "disorder." He made a treaty with one group, and then a few miles down the road he had to reach a new agreement with the next village, because that village did not consider itself bound by whatever had been agreed to by the other. Our people, the White man said, were "ungovernable." They had no natural rulers. So he appointed chiefs to represent the people to him and him to the people. Thereafter, he could say: "Your chiefs agreed to sell half the land you own for nothing. Your chiefs have agreed that you should pay a new tax. Your chiefs have agreed that the women and the goats and the sheep should all be counted, so everything in the district will be counted. See here? Here are their thumbprints. That's how they signed the agreement."

The District Officer, D.O., or District Commissioner, as he was sometimes called, visited the town once a month, sometimes once every two months. One was never quite sure why the D.O. came when he came—sometimes there was a circular announcing his coming, sometimes none. All anybody was told was that our people were members of the British Empire, that we belonged to the King of England and his representatives, such as the Resident and the Governor. So, as soon as the circular arrived that the D.O. was coming, the village went into a flurry of activity to prepare. The women had to weed and sweep the *okasaa*, where the town would meet him. Every member of *ndom alu-alu*, the sodality of married women, had to reach under her hens and find two or three fresh eggs for the White man. Then men usually contributed money to buy a ram. White men didn't eat goat.

The D.O. always came in the morning, before the sun had become too harsh. The chiefs arrived on their bicycles, wearing big striped jumpers and yellow chieftaincy caps.

"*Uru-prisi. Uru-prisi. Uru-prisi,*" the White Man said.

"The D.O. says he is not pleased with you," the *ntaprinta* translated to the assembly.

"*Uru-prisi. Uru-prisi. Uru-prisi,*" the White man said.

"The White man says he is very pleased with you," the interpreter said.

Everytime the D.O. came, the people were told what pleased or did not please him—as if the whole town was now living like a child or a slave, whose purpose in life was to please or avoid displeasing a parent or master.

As soon as the D.O. left, the chiefs took over. Even though everyone had listened to the same message from the White man, the chiefs could make of it whatever they wanted, because they often claimed that the D.O. had given them special instructions during a private meeting.

The Women's War started because the men did not start a war when they were counted and tax was imposed on their heads. The *mbichiri-ezi,* or elder, in every compound became a tax collector. The *kotimas*, as enforcers, terrorized everyone. "*Hoo-sai* your tax re-sheet?"

"Wogu, you have ten adult men in your compound. At seven shillings a head, you owe the Government three pounds ten."

"Nwaigwe, we counted twenty-one front doors in your compound. That means seven adult men. That's four pounds nine shillings. Where's the money?"

If anyone in his compound did not pay, the *mbichiri-ezi* was liable to pay or go to jail, unless he handed over the culprit. So whether they paid or did not pay, whether the *mbichiri-ezi* went to jail or handed over one of his younger relatives, everyone was unhappy at tax time. Men pawned their farm implements or their wives' beads and even committed the taboo of selling their pregnant animals to raise money to pay their taxes.

The War started because that was the third or fourth bad year in a row for everyone, a year of hardship during which palm trees bore little fruit, and the fruit they bore produced little oil, and at the market the oil fetched next to nothing. A villager had to pound six pots of palm nuts to get one good tin of oil. And then when his wife carried the oil to the market the buyers pouted at it. Two years before, the agents had begun testing the oil.

A woman trudged to the depot with two heavy calabashes of palm oil on her head in a sagging basket. The oil trader put a bit of her oil in a tube and warmed it over a fire. Then he added drops of liquid to it and shook it until it turned yellow. Then from another tube he added drops of another liquid and kept adding and shaking until the contents of the first tube were red again. Then he peered at the marks on the calibrated tube and announced to the woman that her oil had failed.

"What do you mean?" the woman inquired.

"No good," the man said.

"What do you mean 'No good?' "

"Just as I said. It is no good. I will not buy it."

"What is wrong?"

"It failed the test. I do not buy anything that is not S.P.O. Your oil is Grade Three." He puts up three fingers. "Even if you give to me for free, I will not take it. What did you put in it?"

"Well, I will not give it to you for free."

"Your own palaver, lady. I would not take it no how." With that, the man walked off to attend to another, more agreeable customer.

"Help me pick up this load, if you please," the woman now said, defeat and disgust written all over her face. Rolling her top wrapper once again into a carrying pad, she placed it on top of her head in readiness for receiving the load.

"After I finish what I am doing," the oil trader replied.

Helpless, the woman waited patiently until the oil trader or someone else was ready to help her hoist her load, and then she would start trudging to another oiler's depot. Miles and hours later, if she was lucky, she found a buyer willing to pay her half of what a calabash of oil was selling for only a year before. "And if you do not accept," the oil buyer haughtily told her, "you can leave the calabashes in your house and soldier ants will consume both them and you!"

Chineke ekwela ihe ojo-o! [God forbid the evil thing!]

Things were really bad. Money was six cowries a head, twenty heads of cowries to a manila, twenty manilas to one shilling, and a shilling bought next to nothing. A length of *Ukwa* cloth cost five shillings, a digit of stock fish two-and-six. Soap was nowhere to be found, and people went back to making soap the old way, burning the stalk of a palm head and kneading the ash with potash. Even yams and cassava were blighted on the farms. At harvest time, a farmer pulled up a yam, and a horde of termites came up with it. A woman pulled up a stalk of cassava and what she found at the other end of it was not fat, dark tubers but rough fibrous roots. Immersed in water to ferment, most of that cassava became puffy and floated on top of the water, its skin soft, its core hard, all of it useless.

The War started because the Government assumed that since the men had been counted without much incident, there should be even less incident counting the women.

The War started because the women felt united in a way the men could not—all any woman needed to know in order to join was that women were at war with the Government. For example, on the day Nne-nne joined, she had been returning from the farm with a basket of cassava roots perched on her head and a few sticks of firewood cradled in her arm when she was accosted by a throng of women, who threw away her basket and her cassava and pilloried her with questions:

"Are you not a woman?"

"Do you not have a monthly cycle?"

"Have you never endured the aches of pregnancy and the pangs of labor and childbirth?"

"So you have little children? Do you think the rest of us are sterile?"

"Do you want Ndom to be counted like goats and chickens and a tax imposed on our heads?"

"Have you not heard that Ndom is at war?"

During the War, the soldiers kept looking for ringleaders, the queens of the termite hills. If these could be found and squelched, they thought, the movement would come to an end. During the trials that came afterward, the Residents and District Officers kept looking for ringleaders. Maybe Oyoyo, the harlot woman at Agalaba Uzo at whose house the women had congregated a month before—maybe she was a ringleader. She lived in the township, was the consort of several important people, including the police inspector and two important Lebanese and *Potokiri* traders, as well as the proprietor of more than one bar. Or maybe Ugbala was a ringleader. She had the carriage of a leader. The other women deferred to her, called her *Daa* and other titles of respect, and hung around her as if her company were a privilege. At the sessions of the Commission of Inquiry, she was an eloquent and fearless speaker.

But in truth Ndom had no leaders. Every woman was led by her own intimate knowledge of their common grief and sense of injustice, by what Nne-nne called Woman's Grief. One by one and all together, they seemed to have known about this grief from the time they were little girl infants suckling milk from their mothers' breasts. They knew about it from the lullabies their older sisters sang in order to quiet them and rock them to sleep on hot, lonely afternoons when their mothers were at the farms:

> Little sister, little sister, please stop crying
> Lest I throw some sand in your eyes!
> Remember the time Grandmother went to prison in the sky
> And set the sky on fire!

Ndom set the sky on fire! Drew down lightning from the sky and set the earth on fire!

Daughters learned of Woman's Grief from their mothers. Married women confirmed it for one another as they toiled together on the farms, stooping to hoe cassava ridges or to pull tubers from the ground, or when they knelt and then bent low with hanging breasts to blow their tired breaths at a fire that refused to catch on wet wood, or trudged from the river with a heavy water pot on their heads and a sick baby on their backs. They were conscious of Grief as they pounded *fufu* for their husbands' suppers or kneaded their testicles to arouse reluctant passions. They knew of it as they squatted to deliver their babies. They knew of it in themselves and they recognized it in one another. *A woman knows what every woman knows!* That was the meaning of *Nwanyi Ibem*, My Fellow Woman, by which they addressed one another during the War.

Insane!

Irrational!

Mass hysteria, like the spirit-induced madness that possesses some of them during some of the juju festivals!

A sudden overflow of premenstrual or postpartum hormones!

Spontaneous combustion!

These were some of the expressions used by the D.O. and the Engineer in describing the war after it was over. But for Ndom, it had been simply war, total war, as inevitable and compelling as a hiccup or belch or the urge to vomit, with every woman a warrior and every village and every town a battleground, as they attacked whatever was part of the Government in their own town or village.

"Ala hentu!" Nne-nne said, continuing to describe the events at the

beginning of the war in terms that made me think of random currents, electric arcs, Van de Graaff machines, and lightning bolts.

Ikputu-Ala, where the first flames of the War were kindled, was ruled by Chief Njoku Alaribe, an excellent example of the type of man we nowadays call His Master's Voice. *Onuru vuru, anugh zia* of a chief, Alaribe was a perfect echo for his masters. As soon as the D.O. said, "Count," he sent a counter into the villages under his jurisdiction. The counter that started the trouble was one Sam-el, a village agent for the C.M.S. Church at Ezi-Ama, who taught Sunday school and church hymns and sat in the shade of the umbrella tree in front of his house on hot afternoons spelling-reading his way through the Bible and lusting after every wife who passed by. Let anyone in the village marry a new wife, and in a few days Sam-el was bound to waylay her on her way to the farm or the stream. "Why don't you come to morning prayer?" he would say, "so I can put your name in the roll book." Every year, the women's festival songs featured Sam-el.

And who was the first person Sam-el wanted to count? Akpa-Ego Ozurumba, whose name was seeped in irony, for, contrary to her name, there had been little good fortune for her in the husband she married. By good sense, Nne-Nne said, she should have been left in peace to continue hoeing the tough row that her *chi* had laid out in front of her. Akpa-Ego was kneeling over a large vat of palm mash, kneading and pressing out the oil, when Sam-el arrived. Her breasts hung heavy; a good observer would have noticed that her turgid, blue nipples meant that she was pregnant, if the observer happened not to notice the bulge of her belly.

Notebook in hand, Sam-el began to query Akpa-Ego:

What is your name?

How many children do you have?

Do you own any goats and sheep?

How many chickens in your chicken coop?

The answer Akpa-Ego gave Sam-el was most fitting. She asked: "Has your mother been counted?"

Sam-el took great umbrage at this and began to *humbug* the poor woman, who was still in a kneeling position and had sweat crawling down her face and the small of her back. After a few more moments Akpa-Ego rose to her feet to face Sam-el, and the two began exchang-

ing insults. Full of importance and high officialdom, Sam-el warned
Akpa-Ego of the severe consequences that would befall her if she did
not cooperate with the instructions she had been given and answer all
questions put to her. He traced the line of authority from himself to
the King of England. Who was she, an illiterate village woman, to
set herself against the King of England?

Sam-el emphasized important points in his harangue by waving his
pen in front of Akpa-Ego's face. At one point, she became so frustrated
with this that she reached back into the vat and smeared him with a
handful of palm mash. In turn, he slapped her. They tangled, and
Akpa-Ego was knocked to the ground.

On hearing of what had happened, Ndom ritually turned an angry
shoulder at this *aru*, this abomination that had occurred, a pregnant
woman knocked down by a man who wanted to record how many
chickens there were in her chicken coop. If Akpa-Ego's husband had
been alive, if he had been the type of husband to whom a wife could
run teary-eyed and say, "Husband, defend your wife's honor," Ndom
might have left it to him to avenge her. But Akpa-Ego was a widow
of a few months, a pregnant widow trying to squeeze out a living
from palm mash that belonged to someone else's husband, a special
widow because of the way she had become a widow. Her husband,
Ozurumba, had hanged himself two months before because the women
of Ezi-Ama sat on him for mercilessly beating her. Akpa-Ego, therefore, was already a ward of Ndom.

"*Ihe!*" Ndom said about what Sam-el had done to Akpa-Ego. "*Kama
ji sii, nku gwu!*" What had happened to Akpa-Ego should not happen
to any woman. Her grievance was the grievance of all women. Her
fight was the fight of all women.

Ndom heaved. The women of Ezi-Ama and all of Ikputu Ala said
War! The women of Onu Miri sent a delegation to Ezi-Ama to find
out what had happened. When they found out, they said War! The
women of Usotuma and Agalaba Uzo picked up the echo and repeated
it. The women of Nsulu, Ntigha, Nvosi, Ama-Achara, Afara, Mbutu,
Okporo Ahaba, and Eberi said War! Beyond the river, the women of
Okpuala, Ahiara, Ulakwu, Owere, and all of Ohuhu said War! Ibibi
women said War! The women of Okirika, Mboni, Opopo, and all the
Salt Water towns said War!

Ndom would not be counted. How many bees are there in a beehive? they asked. How many ants in an anthill? How many drops of rain in a rainstorm? How many drops of water in the mighty Imo River?

Ndom said: British Empire, come and get us! White man, come and get us from your England. Come and get us from your Rest House. Come with your big guns and Munchi soldiers and shoot us. You do not have enough bullets to shoot all of us. You do not have enough prisons to hold all of us. Then after you shoot us, shoot your mother. After you imprison us, imprison your mother. We are Ndom! Undivided! Umbilical cord tied to umbilical cord. Vaginas that whelped the whole human race. Breasts that suckled it and hands that comforted and nurtured it. If we lock our thighs together, the world comes to an end!

Ala hentu!

3

Oyoyo Love

NNE-NNE BEGAN OYOYO'S STORY SOMETIME AFTER midnight. I had
been standing in the doorway once again, staring into the darkness,
and Nne-nne had asked me if I heard something, or if there was
something that caused me to peer with such unusual keenness into
the darkness. "Nothing," I told her. "Just my thoughts." And then
she remarked that I would have made a good seer, if I had been born
in an earlier generation, the way I tended to look into the heart of
things at my age. "Mmmh," I responded, not knowing what else to
say. Then I stood looking at the silhouetted trees, and listening to
the eerie quiet, a quiet so deep it seemed as if someone had said,
"Sssh, quiet!" to all the night animals. It was as if the earth were
one vast chamber and I was standing in the middle of it, and if I
listened carefully I could hear the echoes from the very ends of it.

"I am not saying that everything was all right with the women and
all wrong with the men," Nne-nne said, dispatching a ball of brown
tobacco spit into the corner from where she sat. "No. At about the
time the War started, women were doing things that were once
unheard of for women to do. So much so that discerning people were
wondering what the gods and the ancestors were trying to tell us.

Some of these things might even have been part of the reason for the War. You know how sometimes you eat something that disagrees with your body, and your stomach throws it up? Or how sometimes you may even stick your finger into your throat to cause yourself to throw up when your stomach is upset? Or how the Land reacts with upheavals when a witchcrafter is buried in it?

"Across the river, on the other side of Am'Assaa, the first wife of a famous *kilaki* yielded herself to a singing, dancing beggar, whose face was covered with sores. She was *ndom-misisi* of the highest order, placed on a high pedestal by her husband and held in the highest esteem by all the townspeople—someone who enjoyed a status similar to that of your mother-in-law. Imagine someone like that being straddled by an unbathed beggar. No one knew what spirit possessed her, but the story was that she covered the beggar's face with a cloth while he did his thing to her.

"*Utu-gbara*," Nne-nne continued, causing my eyes to flare in surprise and my lips to part in an involuntary smile. A tee-hee may even have escaped from me. "A woman who goes to live with a man who has not paid a full bride price to her people is mortgaged to a penis. That is what *utu-gbara* is, and it is something that used to happen very rarely and only to the most desperate widows. But then it became quite common among young women. A man would begin making inquiries about marrying a woman—just inquiries, mind you—but before the bride price was negotiated and paid, the woman went to live with the man, and her people were left holding an empty bag. And there were many other signs that something was wrong with the Land. At Omuma a woman gave birth to a nameless thing that had neither arms nor legs. At Itungwa another woman delivered a baby that had grown teeth in the womb. Things that were previously unheard of were happening everywhere, and people were shaking their heads and pulling up their shoulders and saying '*Ihe!* What could be the meaning of all this?'

"But all of these were minor events compared to the one they called Oyoyo. If the other women were running off to be with husbands, Oyoyo was running away from one. The trouble she caused her mother and mother-in-law, and the women of two towns who went to get her back, that is what became legend. Can you imagine a child using the White man's law to sue her own mother and mother-in-law, and the police being sent to arrest them, all because they are trying to correct her behavior? Mind you, she was the one who had become a prostitute, not her mother or her mother-in-law. But the White man's laws are upside down. Nevertheless, when the women of Uzemba trekked to Agalaba Uzo, they did not want to fight the Government. All they wanted to do was to retrieve Oyoyo from the shameful thing she was doing. But then the Government decided to stand in their way, as if prostitution were a noble thing. That was when the women of Uzemba heaved and refused to let that abomination stand.

"I am telling you, Ajuziogu, no one who saw what the women of Uzemba did to the Government at Agalaba Uzo should have been surprised that all of Ndom went to war a few months later. They were not looking for a fight, but when a fight overtook them, they threw themselves into it. As the saying goes, the grass did not soon grow again on the spot where they wrestled with the Government.

"Agalaba Uzo is full of prostitutes today, and one may not even have to go all the way to the township to find a woman willing to sell herself for one moldy shilling, but in those olden days it was something almost unheard of. And this may help you to understand how the women of Uzemba felt about this young woman abandoning her two children and going off into the township to become a prostitute. Once, at our own local Ahia Orie market, a madman named Okpo-Kwee, who had a small hut in a corner of the market clearing, yanked the loincloth off a young woman while the market was in full session, leaving her completely naked and clutching at her crotch with both hands. For some reason, Okpo-Kwee had taken a fancy to this young woman, somebody's new wife, who was minding her own business and doing whatever trading she had come to the market to do. The point of the story is that as soon as it happened, a group of women began chasing Okpo-Kwee to retrieve the girl's cloth from him. Meanwhile another group of women ringed themselves around the girl to protect her from public view. The nearest woman with more than one layer of loincloth pulled off the top one and gave it to her for cover. That is how women are. That is how those women felt who went to Agalaba Uzo to bring back Oyoyo. She was one of them, and so if she was exposing and disgracing herself in the township, that was like exposing and disgracing them. That is why you never see a naked madwoman. A madman may be naked, but almost never a woman. The other women will always get together and cover her with something, for they feel that if she is exposed, then they too are naked in public.

"So it was, then, that Ekweredi, Oyoyo's mother-in-law, summoned together the women of her town and asked them to accompany her to town to bring back her daughter-in-law from the house of prostitution:

" 'Ndom ibem, agree with me!'

" 'Agreed! Agreed!'

" 'Agree with me!'

" 'Agreed! Agreed! Agreed!'

" 'Thank you for agreeing, for consenting to be in accord with me this afternoon. And thank you especially for answering my invitation. The reason I have called all of you together is that the proverb says that when a hunter encounters an animal in the forest that is too big for one person to hunt, he runs home and summons his kinsmen. Well, I have come face to face with a beast that is in part *pagha-pagha-yeghe-yeghe* [a heavy, unwieldy load], in part *enwegh-isi-nwegh-odu* [that which has neither head nor tail], in part *ihea n'adigh otu n'eme ya* [that about which nothing can be done], and I have come to ask you to help me hunt it. As I am a married woman, my fellow married women are my nearest kin. The reason I have called all of you here tonight is already known to most of you. It is about my son's wife. . . .' "

Many of the women sighed. Others made various signs of displeasure. A number muttered, "God forbid the evil thing!" under their breaths.

Ekweredi acknowledged their commiseration and continued speaking. "Yes," she said, "a piece of meat that falls to the ground has unavoidably picked up some dirt. But what do we do with it? Well, because meat is scarce and expensive, we usually pick it up, wash it, and eat it, nevertheless. Is that not so?"

"Yeah. Yeah," the women echoed.

"Yes," Ekweredi concurred. "That is the way it is. A person dons a tight *ogodo* and slaps her backside confidently, thinking that she is fully protected from things that attack one from the back, only to find out she isn't. As you all know, the woman my son married left us some years ago and ran off to Agalaba, where she is now doing

something the mouth finds heavy even to utter. She is offering herself,
I have been told, to every man in the town as a public woman. For
one manila or one penny, I do not know how much the harlot's rate
is in the town, a man can lie with her."

"Shame! Shame!" the women mumbled. Many shook their heads in
despair.

"Yes, it is a horrible shame," Ekweredi concurred. "But what do
I do? What is your advice to me? For a long time, I have had one
mind that told me to consider her spit that has left my mouth. You
know what the proverb says. While spit is in my mouth, it is part
of me, but once it leaves my mouth, then it becomes something that
I loathe. But I have also had another mind that says loathe her as I
may, my daughter-in-law has two children. You know those children;
you have seen them. They look well fed and plump, and could not
look any better if their mother were here. My fellow women, tell me
that what I am saying is not so. Tell me that I am lying!"

"No! No! You are not lying! It is so!"

"Thank you. Thank you for standing witness to the truth of what
I say. It is for these two children that I want their mother back in
this compound. I want your help, *ndom ibem,* in getting her back. I
have a wish to travel to Agalaba in the next few weeks to find her.
I need your company. As the sheep said to the lion in the folktale,
travel is merriest in large company. I want you to go with me. Here
are ten manilas, from me to you as your *ukwu-ozi,* four kola nuts, and
four pepper pods. These two pots in front of you are full of wine.
Ndom ibem, will you travel with me? *Ndewo-nu!"*

"*Ndewo. Ndewo. Ndewo—*"

The first speaker who responded to Ekweredi said, "Certainly!" The
second speaker said, "Of course!" The third speaker named a possible
date for them to travel. Ndom was unanimous. Yes, they said. Of
course they would travel with her. They all understood how she felt
as the mother of a son, a gardener who had watched a solitary shoot
come up weak and prone to be knocked over by the wind, a planter
who had labored to root it firmly, to pack and compact the earth
around the seedling, to help it stand erect and thrive. They all knew
that the reason one trudged to market was not to lose one's capital
but to make a profit. They all understood that even though the children might be doing better under her care than they would with their

own mother, that *njia ka nwa eghu na nne-ya nma* [cuddling best becomes a she-goat and her own kids], no matter what kind of goat she was.

They set a date for their travel.

The object of their quest was Nwanyi-Nma, first wife of Onwu-Ghara, Ekweredi's only son. Nwanyi-Nma's departure was not altogether a surprise to observant people, who had watched her behavior for the last year or so before she left for the township. A woman may take on a lover, and it is not altogether unheard of that a woman plays hide-and-seek with more than one lover at a time, but in Nwanyi-Nma's case, especially in the last few months before she left for Agalaba, man seeking was like a madness.

But then again, Nwanyi-Nma's ending up at Agalaba as a public woman was an eventuality some people claimed to have foreseen. The things she seemed to want, they said, were not on sale in the local markets, in a manner of speaking. As a young pubescent girl, she had been like a banana tree planted in an old refuse pit—large and leafy and luscious. Not the type of wife a careful woman like Ekweredi finds for a son, then pawns everything she owns to pay the bride price for, and then brings home to her own kitchen to groom and mature, so that when she comes fully of age she can be a good wife to her son. Instead, she was the type of woman who would be difficult for one man, no less a mild-mannered man like Onwu-Ghara, to satisfy and hold down. The type of lusty woman who would have made a good third or fourth wife for a man of voracious sexual appetite—big legs, big breasts, big eyes undimmed by shyness, a quick laugh, and a loud, raucous voice that was too ready to bandy flirtatious words with men. Not even a blind man would have passed her without noticing her endowments. Nearly every man with both his eyes stared—many, in fact, muttered fantasies about the likely pleasures of pinning her down on a bed—she was so delectably large, with the smooth, dark, and tender skin of an overripe fruit, such as would burst forth in a spray of delicious juice, if squeezed just a little. She had long, luxuriant dark hair reminiscent of the mixed bloods who lived near the coast, pearly white teeth, and eyebrows penciled by Nature. *"Ojoko,"* some of the young men called her in those early days of her marriage—*"Ojoko-jo nwanyi!"* to signify the little bit of long-limbed adolescent awkwardness still left in her movements and her gait.

Of course, she grew out of that gangliness in a short time, as her joints tightened and her buttocks and breasts filled out to match her frame.

Most people knew from the very beginning that, in Nwanyi-Nma, Onwu-Ghara was overmarried. This was a clear case of squatting in grass much taller than he was. He could not contain her in body or spirit, nor could he fend off all the men that craved her. Luckily, she had become pregnant a short time after marriage, and that first child was hardly weaned—in fact some would say her *ogiri omugwo* was still running—when she became pregnant again. However, after the birth of the second child, Nwanyi-Nma had become too big for any bag Onwu-Ghara could buy or weave. She was found with a man. Then another man. Then a third and a fourth. A wife found at adultery was entitled to a beating of sufficient severity to quell the husband's anger—and a stripping—the husband seized and locked away her clothes, leaving her only the barest covering, so that she was virtually housebound. However, neither beating nor stripping could stop Nwanyi-Nma. After she took her leisurely bath in the morning, applied oils and pomades to her skin and antimony *tirio* to her eyes, not even rags could hide what Nature had given her. Then one day she disappeared, and for about three months no one knew her whereabouts. Then reports reached her mother-in-law and mother that she had been seen at Agalaba, living by herself, plying the harlot trade and making quite a success of it.

About two weeks before they set out for Agalaba, the women of Uzemba took five shillings from their treasury and converted it to one hundred manilas, which they then used as *ncho* money. Delegations were dispatched to all the major towns and villages on the route between Uzemba and Agalaba. Each delegation carried a message: *Ndom ibe anyi,* we are coming through your town in two weeks on our way to Agalaba, where we hope to rescue a daughter and co-wife who has done what the Land forbids. We are leaving with you, on deposit, this signal twig and this sum of money. See by how much you can multiply the money for us, or if you cannot multiply it, then return it to us as we pass through your town. Whatever else you choose to do, we wish to let you know that our hearts will be gladdened if you come out of your houses or simply straighten up from hoeing your farms to wish us a good journey as we pass. If you can spare a gourd of drinking water or a kola nut, we will be grateful for it. We are your fellow women. *Ndom Uzemba*.

On the appointed day, between eighty and a hundred women set out from Uzemba for the trek to Agalaba. At Umu Orisa, six delegates joined their number. At Isi-Ahia, the women came out in force to greet them and wish them well and to return double the *ncho* money they had been given. Okpu-Muo was the same. Village by village, they were met by large delegations, some of which joined them for the trip and others of which plied them with gifts and good wishes, all of which wanted to hear the whole story of their trip and add to it their own stories of all the unseemly things that were now happening in their lives, things their mothers never experienced and their grandmothers never so much as imagined. Again and again the trekkers had to tear themselves away from the overweening hospitality of the delegations that came out to meet them, and in every case the delegation from one village escorted them to the edge of the next village, where the delegation from that village was already waiting. Night overtook them at Ukwu Orji, where again the women came out in force and fed them supper and asked them to stay the night and continue their trip in the morning. They recommenced their trip at cockcrow and passed through several other villages, where they were joined by delegates and were given food and water and many good wishes for the success of their endeavor. "Fellow women, we are with you! We are one with you in your grief and in your travels," they were told again and again.

They reached Agalaba in the fleecy mist of dawn, and paused on the outskirts at a place called Isi Korota, just on the other side of the railway level crossing. There they rested for maybe half an hour and retied their cloths and called out encouragement to one another and once again began singing and thumping on a few drums and ogeles they carried. And then they marched into town.

The address they were seeking was on Ehi Road, about a mile east of Eke Oha, Agalaba's daily market.

"Is this it?" several people asked, when they found the address.

"Yes, this is it!"

"Make sure!"

"Which room is hers?"

Glad to have arrived finally at their destination, the women burst

into a fresh medley of songs, and despite the cautions shouted by
some, some began to knock on different doors around the premises,
causing tenants to come out angry or curious. Ekweredi finally pointed
to a green door at the back of the yard, and many of the women
surged into the yard, blocking the narrow passageway between that
building and the next.

"Is she at home?"

"The door is locked."

"Is she inside?"

"That is impossible to tell."

"Maybe she has not returned from her night work."

"Or she may be inside with someone."

"Why not call out her name?"

"Yes, call out her name!"

"Nwanyi-Nma! Nwanyi-Nma!"

"Nwanyi-Nma, are you in there? Open the door!"

"Nwanyi-Nma, open the door. We are Ndom Uzemba, and have
come to see you!"

"Your mother and your mother-in-law both are here!"

"Call her Oyoyo! That is the name she uses now. Oyoyo Love!"
There were a few titters.

"Oyoyo Love, open for your people. Oyoyo!"

"Do you hear anything?"

"No, nothing."

"I have heard that she is also called Gbom Baby! Call her that and
see if she answers."

"Gbom Baby, come out! Oyoyo, open the door!"

"Break down that door!"

"No, no! We did not come here to break anything."

"Sing, everybody, sing! We will wait for her. If she is inside, we
will wait until she comes out. If she is away, we will wait until she
returns."

In the meantime, one of the tenants of the place had sent for the
landlord, who, on arrival, angrily demanded to know what the women
were doing in his yard. "Who are you?" he asked.

"We are the women of Uzemba, and we have come to see someone
who lives here."

"She is not at home. Can you not see that? Why are there so many
of you?"

"There are many of us because there are many of us," they answered. "What kind of question is that? We will just wait until she returns."

"You cannot wait in my yard. Move out or I will call the police."

"Police!"

"Yes, police."

"Why? Have we stolen from you?"

"You are in my yard. You are trespassing. If you want to wait, wait in the street."

The bulk of the women retreated from Oyoyo's door and veranda and from the backyard into the front yard between the street and the house. Some straggled and continued to bandy words with the land-lord. In the front yard, the singing resumed and grew louder. A lively dancing circle formed, and a crowd of onlookers began to gather and choke the street in front of the house.

A car approached and slowed because of the crowd, and then it stopped. A White woman riding beside an African driver looked on with interest. Noticing her, some of the women, about six of them, trotted to the car and began to dance and gesture in front of her.

"Come and dance with us, White woman," they invited and beck-oned. "Come and join us, fellow woman."

Then the baby in the backseat, cradled in the arms of a nursemaid, caught their attention. "Oh, look at the tiny White baby," they said.

"I have never seen a White baby before."

"Not me either. So this is what little White babies look like when they are really small."

"I used to think White people are like pigeons and vultures. You always see them grown, never when they are small."

Ignoring the nursemaid, who was glowering at their village bad manners, some of the women began to reach into the car to touch the infant. The nursemaid rolled up the glass.

Jumping out from the other side of the car, the driver began shout-ing, "Get out! Get out!" and began pulling roughly at the women whose faces were pressed close to the glass. One woman resisted the roughness. The driver called her a village *ak'akpu* and slapped her. She screamed, more in aggravation than in pain, snatched off her head cover, girdled it around her waist, and declared war on the driver. "You asked for it now, you ashy-bottom kitchen sweeper. You asked for it!" She clapped her hands ritually together, the equivalent of a bull scratching the ground before charging, and screamed at the driver: "Get ready! Get ready to receive me because you just slapped your mother."

Confused and bewildered by these developments, the White woman beckoned to the driver to return to the car, but the choice was not now open to the man, for five or six women had tangled with him, and he was kicking and flailing his limbs to stay free of their clutches. When he managed to struggle free, he broke off and ran. The women chased him down the street, throwing sticks, stones, and abuses after him. When he had put a safe distance between himself and them, he stopped and looked back. Both parties stood in place panting.

Passersby taunted the driver. "*Oga, na wetin kwanu?* How come woman de chase man so? What kind of country we get here now? What kind of man you be? You be man or you be something else?"

The White woman, who had been standing and looking on with her hands firmed against her hips, attempted to return to the car to await her driver's return. Two women grabbed her, one in each hand, and led her to the dancing circle. "Dance with us," they said. "Dance with us."

Not sure how to react, the White woman at first attempted to smile. She had been in the country long enough not to be afraid of these women, and she could surmise from their smiling faces that they were trying to be friendly.

"Dance, White woman, dance with us!" They linked hands with her and danced beside and around her, touching her waist and legs in turn and then touching theirs and making gestures and steps they wanted her to imitate. "Do White people not dance? Are you not a woman? Dance, White woman, dance!"

A police *sajin* and three other policemen, one of them a *kopuru*, arrived. Onlookers, especially men, began to scatter. The police made straight for the White woman, who was standing frozen in the middle of a circle of dancers. "Ex-ooze, Madam," the *sajin* said. "Wass-matter here? Any complain?"

"Yes, yes," the White woman said in a surge of anger. "Everything's the matter. Can you find my boy? My driver? I wish to get the dickens out of here!"

Two of the constables went in search of the driver.

"Madam, any complaints? Anyone molest you? Anyone disturb your peace?" The *sajin* took out his notebook, ready to record a crime.

"No, no," the White woman said. "No complaint. Just find my driver. I am overdue at the Catering Rest House. My husband is waiting for me. Thank you, Constable." With that she dismissed the *sajin* from her attention and then suddenly seemed to remember the baby and trotted off toward the car. The driver came hurrying back, found a winder under his side of the car seat, inserted it at the front of the car, wound a few times, and the car started. He and the White woman drove off.

"Who-sai you women come from?" the *sajin* asked.

"Uzemba."

"Una get parmit for parade?"

"We get what?"

"Parmit. Pa-a-ah-m-e-et! Paper wey say una fit march up and down Government road."

An exclamation of "What?" floated in waves through the crowd as people explained to one another what the officer meant.

"If you no get parmit, then all of you are under arrest," the officer said. "And what give you the audacity to humbug this White woman who just pass?"

An old, deaf woman edged to the front. "What did he say?" she asked a younger woman.

"He said he is going to arrest all of us."

"Why? What have we done to offend the law?" Because she was hard of hearing, the old woman spoke at a fevered pitch.

"You no fit parade without parmit," the *sajin* said very loudly. "Agalaba is Government land. Crown colony."

"But we did not come here to hold a parade," the old woman said. "We have many places to hold a parade without coming all the way out here to hold one. We have come here to retrieve our lost daughter and co-wife. Is that something the law forbids?"

"And if I feel like going to the latrine," the young woman said, "do I need a permit for that?"

"Arrest her," the *sajin* said to his men, motioning at the younger woman.

Two officers lunged at the woman. She tried to get away, but the officers ran her down and handcuffed her.

The mood changed suddenly from uncertain to hostile. The singing and dancing stopped.

"Son," the old woman said.

"I am not your son."

"I do have a son, though," the old lady retorted. "I have four sons, each of them as big as you. What has she done for you to put those iron locks on her hands?"

"All of you women are looking for trouble," the *sajin* said. "You are from the bush and do not understand Government law. I fit to arrest all of you now, but I am having plenty of mercy on you."

"Arrest me," the old lady said, stretching forth her hands. "Arrest me, and then go home and arrest your mother."

"Are you the leader, old woman?"

"We have no leader. No one is a leader. I have lived longer than most of these others, but I am not their leader. We are all women together. What makes each of us woman is the same thing that makes all others women. We have the same slit between our legs, the same two breasts, no one has three; we all squat down to urinate and to deliver our babies."

An officer proceeded to handcuff the old woman. This brought a loud, angry shout from the crowd, which surged forward, threatening to overwhelm the officers. Suddenly someone intoned, "Ndom Uzemba, are you together?"

"Ya-ya-yah!" the women answered in one voice.

"*Kwenu!*" [Agree!]

"Ya-ya-yah!"

"What do you say?

"We say, *Kama ji sii, nku gwuu!*"

"We say, *Kama ihere mee otu n'ime anyi, na nne muru anyi na nna muru anyi gwuu!*" [Rather than shame one of us, kill all of us!]

"We say, *Isi ukazi agbagha-siala!*" [The knot that holds the weaving together has unraveled!]

Head scarves came off heads. Waist cloths, which ordinarily reached down to the ankles, were rolled and hoisted up above the knees and retied *isi-ngidingi.*

Several other women came forward and offered themselves to be arrested and handcuffed. A chant and war stomp began.

"*Iweh! Iweh! Iweh nji anyi! Iweh!*" [Angry! Angry! We are very angry!]

The *sajin* dispatched one of his men to the barracks to make a report and bring reinforcements. As the police officer got ready to go, he discovered that the air had been let out of all the tires of the police bicycles.

In anger and frustration, the *sajin* picked up a whip and began to flail at the women who were now surging out of control. The other officers followed suit. There were shrieks and screams and groans and curses, as the women ran helter-skelter to get out of the way of the whip, but then reconverged when the mad policeman stopped chasing them.

"He is sending for more of his people. Let us send for more of our people," the old woman said. "Go to Eke Oha market and tell every woman you see that we are dead, that the police are killing us for no other reason than because we are women. Tell them to come to our help and rescue us. Go, go to all the villages and towns we passed through on our way here, all the women who wished us a safe journey. Tell them we are dead. If they can come immediately, they may still be able to rescue a few of us. If not, at least will they give all of us a decent burial when they get here, for the sake of our common womanhood? Tell them all we want is their assurance that our bodies will not be allowed to bloat and decay in the sun and rain and that the vultures that live in the tall trees of Eke Oha market will not peck at our flesh. Run and tell them!"

The deaf old lady became like one possessed. Her hands were cuffed but not her lips. Holding up those cuffed hands in the air, she walked the periphery of the crowd breathlessly asking, "Are you a woman?"

'Yes!" the women replied.

"What makes you a woman?"

"What makes a woman a woman is imponderable!"

"Uncountable!"

"Unfathomable!"

"How many women are there in the world?" the old lady continued.

"*Nnu-kwuru-nnu! Igwe!* Innumerable!"

"What is a woman?"

"A knot that is impossible to untie!"

"A river that no one can swim!"

"A knot in a tree that no one can cut through!"

A police inspector arrived at the scene in the company of about a dozen constables on foot. The *sajin* stepped forward and saluted his superior and began to give him a briefing. "Women from someplace in the bush," he said. "They have come to take back one of their number who they say is a harlot. A woman named Oyoyo."

"Oyoyo?" the inspector asked. "The one wey own Lucky Bar for Asa Road?"

"Na him."

"Wetin they say they want for Oyoyo?"

"They say they want take-am to village. A-be say him get two pikin. Anyway, as they arrive and no findam, they decide to wait. Except that landlord say no, they not fit wait in him yard. Too many of them. So they begin to dance in the front yard and in the street and cause commotion. And then they humbug White woman who pass for road."

"Mrs. Peterson! Them be the ones that stopped her?"

"Yessah."

"We just receive complain for station that she get accident, and her motor almost coversize."

The inspector thought for a moment, slapping his staff at his left palm. "Odah! Odah!" he shouted. "Everybody lissen, because what I say I go say only one time! Una de lissen?"

A shriek and then a tumult arose from the back of the yard. "She is at home! She has been at home all this time!" The crowd surged away from the inspector and his orders toward the back of the house where several of the women were pushing at the green door of Oyoyo's room to keep it from closing, while Oyoyo and some accomplice were pushing from the other side in an effort to shut it.

When the police approached, the women on the veranda stopped pushing, and the door slammed shut. The inspector rapped a knuckle on it and said, "Open in the name of the King!" As there was no immediate response, he barked in a much louder voice, "Police! Open this fucking door at once!"

The door opened slowly and slightly. Oyoyo's face appeared in the chink.

"Come out," the inspector commanded.

Oyoyo emerged onto the veranda, and the crowd of women began screaming and whooping. Maintaining a remarkable composure, she said, "Any complain? I do something?"

"Anyone else for house?"

"Ex-ooze officer. I gotto ask—I do something?"

"And I ask you first, anyone else dey for inside that room?"

"Yes, I get guest."

"Tell'am make him commot."

A man emerged, someone apparently known to the inspector, because the two smiled at each other and the man nodded slightly while the inspector greeted him with a joke. "Oga, so na here you tanda?" He was a mixed blood, half *Potokiri* and half Lebanese, with oily dark hair, a white shirt, and khaki trousers. A man of some means apparently, but under the circumstances he could not master the hundreds of eyes that were on him as he retrieved his bicycle from the corner and then waded his way out of the yard into the street beyond.

"You know these people?" the inspector asked Oyoyo. "They say they be your people."

"Yes, I know them."

"This is her mother," someone said. A woman was shoved forward from the crowd. "And this one is her mother-in-law."

"Ezinna," her mother called her, addressing her by her maiden name. "Is this you I am looking at?"

"Nwanyi-Nma," her mother-in-law, Ekweredi, called out. "I gave you that name myself, because I thought you were such a beautiful woman. You are still beautiful. But why have you chosen this life?"

"So," the inspector said, turning around and addressing the crowd of women. He was a man from another tribe and had difficulty with the vernacular. One of the officers began to play interpreter for him.

"You women have broken Government law," the translator said. "The ground where you are standing belongs to Government. You are disturbing the King's peace and blockaded the road and caused White woman to have accident. But Inspector is a kindhearted man. That is why he has not put all of you for prison. Do you want to go to prison?"

No one answered.

"Inspector says he knows you have come here from a long distance and you have children and husbands waiting for you at home. He says if you go now he will forget the laws you have already broken. He will even remove the handcuffs from those who have already been arrested. . . ."

A *kopuru* with two stripes on his sleeve came up and saluted the inspector, and then took him aside and conferred earnestly.

The crowd around the house swelled, stretching from the backyard to the front yard, engorging the two adjacent yards, and spilling across the street to the other side.

"Tell Commissioner the situation is under control," the inspector was instructing the *kopuru*. "Tell'am things a little out of hand when I get here, but everything well in hand now. No more problem."

"Sah, PWD engineer tell'am different. Say the place almost riot. You know Oyibo go believe another Oyibo."

"Just tell'am as I tell you. Tell'am say everything under control. By the time him come here I done finish drive these women away."

The *kopuru* turned and departed on his mission. The inspector turned around and shouted at the crowd, "All right, everybody scatter! Everybody vamoose!"

While the inspector was haranguing the rest of the women, Oyoyo's mother and mother-in-law had pulled her aside for a private exchange.

The two mothers were aghast at what they heard their daughter say. For them, talking to her was a song of grief; for her, it should have been a song of contrition. Instead, however, Oyoyo seemed to boast about being a harlot. There was no shame in her face or in her voice; she did not avert her eyes or cast her gaze to the ground. And she did not cry.

Why, she wanted to know, had her mother and mother-in-law brought such great public disgrace on her by leading all those people to her lodgings? Practically all of Eke Oha market was holding session before her door.

The older women turned to look at each other in amazement, each saying with her eyes to the other: Are you hearing what I am hearing? Then they asked her: Is it not you who has been holding session with your body for all of Eke Oha market?

Oyoyo asked, "Could you not have sent me a message to tell me whatever you wished to tell me? Could you not have come by yourself, or if you like with two or three friends?"

"Perhaps your memory is faulty," her mother replied. "How many messages have I sent to you? And how many has your mother-in-law sent? And who says I must suit your convenience? From what I remember, I gave birth to you, not you to me."

"And I am the one who is taking care of those two children you bore," the mother-in-law joined in.

"Have I not tried to persuade you to let them come and live with me?"

"So they can grow up in a house of prostitution? Is that what you want for your daughter, to become a prostitute when she grows up? Would you have wanted them to be here today to see what we are seeing?"

"What are you seeing here today? Tell me, what have you seen? Except all the people you brought?"

"Something I would have hoped never to see," her mother replied. "Something I thought I would never see. Has anybody else's daughter acted like mine? Has the whole town sent a delegation to recall anyone else's daughter from a house of prostitution? When my friends boast about their children, when they say 'Come, everyone, and see what a household my daughter has built, how many robust children call me Nne-nne because of her, how her crops are flourishing on the farm,' when others say such things, how do I join in the boasting? Perhaps I can ask you to line up all your customers and have them pull down their knickers and trousers and invite the whole town to come and marvel at all the penises that have been inside you!"

"You can say that your daughter is a big businesswoman in the township, that her name is on the signboard of a bar on Asa Road, the biggest street in all of Agalaba Uzo, and that she now has enough money to come home in a few weeks to repay her husband every broken manila that he paid on her account. That after I have paid back to Onwu-Ghara the bride price that made me his wife, I will be a free woman."

"You are a free woman now," her mother-in-law interjected. "Free to every man in this town."

"No, not that kind of free. No-no, ah-aah. I am free to myself. To the men who visit me, I certainly am not free. I cost *bokwu* money, much more than most men can afford. I am a high-class Number A-1 woman. Years ago, when I was a young girl in the village, then perhaps I was free, but today Oyoyo Love is costly. . . ."

The two older women stood dumbstruck while Oyoyo continued: "A man came to me once," she said, "a small crayfish trader in the market, and when I asked him how much money he had he said, Six manilas. I told him that I did not take manilas, that I was not a manila kind of woman, that if he wanted to talk to me he had to have English money, *ego cham-cham*, and he had to have enough of it.

One shilling for one hour. Ten shillings TDB [till day break]. This poor man was so filled with desire for me that he would have given his life to have me. That first day he left *sisi* with me as advance. Next day he came and gave me *toro*, all the profit he made from trading that day. The following day he came back with another *toro*. Now is that not a man who appreciated the hour I gave him?"

"Perhaps we should all leave home and come here and join you and all become harlots?" the mother-in-law said. *"Nwanyi ibem,"* she continued, turning to Orianu. "Can you believe what I am hearing? Do you understand it? If you do, please explain it to me and I will be grateful to you."

Undaunted by their consternation, Oyoyo continued to talk about her prostitution as if she were a *dibia,* an exalted high priestess, and her body a fetish that men paid a high price to come and consult. In the village, she said, did not women often brag about how much they cost their husbands in bride price? When co-wives quarreled, was it not common for one to say to the other: "Our husband spent the last drop of sweat from his brows to marry me. Even till today, he is still paying. That shows how much he values me. But you, you came for almost nothing. And that is what you are worth—nothing! You never had more than one suitor in your life. Even now, if someone bathed you and dressed you and took you to the wife market, you would come home unsold! Your people were so eager to get rid of you that they were willing to give you away for free." What then was wrong, Oyoyo argued, if she got the highest price for her womanhood? Was this not better than *tukwuo-lia* and *utu-ghara,* which the women of the village sometimes engaged in? Besides, no one ever beat her; no one gave her much humbug. The men paid gladly. More than gladly, they paid eagerly. Right now, for example, she had refined her clientele, dropping the junior clerks and the petty traders.

The mouths of the two older women were so wide open that a flock of birds could have nested in them, laid eggs, and hatched their young, and they would not have known the difference. What was their daughter saying? What could have put such thoughts in her? And where did she find the boldness to utter them aloud? They did not recognize her or what she said—there was nothing like it in their previous experiences. Was womanhood for sale? Was there a price on being a wife and a mother? Was the bride price a purchase price for something? When a wife favored her husband with her body, was there a price for the favor? Was it not a gift? Granted, during birth ceremonies, in conjunction with the Ohie N'Ole dance, there was a song that included the line *Ikwe-maam onu ikpu, ma avoro gi ya nvuvo!* [If you give me a good price for my thing, I will even comb the hair for you!] but was that not just a jest?

"*Ogo'm*, Ekweredi, pinch me!" Oyoyo's mother said.

Ekweredi pinched Orianu symbolically on the arm.

"Thank you," Orianu said. "I just wanted to know whether I was still in this world or have died and am living in a different world."

The two women looked at each other and shook their heads. The world they used to know was now doing somersaults all around them and in the process exposing things they could not so much as imagine.

"I did not know the meaning of shamelessness until today," the mother-in-law said. "Now I know."

"I have heard enough," the mother said, and then turning to the mother-in-law, she asked, "Have you not heard enough?"

"I most certainly have," the mother-in-law said, shaking her head, "and I do not have a name for what I feel."

"Same here," the mother said. "What I feel like is vomiting. And as for you, my daughter, that shit you are speaking about, I believe it is backing up from your anus into your stomach and coming out of your mouth. Your mouth, my dear daughter, is spewing shit, and I will not stand here and let you spray it all over me. *Utu gbara,* huh? At least women who succumb to *utu gbara* are old widows who cannot find anyone to claim them. And their mortgage is to one penis, not to all the erect penises in a whole township! And let me tell you this, my former daughter: When your father married me, he could not afford a heavy bride price, so I was one of those women whom some wagging tongues called *nna-l'aka nwanyi*. A wife married on credit, on a handshake and a promise, but I stayed with him and he made good on his promise. When I lay down and opened my legs for him, to conceive you, I did not reckon a price on his pleasure or on your head. That is how you came into this world, a freeborn and not a slave. That is why there was great rejoicing at your birth." She circled her hand ritually around her head, snapped her thumb and middle finger once, and spat "*Tufia,*" to disassociate herself from an unspeakable abomination. Turning toward Ekweredi, she said, "*Ogo'm,* let us do what we came here to do."

"*Ndom, kwenu!*"

"Yah-yah-yah!"
"Kwenu!"
"Yah-yah-yah!"
"We have seen the person we came to see. We have a long way to travel and do not want nightfall to overtake us here. Let us begin to pack her things."

The rest of the women from Uzemba, already smarting restlessly from the several minutes, were only too eager to go into action. There was a rush at Oyoyo's door, but only about a dozen women managed to enter before someone announced that there was no more room inside and advised the rest to stay out and let the dozen do the packing.

"Whatever we cannot put in boxes and baskets, we can carry by hand," someone suggested.

"Yes, yes," many agreed. "There are more than one hundred of us. If everyone picks up one item or two, we may not need to pack anything. *Ivu anyigh ndanda.*"

"Oh no! Oh no!" Oyoyo shouted, dashing into the room and tearing away people who were grabbing her things.

It was at this point that Brockway arrived with six children, three boys and three girls, each carrying a pail of water.

Most people called her Brockway because she was built like a Brockway truck, but she had a litany of other nicknames. Some called her Tank. A few who had been in Kaiser's war or heard or read about it called her Panza. Fada Getz, the Roman Catholic priest, with whom she had had many altercations, called her *Peccata Mundi.* Brockway-Tank-Panza–*Peccata Mundi* was a madwoman, built like a man—a big, strong, and muscular man. She had a loud gravelly voice and deep, sour, bloodshot eyes and a grip that could take two pugnacious boys by the neck, bump their heads together, and instantly call them to order. All of the Agalaba had three water taps; the busiest and rowdiest at the corner of Asa and Jubilee roads was popularly known as Pump Brockway, and was policed by her.

Somehow, Brockway had learned about the mission of the women of Uzemba and had marched six youngsters, each carrying a bucket of water, to the house where Oyoyo lived. "Drink," she commanded the women in her high, hoarse voice. "From the dust on your feet, you must have come a long way and must be thirsty. Everybody drink!"

Brockway served. She lifted one bucket at a time, while each thirsty drinker in turn pressed her lips at the edge of the bucket and drew at the water until her breath gave. "Next," Brockway said, and the next drinker then moved up.

And then Brockway struck a blow for Ndom. It was as happens sometimes, when a person becomes embroiled in an altercation with a dog owner and suddenly the dog bolts out of nowhere and attacks the outsider. Oyoyo was tugging at a chair with two other women, when suddenly Brockway grabbed her by the shoulders, spun her around, and slapped her across the face. With a shriek, Oyoyo hurled herself at Brockway, who hurled her to the ground and proceeded to tear off her clothes. It was an uneven match, but even so, Brockway did not seem intent on pressing her advantage. All she did was strike Oyoyo a few times to subdue her, and thereafter she proceeded to strip off her clothes. When Oyoyo was completely naked, she let her go.

The police, all of whom had migrated to the street at the arrival of one of their senior officers, came running back when they heard the shrieks and the new commotion. Seeing that Brockway was at the center of it all, they gave her wide berth, as none was eager to tangle with her—she had a reputation as a biter who would chew off any appendage that came near her mouth, be it finger or earlobe. Worse than that, a bite from her was guaranteed to infect its victim with her madness. In any event, while the police were hesitating, Brockway, her work apparently done, unstraddled herself from Oyoyo's prostrate body, clapped her hands clean, and began marching her six youngsters back to the pump.

The spell Brockway had cast with the suddenness of her actions lifted as she walked away. Ekweredi took off her top cloth and threw it to Oyoyo, who had turned over on her belly and was sobbing hysterically into the ground. The mother, Orianu, dropped another cloth over her torso. The two women, mother and mother-in-law, helped her up and led her into her room, which was now bare. There they quickly dressed her.

"Ndom Uzemba, are we ready to go?"

"Yah-yah-yah!" the women answered.

"Can anyone remember a song? Why does not someone sing a song to improve our spirits and the atmosphere of this place?"

> Iweh! Iweh!
> Iweh nji anyi!
> Iweh!

"No, no, not that! That is a war song, or a song the men use to go pick up a dead body! She is not dead!"

"*Omutara nwa, zuo nwa ya eeeeh. . . .*" someone intoned.

"Whoever begets a child should train that child. . . ."

After a hesitant start, during which the women tried to find the tune, the song began to roll in waves across the crowd. The two *ogele*s and the three *ekpete*s began to clink and thump and keep time. The women began to move on their homeward journey. Oyoyo's house had been stripped clean; her bedding, clothes, furniture, utensils, and all other belongings were being carried one by one by the more than one hundred women who had come to rescue her. Oyoyo herself was walking in the middle of the throng, reluctantly but without hope of escape, between her mother and her mother-in-law.

A short distance up Ehi Road, a squad of policemen barred their way, with them a White superintendent, before whom all the other police were saluting and clicking their heels. Every policeman seemed to have someone of higher rank for whom he wagged his tail. All tails wagged for the White man. Even the inspector sallied up, saluted, and clicked his heels. The White man nodded carelessly, like a juju unimpressed by a cheap sacrifice. Yes, the women could clearly see, the Inspector might have been the high priest, but the White man was the spirit oracle. And the oracle was displeased, and the priest took a long time explaining and excusing himself.

What the Inspector was explaining was that the Ndom Uzemba insisted on taking Oyoyo back to the village. They had said she had two children, whom she had abandoned. Her mother was the one on her left, and the woman holding her right hand was her mother-in-law. These women were not all from the same village, but were made up of delegates from different towns and villages. They had picked up every belonging from her house and were carrying them item by item, so that it was impossible to order them to put it all back. If he ordered them to put back what they were carrying, they merely broke rank and scattered, making it impossible to control them without much force. . . .

"Can't! Can't is all I am hearing from you, Inspector. What *can* you do?"

"Nothing, sah!"

"Nothing?"

"As you can see, sir, they be legion. Their number pass hundred

and fifty. And they are not like the men. They resist arrest and bite
and fight, and if you arrest some, the others say 'Arrest us too!' And
back there at the house, it be like all of Eke Oha market empty, and
all of the market women come to join forces with these women and
bring them food and fruit. Even madwoman bring them water. . . ."

The superintendent paced for some moments, looking up and down
the street to behold the large numbers of people lining the street, and
it did not escape his notice that the women especially pushed forward
with pride, even ahead of the men and the nosy little boys. They
waved their support and punched the air with their clenched fists and
yelled encouragement.

"Listen, all of you," the superintendent said.

"Odah! Odah!" one of the officers translated. "White man wants
to speak to you."

The White man wanted to know why they had come into town to
break the law.

The women replied that they had not come into town to break any
law, only to escort back one of their number who had brought disgrace
to them. Their mission accomplished, they were now on their way
home, except that he and his police were blocking them.

As they spoke the singing of another large group of women became
more audible in the distance. They were approaching from the opposite direction.

"Inspector, find out who those are," the superintendent ordered.

"Those are our friends," the women replied and began to dance and
make the curious ululating cries they made by clapping their hands
across their lips.

"That's what I said, Sah," the Inspector put in. "These women
bokwu pass water!"

"Do you have any more friends?" the White man wanted to know.

"*Igwe kwuru igwe ndom!*" the women replied. "Those are some of
our friends who bid us safe journey as we began our trip this morning.
If all of us are not home by nightfall, more will come to see what
has happened to the others. . . ."

"What will you do to her [Oyoyo] after you reach home?"

"Her mother and mother-in-law will retrain her."

"She will not be harmed?"

"She needs new training, that is all."

"Let them go," the White man said.

"*Tofi!*" the Inspector said. "You free to go!"

The women broke into cheers and moved forward again as the police stepped aside.

"Escort them to the edge of town," the superintendent said.

The women who brought Oyoyo back from Agalaba Uzo arrived back in Uzemba late in the afternoon, just as Ahia Afor, the town's four-day evening market, was beginning its session. The market virtually dissolved itself on seeing them, as the traders packed their goods and wares back into their baskets and rushed to be part of the *emume* that was about to commence. This was something the likes of which no one had heard before, that village women should travel more than twenty miles into a modern township and rescue one of their number from a house of prostitution. They sat up for the rest of the day and well into the night in front of Onwu-Ghara's house, singing, dancing, ululating, and recounting their adventures for themselves and for the benefit of those who had not gone with them.

"You should have seen what happened between us and the police," some said to the others who had not gone with them.

"Yes, and what happened between us and the White man. We were afraid of no one. He had fifteen or twenty evil-looking police with him but we were not daunted."

"Do not forget the White woman and her little White baby."

"That is right. We made the White woman dance with us. At first, she was reluctant but after a while the music seemed to make her feet lighter."

"What about the madwoman who brought us water to drink?"

"Yes, the madwoman. Talk of someone who swallowed an elephant's heart. She wrestled Oyoyo to the ground before an eye could twinkle! And then stood over her like a gorilla. That was something to behold."

Ekweredi and Onwu-Ghara killed three goats and several chickens to help entertain their guests. Palm wine, *eti-eti*, beer and Coco-Cream flowed liberally, and although hoarse, the women continued to sing intermittently and to thump on the drums.

Oyoyo was given a chair among them and sat sullenly in a semicircle of older women, with no one quite knowing how to treat her, whether as a prodigal or a prisoner of war, and with her not knowing how to feel or relate toward those who accosted her. Her face was

streaked with tears and dirt and the uneven remains of her face powders partially leached by sweat. Some people, trying to be cordial to
her, said hello or welcome home, while others not so sympathetic
simply stood and smiled and shook their heads at whatever private
meaning they were extracting from the scene. For her part, Oyoyo
stared back at them with sheepish boredom, once in a while parting
her lips as if to speak, when someone spoke to her whom she held in
great respect or affection, but then not letting the words form or
escape from her mouth.

Those whose sense of probity had not been fully assuaged by what
had happened to her conversed among themselves, intentionally to her
hearing:

"Maybe she will now let her tail rest in the dust a little bit," some
of the harsher ones said.

"Yes, and take care of those two children she brought into the
world."

"I hear she said that prostitution is just another way of being a
wife?"

"And prostitutes are better than wives because they get paid more
for what they do for men?"

"Do you think she feels any shame at all for what she has done?
How can she sit so calmly among us and not feel like covering her
face or running somewhere to hide? How can she be so bold and
shameless that her eyes do not even dim a little at what she has
done?"

"They say shame is the first thing to go, when a person becomes
a prostitute. If prostitutes felt shame, they would not allow themselves
to be seen in the daytime. It is like night-soil work. Night-soil men
at Agalaba do not wait for night to fall before they come out and do
their work. They do not even pull their hats over their faces."

"What the world has now become! Do such people have wives?"

"Yes, of course. They may even be rich."

"Would you like to be married to a night-soil man?"

"You might, but not I!"

"Do you think she will stay or go back?"

At a point, Orianu, the mother, and Ekweredi, the mother-in-law,
withdrew from the crowds to talk with each other in the yard at the
back of Ekweredi's kitchen.

"Nwanyi ibem."

"Yes, *nwanyi ibem*."

They both reached out and embraced each other, tears streaming down their cheeks. Then they pulled up chairs and sat down on the bald yard a short distance from the water pots.

"Well, we have done it," Ekweredi said, wiping her eyes. "We are home safely."

"Yes," Orianu agreed. "We have successfully traveled to Agalaba Uzo and come back with our daughter. That was quite a tall and slippery tree to climb."

"Yes, it was. And we did it. What I wanted to talk to you about is what do we do now? Our fellow women, outsiders, have done their part. In short time, they will all go home. What shall we do with this girl who found reincarnation with you and marriage with my son?"

"Exactly what I have been thinking," Orianu replied. "Your thoughts and mine have been traveling on the same track."

"Have you reached a conclusion?"

"Yes, *nwanyi ibem*," Orianu said. "As you correctly say, Ezinna is my daughter by birth and yours by marriage. I had her before I gave her to you. I hope you will not refuse me if I ask you to give her back to me for a month or longer. Let me see whether I can reconceive her, give birth to her again, bring her up again, and when she is ready escort her back to your house and offer her anew to her husband."

"I completely agree with you," Ekweredi said. "You can keep her as long as you consider necessary. Furthermore, at your house she will be among her kith and kin and therefore away from the temptation of men, to say nothing of the tongues that will be wagging about all the things that have happened. As happy as I am about all the women who went with us to Agalaba Uzo, and the way we were able to kindle and uphold one another's spirit, I now realize that every person who was part of our trip will walk away with the story, and as well as it may yet end, it is not altogether a story of joy or triumph."

"You are so correct. It will not end with stories; it will be in all the festival songs for this year and maybe even for next. Your name and mine will even be mixed up with both the stories and the songs. The things we said, the anguish we expressed to the hearing of others. *Nwanyi ibem*, did you ever dream that something like this would happen to you someday? I say to myself that this is not the baby I delivered, the girl who grew up in my house with five other children.

The other five are responsibly married—three boys and three girls survived for me. Five have made me proud, but the sixth is a source of shame. On what do I blame it? Did I not feed all of them from the same pot? Did I not discipline all of them the same way? Where did this strange seed come from?"

"Strange seeds are called strange because they are not like the mother tree, and we do not know where they come from," Ekweredi said. "It is something in her own *chi,* my sister, not something you are to blame for. That is why you never catch the smallest hint of blame in anything I say to you. But there is one additional thing I think we should do. I think we should not let this whole affair pass by without looking into it."

"Same thought I was thinking," Orianu said. "Perhaps we can consult a seer together."

"No, not together," Ekweredi said. "You go toward the sunrise and I go toward the sunset. Then afterward we can meet and compare the oracles. The proverb says that if you are running and calling after a person at the same time, if the running does not catch up with him, then the calling will. So, one of us run and the other call and let us see if we do not catch up with this thing one way or the other."

"Yes, let us do that. And after we get to the bottom of it, my daughter will undergo at least one month of cleansing at my house before reuniting with her husband."

"Tell me something, though," Ekweredi said, leaning forward earnestly in her chair and lowering her voice a little. "Was Nwanyi-Nma circumcised after she was born?"

"What kind of question is that?" Orianu asked, her brows lifting and her countenance furrowing with consternation. "Of course she was circumcised. All my children were circumcised."

"Who did it?"

"Ngwahu, a woman who used to live in the next village. She has since died. Why are you asking?"

"It is probably nothing."

"Why?"

"Well, among the things going on, you hear stories. And jokes. When something like this is happening to you, you become the laughingstock of every oaf whose belly is full of overnight palm wine. There is a bad joke circulating that Nwanyi-Nma is not circumcised, that she has an *atutu* as long as a small finger. It is probably no more than a bad joke, but I thought I would ask you."

"Please do not say something like that!"

"I did not say it, *nwanyi ibem,* but it is something that is being said by others—one of many things so heinous I cannot bring my mouth to utter them in front of you. I pass by a group of men and I hear them snickering. I pass by a group of women on the way to the farm or the stream and I hear them whispering. And I know they are all whispering or snickering about something that has to do with my son's wife."

"Please do not let them repeat such abominable filth."

"I tell you, this is filth that greets and follows me everywhere I go. The people who repeat it do not ask my permission to do so."

Orianu stood. "I have snuff," she said, extricating her *amangbo* from a fold in her cloth. "Would you like to share some?"

"Yes, thank you," Ekweredi said, taking the snuffbox from Orianu.

"We will get to the end of this somehow," Orianu said.

"Yes, somehow," Ekweredi agreed.

The following day, Oyoyo went to live with her mother. Her things, including virtually all of her clothes, stayed with her mother-in-law.

For a month or so, Orianu and Ekweredi met frequently to compare notes on what they had learned from the various seers with whom they consulted. By the end of the month they had agreed on a plan: Oyoyo had to be circumcised, or re-circumcised, and the person to do the job was Ugbala.

On the day they selected, a group of eight women followed Ekweredi on the trip to Orianu's house, which they reached about the first cockcrow. For her part, Orianu had assembled about a dozen other women from her village. Oyoyo was roused, and the group marched with her into the high bushes on the outskirts of the village, where no one lived. They set down the things they carried in a clearing that had been prepared beforehand. Water was set boiling on a fire they quickly lit. A mat was laid down and Oyoyo was invited to sit on it. When she balked, she was tackled by several of the women and pinned down on it. Strong hands held her down, limb by limb, while Ugbala knelt between her legs with her specially sharpened *aguba*.

In a relatively short time, the deed was done. Oyoyo was circumcised. Rituals that went with circumcision were performed. *Ogu*s were cast. The women collected the objects they had brought and headed home.

Four days later, Oyoyo disappeared.

About a week after that, word reached both her mother and mother-in-law that she was back in Agalaba Uzo.

While the two older women were wringing their hands and wondering what to do next, three policemen arrived from Agalaba to arrest them. Their daughter had sworn out a warrant against them and Ugbala, accusing them of conspiracy with intent to kill her, among other things.

The policemen were not quite prepared for the crowd that greeted them at Ugbala's compound, nor in fact for the contingent that followed them from the other places where they had made the first two arrests. More than two hundred people, most of them women, filled the open *mbara ezi* and choked the long lane leading to it, so that the constables had to walk through a throng that opened to let them in and then closed quickly behind them. If this place were nearer to town, they would have asked their superiors for reinforcements. They carried rifles with fixed bayonets, but those would have been of limited use against such a large crowd. Anyway, they were encouraged that most of the crowd consisted of women, and that despite their general sullenness they displayed no unusual signs of hostility. In any event, they had done what correct procedure called for in situations like this: They had paid their calls on the local chiefs to inform them of their mission and indirectly to make them accountable for the success of that mission as well as their safety.

As Nne-nne and others told it, the story of Ugbala's arrest, or nonarrest, comes in many versions. The most plausible version says that she came out of her house to greet the police and inquire about their health and the health of their families. Then she asked if they had come to arrest her, and they said yes.

"On what charge?" she asked.

"Attempted homicide."

She chuckled. "I bring children into this world. I have never attempted to kill anyone. But if you say that I have, well, what can I say? You are people of the law. Whom did I attempt to kill?"

"Nwanyi-nma Onwu-Ghara. A.k.a. Ezinna. A.k.a Oyoyo Love."

"How did I try to kill her?"

"Conspiring with others as named. Physical assault. Unlawful restraint. Slashing at her genitalia with a sharp instrument, and leaving her to bleed nearly to death."

The story continues that at this point Ugbala asked if she could be allowed a chance to go to the *otikpiri* to relieve herself. The policemen were chagrined and looked at one another. They were perplexed, even mesmerized by this unusual woman, who drew such a big crowd to her compound and came to meet them resplendent in a *juj* wrapper, wearing *akah* beads on her wrists and ankles and a chestful of *nkamenyi* ivory around her neck topped by three of the largest lumps of pink *nkalari* anyone had ever seen.

"Hankkup," the *kopuru* said.

"No, no hankkup," Ugbala replied in English, causing many in the crowd to titter. "If you choose, you can come and watch me while I do my business. But you cannot put my hands in your locks. If you do, how will I wipe myself?"

The policemen, indecision on their faces, let Ugbala go. Or at least did not prevent her from going toward the latrine a couple of hundred yards from the outer rim of the compound. Here the story has several versions. Some say she simply vanished, others say that the police tried to handcuff her but the cuffs fell off. In any event, Ugbala went to the latrine and did not return.

Onwu-Ghara, beleaguered husband of Oyoyo Love, was in a mild frenzy, his thoughts jumpy. He was not comfortable standing up or sitting down, walking around or standing still. The thought that his mother would spend a night in a lockup and possibly even go to prison for no other reason than attempting to solve the problem of Nwanyi-Nma—that was the worst type of injury that could be added to an insult. It made him furious.

He went into the house of his friend, Ehiemere, but Ehiemere was not much help. The Government was like a big animal, Ehiemere said, like a gorilla. No one could wrestle with it and expect to win. Then Ehiemere roamed further through the forest and found another animal to which he likened the Government. It was like a porcupine. If you tried to grapple with it, it shot you full of spikes.

Did that mean then that he should do nothing? Onwu-Ghara asked.

"You can follow the police to Agalaba tomorrow and see what the charges really are. They may add some or drop some, so that there are more or fewer than what you heard today. Then they will set bail. They can set it high or low, depending on whether or not you *see* them beforehand. Then they will give you a date to come back. Money. You are talking money. How much do you have on hand?"

"If you beat me now, you could not beat more than one pound out of me. I have two unsold sacks of palm kernels in the house, which I bought at Nkwo Ala yesterday and Ahia Afor the day before."

"This is more than a one-pound case, I assure you."

"Can you spare anything?"

"Not very much. Ten shillings maybe. Like you, I went to the market yesterday, and I am going again in the morning. Whatever I have is all tied up right now in bags of *garri*. Until I go to Onu Miri at the end of this market week, my capital will not be released. But I can lend you ten shillings. Have you talked to De-Osu-Agwu?"

"No, not yet."

"I do not believe he is at home now, but you should talk to him as soon as he returns. Persuade him to summon the men of the kindred on your account. While it is still light, perhaps you can go to the evening market and buy a pot of palm wine to place before them. Everyone has heard about what happened, but you can present it to them formally. Useful ideas may come out of their meeting, and perhaps some money."

"Do you know whether there is any money in the *amala* collection box? I was not at the last meeting."

"Seven pounds is what I remember hearing, but I would not expect to find seven pounds in that box if it was opened right now. Between meetings, various insiders 'borrow' *ewerewe* from it, only to replace it just before the next meeting, in case someone asks to have the box opened and its contents counted."

"Even if the money is there, I do not know whether De-Osu-Agwu and the others will consent to lend it to me."

"You cannot tell until you have asked them. Anyway, I think it is something that the kindred should discuss, even if they do nothing. . . . Someone is arriving. I believe it is Chief Onyiri-Dike's houseman."

"*Ndewo nu,*" the man said.

"*Ndewo,*" the other two men replied. "Have a seat," Ehiemere said. "Welcome."

The man did not sit, but held his cap in his hand, turning it on its rim.

"You seem to be in a great hurry," Ehiemere said, placing a chair next to the man's leg and then sitting back down himself. "I will have to ask you to forgive me for kola."

"Thank you for the offer. Which one of you is Onwu-Ghara?"

"I am the one," Onwu-Ghara said.

"It is true that I am in a hurry. I have traveled here on behalf of Chief. Onwu-Ghara, he would like to see you. It is of course because of the little problem your mother has with the Government."

"This evening? It is very late already."

"Yes, this very night. Chief told me not to beat about the bush about why he wants to see you." Shifting on his feet, he bumped against the chair that Ehiemere had placed beside him and decided to sit down in it after all. He carefully placed his cap over his knee. "It is about the three policemen who are sleeping in his house tonight. They are really your guests, not his. Guests require entertainment, and Chief thinks that a sacrifice should be offered by those from whom a juju is demanding it, not by someone else. He therefore says, what do you want your guests to eat for supper tonight? What should they have for breakfast in the morning?"

"Let them eat shit!" Onwu-Ghara said.

"Mmmh," the Chief's messenger grunted deeply. "I know that is not what you really mean, so I will ignore that statement. But as you can see, it is getting late, and I have a long way to travel back. And I am not really here to haggle. Your in-laws have offered a cock and six yams and one guinea in English money as *ogbakwasa*. You can see the yams tied to the carrier of my bicycle and you can hear the cock. Here is the one pound and the one shilling." He undid a fold in his loincloth and held up a red note and a shilling. "This is not really enough for two meals for three policemen who have traveled all the way from Agalaba, but it may do for their supper tonight. You know also that when a person travels on an errand for people who are senior to him, and the people he has gone to visit offer him some kola, it is custom for the messenger to take a piece of that kola back to those who sent him. These policemen have superiors. One of them is a *kopuru* with two stripes on his sleeve. The other two are barefoot policemen. Back in the depot at Agalaba, they have senior people— perhaps sergeant, perhaps inspector—who sent them on this errand. When they return tomorrow, should they be empty-handed when these senior people ask: 'Did the accused offer any kola?' Should they say: 'One of them asked us to eat shit'? I have not even mentioned that Chief is going to a lot of trouble on your account. He has to find three suitable beds tonight for these policemen—you cannot ask a Government constable to sleep on the floor. . . ."

"I do not have anything to give them."

"Is that your final answer? As I have said, I am not here to plead or haggle with you. What is your final reply?"

"The one I have already given you."

"That the policemen should eat shit? Remember I am going to give your reply exactly as you have given it. I suppose you do not care what happens to your mother, whether or not she goes to prison for ten years, whether she will be carrying that shit you are talking about in big buckets from the public latrines on Asa Road."

"I will castrate myself before my mother goes to prison."

"Perhaps you know something I do not know. Something all those other prisoners who eat the Government's beans at Agalaba do not know. If not, then you should start to sharpen your knife at once."

"Onwu-Ghara," Ehiemere called sharply, before the former could say anything else. "Come, let us confer for a moment."

They left the Chief's messenger in Ehiemere's parlor and stepped outside. Ehiemere put his hand on his friend's shoulder to calm him. "Let me handle it," he said. Onwu-Ghara protested, but Ehiemere insisted. "The proverb says that it is better to pay for medicine than to pay for a funeral. Come." He called one of his wives as they marched across the compound toward her house. "Ihu-Oma!"

"D'im oma," the woman answered.

"Bring me a cob of corn."

"To eat?"

"For a chicken to eat. Any cob you can find."

The woman brought a cob and handed it to Ehiemere.

"The pile of yams I have at the back of your house—select the best six you can find among them and tie them with a rope. Then bring them."

As Ihu-Oma turned to get the yams, Ehiemere began tossing out corn kernels to attract the chickens that were roaming the yard. He had his eyes on a cock, which appeared at length and was caught after a chase by the two men and the chief's messenger.

"You should not do this for me," Onwu-Ghara protested.

"I am not doing it for you," Ehiemere said. "I am doing it for myself. Anyway, let us not argue about the sacrifice while we are still in front of the juju shrine, and the juju priest is still standing by." Ehiemere gave the yams and the trussed cock to the chief's messenger.

"What about what goes with it, the *ogbakwasa?*" the chief's messenger asked.

"What goes with it?" Ehiemere asked with a knowing smile.

"*Ego cham-cham,*" the messenger replied, "if I must spell it out for you."

"Let us say that what goes with it is on its way and has not yet arrived," Ehiemere said. "My friend has been caught off his guard by these events and needs to catch his breath. If you consider for a moment what has happened to him: He has lost his wife to prostitution. Now the same wife has sent police to arrest his mother for trying to persuade her to stay home and mind her two children. He doesn't have a wife, no return of bride price, and now mother under arrest."

"My brother, I am just a messenger. As everyone nowadays says, the world we live in is doing somersaults and revealing things I cannot stand to take a hard look at. I did not start it. I cannot stop it. I am just an onlooker, like you, like perhaps everybody. Our world has become like the church people's Bible—whatever page opens up before you that page you read. If your book opens in Psalms, you read 'Glory and Hallelujah!' If it opens for you in Job or Jeremiah, you read 'Woe betide! Woe betide!' What I am thinking now is what I shall tell Chief as the result of the errand on which he sent me. He will see the yams and the cock, but Chief has a barn full of yams. Each of his nine wives has a big chicken coop. I will show him the one guinea from your in-laws, and he will say what about you. You see, what you have given me is like a bowl of fufu without any soup. Or, if you like, a pot of *okpoko* soup without meat or condiments."

"This big cock will make plenty of good soup," Ehiemere said with a laugh. "This is just *ndende-onu,* an appetizer. Tell the chief to munch on it till we come. The hive is full of honey, but it is the middle of the day and the bees are awake. We have to wait till after midnight when the bees go to sleep."

"You are coming?"

"Yes, we are coming."

"When?"

"Early in the morning, if not tonight."

"Your friend on whom this thing has fallen, I notice he is not saying much. Are you sure you are speaking for him?"

"I am speaking for him. It is as the saying goes: The toad's mouth is so full of water he can hardly croak."

"If my mother asks about me," Onwu-Ghara said, "tell her to keep her heart strong until I get there."

"You will be there in the morning?"

"If God permits, and we all last through the night."

After Ugbala had done her disappearing act, the women who had been keeping vigil at her house thronged to the home of Chief Onyiri-Dike, where the police had spent the night with their two prisoners, Orianu and Ekweredi. More than four hundred of these women mounted a rally in front of the Chief's house, singing, chanting, whooping, and enacting mock battles between themselves and the Government's soldiers.

"Is prostitution a virtue in the White man's country?" they asked in song.

"How could a child call the police on her own mother and on her mother-in-law? And if the police were called, why did they bother to answer? Were these good people not entitled to try whatever they could to cure a daughter of an abominable nymphomania?"

The policemen were apprehensive but did all they could not to let their fear show. They had been taught that the law and the Government that they represented were unstintingly vengeful and resolute. That was the only way a handful of policemen could impose discipline on an unruly or malevolent crowd of villagers. They not only had to show force but had to imply even more unseen force behind that which they showed.

"*Ndom kwenu!*"

"Iya-yah-yah!"

"*Kwenu!*"

"Yah-yah-yah!"

"*Kwekwasinu!*"

"Yah-yah-yah!"

"How many of you are there?"

"Countless as the ants in an anthill!"

"Are you together?"

"Undivided! Hand hooked to hand! Umbilical cord tied to umbilical cord."

"And where will this end?"

"Agalaba Uzo, to see the White man."

"What did you say?"

"Agalaba Uzo, to see the White man!"

"*Obe n'ole?*" [What's our destination?]

"*Obe n'Agalaba Uzo!*" [Agalaba Uzo is our destination!]

"*Obe n'ole?*"

"*Obe n'Agalaba Uzo!*"

They began a song, a marching, charging song, in which the incanter asked, "Where will this end?" and the rest of the women replied in chorus, "It will end at Agalaba Uzo."

After conferring with Chief Onyiri-Dike, the police *kopuru* advised the prisoners, Ekweredi and Orianu, to urge the women to go away. "It will be much worse for you if they make trouble," he said. "You will be responsible for whatever trouble they make."

"We did not ask them to come," Ekweredi said. "Ever since you put our hands in these cuffs, have you seen us send for anyone?"

"You can tell them to go away. They will do it, if you ask them."

"Why should we do that?"

"I have already told you. For your own benefit. They are making your case worse."

"*Ndom ibem,*" Ekweredi intoned. "Are you there?"

"*Iyah!*" the women answered in unison. "We are here."

"Did you say you are there? Answer me in one voice."

"*Iyah!* We are here!"

"You can then hear me?"

"Yes, we can hear you!"

"*Nwa-sonja* says I should tell you all to go home. Have you heard me tell all of you to go home?"

"Yes," the crowd answered. "We have all heard you tell us to go home."

Turning to the policeman, Ekweredi said, "I have told them. You heard me tell them."

Turning to Chief Onyiri-Dike, the *kopuru* asked, "Is there something you can do?"

The Chief replied, "I have sent to our Native Court for court messengers. Up to ten of them may be coming to present a greater show of force. For the time being, I can try talking to these women, but many of them are not from this village. I see only a sprinkling that I recognize as coming from this area. The others come from Onu Miri, Ikputu Ala, and even parts of Uzemba. I have no idea what evil spirit is driving them. I have never seen anything like this before, but let me talk to them."

The Chief waded into the crowd of women to talk to them, to master them with his superior spirit, and to show that he was not afraid of their numbers. As soon as he opened his mouth, the women opened theirs and subjected him to the longest, loudest, and most ignominious enactment of *ibi owu* anyone had ever heard. "*Wo-o-o-o-o-o-oh!*" the women ululated. Chief Onyiri-Dike stood transfixed on the spot, his hands firmed against his hips, his teeth gritting, his face furrowed by a mixture of anger and consternation, while waves of ignominy rolled over him. It went on and on, a single syllable in a continuous monotone, pouring out of several hundred mouths in unending waves lasting at least ten minutes. When they seemed to pause for breath and the Chief lifted his head as if to speak again, the *ibi owu* began again and lasted for another ten minutes. More women and men, on hearing it, came from wherever they were to see this phenomenon.

When the *owu* stopped, one woman punched her fist into the air and shouted: "*Oha Ndom kwenu!*"

"Iyah-yah-yah!" the crowd answered.

"If the Chief wants to know why we are here, we are here because three men from Agalaba Uzo have come into our town and kidnapped two of our fellow women and put their hands in chain locks, as if they 'stole something, and our men have not done anything about it. And you that call yourself Chief, you are entertaining the kidnappers. We hear you killed a goat for their supper and a cock for their breakfast. *Ndom ibem, sinu Ala hentu!*"

"*Ala hentu!*" the crowd roared.

"*Sinu Ala hentu!*"

"*Ala hentu!*"

"Where are we on our way to?"

"We are on our way to Agalaba Uzo!"

"Young woman," the Chief said, "I do not recognize your face. Where do you come from?"

"We recognize his face, do we not?" the young woman asked the crowd.

"Yes, we do," the crowd replied.

"What do we recognize him as?"

"*Ogasi Nwa-Beke-e!* [The White man's tattletale!] *Ora otila Nwa-Beke-eh! Wo-o-o-o-oh!*" [The White man's *nyash*-licker!] They broke into the *owu* once more.

Chief Onyiri-Dike stood still and let them wear themselves out. Then he said, addressing himself to the young woman who had last spoken, "I have remarked your face. You will pay for this fit of boldness that has seized you."

"Remark my face too," one other woman said. And suddenly the crowd erupted with women exclaiming, "Mine too! Mine too! Mark my face too!" Some even called out their names, the names of their husbands, fathers, and home villages.

What did they want? the Chief asked imploringly. What had he done to offend them? What quarrel did they have with him? Was he the Government? Did he live at Agalaba Uzo? Did he not, like them, live in the village?

With heckles and catcalls, they answered that they did not see any difference between him and those for whom he wagged his tail. The court messengers under the command of him and his fellow thiefs at Icheku were just like the police from Agalaba Uzo. They were all priests of the same oracle.

"What do you want me to do?" the Chief asked desperately.

"Release Ekweredi and Orianu," the crowd shouted.

"I cannot do that. They have offended the law."

"What law?" one woman asked.

"Whose law?" another asked.

"The White man's law," the chief said. "The Government's law. You, as you stand here now, are offending the law."

"Then arrest us also. All of us, because we are one and the same with the people you have arrested. We are as guilty as they are and as innocent as they are. Why not arrest us also?"

A short time later, the court messengers arrived. With the policemen, they formed a flying wedge and pierced their way through the crowd, with Orianu and Ekweredi in their midst.

The women decided to follow the party all the way to Agalaba

Uzo, walking behind them, taunting and heckling. Throughout the lengthy journey, the crowd was never less than three hundred women. It got recharged often, as some of the women dropped off but others joined up on hearing what the issue was. From junction markets and from roadside farms, women stood or straightened up from their trading or hoeing to look and comment and heckle. Others left their wares or their hoes and walked to the edge of the road to fire insolent questions at the police or shout encouragement to the trekking women.

The group followed the policemen all the way to the depot.

Ndom!

As Major Ogden's car rolled to a stop on the gravel courtyard in front of police headquarters, officers working within adopted the attitudes and precautions common to underlings who expect to be found at some fault by a superior. The briskness of the superintendent's steps when he dismounted—he did not wait for the driver-orderly to step around and open the door for him—notified the officers that a wasp's nest had been thumped, and anybody with a mind to his health had better start ducking.

"Gidiven, sah! Goodday, sah! Afta-noon, sah!"

Down the long corridor, with its bare cement floor and walls painted with whitewash and trimmed with coal tar, heels clicking in salute punctuated Major Ogden's crisp and measured footsteps as he marched to his office.

"Is Inspector Ofodire here?" he asked the last officer who saluted him.

"Yessah. I believe so, sah."

"Summon him to my office. Pronto."

"Yessah."

The inspector appeared in a matter of moments.

"Inspector."

"Sah."

"Why are you a police inspector?"

"Beg pardon, sah. I do not understand, sah."

"You do understand, do you not, that the police is a peacekeeping force. That the purpose of the police is to keep the civil peace?"

"Yessah."

"And you are the Chief Inspector for this district and therefore responsible for its peace?"

"Yessah."

"Inspector, is there peace in your district?"

"Yes. Yessah. There has been no reprot of disorder anywhere."

"No report? Where is Sergeant Madugba?"

"I do not know, sah. I believe in Charge Office."

"He has not reported a disturbance to you?"

"He sent a constable to report of some women from the bush holding a parade in town. But he said everything was under control."

"Everything under control? Step over to that window and take a look. Is everything under control?"

"Seemingly not so, sah. I shall investigate and report back to you. I am sorry, sah."

The Inspector saluted and turned to go. Major Ogden was a few steps behind him, walking a little more slowly. Down the long corridor, other policemen stepped aside and saluted.

At the other end of the headquarters building, the short end of the L, in front of the double doors of the Charge Office, was a crowd of over three hundred women, singing, dancing, and ululating. They covered most of the sandy area in front of the Charge Office where the Bahama grass had been trodden to death by so many accused and their accusers. Some stood, while others sat, around the acacia tree, most of them favoring the shade it provided from the stoking sun. Others spilled into the greener part of the lawn. Two policemen with drawn truncheons stood guard over the steps that led up to the Charge Office, ostensibly to keep the women from entering.

Major Ogden stopped by his car to inform his wife that their trip to the Rest House for lunch would be delayed. Then he cut across the lawn, an uncharacteristic breach of discipline for him and something forbidden to all policemen on the force, and caught up with the Inspector just as the latter was about to begin berating the Sergeant. Other, more-junior officers stood at a respectful distance.

"What's going on here, Sergeant?" the superintendent cut in.

"These bush women, sah. They are protesting an arrest we made."

"Why are they protesting an arrest you made? Who was arrested?"

"Two other women from their village. They are inside being charged. Constables just returned from the bush with them, after much *wahala* by these same women. I do not know what they are drunk on."

"What is the charge?"

"Civilian complaint, sah. Assault. Attempted homicide. Conspiracy with intent to kill."

"Who is the complainant?"

"One woman in town. Businesswoman, who operate a business on Asa Road."

"What was she doing in the village when they assaulted her?"

"Sah, it is a long story, and I do not know the head and tail of all of it."

"Where is the charge sheet?"

"It is under preparation, sah. Not complete yet. Constable," he said to one of the nearby officers, "obtain charge sheet from *kopuru* at the desk, whether or whethern't it complete. Tell'am who want'am."

Taking the sheet from the returning officer, Major Ogden quickly ran his finger down it. "What is this?" he said derisively at a point. "What is this?" he repeated, seeming to lose more hope the more he read, until in the end he was driven to the point of desperation. "Who dispatched constables to go and make this arrest?"

"I did, sah," the Sergeant replied.

"On what basis? What was the prima facie evidence that induced you to send three officers twenty miles into the bush to make an arrest on such a flimsy allegation?" He looked up, but before the Sergeant could begin to answer, he said, "The people arrested are the complainant's mother-in-law?"

"Yessah."

"And mother?"

"Yessah."

His sunburned face wrinkled into tight furrows, while his blond moustache pressed into a thin line against his upper lip. He peered. "Does this say they were trying to what? *De-va* . . . *de-vaginate*—what is this word?"

The Sergeant looked and repeated, "*De-vaginate.* It mean, sah, to cut off . . . It mean what you do to small, small *pikin* seven or eight days old, to cut off part of testicle."

"I believe the Sergeant means 'circumcise,' sah," the Inspector cut in.

Major Ogden paused, and looked at both officers in turn. "Her mother and mother-in-law were trying to circumcise her, is that correct?"

"Yessah, that's what they did. She did not want them to, but they did it to her by force."

"How old is this woman?"

"Plenty old," the sergeant said. "Already born two *pikin*."

"This Miss Yo-Yo, is she not the same woman, the prostitute, whom some women dragged out of town several months ago?"

"Yessah. Same exact one, sah."

"Are these not the same women who came to take her away then?"

"I believe they are the same, sah."

"Release those two at once."

"Sah?"

"I said, discharge them at once!" He cut himself short in midsentence, turned, and marched angrily into the Charge Office. The Inspector and the Sergeant followed. Taking out his fountain pen, he drew two diagonal lines across the charge sheet and signed his signature under the word: *Discharged*. Slapping the sheet on the table, he said to the lance corporal in attendance, "Are these the women?"

"Yessah," the corporal said.

"They are discharged. Uncuff them and send them home." Turning to the two senior officers, he added. "Inspector, Sergeant, report to my office at ten sharp on the morrow."

"Yessah!"

"Yessah!"

Outside, the two released women, Ekweredi and Orianu, were seized by their friends and carried shoulder high through the crowd, which began singing and dancing around the acacia tree.

Major Ogden went before the women and raised a hand to demand attention.

"You women should go home now."

"We are going home," they replied.

"And you will not cause a disturbance."

"Whom were we disturbing before your police came and arrested our people?"

"All right. I will not argue with you. Your people have been released. Now go home."

"We do not want to come back for a case," the women shouted.

"There is no case. Case is quashed. Dismissed."

The women burst into a sustained ovation.

"*Ndom kwenu!*"

"Yah-yah-yah!"

"Sah! Ex-ooze, sah," the sergeant said as Major Ogden was about to climb into his car. "There is another part to this case."

"What other part?"

"It concern one man, husband of the woman in question."

"The same Yo-Yo woman?"

"Yessah. The man, as accused, chase woman down road with big cutlass, with intent to butcher her. If not for police who were in propinquity, she be dead by now."

Major Ogden paused thoughtfully, running the allegation through his mind. He took a quick glance at his wife, sitting in the hot car with a martyred look, trying not to fan herself too strenuously, as the effort caused more of the heat and sweat that she was trying to reduce. "Bring a report on the matter when you come to see me in the morning."

"Yessah," Sergeant Madugba answered, saluted, clicked his heels, and turned to go.

Onwu-Ghara, husband of Nwanyi-Nma-Ezinna-Oyoyo, got three years and six months for assault and mayhem. He was acquitted of the more serious charge of attempted homicide.

4

Woman to Woman— Ugbala and Elizabeth Ashby-Jones

"THE WHITE WOMAN WAS AN APPARITION that emerged from nowhere just before the War," Nne-nne said, speaking of Mrs. Elizabeth Ashby-Jones. "*Saklaa* [a circular] came down from the D.O., addressed to the women, telling us that the White woman was coming and asking us to show her our best hospitality, and help her do whatever she wanted to do. All the towns received *saklaa* and all of them made preparations, but *Nwanyi Bekee* did not visit most of the towns, including ours."

Nne-nne herself first saw Mrs. Ashby-Jones at Eke Akpara market, and remembered that *Nwanyi Bekee* [the White woman] caused quite a stir in the market that day as she waded slowly through the market crowds and stopped at many stalls and asked the price of everything through her interpreters. "What's this? What's that?" she asked in her lispy, thin-lipped way, but she did not buy anything.

"What it was that the White woman wanted to do no one could be sure of," Nne-nne said, "and she never did say for certain even after she arrived. Just that she wanted to observe us and learn about us, how we lived and what we did with our days. She wanted to know how we farmed and how we cooked and how we took turns

sleeping with our husbands. No one minded her much in the beginning—that is, before the War started. Everyone knew that White
people were always doing one thing or another that made no sense to
anyone else but themselves. So if this woman wanted to come and
look at us live our lives, if she wanted to come and peer into our
water pots or pots of fermenting cassava, she could come and look to
her heart's content. But people did follow her travels with interest
and in the markets often spoke of where she had been last or where
next she was going. I think it was also because she was a woman,
and many of us had not been close to a White woman before. White
women used to be a rare sight in those days.

"Uzemba is where she spent the longest time," Nne-nne continued.
"Uzemba and at Ugbala's house in Amapu. It was said that she picked
Uzemba because of Oyoyo. Same reason for Ugbala, in addition to
her fame.

"You remember Ugbala?" Nne-nne asked, her face lighting up in
a teasing smile. Both of us burst out laughing, and then I began
shaking my head.

Yes, I remembered Ugbala. I remembered Ugbala as the tall woman
with the rough voice and the hoarse laugh, the beauty gap in her
upper front teeth, blue *nki* tatoos on both her arms. Ugbala had the
ability to transform herself into a fiery-eyed monster by pushing out
her lips and folding her upper eyelids inside out. Tell any child in
our village that Ugbala was coming, and he could be made to eat
food or swallow medicine that no one could otherwise get past his
clenched teeth. I remembered Ugbala for the thorough physical
inspection she gave me whenever she came to visit my grandmother,
peering ʾinside my mouth and ears, examining my hair for lice and
ringworm, and squeezing my belly to see if any organs were enlarged
or painful. Then came the part that, even at twenty-one, I remembered with a shudder. Ugbala turned me upside down, and holding
me in place between her knees, she pulled apart the lobes of my
buttocks and peered into my rectum for worms, all the while making
comments about how carelessly I wiped myself and jokingly threatening that if I did *anything* in her face while she was looking, she would
poke a stick into my belly all the way to my mouth!

Yes, I remembered Ugbala. I remembered her rolling her eyes or
opening them wide with mock surprise or making faces at everyone's
genitals, calling them nicknames that described their size, shape, and

the direction of their pointing. I remember that older children found her an unbearable tease but dared not show it, for if you frowned or acted offended because of the liberties she took with you, she was apt to say, "Look at him now, daring to be haughty with me. If only I had known he was going to act haughty with me, I could have made a little mistake when I was circumcising him and gone *chook!* with my *aguba*. And cut off the whole thing!" Then she would wink and chuckle.

Physically, Ugbala was a tower of a woman, a rare combination of grace and strength. Men said of her that she had a personality originally intended for a man, but which somehow had found its way into a woman. Regardless of what anyone said, Ugbala was very much a woman. In fact, all aspects of womanhood were exaggerated in her— in her heavy breasts; her long, black hair; her laughing, teasing eyes, which invited flirtation or easy familiarity; and in her tendency to tell bawdy jokes, which sometimes gave false hopes of seduction to men who had no chance of bedding her in a thousand reincarnations. When she smiled, her wide-open face opened even wider; her teeth with a beauty gap in the middle of the upper row flashed, and her head wagged fat plaits of hair that were pulled down beside her ears like grooved horns. Those plaits and her warm rusty complexion gave her the look of a Mami-Wota doll.

Remembering Ugbala from the age I now was, I saw her as the proverbial *okpolu*, a specimen marked by its uniqueness and singularity and produced by Nature to illustrate the ultimate possibilities of which a species is capable. She was the solitary *orji* or *apu* tree whose roots seem to reach down to the very center of the Earth and whose trunk erupts out of the ground and vaults straight upward to meet the sky, attaining a height so great that men could only tilt back their heads to stare and wonder about what went on among its elevated branches. For such a tree, as for Ugbala, Nature usually clears a wide perimeter free of the ordinary.

"Everybody in Uzemba remembers that the White Woman questioned them about everything," Nne-nne was saying, as my mind resurfaced from its reminiscences. "She asked questions and more questions and wrote everything in her notebook. The story by everyone who met her was that she was so busy writing in her notebook that she had no chance to hear what was said to her. And with her *ntaprinta* girls chewing up and spitting out again what she said to people or what people said to her, no one knew for sure what was being said by the other side."

Nne-nne then began sketching a caricature of Mrs. Ashby-Jones in the act of writing, sitting square and erect on a backchair, a notebook open on her lap, a slowly waving Oriental fan in her left hand, her right hand moving furiously across the pages of her notebook. According to Nne-nne, people marveled and whispered to one another about how fast her writing hand moved across the pages. She wrote faster than anyone could dance, faster, it seemed, than her interpreters could talk. Even when no one was taking, she continued writing.

In addition to the dozen or so pages that Nne-nne gave me on that night before I left for the United States, I found more pages of Mrs. Ashby-Jones's notes among Nne-nne's things when I returned home from the United States five years later. Later still, having been pricked by what I read of Mrs. Ashby-Jones's entries, I recovered even more pages of her famous notes from two of Nne-nne's friends. The last group of women who guarded Mrs. Ashby-Jones had divided among themselves not only the locks from her hair and kerchiefs from her frock, but pages from her notebook, as mementos of their historic encounter.

From what the notes themselves showed, Mrs. Ashby-Jones indeed wrote down "everything," just as Nne-nne had said. Whatever her purpose, whether she observed and wrote for her own benefit or that of others, she noted the most curious things and described them in painstaking detail. Her entries ranged from wife beating to farming methods, from circumcision to the contents of water pots, from bare breasts to women's title organizations, from exogamy to hair-plaiting methods.

According to the notes, Mrs. Ashby-Jones was very pleased that the women of Uzemba received her cordially. She had expected them to be wary or indifferent, and the District Officer back in town had cautioned her that they might be surly or even belligerent. "And their numbers!" she wrote exultantly. "They were all decked out in their festival best, in group uniforms of Madras broadcloths and Dutch wax prints . . . and it was wholly a woman's occasion." Their assemblage moved twice, the notes said, first because the village council hall where their meeting began smelled horribly of goat urine, which became unbearable as the heat stoked up, and then again because she wanted to get away from the market square and see the women in their various homes.

The notes also included excerpts from the "Welcome Address" read to Mrs. Ashby-Jones on behalf of the women of Uzemba. "Strange phraseology—stilted transliterations from the vernacular," she commented. It sweeted their hearts more than sugar, they said, that she had decided to honor their humble town with her august and royally esteemed presence. They hoped that she was in good health and had left her father, mother, husband, children, and all the people of her household and village in good health when she left home. They hoped that she would carry their feelings to her people and especially to the Government and explain to them that the "burden of life" was falling too heavily upon them as a result of some of the things the Government did—things like heavy taxes on their men, expensive litigation in the Native Courts, falling prices of palm oil and kernels on which they depended for everything. Since the end of Kaiser's War, they had suffered everything from *mgberegede* [sudden death] to famine. Now their land was no longer fertile; they could no longer afford salt and crayfish for their soups and had been reduced to eating meatless, saltless vegetable pots, which their grandparents used to eat during famines! . . . Could she tell the Government for them that they did not want to be counted like animals? Could she do anything whatsoever to help lift the "burden of life" from their shoulders?

As tokens of their welcome and friendship, the women of Uzemba gave Mrs. Ashby-Jones a ram, several chickens, a basin of fresh eggs, and baskets of fruit. They were especially pleased, the address said, that a fellow woman had come to visit them, that they could address her as *"Nwanyi Ibem,"* or Fellow Woman, and that she could understand their *grief.*

Then they staged a dance. It seemed that the women of Uzemba were determined that every White woman they met would dance with them—Mrs. Ashby-Jones as well as the young woman whom they had met in town when they went to Agalaba Uzo to bring back Oyoyo. As Mrs. Ashby-Jones described her own exploits, at a point during the reception in the market clearing at Uzemba, "a bold, young dancer" reached out and tried to pull her up to join the dancing. At first, she had demurred. However, because the puller was determined and very strong, she was hoisted to her feet. There was a burst of cheering, and then several dancers had surrounded her, grinning, shouting encouragement, and telling her what parts of her body to move. Eager to save time, which she thought was being frittered away in endless welcoming ceremonies, she decided to cooperate rather than continue to resist them.

"Do not stand so erect," one of her dance teachers said.

"Lower your waist," another added. "Squat down a little. Like this, not like that!"

"Hold your hands away from your side. Open your palms and face them downward."

"If you are tired, you do not have to dance furiously. There are different types of dance steps you can do to the same music. For old people and tired people, who do not wish to move or sweat too much, dancing is mostly *amara* and *ibara*—standing in one place and heaving slowly and gracefully. Come on, Nwanyi Bekee, show us your *ibara*!"

"I did my best!" Mrs. Ashby-Jones wrote in an enigmatic conclusion to this section of her notes, her frustration showing through several exclamation marks jabbed at the end of the sentence.

Then the notes continued:

Exogamy, Mrs. Ashby-Jones wrote down as a heading with a double underline. All the adult married women in a village were born in other villages. A girl cannot marry in her own village because all the males in that village are her blood kin.

Was wife beating common? Mrs. Ashby-Jones asked her hosts.

Yes, her hosts replied.

How did they feel about being beaten by their husbands? she further inquired.

How were they supposed to feel? They asked her in turn.

Did they enjoy being beaten?

What kind of silly question was that? they retorted through their comments. Even a dog did not enjoy being beaten.

Why then did they allow their husbands to beat them?

They laughed as they replied that their husbands did not first ask their permission before beating them. They just did.

What, then, Mrs. Ashby-Jones wanted to know, was Ozurumba's offence, Ozurumba being the man at Ikputu Ala, who had been ritually sat upon by the women of that town for beating his pregnant wife, Akpa-Ego. Why did the women of his village single him out for collective punishment?

Ozurumba, the women of Uzemba told Mrs. Ashby-Jones, had gone beyond limits.

Was it true, Mrs. Ashby-Jones asked, that girls were circumcised? Yes, the women of Uzemba told her. Girls too were circumcised. . . . No, they saw no reason why girls should not be circumcised.

So, she had heard about Oyoyo, or the Yo-Yo woman, as she called her, whom they knew by the married name of Nwanyi-Nma and the maiden name of Ezinna. They did not wish to talk about Ezinna and showed their disaffection with her in a most dramatic way. At the mention of her name, many of the women circled their hands ritually around their heads and then snapped their fingers, simultaneously spitting *"Tufia!"* on the ground beside them. They considered her dead and had held a mock burial for her, placing oil bean seeds in her coffin, praying that just as the force of an exploding oil bean pod flung the seeds far away from the mother tree that in her next incarnation she would go as far away as possible from them and their kindred.

Yes, they said, Ezinna-Oyoyo's mother was there among them.

No, they would not point her out to Mrs. Ashby-Jones. However, was there something she could do to set Onwu-Ghara free from prison?

Yes, it was true that they liked to work collectively much more than the men did. *Ndu-oru* meant "work exchange." That was how they, as women, did their farm work much of the time, in twos and threes and fours. Today you and I work together on your farm. Tomorrow we work together on my farm. Today I help you press palm oil. Tomorrow you help me crack palm kernels. But *ndu-oru* could involve more than two people. One woman could work for each of five or six other women in turn. Now, each of those five or six owes her for a day of work. She could then plan to take all of them on a single day to work on the farm of her mother or her mother-in-law or any other woman to whom she owed a favor or with whom she was trying to curry a favor.

Forced to think about it, which was not something, apparently, they had done before, companionship was the major benefit of *ndu-oru*.

From the number of times she referred to it, Mrs. Ashby-Jones seemed quite taken by the expression *ikwa uwa*, or "bemoaning one's fate," or "complaining about one's life's burdens." But the women of

Uzemba insisted that they were not complainers. *Ikwa uwa* was simply a way of chiding fate and encouraging one's *chi* to do better by one. One's personal god, *chi*, was like a goat's udder and needed to be pumped and squeezed before it would yield any milk.

No, they had no leaders. They were all equally women, with no one more of a woman than the others. They all were "cut" the same way, all squatted to urinate and to have their babies.

Yes, women did take titles. The first title every woman took was *nmuzu*. When a woman was the mother of both a son and a daughter, she was a "full mother." When an older woman became a grandmother many times or a great grandmother, she earned the nickname *Nne-Nne Ozuru Umu*. There were also titles of accomplishment, such as the farm title of *Ihie Ede*. A woman needed at least ten approved mounds of cocoyams to become a titleholder in the Ede Society.

"How many here are titleholders?" Mrs. Ashby-Jones asked.

No hands were raised.

"Not one person here is a titleholder?" she asked.

Not a soul stirred, and Mrs. Ashby-Jones turned to her interpreters for an explanation. At length they were able to tell her that the women felt insulted that she should ask them to raise their hands as if they were little children. Her insult was further compounded by the fact that the people she was asking to raise their hands were titleholders. A major reason for taking a title was to earn respect and deference. It was true they had told her they had no leaders as such, but titleholders had privileges, such as first claim to seats at an assembly and choosing the nature and duration of a greeting ceremony between them and nontitleholders.

From her notes, it seems that Mrs. Ashby-Jones breached this point of etiquette many times by asking her hosts for a show of hands or to number one thing or another.

After they had accepted her apologies, they began to ask her questions:

Did women in her country take titles?

She explained that there were queens and duchesses and ladies of the peerage.

Were any titles exclusive to women?

No, she said.

Did she personally have any titles?

No, not a title as such, but she had a university degree, which she had earned after several years of study.

No, she said, university degrees were not exclusive to women.

How did women in her country distinguish themselves?

More or less in the same ways as the men, she answered. More or less.

When she told them how old she was, a large part of the crowd gasped with surprise and said she was a "small child."

Again they wanted to know why she had really come to them, whether she was a spy for the Government, sent out to probe their feelings.

Again she tried to explain to them the nature of her intellectual curiosity about them and their ways, how she wanted to understand them in a *systematic* and *scientific* way. Becoming the interrogator once again, she asked them to explain a typical day, week, month, or season in their lives.

Their days, they said, went from cockcrow to sundown; their weeks had eight market days; a short week had four days; a month thirty days. They planted most of their crops just ahead of the rainy season, which started in the fifth month of the year and lasted to the ninth or tenth month. The dry season went from the tenth month of the year to the fifth month of the next year, and in the middle of it was a dry cold harmattan, which lasted for two months.

Was it true, the Uzemba women wanted to know, that White men liked to suck their wives' lips? There was a feast of giggles when this question was uttered. Was it true, also, that White women became pregnant through the mouth? Was it true that White women had no milk in their breasts and that was why they fed their children cow's milk? Did her husband ever beat her? What was the *grief* of her life—the things she suffered as a woman and a wife? Did other White women look down on her because she did not have a child?

At this point in the proceedings, Mrs. Ashby-Jones apparently moved to change the format of her interaction with her hosts, among whom she had sat in the center of a semicircle. She decided to let them escort her through the village and explain things to her in their compounds and homes. The format of the entries also changed, becoming more elaborate, the handwriting more deliberate and better formed, showing signs of having been rewritten and elaborated in the leisure and convenience of the Catering Rest House or the D.O.'s Rest House at Onu Miri. Where the entries made in the field had many marginal notations and elaborations, the entires made at the Rest House had a more polished and finished appearance. They included:

Nakedness

For early European sailors and other travelers, one of the more interesting spectacles Africa presented was the uncovered female bosom and buttocks. In the various accounts which I have read in journals and the like, the breasts and buttocks of the Bantu/Negro and Zulu woman have received quite a play (or display, if one thinks of the photographs often included), some of it disguised as serious study of anatomical differences between the races. (Hottentot Venus, for example.) Well, anyway, this place is not Eden and the women do not wander about naked. Most, though, are scantily clad. Very modest, I must say, almost to the point of being prudish. They sit, stand, and carry themselves with their own peculiar type of female grace. The hot weather is of course one reason they wear so little. Another is probably the relative expensiveness of fabric. What is sold in the European shops is more costly than most of these women can afford. I have not been able to ascertain how much weaving there was in this area prior to the arrival of the European. Indications are that raffia was woven fairly extensively (into mats, bath towels, kirtles, etc.), cotton less extensively. . . .

The women wear much more clothes than the men, some of whom seem to have the most casual attitude towards nakedness. (In the rivers, for instance, the men readily shed whatever little clothes they happen to be wearing, sometimes the top pieces of their wives' loincloths, and wade naked into the water, and swim and wash unabashedly—no underwear.) When the women choose to bathe in the rivers, they usually do so wearing at least one layer of their loincloths, which unfortunately may become clinging and transparent as they become wet, but which nevertheless give them a modicum of cover. . . . More about the men—I have seen men in the villages wearing something they call ogodo—a six- or seven-inch strip of cloth or raffia weave, passing from the front to the back between the legs and held in place by a rope belt, over which its edges are furled. (N.B. *The women, too, wear* ogodo, *but as an undergarment during menstruation.*)

Ordinarily, *the adult women are clothed from the waist down in a loincloth or kirtle, the latter made of raffia for the poorer women and for the others, who can afford it, of coarse baftlike cotton woven by the Mba-miri women, who live in the Delta. At home and at work or leisure, the women are bare from the waist up. The breast for them is simply a mammary, used for suckling infants. There is no hint whatsoever that these women have any consciousness of their breasts as a sexual organ, as is the case with women in Europe and the Occident. They make no effort to enhance its beauty. Some of the more thoughtful mothers, when they are dirty or sweaty from their work, wash them carefully before allowing their infants to nurse from them. Others don't give a care! A common sight is a woman carrying an infant astraddle her side, with the infant grasping the breast with its little hand(s) and latching onto the nipple with its mouth. One of the pictures I have etched on my mind is of a woman sitting on a low stool beside a cooking stand on which the family supper was cooking, and meanwhile an infant was lying on her lap and suckling from a breast, while her hands were busy pounding something in a mortar, nipping vegetables from their stalks, or stirring the soup with a ladle. Mr. Costain, a PWD engineer I met at the Catering Rest House, painted a similar picture. He described once buying oranges from a woman who had an infant on her back, knitting in her hands, and of course the basin of oranges balanced perfectly on her head, so that both her hands were free for the knitting. And her yarn was stuffed neatly into her blouse above her breast.*

Because of the way they are used and cared for, breasts in adult women are (ugly) *stretched flaps of tissue, heavy and pendulous in women who are nursing, but thin and shriveled among women who are not. They just hang, big and small, equal and symmetrical or unequal and asymmetrical. The* brassiere *is hardly in use in the villages, although I saw maybe a couple in all of my travels, one on a woman who had lived in the township for a while and another on a nursing mother with very heavy breasts, who used it to relieve the weight of the breasts on her back. As a rule, young girls go about with their budding breasts uncovered. Beautiful and firm in their youth and innocence, but not for long! In fact, they tend to go totally naked, until they are "clothed" at puberty. I was told that being "clothed" usually meant that a girl had been "touched" or was no longer virgin. Because these girls live among their own kith and kin—the universal "brothers" in the exogamic village—they are apparently not self-conscious about such nakedness. Yet, pubescent girls are given small strips of cloth which they may use to cover their nakedness, should they become self-conscious before visiting strangers. (See photographs.)*

Farming

Farming is by the slash-and-burn method. The men do the slashing and the women the burning. They dig their cassava ridges the same way their mothers probably did, and through it all seem to have no idea about the principles which underlie their actions or the consequences which occur when they act or fail to act in a certain way. For instance, they let their land lie fallow for several years after cultivation, but will they ever discover fertilizers or crop rotation?

Mrs. Ashby-Jones made a note to ask them that question, and when later she did, they told her that they had not heard of fertilizer as such. Yes, they knew that the longer they left a piece of land fallow before farming it again, the better the yield of crops from it.

Had they wondered why? she asked.

No, they responded. What was there to wonder? It always happened that way. Their analogy was as follows: It rained during the rainy season and was dry during the dry season, so why wonder about it?

Interestingly enough, Mrs. Ashby-Jones noted, in the little gardens they made around their houses, away from the much larger farms on which they spent most of their lives, they used fertilizer without calling it by that name, or even knowing what it was. Such gardens were usually plied with fireplace ash, henhouse, goat house, and general household refuse—and the vegetables they planted in such places usually grew brilliantly. They planted banana suckers in old mud pits which they had filled with general refuse, even sometimes in old, decayed latrine holes, but the *general* principle of fertilization of crops seemed beyond their grasp.

This inability to generalize, Mrs. Ashby-Jones went on to add, was probably the essence of their primitivity, a failure to *examine* life, in Socrates's sense of the word. It was as if Isaac Newton had been sitting in his garden and watching an apple fall without stopping to wonder why apples always fall. They observed and were able to translate their observations into witticisms and proverbs, but never went beyond discrete proverbial observation. No abstraction or series of abstractions linked by some rule of logical formulation into hypotheses and theories. Thinking (cogitation), in other words. How did they think? she wondered.

She recalled something that Mr. Blakiston, the District Officer, once had said about the endless and circumlocutory proverbs used by the men in the villages. Perhaps these proverbs, distilled from life, were like the most primitive principles of science, but they remained unlinked to one another and were never integrated on a higher plane. Africa, Mrs. Ashby-Jones wrote, was full of fields of gold and diamonds, but it had no foundaries or smelting factories. Its gems remained in the form of nuggets, with no one to work them into tiaras, brooches, bracelets, and crowns. The place was full of beautiful flowers and spectacular inflorescences, but no one wove garlands and diadems. No gardens even!

This idea seemed to have gripped Mrs. Ashby-Jones like a fever. It explained everything about them, she wrote, from their farming and husbanding of animals to their treatment of illness and disease. For example, the women kept chickens. The chickens roamed and fended for themselves by scratching in the gardens for worms or kernels or whatever else they could find. They laid a dozen eggs, hatched ten, and of the ten chicks maybe four or five matured. They accepted these four or five as a gift from Nature, and made no effort to control the egg laying or the hatching or to place the chickens in a pen and feed them so they did not roam the bushes and thereby become victim of the hazards that cut their number in half.

Same thing with children, she observed. "I have had ten pregnancies," a native woman would say, "but only four survived for me." A random draw of Nature's cards, it seemed. Did they ever wonder if there was a way to make more survive?

Waterpots

Mrs. Ashby-Jones continued.

In the yard, behind a woman's hut. Covered and uncovered. Placed to catch the rain coming off the smoky roof. Brown water, full of debris and mosquito larvae. When they drink, they simply shoo the larvae away by blowing their breaths on the surface of the water—the larvae dive toward the bottom—and they drink carefully! And if they should happen to swallow a larva, there is no great bother, and too bad for the larva! Storage water pots are intentionally(?) left unglazed, so that there is continuous seepage to the outer surface of the pot, and water in the pot remains relatively cool, because of latent heat of vaporization.

Census

Someone—again—just asked me about the census the Government is planning to take of these women. They simply cannot understand why the Government is so interested in counting them. None of the answers I have given them seems to satisfy them, and I am left wondering whether there exists an answer which would really satisfy them. I have tried to explain to them that it is for the sake of understanding, order, and control—and planning. The Government needs to know how many people live in each district. Government, I said, did not want to leave things to take their own natural, unregulated, and possibly random courses. Good government was based on plans. One could not plan without knowing at a minimum how many people one was planning for. I asked them whether they did not plan their feasts. Did they not, for instance, cook for a certain number of people?

No, they said, stultifying my analogy. What made a feast a true feast was the unregulated superabundance of everything. During a feast, they did not cook with a number of people in mind. They cooked as much as they could, and the idea of a feast was that everyone ate as much as he could— that was what made a feast a feast—how could it be a feast if everything was measured? Plan a feast? That was like a contradiction in terms.

After each answer I gave about the Government's need for a census, they kept quiet, without seeming to have been satisfied—and obviously they were not, for sooner or later the question came up again, directly or in another guise.

The most difficult remonstration I had with these women was on the issue of taxes. The idea of creating revenue, as it is generally understood in Civilization, seems beyond them. I tried, for instance, to explain to them that labor had monetary value, and therefore community labor, which they did for their villages or for the Government (in the days when the Government would order villages to contribute men and women as laborers to work groups) had financial value. Instead of asking them to contribute laborers, the Government could ask them to pay a levy, from which the Government could then pay hired laborers.

No, I said. Such a levy was not a tribute.

No, it was not a fine for some offence they had committed against the Government.

I seemed to hit something of a responsive chord when I mentioned the digging of wells. Water was scarce in this area during the dry season, and they had seen their neighbors able to draw clean water out of a Government borehole during the worst of the dry season.

Medical dispensaries.

Yes, they liked dispensaries, although they did not believe that the White man's medicine could cure their most endemic ailments.

Revenue paid the Government's workers, clerks, and chiefs and others, who were after all their own people.

A hornet's nest. A uniform wave of groans and sighs went up. Some of them spat ritually on the ground—so intense was their antipathy against clerks, chiefs, and other Government workers.

Following the entry about chiefs and court clerks were personal ruminations and conjectures, which Mrs. Ashby-Jones apparently wrote in the leisure of the D.O.'s Rest House. She wondered how "these people," as she frequently called her hosts, on their own cohered and governed themselves, since they were so averse to modern government. Everything about them seemed so loose; everyone seemed to be so independent—free. This was unusual for Africa, really for anyplace in the contemporary world—a sort of village democracy reminiscent of the classical democracies of Greece and Rome, but without fanfare. More classless than Rome or Greece, because there were no patricians or plebs. Because their basic organizational unit, the village, was made up of blood relatives, it was impossible for any man to claim an intrinsic superiority to his relatives. Maybe she was overstating the case, she appended. Uzemba was not Athens, and the people she was focusing on were the women, even though the men were not different.

Yet, there was no discernible hierarchy, except those of age and of course the title societies. Even the idea of using age as a basis of hierarchy was so intrinsically democratic! Everyone had an equal chance to become old and therefore a respected senior. How remarkable!

Remarkable indeed that there might be some principle of coherence and "government" among these people that might have eluded others and was now becoming more tangible in her grasp. There had to be, or else how could they live and function as a people? How could those several hundred women she had been addressing that afternoon be so orderly? This area, unlike other parts of the country, had been without "natural leaders" when the British first arrived—no chiefs, obas, emirs, or obongs. Authorities, unable to deal with this inchoateness and lack of established government or hierarchy, had appointed Warrant Chiefs for them, to act as rulers (really administrators).

How had they withstood better organized outsiders such as Usman dan Fodio and kept the Moslem empires from extending from the Mediterranean to the Gulf of Guinea?

Was there something here—a latent, subtle, and arcane structure in what seemed like structurelessness? If so, was this a primitive, prototypical form of social organization? Newton's first principle of natural philosophy, the Law of Parsimony: More is in vain when less will serve. If any of what they did to cohere, they did intentionally and not as a result of happenstance, then these people could be the world's greatest minimalists, for they had learned how to create structure so diffuse and abstruse that its presence was not externally observable. Like making bricks without straw. Erecting towers without scaffolding. At one time, Mrs. Ashby-Jones wrote, the flourishes of her handwriting betraying the force with which the idea she was dealing with had seized her, the ancients had thought that the brain was just a lump of gray tissue that sat inside the skull without much discernible purpose. They ascribed control of the emotions and body functions to the heart and the other more interesting organs of the body.

If these people had discovered a principle of minimalism, then it extended to their art. They had little or none. What they had was very basic. Their houses were simple and for the most part unadorned. Except occasionally for the houses of the older women and the witch doctors or medicine men, which had simple designs traced into their walls with a finger, while the mud was still wet. No painters or paintings. Few sculptings of clay or red subsoil—usually of ancestors and spirits, often handled rather disrespectfully and left to become eroded and denuded by the weather.

I once, for example, heard a native woman say something equivalent to: Everything (including gods) has its nemesis. What she actually did say was:

While the wooden idols are getting the best of me, the termites are getting the best of them. Rather cheeky way to treat a god, I daresay. One of the interesting sights I saw this afternoon was a fetish hut with a leaky roof, in which the rain had eaten away much of the face of an ancestral figure or god. What a sad god or ancestor, I said to myself.

Not many wood carvings, Mrs. Ashby-Jones further observed. The most common was of a juju called *Agwu*. Few carvers in the area. The carvers were in the Ibibio and Efik areas further to the southeast.

Body ornaments were rare. Boys and girls had their heads shaved uniformly bald, ostensibly for purposes of hygiene. Mothers occasionally cut patterns of one kind or another in a little girl's hair, making paths and furrows through it. The result was usually appalling. At puberty, the girls began to let their hair grow a bit and began to harness it into little tufts with bits of black thread. The older women wore their hair in long, tight plaits, wrapped with black thread and worked into different shapes to suit the type of face.

Occasional earrings and necklaces and glass beads are the most common. Bangles and copper bracelets. Older, well-to-do women wear nkamenyi (*ivory beads*) *in a profusion which sometimes covers not only their necks but also their chests. The beads are on strings of unequal lengths, so that they hang down to different levels on the neck and chest. I have seen women who wore so many of these things that I wondered if they were not in danger of choking from them. Black beads, worn on strings around the waist, are common, worn mostly by girls and younger women, and often given as a betrothal gift to a girl by her intended groom. Pubescent girls who are considered not yet old enough to be "clothed" may use several strings of beads, worn loosely so they ride down on their buttocks, to cover part of their nakedness.*

Red ochre is everywhere as body paint. Women cover themselves with it from head to toe. Two types are in common use, a local variety, which has a deeper maroonish hue and washes off fairly readily, leaving a reddish tint to the skin, especially the palms of the hands and the soles of the feet, and the fiercely red, almost vermilion type, which they buy from traveling Hausa men in the townships.

Indigo is in common use as medicine and as makeup. Children suffering from convulsions are covered with indigo as part of the effort to make them as repugnant as possible for the spirits which are supposed to be haunting them and causing their illness. Young girls use styluslike instruments to paint patterns with indigo on their faces and bodies. Sometimes they take turns grooming and painting one another. It is a lovely sight to see a woman seated on a stool, with her daughter seated on a mat between her knees, while the mother plaits or shaves the girl's hair or decorates her back with indigo dye. I saw instances of not just hair plaiting but also of using a quill feather to dab wax out of the children's ears or using a small knife to scrape tartar off their teeth.

Uri ede—this was one thing which I found among these women which was highly unusual and came close to being an art form. I have never seen anything like it anywhere else before, and I am taking back some samples with me for special analysis. Uri ede is a type of root—a rhizome, it seems— which resembles West Indian gingerroot. They pound it in a mortar and then crush it to very fine paste between two flat stones. Then they blend it with red clay and add some other "secret" ingredients. Then a body decorator comes along and uses the paste to make very interesting patterns on the body of the client. This is probably the closest thing to art that I saw among these people. The person, usually a woman, who is about to be married or to enter a "fattening house," or is involved in some other kind of ceremony which includes a market parade, has to sit up all night or at least for twelve hours to allow the paste to work its effect on the skin. After about twelve hours, the paste is washed off. A most remarkable thing has happened. The skin is no longer smooth but has taken on the patterns drawn on it by being elevated ever so slightly. It is like tatooing without a dye. There is no discoloration of the skin, just the formation of "pustules" and "blastulas." (I looked at a woman's skin with a small magnifying glass that I carried.) This skin decoration lasts for months, fading as the epidermis is sloughed off. Truly remarkable!

I cannot end this account without describing the faces of these women. Generally flat, with a short, wide nose without bridge; flared nostrils; thick, Negroid lips, with no noticeable hue. This being the harmattan season, the atmosphere is relatively dry and the lips are scaly and cracked. They lick their tongues across them often. Some oil themselves liberally—face, lips, hands, and body—with coconut oil, which they obtain by frying coconuts into copra. Generally, they have good, sparkling teeth, which they keep clean with a "chewing stick." They do not use a toothpaste. Deep-set brown eyes. Although they seem capable of excitement and spontaneous cheerfulness, their general attitude is solemn or dour. They are not prompt with a smile and often seem to wonder why you are smiling. It seems they don't want to waste a smile on anything undeserving. Their eyes are perhaps the most remarkable part of their countenance. They stare at you with a bored, droll, almost sheepish and unintelligent look, except that they appear studious and knowing. What one senses is not unintelligence or drollness but detachment and indifference. Even young children are that way. They reveal little through their faces or their eyes, except perhaps that they may be afflicted by a peculiar type of tribal strabismus, which seems to enable them to see more than one of whatever they are looking at, and perhaps like those reptiles which can rotate each eye independently, they may see you from more than one perspective, each picture on a different screen of their dark minds.

Despite the incessant, ritualized complaining of the women—ikwa uwa— which they explained to me at length, they tend to be stoical. I am reminded, though, that these are the people about whom the phenomenon of "Fixed Melancholy" was discovered during the Slave Trade.

From all that she had heard about Ugbala, Mrs. Ashby-Jones apparently had expected her to be a bush queen living in an exotic mud palace, sitting on a throne of split bamboo fronds or polished mahogany, and flanked by stocky, muscle-bound guards, or perhaps an Amazon queen, surrounded by female spear-wielding warriors. As it turned out, Ugbala was fully within normal human scales, taller perhaps than most and perhaps even statuesque by native standards—all around better looking than most, consciously groomed and adorned—loamy complexion, as if hewn from a deeper, redder layer of subsoil than the others—long limbs—long, delicate fingers—well-trimmed fingernails—big breasts—remarkably flat tummy—there were not many fat women in this society—fading *uri ede* designs on her skin—beauty gap in her upper teeth—eyes somewhat almond shaped, with a shade of the Oriental in them, not the flat, oblong, and widely spaced variety that is much more common.

One of the most remarkable things about Ugbala, Mrs. Ashby-Jones noted, was her self-satisfied carriage, a cocky attitude about the head and neck, and a long and measured gait, as if she were marching in a parade rather than merely walking. *She was entirely self-possessed and unimpressed by my presence,* Mrs. Ashby-Jones wrote, *as if the pleasure of my visit were entirely mine, and if I should have decided to turn around and leave, it would not have bothered her one bit.* "Welcome," she said expansively, like a queen holding court.

Mrs. Ashby-Jones then described the welcoming ceremonies in detail, including the kola ceremony. She wrote:

I nibbled at the piece of kola to be polite and sociable but declined the pepper seeds which came with it. Earlier, elsewhere, I had discovered to my dismay how maddeningly hot those little devils were!

"Palm wine?" Ugbala offered, one of her daughters-in-law acting as a server.

"No," I said, again as politely as I could. "It does not agree with my belly." This was a demurral I had learned from Appolonia from other times in the past when I was offered something I didn't dare to eat or drink. What I was being offered now was "palm wine," strictly speaking palm sap, *tapped by the men from the stems of the two common types of palm native to this area—the Guinea palm* (Eleis guinensis) *and the raffia palm* (Raffia vini- ferra). *What is tapped in this area is mostly the raffia and not the other kind of palm. Palm wine is potable when fresh and unadulterated by the red bark of a tree* (ntche), *which they put in it to make it stronger. It tastes somewhat like coconut milk. Of course, there is the matter of the unreliable hygiene of these things. I once saw a wine tapper take down a pot of palm wine from a tree, and to put mildly, I was horrified to see how many flies and bees had drowned in the pot. The man simply skimmed off the dead insects with his cupped hands and then proceeded to transfer the wine into a calabash. They drink that "fresh" and still live!*

"White people have delicate mouths," Ok. said.

[Ugbala received Mrs. Ashby-Jones in the presence of two friends, Ngwanze and Okwere-ke-diya-nkara.]

"Yes," I agreed.

"And bellies too," Ng. concurred. "They like eggs and other slimy things."

"That is certainly true of soft things," I agreed, but not about the slimy part. "You people like hard and crunchy things."

"Yes," they all agreed, laughing, "and we have good teeth to chew things with. Do you have your own teeth?"

"What?" I said, surprised when Appolonia translated the question.

Truly enough, the women wanted to know if I had my own teeth. Yes, of course, I assured them. I became curious about this question and learned later that the common belief was that most White people had false teeth. Two or three White men—the R.C. priest at Agalaba Uzo, one district officer, and a PWD engineer now retired all had false teeth and were the sources of these rumors. I also found that there is quite a collection of false beliefs about White people among these natives. Cf. the questions I was asked by the women at Uzemba about White women not having milk in their breasts, and therefore having to rely on cow's milk to nurse their infants, and having intercourse and getting pregnant through their mouths. Others questions included: White people carrying dread diseases and being the cause of mgberegede, *or sudden death, a reference to the influenza epidemic of 1918, which killed thousands of people in this area. I have heard accounts of villagers turning their faces away toward the bush when White people drove by in a car.*

As seems to have been the case all the time, Mrs. Ashby-Jones became impatient with the extended welcoming ceremonies and the fact that her hosts took their own good time about everything and easily became irritated at the idea of being hurried along by a visitor. Also, Ugbala and her companions were curious about their visitor's incessant writing, and asked her to read back to them some of the things she had written about them.

"We are trying to understand why you are here," Ng. explained.

"Yes, why you are really *here," Ok. added. "Did you come all the way from your own country just to see who we are and to learn our names?"*

"Yes, the sole reason of my visit is to study the women of this area. I did not know you before. The people of my country, both men and women, do not know you. Through the book I am going to write I can enable others who have never met you to meet you."

"In the other villages where you have been, have you found the kind of information you were looking for?"

"Yes, it has been a very fruitful trip so far. Quite fruitful." I decided to hurry up and begin to get in some of my own questions, lest I spend the entire day answering theirs. "I have been looking forward to meeting you," I said, addressing myself to Ugbala. "People have mentioned your name everywhere I have gone. You have quite a reputation and I consider it a privilege to meet you at long last."

"Welcome to my compound," Ugbala replied. "Where have you been and what have people said?"

"I spent the longest time in the town of Uzemba."

"I believe my name would be well-known in Uzemba. I have been there on many a doctoring trip and have quite a few friends there."

"Yes, that is what many people said. You are a well-known dibia."

"Dibia, yes, but God is the healer," Ugbala said, surprising me with her unexpected reference to God. "The best dibia *is only a medium and a vehicle, only an interpreter of the oracle of the gods."*

"Do you feel unusual as a dibia? *I hear that you are the only female one around here."*

"Around here, maybe I am the only one bold enough to stand up in the open and say so, especially say it to the hearing of the men. There are many women who have a knowledge of herbs, which they may keep to themselves or use silently. Okwere-ke-diya here, for instance, has a knowledge of the secret herbs which cure okpo-onuma. *If you wanted to seal a running belly or get one that is blocked to open, Ngwanze has herbs for those. But to answer your question: No, I do not feel strange being a* dibia. *But then in a manner of speaking, I am not a full* dibia. *I am a woman and cannot possess an* Ofo *stick. Without* Ofo, *I cannot rightly shake the divining rattle,* ebe, *and expect it to say things to me. I do not even try it."*

"Why not?" I asked.

"Because 'Why' has a long tail. It may kill me rather than instruct me. . . . I am a woman. That means I must squat to urinate. If I do not squat, I get the urine all over my legs and cloth. On the other hand, a man can stand erect and aim his jet a full step away from where he stands. A woman cannot do that. Boys sometimes play with their water, slashing it this way and that like a sword. Girls cannot do that. I had to lie down for my husband before I could get pregnant with my children. Standing beside him, I was taller than he was, but I lay down for him and accepted his erection in me, because of the way a husband is a husband and a wife is a wife. Which is to say that certain things are a certain way by nature and you get nowhere trying to change them. That is why I am not a dibia. *But there are many things for me to be apart from* dibia. *If I become all of those other things and* dibia *is the only thing left for me to become, then I will consider fighting to become* dibia."

"You feel no sense of privation?"

"No. A goat can wedge itself in a fence and die of starvation while looking at the distant grazing fields beyond the fence. Or it can turn around and realize that the fence which encloses it also encloses a rich pasture."

"If you are not a dibia, *what then do you call yourself?"*

"A healer perhaps. A herbalist. I have a knowledge of herbs and roots which many a man in this area who calls himself a dibia *does not possess. I keep that knowledge to myself. Many men in the past have offered money, if I would teach them certain cures for this or that ailment, but I refused."*

"But you are teaching your grandson," Ok. interjected.

"That is true. Evulobi, my first son's oldest son, has often been my helper.

If one of these days Death should find me, he has a knowledge of many of the herbs and roots I use."
I asked Ugbala: "How did you acquire your knowledge of herbs?"
"My father," she replied.
I was surprised. "He taught a daughter and not one of his sons?"
"No one else, son or daughter, was as ready to learn as I was. I was the one always standing beside him to help him crush and grind things, the one who walked in the bushes with him searching for herbs. Because I had the eagerness and bright eyes of a child, I could spot the herbs we were looking for more quickly than he could. And when his clients came, I was the only person who knew where he kept everything. . . . My husband was the same. He too was a dibia, *and I married him a short time after my father died. In fact he used to be a friend of my father's. . . ."*
"You were then able to combine your father's herbs with your husband's?"
"Yes. After my husband died."
"No wonder you are so powerful," I flattered.
"By the power of God."

Parables and Proverbs

I have heard more proverbs and parables in the last few weeks among these people than I ever care to remember. They toss them out at the proverbial drop of a hat. Most of them are only marginally meaningful—at least in translation. Otherwise obscurans obscurantis! *What is somewhat irksome is the habit of circumlocution that spawns these proverbs, the misdirection, obliquity, and intentional obscurity. Quite frequently, the meaning or insight in question isn't worth the elaborate disguise so tediously constructed around it. I have been told by Appolonia and others that proverbs are "adult talk," and are used to create complexity. Adult men do not wish to be fully comprehended, preferring instead to be enigmatic or prismatic. The African mind has a tendency to go around in circles. It loathes the concrete and the literal, and prefers the parabola to the straight line, myth and spiritism to science. The wheels of the native mind seem to turn hundreds of times in order to travel a short distance. It sometimes tries one's patience to no end to get a straight answer from these people! The problem, I believe, is the difference between complexity and obscurity, between the rhythms etc. which make up a complex musical composition and the random notes that may suggest but assuredly do not constitute a Bach concerto. What the African ceremoniously disguises as deep thinking is to genuinely deep and complex thought what a baby's babblings are to a great poem. (N.B. This probably sounds harsher than I intended and possibly reflects the frustration I feel at this moment. Generally I have a kindly disposition towards these people, especially the women, and believe there is something "noble" in the very simplicity of their lives, but . . .)*

Oratory

It would seem that considerable premium is placed on eloquence, especially on arched language (as noted before). Emphasis, however, is not on loud or boisterous grandiloquence as much as on terseness and whatever else betokens thoughtfulness. It is impossible to say whether a great oratorical tradition exists here, given the clumsy translations provided by Appolonia. All things considered, it would seem this culture has relatively little interest in articulating itself, and is therefore a largely inarticulate culture. Taciturnity is preferred to speech. Speech is slow and deliberate, and the greatest consonance between the mind of the speaker and that of the audience is achieved through the smallest number of verbal cues. Hence their habit of constantly repeating the hortatory ejaculative "Kwenu!"

A Garden?

The place where we sat was a sort of summer shed (much like the ones in the market) next to Ugbala's house—nine sturdy stakes dug into the ground to support the latticework of a roof made of raffia fronds and thatched with overlapping raffia mats. No walls, mud floor, sprinkled with water to suppress the dust, scratched with a broom made of grass stalks.

Much of life here is outdoors, especially in the dry season, because of the heat. Verandas are popular. Shade and fruit trees abound. Chairs are set out for visitors in the veranda or the shade, and moved as the shade moves with the sun. Visitors are rarely received indoors during the daytime, unless it is raining. Rooms are dingy and virtually windowless. It is a taboo to light a lamp before sundown, so no matter how dark it is inside a room, one is often forced to sit in the penumbra of a sticky room during a visit. Realizing this, I always take pains to sit near a doorway when possible, to see my notes and to catch whatever breeze there may be.

Tragedy!!!

Never having borne a child myself, and never having witnessed human delivery before, I am unable to say whether my shock was due to my never having seen this human phenomenon before or the result of my seeing it for the first time in very primitive conditions.

To begin with, a girl came to summon Ugbala. She rose promptly from her place on a split-frond chair, asked some questions of the emissary, and then hesitated a few moments before saying something to Ng., the younger of her two companions. Ng. walked off with the emissary. I was tempted but suppressed the urge to ask what was up. Ugbala continued to answer my queries, but somewhat distractedly. She seemed to await further word on whatever was going on. That word came soon enough. Ng. returned to say the same word quickly, twice: "Gbata! Gbata!" which Appolonia later told me meant "Come on the run! Come on the run!" Ugbala ran into her hut, oblivious of me, and was about to set out with Ng. when I asked if I might come along.

No, she said. One of her clients was deep in labour, and she had to go and see about it. Could I please come back another day?

I would only be too glad to go along with her.

No, she said.

I persisted, trying to convince her that this was a chance of a lifetime for me, to observe and record this most significant human phenomenon.

No, she said, and left me.

After Ugbala was gone, I asked Appolonia to find a bicycle taxi. I put a shilling in the man's hand, and said, "Take me to where Ugbala is delivering the baby."

The compound was abuzz with excitement, with men and women and children conversing in groups. My arrival caused a bit of a stir, but not as much hubbub as would ordinarily have attended the visitation of a European. The focus of attention was on the ongoing delivery. Even so, a man I took to be the owner of the compound came forward to introduce himself, offer me a chair, and make me welcome. However, I had not come to make a social call. The action was where Ugbala and some others were, out of sight, at the back of one of the women's houses. I could hear them. Before Appolonia could arrive to do my interpretations, I walked towards this house and ducked into a veranda, then into a doorway which led into a kitchen. The kitchen had a *back entrance which led to an open, bald backyard, where the birth was taking place. Three or four women were wedged into the back portal, and there was no way for me to get through them—they would not stand aside to let me pass— or even to see over their shoulders, notwithstanding the fact that I signified my wish to see or get past them. These women surprised me. They were not merely interested in maintaining their positions vis-à-vis what they were watching—they actively wanted to prevent me from seeing the same. When I tried to peer over their shoulders, they shifted position to forestall me. Frustrated and somewhat angered, I ducked out of the sooty kitchen into the veranda and again into the open air of the compound, just as Appolonia was walking up in search of me.*

And lo, there was an opening in the fence on the side of the house from which I had just emerged. I made for it, and Appolonia followed quickly on my heels. Yes, indeed, the gate in the fence led to a small cocoyam garden, which adjoined the bald courtyard where the girl was making her delivery. I stood in the garden amidst the withering leaves of cocoyam, okra, eggplant, and other garden vegetables, while observing this great event.

An outer ring of about six or seven women surrounded an inner ring of four, who in turn surrounded the girl in labour. Drawn as if by the force of a strong magnet, I found myself moving closer and closer, peering or craning my neck to get the best possible view of what was going on. The girl was crouching or squatting on top of several banana leaves, wet with mucus and what I took to be amniotic fluid. No one was talking intelligibly, except Ugbala, who was like a surgeon in an operating theatre, moving this way and that, getting down on one knee, peering between the girl's legs, reaching into her body with her fingers, giving instructions and encouragement. She was also perhaps the conductor of an orchestra, directing an eerie chorus of grunts and gutturals. None of the other women spoke at all. They merely grunted and pushed in unison with the girl whenever Ugbala said, "Nyia!" {Push!} I was simply mesmerized by these events, never having been present at a birth before. Later on, Appolonia was able to help me recall and translate some of the words Ugbala used in her fascinating performance.

"Gbuo!" {Now!} she said, and everyone went "Uuummmh!" including the girl.

"Obia-wa-lah! Obia-wa-lah! {It is coming! It is coming!} Nyia!" Uuummmh!

Two women stood behind the girl, holding her up. Another woman squatted in front of her with her hands cupped underneath the birth canal to receive the infant. No gloves. No sterilized instruments. No hot water even.

"Ngwa! Ngwa! Ngwa! Obia-wa-lah! Gbuo!" Ugbala said. {Make

haste! It is coming! Now!} "Ezigbo nwanyi! Omuzuru-amuzu! Dike-nwanyi!" *{Good woman! Complete mother! Strong woman!}*

I turned around to find Appolonia to translate these words for me, but she would not leave her place by the gate in the fence.

"Isi nwa! Isi nwa abia-wa-lah!" *Ugbala said excitedly. (The head of the infant had appeared.)* "Ngwa! Ngwa! Nyia!"

"Nwanyi oma! Nwanyi siri ike! Nyia!" *{Good woman! Strong woman! Push!}*

Uuummmh!

"Ala binu iko! Biko biaria, biaria biko! Nyia!" *{Land, please! We beg you, please! Push!}*

Uuummmh!

"Nyia!"

Uuummmh!

"Ogwu akpogh nkita! Oye n'adigh ihe ovu, adigh ihe ona adawasi! Nyia! Ngwa! Nyia!" *{A person who is carrying nothing breaks nothing when he falls!} Ugbala's voice became more excited.* "Nwa abialah-nu! Obia-lah-nu! Jikere-nu! Le-kwa-ya! Le-kwa-ya!" *{The baby is coming! It is coming! Make ready! Look at it come!}*

The baby burst out! The woman who was squatting in front of the girl caught it and quickly moved her left hand from its shoulder to its bottom so that she now held it balanced between her two hands.

"Hooray!" I shouted in an outburst of natural exhilaration at the miracle I had just witnessed. As everyone else had fallen deathly silent, I could hear the echo of my own voice reverberating in my ears. Everyone seemed to notice me for the first time. Ugbala cast what I thought was an unfriendly glance in my direction. All other eyes were on me, and they all suddenly appeared to be very unfriendly. I wondered why they were not yet rejoicing.

Ugbala reached a finger into the newborn's mouth to clear it, then applied her own mouth to its nostrils and sucked. Whatever came out of the infant's nostrils she spat on the ground. The infant wailed. The men in the outer compound gave a cheer. Someone told them to keep quiet, so they did not continue cheering.

"Nyia!" *Ugbala said.*

Uuummmh!

"Nyia!"

Uuummmh!

"Ayi! Nmere oleke? Obasi ndi n'igwe! Hafuru'm nwam!" *{What have I done? God in heaven! Release my daughter to me!}*

Uuummmh!

Angrily, Ugbala stalked towards me, took me gruffly by the elbow, and nudged me toward a gate in the fence. I must say that I could not imagine an African being this bold with a European, and was quite surprised at her authoritativeness. When she reached the gate, she gave me a rather unfriendly push through it, then gave Appolonia some unfriendly words for me.

Appolonia explained that I was not supposed to be there. I was a stranger and strangers were not welcome at a birth site. Who knew what curses I might be carrying, or what spirits were with or after me at such a delicate moment? The site of a birth was the site of a new incarnation. Worst of all, I had shouted hooray at the most inopportune moment, and now because of that the girl's placenta would not come down.

In addition to feeling affronted and falsely accused, I was chagrined at this most preposterous superstition. Everyone in the place suddenly turned hostile towards me. I wished to explain, but no one was interested in whatever I had to say. I wanted to help. I wanted to offer medicines from my medicine kit. I wanted to make a gift to the new mother and babe. No takers. The women who were in the front of the house were now each in a séance of private prayer—iju ogu. The men, too, had stopped their banter and chatter and the passing back and forth and snuffboxes and palm wine. Everyone seemed to be praying. I was suddenly an outcast, and there was no one to whom I could offer my good intentions.

A short time later, word came from Ugbala that I should leave.

I expressed a wish to see Ugbala, but they would not let me. Several women barred the gate in the fence. I thought I would simply wait until things calmed down. However, they told me to leave immediately, for I had already brought enough bad luck to the place. After waiting for a while in anger and frustration, I thought it best to return to Onu Miri, where I was quartered.

That night, I did not sleep well at all but was haunted by the specter of what I had seen at that birth site. Early the following morning, I paid a messenger to go and find out what had happened. No change in the situation. That placenta was still stuck in the girl. Despite my schedule, I decided to go to the place to see what I could do to help. I bypassed Ugbala's compound and went directly to the girl's home. Her husband and his people were not as hostile as I had feared, but they would not let me see the girl directly. I could hear her grunting, though, in an adjacent room, in the company of several women muttering comfort and encouragement to her. They accepted the money I offered them, but not my advice to take her to the Government

Hospital at Agalaba Uzo. I was even ready to draft a note to Dr. Pearson, whom I had met previously.

"Come on! Come on!" I said in exasperation. "Don't be so bush!" But my urgings did no good.

Several things struck me rather forcefully as I tried to persuade these people to take this girl who was prone to die of some infection if she was not promptly cared for to the hospital. One was the extent of Ugbala's power over this situation and over these people, even when she was not present. Another was the anxiety with which I awaited Ugbala's return. I had, for some reason, become afraid of her, afraid that at any moment she would suddenly return and scream at me: "What are you doing here? I thought you were gone!" I was like a schoolgirl who had been caught at some bad behaviour and was afraid of further reprimanding from the headmistress. Odd feelings, I thought, for a European to feel towards an African. And finally there was the very real problem of a young woman lying on a mud bed with an undelivered placenta in her womb and a piece of cut umbilical cord sticking out of her body. While I totally rejected their superstition that my shouting hooray was the reason for this predicament, I was disheartened by my own inability to do anything genuinely helpful in the situation.

When Ugbala returned, I was surprised that she was not as hostile as I had feared.

"She needs to go to the hospital," I said.

"What for?" she said. "What man's hospital knows how to handle such things as this?"

"Of course they do," I protested. "Give her a chance. If since yesterday you have not been able to help her, give someone else a chance." That seemed to get to her. Behind her smooth oiled face, behind the languid eyes, something was happening. I persisted: "Will you?"

She turned sharply and glared at me and walked off without an answer.

To make this long, sad story short, they did take the girl to the hospital at Agalaba Uzo, not that day but the following day. By then, of course, it was too late. Infection had set in. She died in the hospital. "Septicemia" said a note I received from Dr. Pearson, the medical officer in charge of the hospital.

This incident saddened me and cast a pall on the rest of my visit to this area. I withdrew to the Rest House for a couple of days, to finish writing down my notes and to make plans for the remainder of my trip. I resolved to see Ugbala again and did so about a week later. I took a bicycle taxi to her house without previous appointment and was fortunate enough to find her at *home. She was reluctant, but I persuaded her to talk, and I am glad that I went because this turned out to be one of the more fruitful conversations between us. She was reflective when I asked her if she lost patients often in childbirth.*

"It does happen sometimes," she replied.

Was it often due to the placenta not coming down?

Sometimes that, sometimes other things. This young woman's death was the only one of its kind to occur in her practice during the past two years. This was the most dreaded form of death for a woman. Women swore by it. Men swore by their climbing ropes—Ugam chaa! Women said: May I be strangled by the umbilical cord of the baby I am birthing, if I do not keep my oath!

Men went to war, Ugbala said, and placed themselves at the risk of injury and death and of being captured by their enemies. They also stood to win acclaim for their valour and courage and could bring back trophies, prisoners, and loot. Men also went hunting and brought back the carcasses of wild and dangerous animals. For a woman, the battlefield was the backyard where she gave birth. That, too, was the forest of the hunt. For a woman to lose a child at birth or even to experience difficulty in delivery was the equivalent of a man being found a coward by his fellow warriors. Dying in childbirth was the worst fate a woman could suffer, and was usually the result of some curse she carried from a previous incarnation. Motherhood was the first title a woman took. All others came later.

A bit of a surprise: Ugbala asked me, "Did you write about this unfortunate young woman in your book?"

"Yes," I admitted hesitantly.

"You must tear it up," Ugbala said.

"Why?"

"You were not supposed to be there, and that young woman's travail was not meant as a spectacle for strangers. Especially now that she died in it, you cannot write it in a book for all to read."

"I am sorry," I said.

"Yes," Ugbala agreed, lifting her eyes to stare me squarely in the face. "But you must be more than sorry. Will you tear up the pages?"

"Perhaps. When I get home," I said. "At least I will consider it."

Ugbala looked in my face again, seeming to search my eyes for sincerity. "Her spirit may become displeased with you also."

I did not answer further and was relieved that we went on to something else.

Also, on this occasion, as we talked, we walked around to a fetish hut at the back of Ugbala's main house, past a bald backyard. There are no lawns in Africa—except near the European quarters! Beside the fetish hut was a herb garden dominated by a large bougainvillea bush. I was quite surprised by this—the garden that is—but especially by the bougainvillea and the other "European" flowers which grew in this garden. The idea of a garden is not something I had learned to associate with Africans, and maybe this was not really a garden in the real sense of the word. Still, here it was. Because it was already December, the driest, if not the hottest part of the year—in fact the harmattan was about to set in—many of the shrubs were withering. Ugbala seemed surprised at my surprise. She was after all a herbalist, she said, and it was therefore not unusual that she should have a herb garden. When she went into the forest to look for herbs, she often transplanted rare ones, so she would have them on hand when she needed them and would not have to go looking for them. I asked: What about the bougainvillea, the hibiscus, sunflower, and pride of Barbados (Caesalpina Pulcherrima)? *Those, she said, belonged to her grand-children, who were enamoured with these "foreign" flowers.*

At a point I asked Ugbala to estimate how many children she had delivered in her lifetime of practice. She went stone silent, and I was reminded by Appolonia that this was a "number" question. I begged her pardon and probed elsewhere. Had she been a widow a long time?

Yes.

How long?

A very long time.

In that she had succeeded so well among her friends, married and unmar-ried, did she like being a widow?

Did I like being a childless woman? she inquired of me in turn.

I swallowed hard and on second thought conceded that maybe my question was not the most tactful. In any event, I said, why did she think she had succeeded so well? Why was her reputation so widespread?

Her answer: Why is one puppy bigger than the rest of the litter? Why does one plant, one fluted pumpkin, for example, grow larger than others on the same vine, or one tree taller than others in the same forest? Chi was her answer, the personal god. To say otherwise would be to imply that she had planned it that way, that her success was the result of her own designs. She cited the recently dead woman as an example. That girl had been relatively tall and physically strong, yet could not deliver her baby successfully. On the other hand, the most recent delivery she had assisted at during the week was by a tiny, tiny woman, but the baby—a large baby too—shot out of that tiny woman without a hitch or difficulty. This latter woman, Ugbala said, was so tiny that everyone was wondering in what part of her womb she could have hidden such a large baby. That was the way of the gods, she said.

I agreed with her about fate and providence but then tried to point out that man could understudy nature and, when possible, get the better of it. That, in fact, was what she herself did. Her skills as a midwife, her pharmacopia of curative herbs, all demonstrated an attempt to alter the course of natural phenomena and to engineer an outcome we would prefer. A successful farmer, even a casual gardener, did not sow his seeds without selecting the best from his stock. He did not sow at random but selected a fertile spot for his garden. The success of Western civilization, I said, was built on replicating and repeating previous success.

Yes, Ugbala said. The White man had succeeded in many things. Most of all, he had captured God's thunderbolt in a bottle. This last statement startled me because of its suddenness and poetic succinctness. I asked Ugbala for an explanation. She meant cannons and shells and rapid-fire guns. Because the White man had harnessed these secret forces of the gods, he could masquerade like Ekpo Amadioha, *and impose his will and whim on everyone, or he could demand tribute and gifts and sacrifices from all those who would stay in his good graces. A most remarkable observation, I thought. These people do not see civilization as we do, nor do they view the White Man's Burden or civilizing function the same way we do. (The towns in this area seem to have poignant memories of some particularly brutal lessons taught them by the Government under the Disaffected Area, Peace Preservation, and Collective Punishment ordinances.)*

I tried to probe Ugbala further on this point, but she recoiled, seeming to have said more than she intended in the first place. She did hint, however, that one of the women who had been with her at our first meeting, Ok. or Ng., had years before lost a father or grandfather on the other side of the river, when an army detachment had opened fire on a crowd of unarmed villagers. They remembered it as an ambush by the Government and insisted that the villagers had been unarmed and come out to meet representatives of the Government for a discussion of grievances. Whatever the actual case may have been, these women saw the action of the Government as treacherous. . . .

Did the native women sometimes cuckold their husbands?

Ugbala chuckled heartily at this question, the beauty gap between her incisors flashing. Then she said, "This is a question you should ask the men. I do not wish to betray any secrets." Then she went on to say, "There is no taboo against a woman's taking a lover. It (adultery) is not an offence against the Land, but something between the woman and her husband. If he catches her, her accounting is to him, not to others or to the Land."

"Does that happen often?"

"As often as there are men who want someone else's wife as a side dish, and most of the men do." Ugbala explained further that adultery was strictly a woman's offence, since men could marry many wives. If a woman objected to her husband's having a lover on the side—how could she object too loudly, since she already shared him with several other women?—the man could marry the erstwhile lover and make her a full-fledged co-wife of the objector.

"Do you have any lovers?" I dared to ask Ugbala, and was surprised that she was not as offended as I feared she might be.

"Tell me about yours first," she replied. "Especially since you do not have a husband and are younger than I am."

"Does that mean that you have a lover then?"

"I am a woman," she said, "and old enough to be your mother. You would not ask your mother about her lovers, would you? Anyway, I am a woman, as I say, and have known a few men in my life. If a man comes along now who can persuade me to lie down for him, I will gladly do so. But believe me, I take some persuading." Her spirits were so high that she broke into a song, which Appolonia told me was a young bride's song. Because of the difficulties we had with the translation, I had her copy it down for me in the vernacular for more effective translation at a future date. It went like this:

> Onye, onye-O ga'lum di?
> Iyomiri! Yomiri! Iyomiri! Yomiri!
> Obu Okoro-bia ga'lum di?
> Iyomiri! Yomiri! Iyomiri! Yomiri!
> Ya'mata sa-ya g'alum di!
> Iyomiri! Yomiri! Iyomiri! Yomiri!
> Ya weta mkpisi-akwa, weta edegere-akwa
> Tukwasa'm n'okpa!
> Ogwu nkpom n'uzo, ntiwa D'im Eze! D'im oma!
> Aka n'akpo okoro!
> Onye-ijeh ngata nma n'oga agwa'm agwa!
> Iyomiri! Yomiri! Iyomiri! Yomiri!

The best translation I could get of the song for now is as follows:

Whatever man thinks he wants to marry me
Iyomiri yomiri chorus.
If he is truly desirous of marrying me,

He must buy a length of rare and expensive cloth and lay it against one of my legs.

Then another length of rare and expensive cloth and lay it against my other leg.

Then waist beads for my waist. Necklaces for neck. Earrings for my ear. Bracelets for my arms.

So that if I happen to be walking along a road and stub my toe against a root, I will have no problem blurting out his name:

My husband the chief!

My husband the go-getter!

My husband who covers me with good and expensive things!

My husband who is always telling me to come inside!

Because his beehives are full of honey!

Turning our attention to Oyoyo, I asked Ugbala, "Have you known her all her life?"

"No," she said. She had not delivered Oyoyo, or she would have been circumcised shortly after birth.

Why were girls circumcised? I asked her.

For the same reason boys were circumcised, she replied.

Which was?

For hygiene, and to prepare them for clean, fruitful coitus. White women were not circumcised? she asked me in turn.

No, I replied.

"Not ever?" she asked, eyes widening and brows lifting.

"No," I replied. "There is no reason to."

"H'm," she said, and fell silent for several moments, at the end of which she said, "H'm" again. Then she asked, "What about White men?"

"Most are not," I replied.

"Not even men!" she expostulated, then paused as if to imagine it. Then she added, "Few women here would allow an ngolo *inside their bodies."*

"Why not?"

"It is just not done. Men are supposed to be circumcised, usually eight days after they are born, which is usually four days after the stalk of the umbilical cord falls off. If a child is sickly and cannot be circumcised as an infant, then it is done as soon as he gets well."

"What about girls?" I asked.

"Same thing," Ugbala replied.

"But clitorectomy," I insisted, "does not improve a girl's hygiene the same way cutting off the prepuce improves a boy's hygiene."

Ugbala remained unconvinced. An uncircumcised woman would remain undesirable to most men, who would say she was "thorny" and could cause impotence or other sexual problems.

Was that the problem with Oyoyo? I asked.

No, Ugbala said. At least not the part having to do with men finding her desirable. She thought Oyoyo's problem (i.e. her uncontrollable sexual desires) was more likely something she called ohiri. *She tried to explain the phenomenon, but I had difficulty grasping it through Appolonia's translations. The best I could gather is that an* ohiri *is a "phantom child" or a "devil child," usually marked by an overabundance of natural gifts—beauty or strength or eloquence or good fortune. Most such children did not live to adulthood but tended to die suddenly in infancy, usually following a short illness or what everyone mistakes for a minor ailment. If the parents of such a child are alert and can have a seer confirm for them early in the child's life that he or she is an* ohiri, *they can do the necessary things to keep him or her alive.*

The necessary things being?

Sacrifices. Scarring and deformation, to make the child imperfect. Usually cutting deep tribal marks on the side of the child's face was sufficient. Sometimes it took cutting off the tip of the child's little finger. When the child was no longer perfect, the ohiri *spirit would abandon him.*

Was Oyoyo an ohiri child?

Ugbala demurred on an answer. I had been dealing with her long enough now to know when not to press her. Later, when I returned to the issue in another guise, I was able to ascertain from her that Oyoyo, she believed, was driven by an undisciplined spirit, and since she was not Nwanyi-Agwu, *i.e., dedicated to the spirit Agwu, she had to be an* ohiri. *A normal person does not do what she (Oyoyo) has done: abandoning her children, running off to become a prostitute, calling the police on her own mother.*

If that were the case, I asked, had circumcision cured her?

Ugbala could not be sure, but she thought so. She had heard that Oyoyo no longer had the fire of desire burning in her, and was now carrying on her prostitution more out of habit than anything else.

We talked in general about many other topics, having to do with sexual mores among the women and their relationships to their men. One of the things of note which Ugbala mentioned was that there was a time when it was considered a taboo to have intercourse in the daytime or outside a house. Nowadays, she said wistfully, people did both, as they now did many other things they did not do before. And because people no longer complied with custom as they used to, strange seeds and weeds were being thrown up by their land. Birds cried out at night whose voices no one could recognize. Weeds grew everywhere. She pointed out clumps of tough weeds growing in her garden. "They grow everywhere," she said, "and the dry weather does not even kill them!" Things were hard. Children were born past the time they were due, some of them already having grown teeth in the womb. It was all an omen of a coming upheaval, she said. A famine or a drought was on the way. Or a blight of locusts. Or were White people getting ready to fight another war? And again kill everyone with poison gas and disease? . . .

This was simply a remarkable woman. I wish I had the opportunity and the ability to converse at even greater length with her—in English—so that what we had to say to each other would not be obscured by tedious translations.

5

The
Impossible Wife

THERE WERE TWO VERSIONS TO THE story of Ahunze, one told by the
men, who called her *Nwanyi Enwegh Nluma* (Impossible Wife), and
another told by the women, who saw in her gentle manner and tough
spirit an example of what was best in women. *"Anya nlecha-a nwa-ite,
ya foro kuwa!"* Nne-nne said of her that night. "You can stare as
much as you want at the little but very hot clay pot. However, all
you can do is stare. You cannot pick it up off the fire and smash it,
because you don't dare!" Nne-nne called Ahunze a domesticated bush
cat with covered fangs and retracted claws, an *uvuvu* caterpillar that
looked soft but stung fiercely when squeezed. "If any one woman can
be said to have started the War," Nne-nne said, "then that woman
was Ahunze, even though she did not see the fighting. *Awtu-aligh-li,*
if ever there was one, who showed the truth of the saying that a
woman has to say yes to a man for him to get anywhere with her.

As Nne-nne repeated Ahunze's story, I could not help smiling at
the parallels she seemed to draw between this legendary woman and
herself.

At about the time the War began, Ahunze was a woman of grand-
motherly age, dark complexioned and considered pleasingly small by

people who liked her, but nicknamed *atu ukwu* by her male detractors—a woman with thin ankles who seemed to grow spikes on her heels, and who, according to the proverb, caused her husband to die at an early age. Surely enough, Ahunze's husband, Madu-koma, had been dead for about ten years, and the circumstances of his death, who or what killed him, were topics of common gossip and conjecture, especially as Ahunze continued to live a defiantly independent life in the village, set apart from the other widows by the fact that widowhood seemed to favor her much more than married life.

Ozurumba, Ahunze's late husband's brother and therefore the man most entitled to inherit her as wife, had pressed his claim. That she said no to him really surprised no one—Ozurumba was that sort of man. But then, after Ozurumba, several other men in the compound had made their advances. Ahunze gave all of them polite but firm rebuffs. *Ine,* the men had thought at first, a woman's ploy to heighten a man's desires by appearing difficult. She was a good-looking woman and a seasoned trader, and with so many men interested in marrying her, it was not surprising that she may have wanted to raise her price by playing them against one another. Custom allowed her to choose whom she pleased. What custom did not allow her, however, was the choice of emerging from the mourning house and declaring that she did not wish to be anyone's wife. Anyone at all.

Impossible, the men said. Something unheard of, that a woman, no less a widow without a son, could rebuff the entire manhood of a village. Simply unheard of. In their chagrin, the men took to saying that she had not been well brought up, that she had not been fully and properly husbanded by her late husband, that he had not taught her the kind of humility and discipline that turned a strong-headed woman into a gentle and agreeable wife. All of this was probably a result of his being gone much of the time, as a migrant house builder in the obscure towns on the other side of Usotuma. In fact, Madu-koma had met and married Ahunze in ways that were not exactly customary, and although she hailed from Umu-Ichima, not far away from Ama-Nkwo, he had met her in a market near Diobu, on the edge of the Salt Water area, where at the time he was an itinerant house builder and she was a house servant and baby nurse to a court messenger. According to the stories told by Nne-nne and others, Ahunze and Madu-koma had overheard each other speak one day at a market and recognized from their accents that they came from the same area. And for as long as their marriage had endured, it had been touch-and-go—Madu-koma had touched home periodically, stayed only a few weeks, and then had gone off again.

When none of them was left who had any further hope of bringing Ahunze to wife, the men of Ama-Nkwo moved to make her feel the sting of their annoyance. They visited her as a group one day and carried away all of her husband's possessions, even those few belongings of her husband's that tradition would have allowed her to inherit as a childless widow. In a manner of speaking, they took everything but the kirtle with which she emerged from the mourning house. That, however, was only a beginning. Her chickens began to disappear. Her goats were poisoned. At night, stones and sticks fell noisily on the roof of her house. Throughout the village, a rumor started that she had poisoned her husband.

Hearing of her plight, her relatives from Umu-Ichima, her maiden village, came to get her. She stayed there several months. Ordinarily, that should have been the end of her story at Ama-Nkwo: a childless widow made uncomfortable by her husband's relatives returning to her maiden village for safety, where a man from another village took a liking to her, married her, and returned the original bride price to her former husband's relatives. What had happened to her up to this point was the common fate of a childless widow, or in fact any widow who did not want to marry one of her dead husband's relatives. However, Ahunze wanted to return to Ama-Nkwo, her husband's village.

The men of Ama-Nkwo wondered why. Ahunze's relatives in Umu-Ichima asked why.

Her answer was a shrug of the shoulder.

Was there a special reason why she did not want to get married again? And if not to one of the men who pursued her at Ama-Nkwo, why not a man elsewhere? "You cannot go back to Ama-Nkwo," her relatives told her. "You are a woman, and your husband is dead. Women do not inherit their husbands. If you had a child, a son, you could return to protect his claim to his father's belongings until he was old enough to protect it for himself. As things now stand, you do not even have a claim to the house in which you used to live. What business do you now have in that village, if you are not anyone's wife?"

"The things they have taken from me were really mine, not my husband's," Ahunze said in reply to her people. "They are things I earned on my own efforts. The pieces of land and the palm trees that people pledged to me and for which they still owe me money, those were really mine. I earned them from trading."

From being puzzled but understanding, Ahunze's relatives became peeved and impatient. They said to her and to one another that her years of living away from home, of growing up in the unstable towns near the coast, had left gaps in her common sense. She reasoned like a foreigner. "Whatever you earned," they told her sternly, "you earned in your husband's name and as his wife. Now that he is dead, whatever was his belongs to his brothers. If you had any loose money, *ego cham-cham*, in your hand, you could take it away if no one knew about it. But a woman does not claim land or palm trees in her husband's village, unless she does so in the name of her husband or of a son. It is not done. No matter how she acquired them. You left Umu-Ichima, where you were born, to go to Ama-Nkwo as a wife," her relatives said. "If you are no longer a wife, then you have no further business at Ama-Nkwo."

"But the people who pledged those palm trees to me know that the money I gave them did not come from my husband."

"Ozurumba, your husband's most immediate brother, can claim those lands and bushes on his behalf, but not you. If you had agreed to marry Ozurumba . . ."

"I will not marry Ozurumba!"

"If you would be friendly with him and work out an arrangement with him, a type of *agbata eke-eh*, he could claim the lands on his brother's behalf and give you a portion."

"Give me a portion of what is already mine, as if he is giving me a gift?"

"That, or you will lose all of it. Why not consent to be the man's wife, if only in name and appearance? Is he so bad? You can continue your trading from his compound, and if you do not like him as a woman likes a man, you can take a lover on one of your trade routes, if that is what you wish."

A delegation traveled from Umu-Ichima to Ama-Nkwo to talk to Ozurumba. He was very agreeable to having Ahunze return, for he saw this as a first step to her ultimate consent to marry him. He may even have offered to rebuild her house himself, as a way to further his interests, but she expressed a reluctance to have him do so, and for his part, he did not wish to waste an expensive and time-consuming effort. In the end it was her brothers who formed work gangs and traveled to Ama-Nkwo daily, until the house was completed. Then a delegation from Umu-Ichima escorted her back and left a message with her husband's people, which said: "Ahunze is our daughter and sister and lives as a widow among you. We are holding you responsible for her health and well-being."

Further insulted, the men of Ama-Nkwo replied: "Ahunze is our widow and our wife. As long as you owe us for her bride price, we do not need your instructions on how to treat her in either capacity. If it pleases us—in a manner of speaking—we can cut her throat, cook her, eat her, go to the latrine unhindered and pass out her remains, and you cannot do anything about it!"

Now feeling that their collective beard had really been tweaked by this woman and her people, the men of Ama-Nkwo were in the midst of hatching their biggest conspiracy against Ahunze when a horde of wild bees attacked their assembly. Ekwu-biri, the oldest man in the village, and Aja-Egbu the next oldest, nearly died from beestings. More than half the men of the compound had their eyes and mouths swollen shut by beestings. But that was not all. Ekwu-biri was kept out of his house for three days by bees, which swarmed around his door posts.

Seers, who were consulted about these strange events, divined that Koon-Tiri was responsible.

"Koon-Tiri!" people repeated, as their hearts quickened with apprehension. Mere mention of that name in those days used to cause grown men to shudder, for until he was killed by a bolt of lightning five or six years later, Koon-Tiri was probably the most feared man in the area. Nicknamed *ghakuru nwoke, ghakuru nwanyi,* or Centipede, Koon-Tiri had a sting as painful as a centipede's, whenever and wherever anyone touched him. *Dibia* of the highest possible order according to native rites, who became a churchgoer when the RCM church moved from Agalaba Uzo to the villages, he had a statue of the Virgin Mary on a shrine at the back of his house, and next to it a collection of wooden *agwu*s artfully carved by someone from the Ibibi area and arranged in a circle like a group of elders in conference. Then there was a third shrine, dedicated to Mami-Wota, wrapped in endless coils of river snakes. A candle and incense burner and frequent burial ground goer, Koon-Tiri was reputed to be in league with several occult powers—local spirits, Mami-Wota, and Dee-Lawrence. According to the stories that were rampant in the surrounding villages, only three copies of the notorious *Sixth and Seventh Books of Moses* existed in all of Africa. One was in Egypt. One was held by a woman in Sierra Leone. Koon-Tiri had the third copy.

Among the wonders that made Koon-Tiri legend, thieves who went to his house one night—they came from a distant town and apparently did not know whose house they were robbing—fell under a spell and were found warming themselves by a log fire the next morning, unable to leave until he lifted the spell more than a week later. In the meantime Koon-Tiri had exacted a week's worth of slave labor from them. They uprooted two trees, mended his fences, thatched his roof, and dug a new latrine for him. According to another oft-repeated story, Koon-Tiri once unleashed evil spirits on Fada Getz, and the Roman Catholic priest lost his voice in the middle of singing a High Mass and did not recover it for several days. There were many versions of this story. Some, who claimed to have been at the scene, said that the priest was reciting the Sanctus when his voice simply disappeared from his throat, and he tried and tried but nothing came out. Others said that it happened at the elevation of the Host, and that the Host turned into a pool of blood on the altar. That was the kind of legend that surrounded Koon-Tiri. Anyone with no better sense than to tangle with him had a funeral scheduled in his near future.

What the people of Ama-Nkwo came to learn after the visit by the bees was that Koon-Tiri was a cousin of Ahunze's on her mother's side, and his word of personal advice to them was that anyone who harmed Ahunze had better never leave his house, because a swarm of bees would be waiting for the person.

"And so," Nne-nne said, "among other things, Ahunze also became known as the untouchable 'sister' of a mean 'brother.' She continued to live among her late husband's people, unhusbanded, childless, and for the most part unbothered. However, when the new Government road from Icheku to Omahia came through the village, the men of her husband's compound took their wives and children and moved to new sites near it and abandoned her to her own devices amid the ruins of the old compound. Such isolation should have been enough to cause any other woman to flee, but Ahunze stayed put. Shaking their heads at her incomprehensible behavior, but willing to do what they could for her, the people of her maiden village sent her two younger brothers, Nwa-Nguma and Odogwo, who were just then growing into adulthood, to stay with her for company and protection."

In time, Ahunze prospered in the cloth trade beyond what was imaginable for a woman. No other trader anywhere nearby, not even the Aro traders who lived at Onu Miri, had a stack of *ukpo* or *juj* cloths as rich and colorful as hers. She had the unwomanly boldness to travel to distant markets, past Usotuma and Agalaba Uzo, all the way to Akwete and the towns of the Salt Water tribes—places she knew about from her days in Diobu as a baby nurse—and return with durable broadcloths and florid European wax prints. Men and women from far and near regularly mobbed her market stall to buy her latest acquisitions, and in time virtually everyone in Ama-Nkwo owed her money or favors, and her house was filled with objects that borrowers left with her as pledge for the money they borrowed or cloth they bought on credit. She owned cassava farms, which other women frequently planted and weeded for her to work off their debts. She even owned palm trees—something unusual then for a woman. For example, the eight or ten trees around her house used to belong to a man named Ufomba, one of the men in her husband's compound, until one day Ahunze was taking a bath at the back of the house and was alarmed to see a young man begin to climb one of the trees.

"Come down," she shouted to the young man, "until I finish my bath. How can I sit here naked with you up there?"

"I am already on my way up," the man said, "and I have many trees to climb. I promise not to look your way."

"No! No!" Ahunze protested, as the man continued to climb, casting a glance in her direction and then smirking. Then in anger she had stood up, turned squarely toward the young man and yelled: "Here! Go ahead and get an eyeful of your mother's nakedness!" Then she picked up her cloth and fled into the house without finishing her bath.

A few weeks later, when Ufomba needed money to pay his tax, Ahunze took those palm trees in pledge for one hundred manilas.

Men shook their heads in disbelief at what this one woman could do. Her fellow women marveled. As a creditor, Ahunze was neither unkind nor condescending, and most important for those men who were desperate enough to approach her directly, she honored confidences. So even though many disparaged her publicly, many privately

regretted that her excellent wifely qualities went to waste unhusbanded. Had she forsworn intercourse with a man as part of the pact
with a spirit that made her rich? Was she touched in the head? Was
it true that she had made a pact with the river goddess, Mami-Wota,
and had given up marriage and childbearing in return for success in
trade? Was it true that Mami-Wota had killed her husband and
yanked the fetus out of her womb, when she had the miscarriage a
couple of months before her husband died? Part of this pact, so the
rumors went, was that if she ever lay down with a man she would
lose her trading skills as well as her wealth.

So, Ahunze had continued to live at Ama-Nkwo, all by herself in
an ancient compound where her dead husband's relatives had abandoned her, a woman whose courage was legend, whose life was
shrouded in mysteries and whispered stories. Her gentleness of manner
and kindness of spirit made her an enigma. Some tried, but no one
could accuse her of witchcraft and make the charge stick. There was
a time, though, less than a year after she returned to Ama-Nkwo
from Umu-Ichima, when she was on a trade trip to Agalaba, and the
women were supposed to weed and sweep the market clearing at Ahia
Orie in preparation for a visit by the District Officer, and she could
not be there. As was custom, the men ordered that one of her goats
be killed as a fine, and soup was made of the animal at the public
clearing. A few days later, a near epidemic of diarrhea broke out in
the town. Everyone quietly took notice, and no one ever again killed
any of her animals or seized any of her belongings to satisfy an infrac-
tion. Instead, she reached an understanding with the elders that when
she could not be present for some collective work required of the
women, she could satisfy her obligation by paying someone else to do
her share of the work or by contributing a pot of palm wine for the
relish of the whole group, who then absorbed her share of the work.
"*Uvuvu* was her other name," Nne-nne said. "She stung fiercely if you
so much as touched her wrongly."

When Ahunze was away on her frequent trade journeys, no one,
neither thief nor curiosity seeker, bothered her compound or her
belongings. People, who in their wanderings through the adjacent
bushes, came in sight of the thatch roof of her house, took that as a
sign to retreat or turn in another direction. Many were the stories of
strange sounds heard in those bushes near her house, unnatural and
disembodied voices and awesome apparitions. Children looking for

firewood, mushrooms, snails, or *ukazi* always took care to avoid that vicinity. Anyone who ventured too close to Ahunze's house was asking to be ambushed by evil spirits, especially Mami-Wota, who could appear in any disguise, as a harmless animal or beautiful woman, always given away though by the magical aura of her "Six Flowers" scent. Adults reminded themselves and pulled their children's ears to remind them never to pick up anything of value near that house, as these were likely to be ritual objects apt to bring a curse on whoever found them. Even so, people often reported having found phantom money or other objects near there, English money, not manilas and cowries, only to have them disappear into thin air or turn into a puddle of water where they had been left for safekeeping.

Nwa ohiri, everyone said. Money rained down on her. Things bloomed on her fingertips. The yams, okra, and cassava planted on her farms grew better than crops on anyone else's farm. Greeting her early in the morning gave a person good luck for the rest of the day. Palm nuts harvested from her trees soaked with oil. Yet, she had only herself to enjoy all this, no husband and no children. Despite their fears, despite even their jealousy, the women of Ama-Nkwo often sought favors from her, cloth bought on credit, a gift animal for a child to take care of under an *nli* arrangement, a basket of cassava from a farm, and sometimes money to borrow. In desperate cases, even the men approached her for loans, although they were more apt to send their wives to borrow for them from her.

Yet, because of her "strangeness," people dealt with her from an arm's length. Among the women of Ama-Nkwo, only Ozurumba's forlorn and battered wife, Akpa-Ego, had the freedom or maybe desperation to seek out Ahunze openly and regularly. Akpa-Ego fastened to her with a mixture of awe and admiration and eagerly sought to play the roles of daughter, confidante, and apprentice. She came seeking to borrow money or a piece of cloth to wear to the market, salt, or a condiment for her soup. In return for what she borrowed and had no hope of repaying, she often offered to wash, weed a farm, or crack palm kernels for Ahunze, with Ozurumba resenting the relationship all the while, even though he often benefited from it, for whatever his wife borrowed she often borrowed for the two of them.

This strange friendship between Ahunze and Akpa-Ego had begun—if what existed between them could be described as a friendship—when Akpa-Ego was a very young bride, in fact a child, barely into puberty.

She possessed a kind of virginal innocence and awkwardness, added to a touch of personal coarseness of manner, which suggested that she had not been brought up in an attentive mother's house. But she was a hard worker—and very strong—and could heft a bundle of firewood or a basket of palm nuts or cassava onto her own head without anyone to help her. Ahunze, in a manner of speaking, had adopted her.

Then one day, at about the middle of the fifth month of the year, the year being 1929, Akpa-Ego came to visit Ahunze. Her jaw was swollen and her right eye blackened, meaning that Ozurumba had recently been displeased with her. But this occasion was not to be routine.

"Get a stool from the kitchen," Ahunze said, motioning with her head while assessing the visitor. "I am cooking out-of-doors to get a little of this breeze that is blowing." She fanned her face with both hands.

Akpa-Ego set down the stool and sat attentively on it as if awaiting an order to commence speaking.

"What did you do this time to offend your husband?" Ahunze asked.

As if that was the cue she had been waiting for, Akpa-Ego began sobbing. "If I did something to provoke him, at least I would know how I roused his anger. But I do nothing at all and he still beats me. When I go to the market I do all my buying and selling in a hurry and rush home like the mother of a sick infant. Still I get a beating for coming home late. Perhaps I should just stay home and never go anywhere. Perhaps I should never go to the market? . . ."

Akpa-Ego paused, but Ahunze did not take the opportunity offered her for a comment. She had heard these complaints many times before. Akpa-Ego was like a stray animal that had followed her home, a young bird with a broken wing, an orphan child paddling by herself on a deep and turbulent river.

"What do you think I should do?" Akpa-Ego asked directly, when it became obvious that Ahunze would not volunteer a comment.

Ahunze looked up at Akpa-Ego's expectant eyes and shook her head. "I do not know what you should do. Can you see out of that right eye?"

"Yes, I can see out of it now, but last night I was seeing things divided." Akpa-Ego's eyes were slightly crossed, the result, she often said, of a convulsive fever she had had when she was a child. This afternoon, their darkened orbits made her look like a sad lemur.

Ahunze sat on a low kitchen stool, her legs stretched out in front of her and crossed at the ankles, and her hands moving deftly to pinch tiny *uha* leaves from their stalks and deposit them in a bowl. She had set a cooking tripod on the bare yard in front of her house and was cooking a pot of soup on it over a wood fire.

Tears began streaming afresh from Akpa-Ego's eyes, and she was making no effort whatsoever to wipe or restrain them. She too sat on a low stool, but on the other side of the fire; her legs were drawn up; her *lapa* was folded and tucked between her knees; her head rested in the palm of her left hand, whose elbow was anchored on her knee. "I do not know what I can do to please Ozurumba," she said. "I am like a slave. Everything I do is wrong. Last week he was complaining that weeds were choking his yams, so I spent all of the next day at the farm weeding. Late in the afternoon I came home and took a quick bath and rushed to the evening market to find a piece of fish for his soup. I went like a beggar from one stall to another to find someone willing to sell a piece of fish to me on credit. Later, I was in the middle of making the soup when he came home. I received a beating."

"What for did he beat you that time?"

"What else, except not having his food ready? Last night's was about money. He wanted threepence to pay the bicycle repairer for patching the tube of his bicycle. I told him I did not have threepence. He did not believe me and went through the house turning over everything." She giggled through the tears in anticipation of what she was going to say next. "He even lifted a hen that was roosting in a corner of my kitchen, to see if I had hidden money underneath the eggs. And he got his fingers stuck in the hen's refuse."

Ahunze shook her head in unbelief and joined Akpa-Ego in the laughter. "Where did he think you got the money?"

"I do not know, but probably he was thinking that Da-Oyidia had paid me for the two days I had just spent cracking palm nuts for her."

"What a shameless eunuch! I wonder if you had a lover and your lover gave you money, would he take it from you?" Ahunze sighed and shook her head again. "One of these days, he will lose you and then find himself without a wife."

"That is right," Akpa-Ego said with determination. "Last night, I told him I may run away someday. But he said I was not going anywhere, because no one wants an ugly and barren woman like me."

"Looking as you are today, it would be hard for anyone to want you. But that is because of him. You are a young woman. Your skin is smooth and your face is pleasing enough, when it is not bruised and swollen. In your natural self, there is nothing wrong with you that could not be overcome by grooming and a few new things to wear." Ahunze's eyes narrowed, and she pointed a finger at Akpa-Ego's waist, as she said: "No one would look good in that faded and dirty *lapa* you are now wearing." One corner of Ahunze's mouth curled up in disgust as her eyes passed over the rest of the *lapa*. "And you may not be a barren woman as much as he may be an impotent waif of a man."

"I wish you could tell him that. You or somebody. I wish I had the courage to tell him that. I think many things in my mind that I cannot bring myself to say to him. I do not know why I don't say them, since he beats me anyway whether I say something or not." Her face and shoulders tightened with emotion. "Why is my fate the way it is? Is it because of something I have done? A curse I am carrying from other incarnations? Am I not a wife like other women? Is there anything they do for their husbands that I do not do for mine? Why then must I do day-work for other women, crack their palm nuts, and weed their farms and get my supper from what I can pick from between their teeth?" Large teardrops fell from her face to the ground.

"What is a man's lot by fate should not be held against him," Ahunze said, "so one cannot say that Ozurumba's poverty is a crime. But when he asks you why you do not look like one of Chief Enye-Azu's wives, you are entitled to ask him why he himself does not look like Chief Enye-Azu. And he has to put a child on you before you can bear one for him. Does he do well what a man is supposed to do?"

Akpa-Ego tee-hee'd.

"Does he?" Ahunze insisted.

Her head bobbing up and down in assent, Akpa-Ego said, "He manages well enough."

"Manages?" Ahunze exclaimed in mock alarm. Both women

laughed. "But does he really get to you? You are a young and strong woman, you know, and he is such a waif of a man."

"I have never had another man," Akpa-Ego said, smiling shyly, "so I do not know how anyone else feels." She paused thoughtfully, as if to imagine how another man might feel. Then she said, "True to God, though, I wish I could conceive. Sometimes I feel sorry for Ozurumba that I have not given him a child."

"Stop feeling sorry for him and feel sorry for yourself!" The statement escaped from Ahunze with more vehemence than she had intended. She sighed and attempted to amend it. "What I mean is, you are a good wife, Akpa-Ego, a better wife perhaps than Ozurumba deserves. It is not necessarily your fault that you do not have a child."

"But is it not always a woman's fault? She is the one who is supposed to become pregnant. Does not the proverb say that after a man has entered into a woman and left his seed in her, he has done his part, and if she does not become pregnant she *alone* knows why not?"

"Yes," Ahunze said, "but there is another proverb which says that there may be more than one reason for a bad haircut: The barber may not know what he is doing, or maybe his razor is not sharp. Ozurumba's first wife never had a baby for him either, but after she left him she had a houseful of children for her next husband."

"That is true, isn't it?"

"Yes. She is married to a man at Amapu named Wogu."

"But all the seers Ozurumba has consulted have said that it is my fault that I have not conceived. As you know, it is supposed to be because of a coin I picked up when I was a child, a coin used in sacrifice by a woman trying to shake off a curse of infertility."

"Perhaps the seers have not seen the situation correctly."

"That is possible too, is it not?" Akpa-Ego agreed. Then noticing that Ahunze was staring at her, she remained silent until the assessment was over. Then she said, "I will not ask you if I am pretty, because I have looked in the mirror, but do you think any other man would *really* want me?"

"Why not?" Ahunze asked. "Why not? In all the years you have been a grown woman, has no man made eyes at you?"

Akpa-Ego chuckled at the thought, then after seeming to take inventory of her experiences said: "No. No one I have noticed."

"The fact that you did not notice it does not mean that it did not happen. As the *akuku* goes, even Nwanyi Uguru could find a man to look past her face and get her pregnant six times."

"Do you think, then, that I should leave Ozurumba?"

Ahunze shook her head and smiled wryly. "I keep telling you that that is advice you will never receive from me. I will not be the person who advised Ozurumba's wife to leave him. As everyone knows you come here often, if someday you stop coming here and it is because you have found a husband in another town, I want to be able to swear that I did not induce you to do it."

"Is it true that he tried to claim you as wife after your husband died?"

"He is my husband's brother, as you know. I was a new widow, and all the men of the compound made their claims. But here I am. As you can see, I did not marry anyone."

"I wish I could be as strong as you," Akpa-Ego said. "You are able to live here all by yourself, with no one to tell you when to come or to go. You have your own trade and more money than many men. All the women of this village envy you, as I am sure you know. And many men too! . . . Tell me something: Are you not ever afraid of living here by yourself?"

"Sometimes and sometimes not," Ahunze replied. "The way I live has become a habit with me. You know what the proverb says: What gives the child the itch has also given him fingernails."

"I truly wish I could be like you."

Ozurumba stopped a short distance from his wife and proceeded to render her worthless with a long scowl, while for her part, Akpa-Ego was overtaken by a series of what seemed like spastic motions as she attempted to comport herself. She began smiling, then switched off the smile, and tried several other faces in quick succession—all of them rendered ugly by her swollen eye and blistered lips. In the end, she did not know which expression to hold. She began saying *"Ilola,"* but the word became ensnared in her throat between syllables. She cleared her throat.

"Where have you been all day?" Ozurumba demanded.

"At the old farm to harvest cassava. After I returned, I had to clean the cassava. Then I trekked to the stream twice for two pots of water, so I could start the cassava soaking. I became very tired. I do not have any help. . . ."

"Help!" Ozurumba shouted. "Help? Is that what you said? Who is supposed to help you? Have you borne any children, or am I supposed to hire a servant for you? Hah? Hah?" He cut himself short, advanced on her, and slapped her with such force that she was knocked over along with the stool on which she was sitting. "Hopeless woman! Because of you I am scorned throughout this village as the wine tapper who has tapped every type and size of tree, but cannot tap a child out of his own wife!"

Akpa-Ego yelped in pain, writhing and whining where she lay on the ground. Ozurumba stood over her, with a mind to administer more punishment, but for one hesitating moment unable find a suitable spot to apply it. Akpa-Ego's prostrate form was out of the reach of his eager fists. "Tell me," he screamed. "Tell me why I should go all day without food? Huh? Huh?" He punctuated each query with a kick, using his heels to keep from stubbing his toes. She lay curled up into a lump, her knees pulled into her chest, her arms folded over her head. Thoughtful enough not to kick her in the belly or chest, he stepped around to the other side and began to kick her in the buttocks and the back.

"Ozurumba, you have kicked her enough!" Ahunze said, taking a couple of steps forward. "If you have a mind to kill her, then wait until she returns home, so you can kill her in your own compound. Do not make me a witness to it."

"It will help your health to stay out of this!" Ozurumba shouted. "I have not yet done what I am determined to do to you someday for corrupting her. Here you are, cooking supper, even though you do not have a man to cook for, and she is sitting beside you idle. Why did you not tell her—advise her like a mother or older sister—to go home and do her wifely duty?"

"Why do you not go home, Ozurumba, and think of how to be a good husband to her? I am sure she will think as hard about how to be a good wife to you."

"How would you know anything about it? You will teach her? Is it not true that a person can only teach what she knows? What can you teach her about being a wife? Whose wife are you?"

For a few moments, their eyes dueled, and then turning away,

Ozurumba reached down to pull up Akpa-Ego, who, thinking that more blows were about to fall on her, curled into a tighter knot and whined like a terrified puppy. "Get up! Get up!" he shouted, as he grabbed her hand in both of his and tried to pull her up. Two or three times he managed to heft her torso off the ground, but as soon as he relaxed his effort, she slumped back down again. Finally he gave up the effort and addressed himself once more to Ahunze. "What are you training her to become? Huh? A witch just like you, is that what you want her to become? Are you giving her instructions on how to kill me?" With that, he turned around suddenly and began walking away.

Ahunze watched the receding figure of Ozurumba with a sudden surge of contempt and revulsion. A triangle of old loincloth that barely covered the compact lobes of his buttocks swayed from side to side in rhythm with his footsteps—the light and springy footsteps of a tree climber and wine tapper who weighed little and walked on high arches, as if his heels never touched the ground. Ahunze became amused as she recalled how, a short time before, Ozurumba, in his efforts to pull up Akpa-Ego, had been extended to the limits of his strength and how his ribs had appeared on the verge of breaking through their cage. A full smile broke over her lips as a thought occurred to her: Because Ozurumba never had more than one loincloth at a time, she could remember in sequence the design on each of the last several cloths he had owned, beginning from the present one with its patterns of snails and seashells. Yet, Ozurumba was a man, she thought. Being hung with testicles made him so.

"You have seen for yourself what he does to me," Akpa-Ego said.

"Someday, he may reach up to strike you and find that he cannot bring his hand down."

"Can you do that?"

"Just a manner of speaking. . . . Well, you have sat with me through the preparation of my soup. Eat supper with me."

"Can you imagine what Ozurumba would do if he came back here and saw me eating supper with you?"

"You can take back some soup for him. I have more than enough."

"He will say that he deserves better than some borrowed soup that has been trekked along the village footpaths in an uncovered bowl. Especially soup made by you."

"Take it anyway. I will put it in a bowl for you and cover the top with an *etere* leaf."

Some weeks passed. Then one day, at about the beginning of the rainy season, Akpa-Ego came to *Ahia Afor* wearing a new *mara-suru* outfit, which became her immensely and drew many compliments from the women at the market. "A good spirit has ambushed Ozurumba," they said, "and he has decided to invest in the beauty of his wife!" Some teased Akpa-Ego about the smoothness of her skin and what they said was a suspicious glow in her complexion. Others called her a former weed patch that had magically turned into a well-tended garden. Was fruit on the way? She caused quite a stir in the market that day; so rare was it to see her in new clothes. Even more remarkable for Ahunze, who watched all this hubbub with delight, was how Akpa-Ego seemed to enjoy herself and freely yield to laughter, how womanly alluring she became when heartfelt laughter shook her bosom and brightened her face. The surprise of the occasion, though, was the *mara-suru* outfit. The cloth from which it was made had been bought from her, but not by Ozurumba.

Not too long after that day at the market, Akpa-Ego visited Ahunze and excitedly announced that she had become pregnant. Amid the hugs and exclamations of surprise, Ahunze remarked, "Ozurumba must be very happy."

"At first all he said was that it was about time I conceived, but since that time he has begun to treat me much better than before. I do believe he is happy."

"How many months are you?"

"I have skipped three times."

"You do not seem to be as happy as I would have thought."

"I am happy," she said, then added, "very happy," as her smile enlarged. "But there is something." She stopped to gather and weigh her thoughts. Drawing her chair closer to Ahunze and looking around nervously, she said, "I am not sure the child belongs to Ozurumba."

"No?" Ahunze's eyes narrowed. "You are not sure, or you *know* it is not his?"

"It is not his. Perhaps I should not have told you, but my chest was near to bursting from keeping it to myself. I needed to tell someone."

"You took a lover?"

"Yes, after a conversation you and I had about how you were sure other men had looked at me without my noticing, I began to notice that men in fact looked at me. Do you remember how you said you were sure some other man besides Ozurumba would find me desirable?"

"I remember saying that, but I did not mean to advise you to find a lover."

"I did not think of it as advice; it was more like reminding me of something I should have thought of myself. After I left here, I began to watch how men looked at me. I was surprised that more than one gave me a second look." Her face was stretched and her cheeks inflated by laughter she was having a difficult time restraining. When she stopped laughing she said: "What troubles me now, though, is that sometimes I feel guilty. I am happy that at last I have conceived, but then I also feel guilty because I have allowed another man to touch me. I feel bad when I see Ozurumba rejoicing over a baby that is not his."

"Is there not a proverb about all the men who have rejoiced at pregnancies that were not theirs and given heartfelt names to sons fathered by others?"

Both women laughed. Then Akpa-Ego said, "What confuses me is that I enjoy the other man more than I enjoy my husband. Revenge I can understand. You know how sometimes in a fight you absorb many blows from someone who is stronger than you, but in the middle of it all you manage to land one good blow, which makes your opponent grimace with pain? When the fight is over, you forget all the times you were hit and remember only the one blow that you landed. That is how I felt when I found out I was pregnant. I had something I could hold privately in my heart as my revenge on Ozurumba for every unkind thing he has ever done to me. But there is more than that. I *enjoy* the other man. *It* is different with him."

"Enjoyment is not a bad thing, is it?"

Both women laughed.

"But so now you have your revenge, and perhaps for the first time in your life, a man has tickled you at a soft spot and made you laugh. Everything should then be all right."

"It should be, but Ozurumba has stopped beating me. It feels strange not to be beaten. Look at me, I have no bruises, no aches or

pains anywhere. My eyes are not puffed and my lips are not split."
She patted and fingered herself joyfully as she spoke.

"I could say no sane man, not even the worst beater, lays hands
on a pregnant woman," Ahunze said, "but I know better."

Ahunze's statement hung heavily in the ensuing silence. Akpa-Ego
studied her, then asked the question she was trying to suppress.

"The pregnancy I have heard that you lost a long time ago, was it
because of something your husband did?"

"Yes."

"He beat you?"

"Yes."

"Oh God," Akpa-Ego exclaimed. Then after several moments she
added: "I am very sorry." Her manner became deeply thoughtful,
even solemn, and as she continued to stare at Ahunze, she was thrilled
for a moment to realize that their usual positions of sympathizer and
sympathy seeker were reversed.

"That is all right," Ahunze said. "I recovered. All the wounds have
healed."

Akpa-Ego tried to think of subtle questions to ask to induce Ahunze
to say more, so she could link the fragments of a life story that was
beginning to take shape in her mind. At length she sighed, her
face switched gears, and she returned attention to herself. "Suppose
Ozurumba never beats me again?" she asked almost wistfully.

"Then you will thank your God for your wholesome and pain-free
body. But what has stopped Ozurumba from beating you may not be
your pregnancy."

"What then, if not my pregnancy?"

"You may have put a thought in him, a second thought. Did you
say anything to him recently that you had never said to him before?"

"I have said something about leaving him. You think that is it?"

"That could be it. That probably is it."

The atmosphere around them thickened. Each woman knew that
neither was really thinking about Ozurumba at this moment. Rather,
there was something else tangible but elusive, which had bumped
against their common consciousness like an object in a murky pail of
water, and now they were groping about, to bump into it again and
perhaps grasp it.

"Once it is born this child will always be there, always another
man's child," Akpa-Ego said, breaking the silence.

"Yes, that is the way things are," Ahunze agreed. "If you begin to feel guilty, then remember all the times Ozurumba beat you in the past. And he will probably beat you again someday."

"My mind is not so much on the beating now as it is on the baby, although I ask myself what I would do if I lost it the way you lost yours. I would probably go mad." She pulled up her shoulders against her neck and shuddered at the thought.

"I hope that never happens to you."

Akpa-Ego thought silently about how it might feel to lose a baby, then shook her head to dislodge the thoughts. With her face returning to normal, she said, "I would like to tell you about my lover but right now I cannot bring myself to do it."

"I have met your lover," Ahunze said. "That *mara-suru* you wore to the market some months ago, who else sells fabric around here?"

Akpa-Ego's eyes flared in surprise. She said, "When he told me a tailor at Agalaba sewed the blouse, I thought he bought the cloth there too. It never occurred to me that he might have bought it from you." Her eyes narrowed with thought. "I wonder, does anyone else in the village know? Did anyone see him buying the cloth from you?"

Ahunze's shoulders rose and then fell together in response. "I do not know," she said.

About a week later, Akpa-Ego visited again, and this time told Ahunze that her lover was planning to place the refund of Ozurumba's bride price in the Chief's custody.

"Have you consented to marry him?" Ahunze asked.

"I have not yet given him my final reply because I am confused. I want to marry him and I do not want to marry him. Everything has come upon me so suddenly that I have not thought all of my thoughts to a conclusion. Perhaps you can help me to make up my mind."

"I am much too involved in this already. How will I answer all the tongues that will begin to wag after you leave? Everyone will say I encouraged you to leave. Could I swear that I did not?"

"Do you think it is wrong for me to look for a better husband? Am I not a woman? Do I not have a woman's desires?"

"What your desires should be is not for me to say."

"That is not much help," Akpa-Ego said, causing Ahunze to jerk up in surprise. The tone was uncharacteristic of Akpa-Ego and close to insulting.

"It pleases me that you know what type of help you would prefer, but I do not mind if you find it somewhere else."

"I am sorry. I did not mean to offend you. Let me go away." She stood up, started to say something, then hesitated, with her mouth hanging open. Then she spoke: "Forgive me about what I am about to say, but I had no other choice in doing it. When Ozurumba asked me how I came by my *mara-suru* dress, I told him you gave it to me for free."

At first Ahunze was too stunned to speak. She made several false starts before she could finally say, "You cannot lie on me. You cannot make me a part of all the things you are doing."

Akpa-Ego stared at her for a long time and then said, "I am sorry." Then she began walking away.

Not long afterward, Akpa-Ego received the type of beating which people commonly say should not be given to a person made by God and delivered painfully by a mother. Ahunze was getting dressed to go to Eke-Ngwu market when Akpa-Ego appeared. And quite an apparition she was, so battered and disheveled she could not have been sold for a broken *anini*. Her face was covered with bruises. Her good eye was a large lump. She spat blood from her cut tongue and split lips, and she was naked except for a strip of old cloth around her waist. The bulge of her pregnancy hung recognizably beneath her rib cage. As she tried to tell Ahunze what had happened, her words were unintelligible, because of the condition of her tongue and lips.

Ahunze did not know which of ten different impulses to follow, among them the impulse that she just wanted to be left out of Akpa-Ego's troubles and simply be able to go to the market this evening, sell a few strips of cloth, collect from those who owed her, come home, eat a casual supper, and go to sleep in peace. But by far the overwhelming impulse was anger, and this gave rise to a sudden thought: Take Akpa-Ego to the market with her and let the other women of the town see her; tell them she had seen a snake too big for her—as the proverb said—and seek their help and advice on killing it.

"Go to the market looking like this?" Akpa-Ego rasped, looking herself over.

"That is how you came here, is it not?"

"But your house is not the same as the market. At least give me a piece of cloth to wear."

"Just a piece of cloth? Why not let you take a bath first? And maybe wait for your wounds to heal? I will not give you anything to wear. Come on. We go as you are, or you go away."

Akpa-Ego began crying, but Ahunze was resolved.

At the market, Ahunze shoved Akpa-Ego at the first cluster of women she came upon. They vented their horror in outbursts and ritual spitting and calls on various gods to save them from ever doing anything for which they could be so badly mauled.

"What happened to her?" the women asked on top of one another.

"I do not know," Ahunze replied. "She is Ozurumba's wife, as you all know. Ask her."

"This is a human being?" one of them asked.

"And someone's wife?" another said.

"And somebody's daughter?" another asked.

"Who could have done something like this to a pregnant woman?"

"She could lose the pregnancy."

"Is she a slave or a wife?"

"What did she do?"

"What possibly could she have done to deserve this type of treatment?"

"The same man who beat her, is he the father of the pregnancy she is carrying?"

"God forbid this kind of beating. A man may beat his wife, but even a goat should not be beaten so badly."

"This is surely not a way to marry a wife."

In a few minutes, nearly half of the women in the small evening market were clustered around Akpa-Ego, talking excitedly and sharing their own experiences of beatings by their husbands. As they came and went from where Akpa-Ego sat, a theme emerged from their comments: "This is not how to marry a wife!" the women repeated to one another. "No, this is not how to marry a wife!"

Ahunze started a signal twig, to be passed from woman to woman until every woman in the market had handled it and understood its meaning—they were collectively aggrieved by what Ozurumba had done. They would collectively escort Akpa-Ego home and meet the husband who had done this thing to her. They went through their trading hurriedly and then congregated at the corner of the market.

"*Oha Ndom kwenu!*" someone intoned.

"*Yah-yah-yah!*" the rest responded in unison.

"The Solidarity of Women say yes to me!"

"*Yah-yah-yah!*" the women replied all together, making the hissing sound of swarming termites.

"Ndom, agree with me!"

"*Yah-yah-yah!* We agree! We agree!"

Ozurumba was not home when the women arrived in his compound. They laid down their market baskets under a tree in a corner of the compound and began singing and dancing in front of his house.

> *Ozurumba, Ozurumba, you like to beat your wife!*
> *You will beat all of us tonight,*
> *Until your arms fall off!*
> *Ozurumba, Ozurumba, you have the biggest prick in town*
> *You will fuck all of us tonight,*
> *Until your prick falls off!*

Not long after the women's arrival, Ozurumba returned with a bundle of goat grass, which he threw down angrily, as he demanded to know what the women were doing in his compound.

"We have come to be your wives," the women said, "to give you forty women to beat instead of one." They surrounded him in a tight circle and began to sing more loudly.

"He has a machete! He has a machete!" they sang jeeringly. "He is going to cut us! He is going to cut us! He is a headhunter and is going to behead us! Go ahead, headhunter! Behead us!"

"Cut me first! Cut me first!" the women jeered in turn, as they pressed so tightly around him that he could not move at all, nor could he raise or flail the machete he had in his hand. The women were now so close to him that they were bumping into him directly. Then they wrested the machete from him and passed it to the fringe of the group. Soon the largest he-goat tethered nearby was bleating desperately as some of the women slit its throat. Ozurumba tried to struggle free but could not. Unseen hands jerked off his loincloth so that he was completely naked.

A roar of laughter and applause arose from the women as the strip of loincloth passed as trophy among the women. They began chanting:

Ozurumba! Ozurumba! Wonderful husband!
You are such a great husband,
You will marry all of us tonight!
You will marry us!
Yes, and feed us!
Yes, and clothe us!
Yes, and fuck us!
Yes, and impregnate us!
And we will all deliver for you,
A big tribe of children!

The women pushed Ozurumba to the ground and spread him out, face up, holding his hands and legs so he could not struggle free. Then they took turns at sitting on him, pulling up their cloths and kirtles to their bare buttocks and planting their nakedness on every exposed element of his body.

Hearing the commotion or missing their wives, the men soon began to gather around Ozurumba's yard. The first of them to arrive shouldered his way into the throng of women and rescued Ozurumba. His loincloth was restored to him. Aja-Egbu, the oldest man in the village, assumed control of the situation. "What has happened here?" he asked.

Several women began speaking at once.

"Heyi! Heyi!" Old man Aja-Egbu exclaimed. "May the gods of this village and the spirits of all our ancestors avert their eyes from this abomination! I asked what happened, and with more than twenty men standing here, the women begin to cackle like partridges. Have we all lost our testicles? Are you now our husbands and we your wives? The White man has taken over our land, it is true, but are the women now going to take whatever is left of us? Let a man speak! Who was here first? Who saw what happened?

Several men spoke in turn, each stating what was happening at the point he arrived on the scene.

"Ozurumba, do you wish to enlighten us?" Aja-Egbu said.

"No," Ozurumba grunted angrily. "How can I speak about this unspeakable disgrace? I cannot add to it by standing here in front of all these women, as if this were a trial, and then telling you what they did to me. It is Ahunze, that witch who is now hiding behind the others. She instigated the whole thing."

"No! No!" the women shouted. "No one instigated anything. We all came on our own. No one brought anyone else."

"I have stomached enough interruption from you women," Old Man Aja-Egbu said. "It will cost you a cock if I catch your lips moving before I have authorized you to speak. Now, which of you has something to say? Raise your hand and I will recognize you."

No hand was raised, but Akpa-Ego was shoved forward.

"*Obasi ndi n'igwe!*" Old Man Aja-Egbu exclaimed in horror. "What has happened to her?"

"Her husband," several of the women exclaimed. "Ask him what happened to her."

"Is she not pregnant?" Aja-Egbu continued, narrowing his eyes. "Is that not pregnancy that I see?"

"Yes, yes," the women chorused. "Four months of pregnancy." One woman added that the fourth month was a bad month, a risky month, for her and for many other women she knew.

"Are you pregnant?" Aja-Egbu asked Akpa-Ego.

Tears raining down her eyes, Akpa-Ego nodded several times.

"How many months are you?"

She put up three fingers and tightly pressed her lips together to keep from bursting out aloud.

"Ozurumba, are you sure you do not wish to say anything?" Aja-Egbu asked. "I do not know what your wife has done to you, but is there anything you wish to say? The proverb says that a man does not enter into a woman's thing and afterward pinch it spitefully. Another proverb also says that if you treat a woman fondly, then she can gladly wrap herself around you. What is the explanation for this thing you have done?"

"There is nothing I wish to say at this time," Ozurumba replied.

"Is this matter over then?"

"No, this matter is not over. I have many things to say, but not now."

"Come on, then. Let the men talk by themselves. You women can return to your kitchens and cook supper and mind your children."

"What about her?" one woman asked, pointing to Akpa-Ego. "What will happen to her? Where will she sleep tonight?"

"Where does she usually sleep?"

"Surely not in the house of the husband who has treated her so badly. She is now the ward of Ndom, our refugee, whose safety is now our sacred duty."

"Let her sleep with her friend, Ahunze."

To everyone's surprise, Ahunze shook her head. "Let her sleep with someone else. As the proverb says, everyone blames the riverside monkey for every twig found floating in the river. Perhaps it would be best if she slept in a compound where a man is present."

Several eyebrows were lifted. "Strange to hear you say that," Aja-Egbu chuckled, "but I believe you are correct. She can sleep with one of my wives. Now all of you women return to your houses."

"What about our goat?"

"Your husbands will clean and apportion it."

"No one will clean or apportion anything, unless I am first told how I will be paid for the goat," Ozurumba said.

"That goat belongs to Ahunze, anyway," someone said. "Is it not the offspring of the *nli eghu* that Ahunze left in the care of your wife?"

"This was my share of a past litter. The goat is mine. Or my wife's. I am the one who feeds and cares for it."

"Anyway," Aja-Egbu said. "The goat is dead. What are you going to do with the carcass?"

"Sell the meat in the morning in the market. And make every woman who was here tonight pay for the difference between what I can get for it and what I believe it is worth."

Ozurumba followed the rest of the men sullenly to Aja-Egbu's *ovu,* where they all sat down and shared kola nuts, pepper seeds, and the evening palm wine. Then Aja-Egbu asked Ozurumba: "How did you become so angry that you nearly beat your wife to death?"

With reluctance, Ozurumba explained that he had "discovered" his wife with another man. Not really discovered her as much as suspected that she had taken a lover. Then he had asked her a direct question, expecting her to deny it, but rather than deny it, she had affirmed it.

"You asked her if she had a lover and she said yes?"

"Yes."

The men shook their heads and expressed their unbelief in various other ways. What was the world coming to, many of them wondered, that women no longer respected, let alone feared their husbands? A man asks his wife if she is having an affair, and she has the courage to look him in the face and say yes.

"Was this before or after she became pregnant?"

"I do not know. I still have not got to the bottom of the whole thing."

All present recognized that the question itself was pregnant, but no one showed any interest in pursuing it further.

"The woman I married used to be obedient and respectful," Ozurumba said, "but she has come under the influence of that Mami-Wota witch, who lives by herself at *okpulo*. A good goat that goes foraging in the company of a bad goat soon learns bad habits. The spirit I now see in Akpa-Ego is the spirit of Ahunze, a spirit of defiance and rebellion."

"But Ahunze herself is not known to consort with lovers, even though she is a widow. How could she teach your wife anything she herself does not practice?"

Different men made comments in turn.

"Each husband here tonight should talk sternly to his own wives," Aja-Egbu said. "Women used to sit on people a long time ago, but I have not heard of it in recent times. Anyway, I was not pleased to see the way their eyes were shooting sparks tonight. They are still women and wives, no matter how they think they have been aggrieved, and we cannot have them running rampant and doing what they please. But for you, Ozurumba, the proverb says that we first drive off the fox, then we come home and blame the chickens for wandering too close to the fox's lair. The women are not here now, so I can address you as a man to another man. A man is entitled to beat his wife, but not meanly. You punish a wife the same way you punish a child, carefully and with a light hand. You do not simply let go fist or a kick and let it land wherever it may. Were you pleased with the way your wife looked tonight?"

"No. But she deserved even more of a beating than I had a heart to give her."

"Of course you were not pleased. She is your wife, with her broken lips and her swollen eyes and her missing teeth. After you have beaten her into such a state of ugliness, you are now the husband of a very ugly wife with a big window in her upper teeth. If people laugh at her, are they not laughing at you too?"

"No one likes to be married to an ugly woman," someone else chimed in in support of Aja-Egbu.

"I dress my wives before I dress myself," another man said.

Ozurumba stood up angrily. "The women were right then in doing what they did to me? Am I now being blamed for what I did to my own wife? Which one of you would break out in a fit of happiness if he caught his wife with another man?"

"No one," Aja-Egbu said. "But we are saying that a person restrains himself, even if he is angered. A woman's head is now equal to a man's head. If you are beating your wife, something you are entitled to, and land a blow on the wrong spot and she collapses and dies, it is your head to pay for it."

"Yes," another man said. "The White man's law does not even distinguish between the slave and the freeman, between the *osu* and the *diala*. Remember what happened to Chief Uka-Umunnah of Umuvoh."

"Are the men of this compound then saying that I do not deserve any recompense or even an apology from the women for what they have done to me? They sat on me. They urinated in my house."

"What do you want us to do? You should not have let them do it to you. You should have struggled free. After they have done it, it is like a market vulture carrying away a piece of meat from a butcher. The vulture is an outlaw. When they band together and are of one mind, women can be like outlaws. They can claim the sacredness of Edoh, which no one can touch. It is truly a wonder," Aja-Egbu continued, "those women out there tonight and their solidarity. If they had defied me and refused to go home, what would I have done?"

"Snatched a whip from somewhere and scattered them," one young man said.

"Whom would you whip first?" someone said to the young man who had just spoken. "Your mother, or another woman who was your mother's age, and who was present when you were born and saw you walking around when your penis was no larger than a bottle stopper? Is that the person you would take a whip to?"

Laughter coursed through the group. "Yes," someone else added. "And would you whip someone else's wives or just your own?"

"In that case," the young man said, laughing, "everyone whip his own wife then."

"To what avail?" Aja-Egbu said. "Every woman who has gone behind a house and squatted down and delivered a baby has become a priestess of the goddess Edoh. When they band together, they are as immovable as Edoh."

"What about that childless Ahunze who started all this?" Ozurumba asked.

"How did she start all this?"

"It was she who instigated all the others to come to my house."

"How did she do that?"

"I do not know."

"I hear they passed a signal twig at the market."

"Ozurumba, you are still looking at the ground where you fell rather than the stump that tripped you in the first place. Your wife, in the condition we saw her tonight, was not a wholesome sight."

"De-Aja-Egbu," Ozurumba said desperately, "please dismiss this assembly."

"The assembly is over," Aja Egbu said. "Ozurumba, what are you going to do?"

"Something, but I have to reckon my thoughts."

"Reckon well, especially if you are thinking of Ahunze. I do not have to tell you that she belongs to someone. I believe you know of her brothers. The one who is a wrestler is inhabited by demons you do not wish to tangle with. The other has money and is looking for someone to take to court. I do not know which one you would prefer to tackle, but as the proverb says: Before you challenge a gorilla to a wrestling match, you should make sure of your skills. And apart from her people, who may be half a day's travel away, that woman has something inside her that gives her the courage to live as she does. I do not know what it is, but it is something that commands a second thought before you decide to fight with it."

By himself that night, Ozurumba felt severely aggrieved, as much by Aja-Egbu and the men of the compound as by the women who had sat on him. How could the men side with the women against him, men that were supposed to be his kin? If the women stood together in sodality with Ahunze and Akpa-Ego, why could he not count on the men to stand with him?

A disgrace beyond repetition had been visited upon him, the ignominy and shame of a lifetime. Their smelly and sweaty bottoms on his face, their rank wetness and the prickly hair of their things in his mouth and eyes! Unspeakable abomination. He would rather have fallen into a latrine. How could he ever show his face in public again?

As for the men, they had dared to judge him a bad husband and implied that he deserved what he got. How could they? What did they know about the rest of the story, for example that the child Akpa-Ego was carrying was not his? Perhaps he should have told them that. But how could he have done so, without exposing himself to the possibility of their ridicule? He had never fathered a child, and now the pregnancy his wife was carrying was not even his.

Money, or lack of money, was probably the reason Aja-Egbu sided so consistently with Ahunze tonight. He probably owed her money. Or he was hoping to borrow from her for the coming feast of Ofor, during which the family gods would be demanding so many sacrifices. What a world it now was when an *isi opara* and *mbichiri-ezi* depended on loans from a widow in order to make sacrifices to the family gods! He thought briefly of the rumors that he was interested in marrying her. Could he be? That would be another reason for him to try to ingratiate himself with her. How did it happen that none of the others said anything on his behalf? Were they all against him? What had he done to earn their ill will?

Ozurumba set a pot of water to boil and bathed himself thoroughly. Afterward he felt a little better. Hungry, he searched the kitchen for food. The fufu mortar was empty; there was no soup in the soup pot—it was washed clean and inverted to dry. The hanging basket over the cooking stand had nothing in it.

There was a rap on the door. He looked up. "Who is it?"

"Me," said a boy's voice. It was Ukiro, Agbara's son. "De-de says you should come and put the evening *efe* to the wine tree and empty the pot or it will overflow by morning."

"Tell him it is late, and I am looking for something to eat. I will not climb any trees tonight."

He followed the boy's shadow with his eyes until it was totally absorbed by the darkness. Then he stood looking at the sky on which a partial moon was being rolled over by successive formations of high, rainless clouds. The fruit trees sat silently in silhouette, while the extended fronds of the palm trees hung limply in the dewy night air.

He reentered his house and found a yam and returned with it to Akpa-Ego's kitchen. The fire he had kindled earlier had gone out, and because he had built it with palm fronds, it had left no hot coals or embers. He weighed the prospect of wasting a match and some kerosene trying to light a new fire or of going to some woman's kitchen in search of hot embers. Despairing, he dropped the yam into a nook and decided to forgo supper.

Tears came to his eyes, as he sat on a chair in the yard in front of the house in the dark. After a few minutes of fighting with mosquitoes, he resolved to go to bed. In his parlor he found a small gourd of morning palm wine and inverted it over his mouth and kept gulping until his breath gave.

In bed he felt a strong and strange craving for a woman. As he focused on his desire, he realized that it was not for his wife, nor for just any woman, but for Ahunze. Ahunze who had teased his imagination for many, many years. He saw her in his mind's eye as earlier that evening she had stood apart from all the other women, looking on but not participating in the shouting and chanting, her eyebrows lined with rare mascara bought in the daily market at Agalaba Uzo. Her *akisi* head scarf without duplicate, obviously selected for herself during her travels. Her hands—hands that never dipped in a smelly cassava pot, because she ate *garri*, like the *Ijekebe* people who lived in the township—soft and not callused from farm work or picking palm nuts from thorny heads. Her sense of dignified detachment! She was a woman fit to be a chief's wife, and if someone had commanded him to choose a woman out of that horde that had besieged his yard that evening, there was no question whom he would have chosen. If someone were to ask him now how he wished to be recompensed for the disgrace he had suffered that day, his reply would be: "Give me Ahunze, and I will be satisfied." Straddling her, planting his member inside her, would put him in touch with a source of nourishment such as his heart craved but had never known. He would draw strength from her, and even now as he thought about her, he could feel the strength begin to well up in his muscles, his veins begin to gorge with it. He could feel it rising upward in his chest, all the way to his head. He thought perversely: Had she also sat on him?

But she was the one who had instigated the others against him! How could he feel anything for her but pure hate? Not only had she denied herself to him, but she had probably alienated his wife and induced her to stray with another man. His mind flitted about for a proper mode and level of redress. He thought of killing her and setting her house on fire. He probably could not bring himself to kill, but certainly he could set her house on fire.

Yet, how to explain her kindness, the numerous things that she had lent to Akpa-Ego, the goats and chickens she had left in her care as *nli,* so that when they produced offspring the two of them could divide the flock or the litter. More than two or three times, in fact more times than he cared to remember, he had sold some of these animals or pretended that they were lost, so that Ahunze did not even receive what was due her as owner. And yet, she did not seem to mind. Why did money multiply in her hands, when it seemed to vanish into thin air from everyone else's? Was she really in league with Mami-Wota? Did she have a shrine in her bedroom?

No. No. There was nothing he could do that in life would give adequate redress to what he had suffered at the hands of these women. His shame was beyond remedy. He fell asleep but slept fitfully, awaking with terrifying starts, falling into deep pits and off tall trees in his dreams. At last waking up with a resolve, he grasped his machete from under his bed, tucked it under his armpit, and wondering whether the cock had crowed, he stepped into the dewy morning air toward *okpulo,* where Ahunze lived by herself. Approaching her house, he was surprised to see the glow of a lantern through a partially open doorway, then the figure of a man. It surprised him only briefly to see that the man was Aja-Egbu. So, he thought. This explained the old man's partiality of the evening before. Old Man Aja-Egbu ambled past Ozurumba where he had ducked behind a *uha* tree near the edge of the compound. He then got up to do what he had come to do.

"So Ahunze yielded to De-Aja-Egbu?" I asked Nne-nne.

"No-no," Nne-nne said. "That is the funny part of the story, the part with the double twist of irony."

As Nne-nne related it, the "funny part of the story" was the actual encounter between Ahunze and Aja-Egbu, and the "double twist" was that Aja-Egbu was forced to tell the story in all its embarrassing details as a condition for recovering from an illness, a short time after the fateful events of that night. Seers who were consulted about his illness said that the spirit of Ahunze was holding him for ransom, and he would not recover from illness unless he divulged the entire, detailed truth. What had happened was that after that night, Aja-Egbu had allowed the false impression to stand throughout the village that he had bedded Ahunze, something which apparently grieved her spirit.

"So, what actually did happen between them?" I asked Nne-nne.

As Nne-nne told it, what actually did happen was that Aja-Egbu left his house that morning thinking to himself that there was a woman nearby, a *mere* woman, though strange as any woman he had ever seen or heard about, shrewd in a way a woman was not supposed to be shrewd, and tough as tortoise's shell, who had all the money he needed to save his face from the public disgrace that was staring at it because of the tax money he and his friends had misused as *ewere-ewe*. A woman unhusbanded. Fallow ground. Rich, fertile, fallow ground, unfarmed for years, just lying there useless, while there was a famine in the land!

Would she appreciate how much of his dignity he was suppressing as a man and as an elder in leaving his bed so early in the morning and walking through the unhealthy morning mist to come to her house, instead of sending an emissary to summon her to him? Did she have a soft spot he could press?

Ahunze let Aja-Egbu in after a long exchange across the locked door.

"I will not beat about the bush," Aja-Egbu said, after he sat down. "I did not lose my way and end up here by accident. Nor did I come simply to inquire about your health. Rather, I have important things that I have come to ask you."

"You have both of my ears," Ahunze replied.

"You are a remarkable woman," Aja-Egbu said. "Yes," he agreed with himself. "But still you are a woman, and not so old that the things of life that usually matter to a woman no longer matter to you. Even I, at my age, which is a few years more than yours, am not so old that my eyebrows no longer lift up or fall down. I want you to know that I have always admired your good sense. Of late I have even come to admire your toughness. You have been the dry, fibrous piece of meat that the proverb speaks about. The more you are chewed, the larger and tougher you have seemed to become."

"I do not at all consider myself tough," Ahunze replied to Aja-Egbu. "I am merely an orphan child such as the proverb speaks about, who when given a little bathwater, knows only how to bathe his belly."

"You must not misunderstand me," Aja-Egbu said, "or think of me as a flatterer. This admiration I am speaking about is something recent, where I am concerned. It is like what happens when a father has been trying to discipline a hardheaded son, and such a son for years has insisted on doing things his own way. In time the father gives up, thinking that life will discipline the boy in a way he never could. But in the end the child wins the bet and makes out well despite what the father or anyone else would have forecast for him. At that eventuality, the father can only shake his head and say, 'Live and learn.' If a man tells you that he can dive into a river and catch an eel with his bare hands, you are entitled to laugh and scoff, but if right before your eyes he dives in and comes up with an eel wiggling in his grasp, you have to eat your words. I believe you know what I am talking about. You have proved yourself. You have won your case."

"I was never trying to prove anything. I was never really trying to be anything other than what my *chi* has ordained for me. Nevertheless I am very happy to hear what you are saying. If indeed you are saying that the men of this village no longer see me as an enemy, then my heart is rejoicing inside me. I never wanted to be anybody's enemy."

"No one ever saw you as an enemy. You simply did not behave like a married woman. Or like a woman. A woman is like *mgbalala* plant. Sometimes she flourishes and flowers on the ground, but most of the time she wraps herself around a man to get to the sunlight. But you have been different and have done quite well by yourself."

"I know what I have suffered, but, as you say, I have no knowledge of what I have been spared. But thanks to the gods, I survived."

"You more than survived. You have continued to flourish. You are as strange as the Nameless Tree of Egbelu-Mbutu. Somewhere inside you is buried a secret stone. What is it? What is your secret? Can I touch it? Are you a woman? Do you urinate standing or do you squat to urinate?"

"Do I not look like a woman? I am a woman, and I feel like a woman."

"Let me touch you," Aja-Egbu said, "so that I can reassure myself that your responses are the responses of a woman, that your heart is not made of iroko wood, and that those hairs I see on your arms are not really the quills of a hedgehog. So that if anyone to my hearing ever asks, 'Is she a woman or what?' I can answer 'For sure!' from what I *know*. Let me be your lover."

Her eyebrows lifted.

"Or your husband, if you prefer."

Her eyes widened.

"Come and live in my compound. You will still have everything you have now, and in addition the protection of the fence that now keeps my wives from the dangers of life."

Ahunze shook her head and then chuckled. "Do you wish to be my lover or my husband?" she asked.

Aja-Egbu smiled, then got up from where he sat and went to her, and stood, stooping in front of her. "You are a woman that stirs desires in a man," he said, "even a man like me whom old age has begun to clutch by the heels. *Akwa-eke,* rare as a python's egg—that is what you are, and right now, I want you to coil around me as I snake up inside you. I want you to be mine and to call me yours, whether as my *iko* or as my wife. Whichever way, I want you to belong only to me. The greatest joy of my life would be to have your legs curled around my waist and your face next to mine as I ask you to repeat my name to me in the heat of your passion."

"You sound like a lover," Ahunze said with a chuckle. "And at that, one that is less than half your age. A lover," she said, "is a rare dish, a festival dish one eats only on occasion. A husband, on the other hand, is a daily staple."

"Tell me," Aja-Egbu said earnestly, "do you not feel the least bit of attraction for me? I realize that the light in my eyes has dimmed a little because of age, but as the proverb says: This piece of rag you now disdain was once very expensive Ukwa cloth."

"I have feelings," Ahunze told him, "but they have become like well-trained children. I am their mother, and they do only what I tell them."

They bantered for a long time and it seems that Old Man Aja-Egbu could not decide which of the two things he had in mind was more important to him—to borrow money or to bed Ahunze. And then at a point, it seems that he became frustrated with her, thrust her into bed, and fell upon her.

She slammed her fists into his face and then scratched wherever her hands came in touch with his skin. However, his weight kept her from struggling well, and meanwhile he was trying to insert his body between her legs and his tool into her. With an effort, he unknotted her legs, but then she turned on her side. Their struggle continued for a long time. By sudden switches and turns, she made him miss his aim again and again. They began calling each other names. She called him an old man with a weak erection, who had no chance of penetrating a virgin.

"Virgin," he scoffed. "*Akpuru* disease is what you may have, not virginity. And as if virgin is a good thing for a woman to be at your age!" He called her a witch, who needed intercourse with a man to make her human and woman again. "Fool!" he exclaimed. "You should be singing to me, as your mother must have taught you to sing to a man while he was having you. Have you forgotten? Sing to me! Encourage me!"

Tired, Ahunze lay still, her legs stretched out flat underneath Aja-Egbu, who lay lizardlike on top of her, breathing hard, unwilling to take his weight off her lest he lose whatever advantage he had gained. In a few moments, his chest pumping a little more slowly, he scooted down to a kneeling position, pulled her legs up and apart, and placed his body between them. "Hmmm," he might have said, if he had found the breath to utter a sound, for she seemed to have yielded, an animal paralyzed by a python's venom, ready to be swallowed. She just lay there.

But Aja-Egbu was physically exhausted. His erection was gone, lost in the struggles with Ahunze, and tired as he felt, he had despaired about his ability to get it back. "Sing to me," he said, as he pulled up to her, hoping that contact between the tip of his instrument and hers would stir his erection again. "Sing to me," he said desperately. "Did your mother not teach you any songs to sing to a man as he entered you? Encourage me!"

She made no response, and he shook her. "Hey, is it not you I am talking to?"

"What do you want me to do?" she said at length.

"I said, Sing to me!"

"But you are not inside me."

"Help me get inside you then."

"How? What do you want me to do?"

"Sing! Caress my instrument. Do the things a woman does. Circle me with your legs. The reason I am not inside you is that you are not singing and encouraging me."

"Here are my legs. Where do you want them?"

"You are trying to shame me? Is that it?"

"How am I trying to do that?"

He slapped her.

She reached back with both hands, fists clenched, and struck him between the eyes with all her might. He gasped from a mixture of pain and surprise, expelling a long, heavy tide of air from the pit of his belly. With a heave, she shoved him aside and extricated herself from the bed.

Aja-Egbu was speechless. He shook his head in disbelief, and continued shaking it because Ahunze's actions were so unbelievable. After a long time he was able to say, "*Ikpe nkaraa gi!* You are entitled to insult me because the world has turned upside down and we now look at things backward, like toddling infants bending over and peering between their legs, but are you not old enough to realize that it is a man's privilege always to be right? And especially an elder's? Are you so old you could not have been my daughter? Is it not still an insult for a daughter to try to win an argument from a father? But you are a woman, yes, and this, my loincloth, is my dignity. I had to take it off and cast it aside before I crawled into bed with you."

Nne-nne told the story of the bedroom encounter between Ahunze and Aja-Egbu with such relish and fervor that one would have thought it was something that happened to her. And as I looked at her with the wan smile on my lips, she could not have guessed that I was not thinking of Ahunze and Aja-Egbu but of the late-night secrets between her and my grandfather, the intimate whispers I had heard them exchange as I lay on my mat on the floor and they on their *agada* a short distance away—Nna-nna saying, "I think he is asleep now," and she replying, "I do not think so. Wait a while longer."

The end of Ahunze's story was not a happy one. Rejecting Aja-Egbu was the last thing she did, for Ozurumba was waiting outside with a sharpened machete. A good woman died at the hands of a feckless man. He hacked her to death and set her house on fire. However, even though Ahunze did not see the War, the women of Ama-Nkwo, Umu-Ichima, and all of Ikputu Ala fought it in her name and with songs dedicated to her. Some even said that the premature infant that Akpa-Ego delivered on the day the War started in Ikputu Ala was a reincarnation of Ahunze.

As for Ozurumba himself, he never allowed Ahunze's people from Umu-Ichima or the police from Agalaba Uzo to get to him. A young boy, Ukiro, who had been sent to get him to come and tap Agbara's wine tree, found his door open and his body dangling from the end of a rope that was tied to the rafters of his parlor. The boy took a second look to make, sure, opened his eyes wide in horror, then screamed and broke away at a dead run. Agbara and two other men followed Ukiro at a trot to see for themselves the spectacle that had stolen the boy's breath and garbled his words. They confirmed that Ozurumba had hanged himself, slowly shut the door, and then went to find the rest of the men of the kindred.

Ala hentu!

All of these things happened about two months before the War started, and together marked a turning point in the seamless history of the times, and as some people would say later, a turning point almost as significant as the sighting of the first White man in the area. As Nne-nne put it, most people go through their lifetimes without ever hearing of a murder or suicide. For a murder and a suicide to occur at the same place at the same time—that was an abomination that dwarfed the imagination. Sacrifice upon sacrifice of expiation was offered by anyone who had anything to do with any part of it. The seers who were consulted by individuals and by groups cautioned everyone to beware and to keep eyes wide open and ears to the ground. What had occurred was but an omen of even worse things to come! How could anything be worse? people wondered. Wait and see, the seers replied.

What they were to see came two months later, Nne-nne said. The earth heaved as the earth had never heaved before. In the same place, Ikputu Ala, starting in the very same compound, with the same people—those of them who were still alive—Aja-Egbu and Ozurumba's forlorn wife, Akpa-Ego. It was Akpa-Ego who was kneeling by a vat of palm mash, when Sam-el, the counter, arrived with his notebook and began to humbug her with questions. And that is how the War started.

Ala hentu!

6

At War!

"GOD FORBID THE EVIL THING!" EVERY woman said on hearing what had happened to Akpa-Ego. "What kind of place do we now live in such that a pregnant woman cannot be left alone to hoe in peace the long ridge that fate has marked out in front of her, without a man coming with pencil and paper to ask her how many chickens there are in her chicken coop?"

To the last one of them, the women wanted to see Sam-el, this unstoppable counter, so they could talk to him and give him a chance to count all of them together. And count all the blows they would rain on his head!

"He will not have a head when we finish!" many of them said.

"Yes, his head will belong to me!"

"His right leg is mine!"

"I get his left leg!"

"His right hand will hang over my cooking stand!"

"His left hand belongs to me!"

"There will not be enough of him, this Sam-el, for all the women who want a piece of him!"

A group of the women were attending to Akpa-Ego inside her

house. A few others sat on a mudbed and a couple of dusty chairs on the veranda. Two women were wedged into the doorway, effectively preventing others from going freely into the room where Akpa-Ego lay. Half a dozen women sat askance on the half wall of the veranda, muttering prayers and incantations, some with their faces and feet outward, others with their faces and feet toward the interior. The rest of the women milled around in front of the house, talking in groups, dancing in circles, ululating by clapping their hands across their open mouths. From time to time, someone emerged from the interior of the house to announce Akpa-Ego's current condition—and word of it filtered toward the outer fringes of the crowd: She seemed comfortable but she was still bleeding.

Ugbala had been sent for and was on her way.

Two delegations had gone out to seers to consult the spirits and the ancestors about the meaning of all that was happening. Sighs and expostulations filled the air.

"*Ihe!*"

"*Ihem kwa!*"

"*Ayi!*"

Meanwhile, the crowd of women continued to grow, as those attending the village's eighth-day evening market heard the news, gave up trading, and hurried to the compound.

"Say it is not true, what I am hearing," each woman said ritually on arrival, as other women helped her down with her market basket.

"Yes, it is," the others answered in chorus. "It should not be, but it is."

"No-no," the newcomer said in ritual protest.

"Yes," the others replied. "It feels heavy on the lips to utter it, but it is true."

The story of what had happened between Akpa-Ego and Sam-el was retold again and again, to the exclamations and cries of unbelief from each newcomer and first-time hearer. "Is there not anyone who is safe anymore?" the hearers exclaimed. "Is there not anyone who is considered sacred and untouchable? Not even a pregnant woman? Why is it so important for them to count women, if it is not to tax us?" From the possibility of a tax, the complaints grew to include everything that was wrong with their world—death of children, infertility of soils, the blighting of crops, the cost of things sold in the market—a cup of salt, a parcel of crayfish, a length of codfish when one could be found, an inch of bar soap, ten sticks of matches, a bottle of kerosene.

The men sat or stood in a group around the compound's big *ovu,* casually watching the women, talking among themselves and wondering when this little commotion would be over, so these women would go home and cook their suppers and put their children to bed. However, as the crowd swelled, as the arriving women seemed to pay no heed to their husbands but to the other women present, as their spirits rose and some of them began talking of going to Chief Alaribe's home, the compound's elder, Aja-Egbu, decided that it was time to tell the women that enough was enough. He told them, adding that while it was all right to voice a grievance about what had happened to Akpa-Ego, he would not let them use his compound to plot anything against the Chief or the Government. "If there is trouble," he said, "we do not want this to be the compound that the Government burns down."

"So what do you want us to do?" one of the women asked.

"Go home to your own husbands' compounds," Aja-Egbu said. "You have visited your co-wife whom some misfortune has befallen, and you have given her your sympathy and condolences. Now it is time for you to go home. As the proverb says, a guest at a funeral does not wail more loudly than those who are bereaved."

"Who is mourning Akpa-Ego, if not her fellow women? What man in this compound is her defender?"

"Is whatever needs to be defended in this village now being defended by a group of noisy market women?"

"If the men of this village do not do what men are supposed to do. We are not refusing to leave, but answer this question for us: After we leave, what do you propose to do about this pregnant woman who was kicked in the belly?"

"She was not kicked in the belly. Were you there to see her being kicked in the belly?"

"Where was she kicked, if not in the belly? She is bleeding to death, and the child in her womb may be dead. Is that because someone rubbed her gently on the belly? How hard does she have to be kicked before the men of this compound would show their displeasure?"

A woman from within the crowd shouted a proverb: *"Amara akagh gburu oke madu!"* [Knowing what is right but not saying it is the downfall of old men!]

"That is correctly spoken," Aja-Egbu said. "The other half of that saying is *Aka-a anugh gburu onye ogbede!"* [Not heeding what has been said is the downfall of youth!]

Not able to persuade the women to leave—in fact, it seemed that more women were arriving from some of the outlying villages—Aja-Egbu sent a messenger to Chief Alaribe's house to report what was going on, to assure the Chief that he had nothing to do with it, and to urge him to come in person or send an emissary to observe the situation.

At about the same time as Aja-Egbu's messenger set out, a throng of women decided to go looking for Sam-el. The CMS church where he was a catechist was situated on a small compound near the road junction on the far side of the Ezi-ama market clearing. The women arrived singing and banged noisily on the door. No answer. They walked around to the kitchen and knocked on the door. No answer. They went to the church building and peered inside. There was no sign there of Sam-el. The women set down their belongings in front of the house and continued singing. Some began dancing and whooping.

"Iweh! Iweh! Iweh nji anyi! Iweh!"

As dusk began to descend, some gathered twigs and fallen branches and lit a bonfire in front of the house. A short time later, wailing was heard coming from the direction of Aja-Egbu's compound. Ugbala had arrived and had helped Akpa-Ego deliver her dead baby!

"God forbid the evil thing!" the women said ritually, turning an angry shoulder in the process. "Where is this Sam-el so that we can show him how to kick a pregnant woman in the belly?"

"Perhaps he is at the Chief's house," someone suggested.

"Maybe. Let us go there and look for him."

As the women walked off into the dusk, one of them tossed a flaming stick onto the roof of the agent's house. They had hardly reached the road, when they heard a fresh uproar from the direction of Aja-Egbu's compound.

"Ihe," one old woman said.

"Ihem kwa!" another old lady answered. "Something new is going on."

"I wonder what it is."

"Let us go and see."

The women broke into a trot as they neared the compound—the noise was getting louder and louder. Chief Alaribe was there, with Sam-el and four court messengers. It was their arrival that had thrown the women who were still left in the compound into an uproar, especially as they had not come to offer apologies or condolences but in fact were talking of making an arrest.

"Arrest?" every woman who heard the word repeated in utter disgust. "Arrest?" Eyes narrowed and faces screwed up. "Kick her in the belly and cause her to lose her baby. Then arrest her?"

Ugbala was bantering with Chief Alaribe when the larger group of women returned. No one was prepared for the sudden eruption of feeling that exploded on the scene when this larger group returned. Small groups of women surrounded the court messengers and began abusing and berating them, wagging fingers in their faces and calling them ungodly names. More women poured into the compound, each new arrival primed to vent personal animus on these representatives of the Government. At one point, one of the court messengers grabbed a woman's finger that had wagged too close to his face and gave it and its owner a rough shove. Recovering her balance, the woman threw herself at the officer. Other women closed in on the court messenger and wrestled him off his feet. The other officers were attacked by throngs of women. The same fate befell Sam-el.

Seeing what had become of his companions, Chief Alaribe ducked into Aja-Egbu's house and barricaded himself inside.

Bicycles belonging to the messengers and the chief were attacked with clubs and pounding pestles and demolished.

A man returning from an errand somewhere came running and screaming: "The mission house is on fire! The mission house is on fire!"

"*Ihe!*" Ugbala said. "I am going home."

"Stay," the other women urged. "This is your home too."

"No," Ugbala said. "This is not something I should experience outside my own compound. I have done all I can do for Akpa-Ego. She has lost her pregnancy, but she will live."

Chief Njoku Alaribe made his way out of the compound through a back entrance. From thence he found his way home, on foot. However, no sooner was he home than his compound was besieged by hundreds of women. They had lost all couth and were in no mood to listen to anything, reason or unreason. The reflections of the torches they carried danced wildly in their eyes. Because it was December, the harmattan season, things readily caught fire.

The war had started. *Ogu Ndom* is what they called it. Every woman was in it by mere reason of being a woman.

Ala hentu!

"Da-Ngwanze, *gbata! Gbata!* Open the door! Open the door!"

"Obalanze, is that you?"

"Yes."

"What is the matter?"

"Open the door! How can you be asleep at a time like this?"

"Because I went to bed last night and closed my eyes! Come in. Come in. What is the matter? Was that you jingling the cowbells at the *gadaga?*"

"Yes."

"Who let you in?"

"Your husband."

"I see. Come in. Sit down."

"I cannot sit," She glanced at the open door, beyond which stood Nnab'ugwu, Ngwanze's husband.

"Is someone ill?" Nnab'ugwu asked.

"No," Obalanze replied. "Everyone is well."

"Obalanze just wants to drop something in my ear," Ngwanze said, trying to encourage her husband to go away. "Woman talk."

"This is so early in the morning that whatever it is had better be good. A woman does not wake up a whole compound early in the morning just to share some gossip."

"I am sorry," Obalanze apologized, eager to make him go away. She watched him walk out of earshot and then turned suddenly to announce to Ngwanze: "They have *Nne-dim.*"

"Ugbala?"

"Yes."

"Who has her?"

"The police. They just left with her."

"Just now?"

"Yes, just now. I followed them to the fork in the Egbelu Road, and then I ran here. I did not know what else to do."

"Why did you not raise the alarm?"

"We just did not think of it. It happened very suddenly. They just came all of a sudden. Someone jangled the cowbells at the outer gate of the compound, and one of the men opened it. There were six policemen, and they had guns."

"Police and not *kotima*s?"

"Yes, police. They had blue uniforms, not khaki."

"So this is a big case, a White man's case. And there were six of them?"

"Yes, six. And they all carried guns."

"Did they say anything? What did they say she had done?"

"They did not say. All they said was, 'Come with us!' "

"And she consented to go with them?"

"You know *Nne-dim*. Even at the point of a gun, she would not die without having her say. She cursed them and abused their mothers and at first refused to go with them. But two of them grabbed her and put hand-locks on her, while the other four held their guns at the ready."

"What did those four men do that she is the mother of? Is your husband home?"

"No, my husband rose early to take a basket of coconuts to Onu Miri. But the other three were home. They talked to the policemen, but what could they do against six repeat-guns? We must do something, Da-Ngwanze. *Nne-dim* is *dibia* and cannot spend a night in a prison."

"Yes, we must do something. While I put on my clothes and think, go to the next compound and alert Okwere-ke-diya. Tell her what you have told me, and then add that the war she and I were talking about as rumbling in other villages seems to have reached us. *Ala hentu!* If they can get Ugbala, they could have any of us! . . ."

"No, if they have her, they have us!"

"Tell any women you meet on the road that the war has reached us. Ndom Amapu is at war with the Government. Ndom is at war with the White man. Afterward return to your own compound and have the women there raise an alarm. Scream! Let every woman everywhere hear it! Then come back here!"

"Back here to you?"

"Yes. While the others are carrying on with the outcry, I want you to sneak off and return here. Do not tell anyone where you are going."

Soon afterward, the alarm was sounded in Ugbala's compound. People, both men and women, scrambled out of bed to find out what had happened. Very soon, the word was on every lip: "They have Ugbala. They have arrested Ugbala for no good cause. She was in her bed sleeping and they came and woke her up and arrested her. The police kidnapped Ugbala and are taking her to Agalaba Uzo. The White man has Ugbala!"

While the women of the village were stomping in Ugbala's compound, messengers were sent to all the kindred villages. Ugbala had four married daughters. To each of them the word was "The police have carried off your mother! If you think something should be done about it, summon your fellow women together, and let the earth heave where you are."

Very soon, the earth was heaving in those four villages, and in all the other villages where Ugbala's name was well-known. And in the villages through which the messengers passed.

"Okwere-ke-diya."

"*Iya*. Ngwanze."

"You have heard what I heard?"

"Yes, I have heard. Obalanze just left here." Okwere-ke-diya-nkara was continuously shaking her head.

"I knew when that White woman came here some weeks ago that something would follow in her wake."

"Same thing I was thinking—that she probably has something to do with it."

"As for me I am not wondering. I know it for a fact. It is as the proverb says: Whatever animal left these droppings also left these footprints."

"We must do something."

"That is why I sent for you. Do you have an idea?"

"You seem to be more than one step ahead of me. Why not let me hear your own idea first?"

"I think we should find the White woman and ask her some questions. Maybe we can obtain her help to get Ugbala released."

"H'm."

"H'm what?"

"H'm just to say that I was thinking. The plan sounds good, but how do we find her? Is she still around?"

"Someone saw her at Icheku in the last two days. Perhaps she is still there. Obalanze is ready to do anything we tell her. My idea is to send her and Nkalari to Icheku immediately."

"Why not let everyone go to Icheku? All of the women of the town together in solidarity."

"Are you afraid?"

"No, just cautious."

"Even if we did that, I would still send Obalanze and Nkalari ahead. Pack two bags, one public and the other private, like carrying a sword and concealing a dagger."

"I should say we need a third young woman, or even a fourth."

"Not more than four, though. We do not want to be too visible. Maybe the two we send from here can find two other women around Icheku."

"Can we trust people we do not know?"

"We are all in this together. I do not know any woman who hears what has happened and how it has happened who would not eagerly join the cause. We especially need women from near Icheku who would know the byways and the less-traveled paths. Are there no women from around here who have relatives near Icheku?"

"Akwa-eke Onyendi is from near Icheku."

"That is correct. And she is a sensible girl too. So that is it. Everything is set. But I wonder if the White woman is guarded."

"She was not guarded when she came to us, but I am sure a nightwatchman sleeps outside the gate of the Rest House. Even so, if she is still the way she was when she came to us, she will not be difficult to snatch."

"We must instruct them firmly about what to do or what not to do after they catch her. One other thing bothers me: Will they not be recognized?"

"Here is your answer: *uri*. Their faces will be covered with *uri*."

"But if someone sees four women walking down the road, their faces covered with *uri*, will he not think something is unusual?"

"Not if they carry an *avo aja* filled with ritual objects. They will look like they are on their way somewhere to make a sacrifice. And if they carry a little twig across their lips they can keep from having to answer any questions."

"Maybe all of us should cover our faces with indigo, anyhow."

"Good idea. That way we will all be difficult to recognize."

"All right! All right! I feel the earth shaking under my feet. My heart is drumming and my ears are humming. *Ayi!* No one is playing any music for me, but still I feel like I am dancing. Ugbala, we are on our way! Look out, White man! You may think you are the greatest dung beetle in the world, but I am sure you have never rolled the shit of a woman who has a running belly! You will see! You will see!"

"*Nwanyi ibem!*"

"*Nwanyi na ibe ya!*"

"Are you not excited?"

"My blood is on fire, but I must try to contain it. The whole village is on fire. Women are crawling out of their homes like ants out of an anthill."

"Well, you should know why. Their strong house has been attacked. Their ant queen has been carried away. Here, let me have the indigo."

"Let me cover your face for you. You can cover mine afterward."

"Here is my face."

"Here is mine also. Maybe we can save some time if you do mine at the same time as I do yours. Put down the bowl over here where we can both reach it."

"We shall not tell anyone about the White woman?"

"No, we shall not tell anyone. There is a saying that a whisper shared by more than two people is no longer a secret. What we are doing is something we have been prompted to do by our hearts. If it succeeds, we will share the success with others. If it fails, the failure will be on us."

"It will not fail. The gods always put a limit on evil. Evil may succeed for a while but never in the long run. We have done nothing to the White man. He cannot make the same claim about us. *Ogu* is on our side. We are not in his country trying to count his chickens and his mother. He is in ours trying to treat us like animals. *Obasi ndi n'igwe!* Be the judge between us and this man."

"Can we trouble you for a drink of water?" one of two women passing by said.

"Here is water," Ngwanze said, shaking a drinking gourd and then offering it to the nearer of the two women.

As her companion was taking her gulps, the other woman said, "Have you heard?"

"One hears many things," Okwere-ke-diya-nkara said cagily.
"What have you heard that we should hear?"

"All of Ikputu Ala is on fire," the woman said. "Ndom Ikputu Ala
burned down the mission church, sat on the agent, stripped four
kotimas naked, and besieged the compound of Chief Njoku Alaribe."

"*Ala hentu!* Is that so?"

"This is my sister's child here," the older woman said. "My sister
sent her to tell me. Is that indigo you have in that bowl?"

"Yes."

"Let me have some."

"Child, what did you see?" Ngwanze asked.

"All the women in our village are now at the Chief's house. They
were there all night, all the women, excepting no one, even old
grandmothers who had been sick and in bed. They all wanted to
be part of it. No one slept throughout the night. These clothes I am
wearing now, they are the clothes I wore to the market yesterday. I
was helping my mother to cook supper when the outcry started.
We ran out together leaving our pot on the fire and have not
returned home since. All the compounds, not just ours, are empty
of women."

"Here," the aunt said, "let me put some indigo on you."

"You think you should?" Okwere-ke-diya-nkara asked. "She is a
mere child."

"Fully a woman and only partly a child," the aunt said. "She is
likely to have her period any day now. This is war. All of Ndom is
at war, the young as well as the old. It is like *Amuma Muo*. One does
not elect to be possessed by spirits. The spirits simply overtake a
person without seeking his permission. . . . What about the two of
you? You seem to be the only ones here. Are you late in joining the
others or what? How could they do this thing to Ugbala? What will
Ndom do to avenge what has happened to her? I came here because
of her, and because this place is nearer to me than Icheku, even
though my sister is there."

"Tell us, child," Ngwanze broke in, "what did you see on your
way here?"

"Women," the girl said. "Everywhere women. Not many men. The
men I saw were standing in groups and shaking their heads at things
they did not seem to believe. Every woman I saw was talking or
walking fast. Near the village of Umu Idika, a group of women

wanted to force me to join them, until I told them that I was on an errand from my mother to her sister. They told me to add to the message for my aunt the fact that the earth was heaving at Umu Idika. And that the sky had caught fire. They asked me where I was from, and I said Ama-Nkwo in Ikputu Ala, and they hugged me. I passed by Orie Amorji, which should be in session today, but hardly a person was there."

The noise swelled as they approached Ugbala's compound. It was like the noise of a market in session, except louder. Much louder. And the general din was punctuated by sudden, loud outbursts, chants, songs, dances, and foot stompings.

As the three women and the girl arrived, the word *uri* emanated from every mouth. "*Ndom huo uri!*" several women said at once, and a flurry of activity began at once, dedicated to preparing bowls of indigo paste for every woman to cover her face. All the indigo trees in the town yielded their pods. The women sat and stood in twos or in larger clusters, passing the bowls from hand to hand and blackening one another's faces. In about an hour, the crowd turned into an eerie sight; each face was now a black surface marked by a pair of glistening eyes and a red orifice where the mouth used to be.

Ndom!

This was not a festival. Not a parade, not a show, but a War.

Who was the enemy?

Government. The White man and his chiefs and his counters.

"Let us go to Icheku and put some questions to the court clerk and the chiefs," someone suggested.

"No, let us go to the homes of the chiefs and question them one by one, starting with our own chief Ogbu Agu."

"Ndom *kwenu!*"

"*Iyah-yah-yah!*"

"*Kwenu!*"

"*Iyah-yah-yah!*"

"Who are you?"

"We are Ndom."

"How many are you?"

"The White man wants to count us, but there is only one of us. Ndom is one, uncountable upon uncountable, but still one. Undivided."

"Do you swear to that?"

"With one voice, with one heart, with one birth canal through which everyone enters this world, with two breasts that suckle the whole world, squatting as we do when we deliver our babies, by the cord that binds us to our unborn infants, by the afterbirth through which we dedicate them to the Land, we swear, if ever we should backtrack or double-deal, or double-cross, or double-talk on the rest of Ndom, if we should in any way breach the solidarity of Ndom, may we be strangled to death by the umbilical cords of the babies we are birthing—in this incarnation, and in all our future reincarnations. And what we swear, we swear for ourselves, our mothers, our sisters, and for all our female relatives."

"Ndom!"

"No one travels without the others. *Ije nka nma n'ogbara!*"

"What do you see?"

"We see the sky catching fire!"

"What do you hear?"

"We hear the earth rumbling."

"What do you feel?"

"We feel our hearts filled with pus."

"What do you do?"

"We must squeeze them until the pain stops."

"What is your grief?"

"Ndom has seen more than eyes can bear or mouths can utter."

"What is your burden?"

"Unbearable. But no burden is ever too heavy for a horde of ants."

"And where are you headed?"

"To the chief's house!"

"Where?"

"Chief Ogbu Agu's house!"

When every member of the crowd was caught up in the thrall of the chant, the women set out on the run for the chief's house. When they reached there, the chief had left for a court session at the Native Court at Icheku. His compound was protected by a group of his friends armed with machetes, clubs, and whips. The women fought a shadow battle with them for a while but then decided to head toward Icheku.

About a quarter of a mile from the Native Court at Icheku, the women broke into a run, with the younger and the more spirited among them leading the charge. The chiefs were discussing what to do about the directive the D.O. had given them to count the women, in the light of what had recently occurred in Ikputu Ala, when they heard the approaching din. A court messenger reported to them that all the roads leading to Icheku were clogged with women. The Head Chief suspended the session. The chiefs stepped out into the yard in their long, striped, and embroidered jumpers and stood in a cluster behind a cordon of a dozen court messengers armed with batons and several yard laborers carrying whips. In spite of what they had heard about Ikputu Ala, they assured themselves that these were only women, armed with sticks and pounding pestles, motherly and wifely windbags capable of a lot of noise but not much harm. Chief Ogbu Agu said to a colleague, "There is none of them that catches a good slap on the face or the snap of a whip on her legs who will stand and fight. Fight with what?" he asked scornfully.

As the vanguard of the crowd reached the open space between the road and the courthouse, the head court messenger raised his hand and shouted the White man's magic word: "Halt!"

The crowd kept coming.

"Halt!" the head messenger repeated. "Halt! Halt! Halt!" he shouted as if to muster more force through loudness and repetition.

Like an unstoppable locomotive, or rather like a river in flood surging in from everywhere, the women rolled over the court messengers, beat them, tore their uniforms, and sat upon them. As for the chiefs, they broke and ran helter-skelter into the adjoining bushes, with the women in hot pursuit.

Ndom!

The women occupied the courthouse, smashed the dock and the chairs, set fire to the records. The adjoining lockup cells were breached, half a dozen male prisoners set free.

At the messengers' quarters, the women came upon one woman who, because she was nursing an infant, had been unable to flee with the others. The first of the women to get to her took the infant from her and held it aloft for the others to see. The crowd cheered.

"*Uri! Uri,*" someone shouted. "*Huo ya uri!*"

"Who has the indigo?"

A bowl of indigo paste was passed forward, and the court messenger's wife and baby were smeared, thereby being inducted into the solidarity of Ndom. A cheer went up at the induction, and for the sake of the mother and her baby, the messengers' quarters escaped being torched.

With much of its energy still unused, the crowd still smarted for things to do. They sang. They danced. They stomped. They held mock trials.

"All the way to Agalaba Uzo!" someone suggested at one point. "To find Ugbala and rescue her."

That uproar was aborted quickly, being replaced by an even louder and longer one. The chanting and foot stomping rose to an ear-splitting crescendo:

"*Iweh! Iweh! Iweh nji anyi! Iweh!*"

The message they had just received, the cause of the sudden outburst, said that the White woman, Mrs. Elizabeth Ashby-Jones, was missing.

District Officer Dennis Ogilvy ("Dog," as his African underlings secretly called him) was unresolved, even a bit nervous, as his truck approached the crowd. He wore what appeared to be parts of different uniforms assembled in an effort to make one whole uniform—khaki shorts stiff with starch and shiny from the excessive heat of a washerman's iron, a sweat-soaked white shirt through which his pink skin was visible, brown socks, heavy army boots, and a broad-brimmed Australian bush hat with the left side pinned up and an adjustable leather strap hanging under his chin. He was accompanied by a ragtag force of about twenty men, half of them court messengers in khaki uniforms, brown leggings, and no shoes, and the other half stewards, cooks, and yard laborers. The District Officer, rifle in hand, rode in the covered compartment of the kit-car beside a driver, his men in the lorry's open back.

The crowd of women parted slowly to let them through and then closed again behind them, totally swallowing them. Their shouts were deafening, their darkened faces menacing.

When the lorry came to a stop beside the courthouse, the D.O. climbed to the top of the cab and from there began to address the women. His men formed a defensive circle around the lorry, using their guns to shove back the women.

Where was the White woman? the D.O. wanted to know.

Where was Ugbala? the women shouted back.

Ugbala was in protective custody, the D.O. said.

What kind of protective custody? the women wanted to know. If that was another name for prison, what had she done to offend the law?

That, the D.O. replied, would be determined during a trial. Her guilt or innocence would be established according to the law. Now what about the White woman?

They knew nothing about the White woman, they shouted back. They were not even interested in the White woman. All they wanted to know was when Ugbala would be released. In addition to that, they did not want to be counted.

They did not want to be taxed.

They wanted better prices for their palm kernels.

Also for palm oil.

They wanted the prices of imported goods to fall—stock fish, kerosene, soap, and cloth.

They wanted the Native Courts to be abolished and the chiefs sacked.

But the chiefs were their own people, the D.O. countered.

But they worked for the Government, the women replied in heckles and catcalls. They were corrupt and oppressive.

All right, the D.O. said. He had heard their grievances and would review them when he returned to his office at Agalaba Uzo. Would they be willing to meet him again in exactly thirty days? Would they now return peacefully to their homes and not cause any more damage to Government property, and they could have the assurance that he would meet them in a month to discuss their grievances?

No! They wanted immediate action. They would not leave until they had the promise that they would not be counted, that the chiefs would be fired.

Late afternoon on a warm, but not too hot December day. Everything but the evergreens was scorched and dusty—every movement kicked up a small cloud of dust. The D.O. lifted his hat to let the air cool his scalp a little. The crowd was so large. Those of them who were near him responded to him directly. Others near the periphery of the crowd were not under the command of his voice, and even if they had been near enough, his words lost all impetus in the translation rendered by his interpreter. He carefully laid down his gun beside him, formed his hands into a funnel around his mouth, and aimed his words this way and that at the crowd. Do you hear me? he asked desperately. Do you hear me?

We hear you! the women responded. We hear you well!

Do you have the White woman?

Do you see any White woman here?

That is not my question. I say: Do you have the White woman?

We say: Do you see any White woman here?

You are trying my patience. I did not come here to bandy words with you. If I go away now, I will return with soldiers—plenty *sojas,* he added in pidgin English—and maybe then you will answer me more politely.

Our patience is already worn out, the women replied.

Listen, I am willing to have fair exchange with you. If I give you Ugbala, will you give me back the White woman?

Give us Ugbala first. Then we may help you look for the White woman.

Do you know where the White woman is? Have you seen her?

If you do not know where she is, then she must be lost.

Mr. Ogilvy swore and uttered a barrage of obscenities. He looked over the crowd, but as was common with these people, no one was in charge, no one could speak for the others or make a commitment on their behalf. If they acted a certain way, it was out of a sense of belonging together. What they shouted back to him were heckles and catcalls. There wasn't even a way to use their responses to figure out what they knew or did not know about Mrs. Ashby-Jones. He weighed the possible consequences of seizing three or four of them as hostages until the rest produced Mrs. Ashby-Jones. But then he thought, They may not really know. Another group further up the road could have Mrs. Ashby-Jones. Even if they knew her whereabouts, he wondered if he was prepared to apply the degree of coercion sufficient to compel them to reveal what they knew. No, taking four of them would complicate things. How would they be transported—the truck was already full? How would they be guarded? Above all, there was the question of reaching into this restive crowd and grabbing four or five of its members and driving off with them in handcuffs. The rest would surely burn down the courthouse. If only they had been men! The men were so much easier to deal with! Where did all of these bitches come from anyway? Why didn't they disappear back into their smelly huts!

A commotion arose on the north edge of the crowd, in the area adjoining the great bushes. There were whoops and shouts and a stampede, a chase and then whoops of victory. Someone had spotted the chiefs, who had been encouraged out of their hiding places by the District Officer's arrival. They lived to regret it.

7

Woman to Woman

"NDOM!"

"Ndom *ibe!*"

"Is that you?"

"Yes, that is us!"

"Us? Are there many of you?"

"Uncountable many."

"What is your name?"

"My name is *nwanyi*. I squat to urinate and to give birth to my babies."

"And what is the name of this village?"

"This village has no name that I recognize. *Ala hentu!* When the earth heaves, it does not stop heaving at village boundaries. Ndom is one! All villages are one!"

"Let me hear your oath."

"If ever I should betray the secrets of Ndom, may I be strangled to death by the umbilical cord of the babies I am birthing. In this incarnation and in all my future reincarnations."

"Good. I have performed my part of the oath, taken the noose from around my neck, and placed it around yours. If you wear it honorably, it is a garland for a parade. If you do dishonor to Ndom, it becomes a hanging noose. Here she is, all yours. We have not harmed her but have considered her sacred, as a refugee is sacred to us. Do not let her escape. Feed her soft things like eggs and papaw that is overripe. If you find a coconut, give her the juice from it. We did not have enough indigo to cover her completely, so she is in blotches as you can see, and her head is full of razor nicks. The cloth she is wearing is an old one of mine, and anyone who knows me would identify me with it. If you had a replacement, I would ask to take away mine. On second thought, I will! Ndom *ibe*, forgive me! *Chi nwanyi beke-e* [White woman's personal god], forgive me. I did not mean to leave you naked, but I must have my cloth back." She snatched the cloth off Mrs. Ashby-Jones, leaving her naked from the waist down.

"Mention no names, as you talk in her presence, for she is not completely deaf. The girls who traveled with her have taught her a few words of our language. You do not know me or the name of the village from which I come. I do not know you, although I had to know the name of this village to find you. But beyond bringing her to you, I know nothing else. If you should decide to take her to another village, I do not know what village that will be, so our chain cannot be longer than two links. The proverb says that when a journey turns out well, everyone claims to have come on his own, but if a journey should turn out badly, everyone remembers the person who induced him to make the trip. I have no instructions to give to you. Ndom is a snake with a thousand heads! Ndom!"

"*Nwanyi na ibe-ya!*"

"I am gone!"

"Go well! . . . But wait," Ngwanze said. "*Nwanyi ibem*, wait for a moment. Tell me," she began and then hesitated.

"*Nwanyi ibem*, please hurry. I have dozens of farts that are backed up in my belly all awaiting their turns to come out."

"Yes. I just wanted to let you know that you have done what we had in mind to do. We had decided to snatch the White woman, but you snatched her before we could."

"Goes to show you, all of us are palm wine from the same tree."

"That is so. It is as the saying goes. Palm trees that come from the same soil yield the same type of wine."

"You said it correctly. Shake my hand."

"An embrace, my sister. That is the woman's way."

"*Nwanyi na ibe-ya!* An embrace then for sisterhood, but the handshake is for the feat you have accomplished."

"Ah yes, someday I may flounce before *ukom* drummers and tell of the feat, or I may tell it quietly to my grandchildren. We may yet be stung, but for now the honeycomb is full of honey and the honey is sweet."

"Have you heard any news?"

"There is more news than I can tell you, and it is not all good."

"It is not about Ugbala, is it?"

"Not directly." She exhaled. "I wished I would not be the one to tell you. One of those you sent, the name I heard is Nkalari."

"Oh God! They arrested her?"

"No, worse. They killed her. Soldiers jumped out of a lorry and began shooting. As of now, no one knows how many died and how many were wounded."

"Almighty God forbid the evil thing! But how then do you know about Nkalari?"

"The one sent with her managed to escape."

"We sent four."

"Yes, so we found out later. The other two are on their way home. The third person we do not know about, whether she is alive or among the dead, but she is the one who told the crowd at the courthouse that Nkalari had been shot by the soldiers. The soldiers had stopped to destroy some villages on their way, so she was able to get to the courthouse ahead of them."

"I wonder if that was Obalanze."

"No, it was not. Obalanze is alive. She and someone else are on their way home. They were unharmed when we saw them. Our route must have been shorter than theirs for us to get here before them. Or they were delayed for some reason. But they are safe. They are the ones who told us of the mission on which you sent them. They divided into two teams, two of them to snatch the White woman, two to snatch her companions or make sure they didn't raise an alarm or get in the way."

"You do not know who is dead?"

"Many are dead. I cannot know the number until I get home. I must go now."

"Go well!"

"Okwere-ke-diya!"
"Ngwanze!"
"The war has taken one of our daughters!"
"Yes, maybe more than one!"
"Many of our fellow women!"
"It is not a joke!"
"No, it is not!"
"What shall we do with her?"
"I do not know, but the thoughts that are going through my head are not pleasant."
"Not mine either."

The two women snatched leafy boughs off nearby bushes and laid them on the ground to make cushions, and then sat on them, each of them facing Mrs. Ashby-Jones at an angle. Ngwanze motioned to her to sit down. She moved to comply, using her notebook to shield her nakedness. She looked at the rough ground, first at one side of her, then at the other, and made as if to squat, but was unable to do so. Sighing, Ngwanze stood and broke off a cluster of leaves and laid them on the ground; then she yanked the notebook out of her hand, and dropped it on the leaves, opening it to make a wider sitting area. "Sit down," she said to Mrs. Ashby-Jones, who slowly began to lower herself to a sitting position but could not find one that was both comfortable and decorous.

Okwere-ke-diya stood, then motioned her to stand. "Stand up," she said, "Up! Up!" she repeated, motioning with her hands.

Mrs. Ashby-Jones stood. Okwere-ke-diya undid her headtie, snapped the cloth in the air, and then began tying it around the White woman's waist. "Watch how I tie it, so you can tie it for yourself. Do you understand what I am trying to tell you? Look, you hold the edges like this. Do you see? Then you twist the top part over the lower part. Then you pull it tight. Do you see? Try it. Try it and let me see. Otherwise you will have to walk around naked and sit on the coarse ground with that soft bottom of yours. Come on, stop looking so sheepish and try it."

"Leave her and it alone," Ngwanze said. "When she gets tired of being naked, she will learn how to tie it."

"Wait, I think I hear a noise! Someone is approaching. Do you hear anything?"

"Yes. Lower your voice, and get ready to run."

"Whoever it is has heard us by now."

"It is a woman. I can see her darkened face. Obalanze, by her walk and the attitude of her head. Thank God!"

"Obalanze, is that you?"

"We are not supposed to mention any names because of her." She gestured toward Mrs. Ashby-Jones by switching her lips in the White woman's direction.

"I do not care. She cannot remember anything without her writing stick. Obalanze, are you by yourself?"

"Things are not good," Obalanze said, dropping to the ground in a kneeling position, as tears streamed down her cheeks. "Things are not good at all."

"We know. A woman from Uzemba brought *her* here and told us what happened." Ngwanze and Okwere-ke-diya knelt on either side of her and placed their hands on her shoulders.

"Who was with you?" Ngwanze asked. "Who got shot?"

Obalanze shook her head, flinging tears this way and that. She wiped first the palm then the back of her hand across both eyes. Then she began pounding the ground and sobbing.

"Tell us, tell us," Ngwanze persisted.

"Nnete."

"Oh my God," Ngwanze said. "So Nnete Ufomba was the person you found to go with you."

"Yes," Obalanze replied through her tears. "And what makes me feel so bad is that I had to persuade her.. She was afraid and did not really want to go, but I made her."

"You did not make her," Okwere-ke-diya said. "Do not blame yourself."

"Her four young children are now without their mother."

"God. That is bad."

"Yes," Ngwanze agreed. "That is bad. Tell us, what happened? Did the soldiers come upon you all of a sudden?"

"Yes, we were in the big bend of the road before you enter the town of Onu Miri proper. We were walking apart, just in case something came up, and I was ahead of her. Before that we had divided into two teams, she and I in one team, Nkalari and Ezi-Akwa in the other team. All of a sudden, voo-oo-m, a lorry came up from behind, and the soldiers in it began shooting at us. They came upon her first and she did not have a chance to run away or to hide in the bush. What saved me was that they slowed down a little bit and did not seem to know at first whether to catch her or what. I saw some of the soldiers make like they wanted to jump off the lorry. And then tah-tah-tah, they shot her. I dashed into the bush, but that is not why I am alive now. The reason I am alive is a big *uruh* tree behind which I hid. Many of the bullets they shot into the bush hit that tree, but lucky for me, I was on the other side of it. From this day onward, for the rest of my life, I will always be grateful to the *uruh* tree. Everytime I see one, I will stop and thank it for saving my life."

"What about Nkalari and Ezi-Akwa?"

"I do not know, but I think they are alive. They were not the ones who brought *her* here?"

"No. The people who brought *her* here were from Onu Miri. It seems we and they were thinking the same thing, and by the time you reached the courthouse, they had already captured *her*."

"What are we going to do with her?" Obalanze asked. "Why is she standing over there like that with your loincloth on her shoulder?"

"I gave her the cloth to cover her nakedness," Okwere-ke-diya said. "It seems she does not know what to do with it. What else did you see at Onu Miri? We received word that the whole place was on fire."

"More than on fire, but it did not really start until the soldiers had come and gone. You see, the soldiers drove up to the courthouse, after setting some compounds on fire. There were hundreds and hundreds of women in the place, and everyone was thinking, this is it. But a White man drove up from the other direction of the road and after he talked to the headman of the soldiers in the lorry, he and they drove off toward Usotuma. It was then that the women at Onu Miri attacked the Patterson-Taylor place."

"They set the palm oil drums on fire, we heard," Ngwanze said.

"No," Obalanze replied. "Not the oil but the pyramids of palm kernels that they had piled up in bags in the yard. They uncapped the oil drums and then rolled them down the hill toward the river. Really, I saw only part of it. I was all the while thinking of Nnete's body lying under a tree on the side of the road where I had dragged it. I could not carry her all by myself and come all the way home to tell you what had happened."

Ngwanze and Okwere-ke-diya patted her on the shoulder. "You have done well," they both said.

"You have been very brave," Ngwanze added.

"Yes," Okwere-ke-diya said. "You have been very brave, but we must think of a way to go and retrieve Nnete's body and give it a decent burial. We cannot let the hyenas get to her."

"Is it us or her husband and people who are going to bury her?" Obalanze asked.

"You know, that is a question for which I do not have an answer. What do we say to her people when we bring her body back? To whom do we give it? She is a woman, yes, and as such belongs to all of Ndom, but Ndom has not been at war before, at least not in the memory of any of us who is now living. So what does one do with those who die at the hands of the enemy?"

"All I know," Ngwanze said, "is that we must find a way to bring that body back, so that it does not rot in a strange place in shame. Or become food for bush animals."

"Yes, that we must do," Okwere-ke-diya said. "After we get it back to our own town, we can decide to whom it belongs."

"What are we going to do with *her?*" Obalanze asked again, referring to Mrs. Ashby-Jones. "Are we going to kill her?"

The two older women turned sharply, both of them at the same time, to look at Obalanze.

Ngwanze said, "If we are going to do anything to her, we are not going to announce it first, to her or to ourselves. Do not talk like a child."

"We are not going to do anything to her, except keep her," Okwere-ke-diya said. "For you, though," she added, placing a motherly hand behind Obalanze's neck, "I wish you could go somewhere and rest. You have seen more than one person your age needs to see in one day. You have been near death and seen his face."

"But will she not recognize us later?" Obalanze asked, bending her head toward Mrs. Ashby-Jones.

"Let us worry about later later," Ngwanze said. "Anyway, what does it matter if she recognizes us? We *too* recognize her. I do not believe she can recognize anything, though. She is almost half dead with fear, and we have the indigo on our faces. The two of you sitting in front of me now, I could not tell who you are if I just walked up to you from somewhere. Even *she* does not look like herself. Look at the way her head is shaped without all her long hair to cover it."

"Without her eyeglasses, she does not seem to see well," Okwere-ke-diya said. "She squints all the time and even walks with unsteady steps."

"I almost feel sorry for her," Obalanze said. "She looks like such a sorry *nwa-eleghe-le.*"

"In spite of what you have seen today?" Ngwanze asked. "Your nature is much kinder than mine, because I do not feel sorry for her. After all, we have not been sent to escort her on a market parade. We are at war. This is war. Ndom is at war, and it is her and her people who have caused it."

"That was why I asked the question I asked before," Obalanze said.

"We are not killers," Okwere-ke-diya said.

"True," Ngwanze said, "but with half my mind I wish we were, because the White man is a killer. If he were to come upon us now, would he join us in this debate or would he shoot all of us down with his rapid-fire gun? Even *her*, pitiful as she looks standing over there, if she had one of those little *riva-riva*s that they sometimes carry in their pockets, do you think she would hesitate to shoot all of us down?"

"I hear what you are saying," Okwere-ke-diya said, "and you are probably correct. But we are what we are and the White man is what he is."

"My question is: Can we fight him and hope to win with one hand folded behind our backs? As both of you know, my maiden village is across the river. I never knew my grandfather because the White man's repeat gun sent two bullets through his head. He died at the *okasaa* at Afor Ibeku because the White man had invited the whole town to a meeting. The men went wearing their best clothes, carrying no weapons, to meet with the White man. As they sat or stood in the market clearing, the White man and his soldiers drove up in lorries and began shooting. . . ."

"Do not say anymore," Obalanze said, shrugging her shoulders to suppress a shiver. "That is giving me goose pimples." She shook her head violently. "Nnete's death face is haunting me. One of the bullets went through her neck. Right here." She fingered a spot on her throat.

"I am sorry," Okwere-ke-diya said.

"Try not to think about it," Ngwanze added. She broke a branch off a nearby *ntikirinkwa* bush, peeled the bark off it, chewed the end to a pulp, and began scrubbing her teeth with it.

"Are you afraid?" Ngwanze asked.

"No, it is not fear, but something else to which I cannot give a name. I felt much better when I was in the middle of everything. My blood was boiling, and I could hear my heartbeat in my ears. It is different, sitting here as we are and just talking and waiting. I cannot describe how I feel."

"Men who have been at war always say that the preparation and the wait are the hardest part."

"I keep thinking of Nnete's body lying on the side of the road in shame," Okwere-ke-diya said.

"Me too," Obalanze said.

"I hate to send you off again, after all that you have gone through during this one day, but that may be better for you than just sitting here doing nothing. Tell me, did you see anyone at all, man or woman, while you were on your way here?"

"I saw a few men whom I recognized, but I am sure none of them would have recognized me from the distance at which they saw me, with the indigo on my face. All they could tell, I am sure, is that I was a woman, but not who I was. I kept darting in and out of the bush, traveling on the road when I thought no one was coming, darting into the bush when I heard the slightest sound of someone approaching."

"That is good," Okwere-ke-diya said. "That is very good. Do you think you can sneak up to Icheku and leak the news of what has happened to Nnete? I believe, since we have not heard their noise, Ndom Amapu must still be at Icheku. Let them know that Nnete has died and that her body must be retrieved."

"They must already know by now," Obalanze said.

"How? You came here by way of Icheku?"

"Yes, I went to Icheku to look for you, when I heard the news that Ndom had driven the chiefs from the courthouse into the bush. I saw Nkalari and Ezi-Akwa there."

"They are alive?"

"Yes, both of them are alive. They said, 'Where is Nnete?' And I had to tell them what had happened."

"What did they say?"

"Nkalari began crying."

"It is not a good idea to let everyone know that we have the White woman," Ngwanze said. "Do you not agree?" she asked Okwere-ke-diya, lifting her brows.

"I agree," Okwere-ke-diya said. "We do not want *anyone* to know that we have the White woman. The first reason is obvious. The second reason is that we may not have her for long."

"I agree that we should kill her," Obalanze said. "If that is what you mean," she added.

"That is not what I mean," Okwere-ke-diya said, "and you are only agreeing with yourself. You seem to have killing on your mind. Have you killed anyone before?"

"No."

"Of course, you saw someone killed today. Was that not your first time?"

"It was."

"I have never killed anyone myself, but I have lived long enough to realize that it is not easy. If I told you to go ahead and kill her, as she stands over there now, do you think you could do it?"

Obalanze looked Mrs. Ashby-Jones over from head to toe. Then she said, "I think I could close my eyes and do it."

"But not with your eyes open?" Ngwanze chuckled.

Okwere-ke-diya cut in. "I do not think you would have the stomach to kill her, in spite of what you say. Not with your eyes open or closed. Would you hit her with a stick or hack her with a machete?"

"I do not know," Obalanze answered skeptically. "I very much think I could. I would not ask anyone to dare me on it, not after what I saw those men do to *Nne-dim* this morning and Nnete later. My belly is right now dry of all mercy."

"I do not doubt you," Ngwanze said. "And I do not mind confessing that my own thoughts about her are not very kind."

"If you go to Icheku," Okwere-ke-diya said, "bring back news of what is going on, so we can decide what to do with her. As you go and come, keep your ear to the ground and hear whatever you can. Especially listen for news of soldiers and any news of your mother-in-law. If you come back before nightfall, wait here for us and we will find you. If night overtakes you there, then come here early in the morning before the dew has dried from the grass. In everything you do, continue to be careful. Let me hear your oath before you leave."

Obalanze placed one hand ritually across her breasts and the other on her crotch. "If I should ever betray the secrets of Ndom, may I be strangled to death by the umbilical cord of the babies I am birthing, not only in this incarnation but in all my future reincarnations."

"Do not forget that this is not only about being brave but also being discreet and loyal," Okwere-ke-diya said. "I would have preferred to go to Icheku myself, but I am not sure I can trust the two of you with the life of this woman."

The two older women embraced Obalanze in turn and watched her wade into the bush on her errand.

The two then turned to Mrs. Ashby-Jones, who in the meantime had eased herself into a sitting position and was leaning against the *uru* tree they used as shelter. It was the middle of the afternoon; *nsa-nsa* flowers had opened and the shadows had begun to lengthen. Flights of *okiri-ekwe* were coming and going from the branches above, to feed on the succulent fruits of the tree that were in season. *"Ezi amuru! Ezi amuru!"* they kept whistling in the proverbial language that was supposed to have kept their species from learning how to build a nest as good as the weaver bird's. "Teach and learn! Teach and learn!"

"What have you learned?" Ngwanze asked Okwere-ke-diya.

"That when you wake up in the morning, you do not know how you will go to bed that night."

"That is so true. Look at where we are now, compared to where we were this morning. This was supposed to be a day on which I would crack a basket of kernels and go leisurely to the evening market to see if I could find those who owe me money."

"What do you think about *her?* What do you think she had planned to do today?"

"Spy. Find people to ask questions. Write in her notebook. But she is not writing now."

Okwere-ke-diya exhaled heavily, as she turned to Mrs. Ashby-Jones. "White woman," she said, placing one foot on a nearby log, her elbow on the raised leg and her head in her hand, "you look so pitiful I cannot help feeling sorry for you. In spite of everything. I realize you cannot understand me, but is there any way you can get a sense of what I am saying to you? I wish you were strong. There is no pleasure in defeating someone who cannot fight back. I even wish you were not a woman. If you were a man, I do not think I would have to close my eyes, as Obalanze said, to be able to hit you on the head with a stick and kill you. But you are a woman."

"There is not much that is womanly about her," Ngwanze said. "Look at her. Those breasts have never suckled an infant, and those hands have only written things in her notebook; they have never comforted nor cuddled an infant. If right now she could somehow hear our language, and we began to talk to her about womanly things, what do you think she would do? Answer me, what do you think she would do?"

"She would probably take out her notebook and her writing stick and begin writing down what we said."

"So true, so true. In the conversations she had with us, in all the places where she has been, has anyone heard her ask womanly questions? The questions she asked, were they not the same ones that the Government's counters are now asking? How many children do you have? How many goats and chickens? I tell you she is one of them."

"I do not believe she is a spy," Okwere-ke-diya said. "Are you a spy, White woman?"

"Explain this to me then," Ngwanze said. "She arrives from no one knows where, and begins going from village to village just like a D.O. A few weeks later, the Government's counters arrive. Does a spy not always go ahead of an army? And she does not talk to the men but only the women. If you were sending a spy to spy on the women, would you send a man? Would you not send another woman, so as to win confidence and lower suspicion?"

"Maybe you are right," Okwere-ke-diya conceded. "But if she is a spy, I wonder what she has found out."

"Who knows? But whatever it is, it is all in that notebook of hers. But does she not look strange to you, though?"

"She certainly does. She is almost frightening because of the way the indigo has reacted with her skin, with the red of her lips and eyelids showing through, and the glassy sparkle of her eyes moving back and forth. She looks like a phantom animal."

They watched her silently for several moments, and at length Okwere-ke-diya said, "She is a woman nonetheless. Especially now that she is not wearing her own clothes. Those breasts may never have nursed an infant but they are a woman's breasts. That slit between her legs is a woman's slit, and when she first got here from Onu Miri, she was crying. She probably has experienced some *grief* in her life. Whatever *their* kind of grief is."

"What are you doing?" Ngwanze asked, alarm in her voice.

"I believe we can take these bindings off her feet. I don't believe she is going anywhere barefooted in this thorny forest."

"Left to me I would not take any chance with her," Ngwanze said. "She may be stronger than she looks, and more resourceful too."

"Those are not the eyes of a person who is thinking of escape. Or of anything. I think her world right now, like ours, is turned upside down."

"*Nkita biam-biam ntachara oba akwa*" [The harmless looking dog is the one that stole the eggs], Ngwanze said.

"I do not think so," Okwere-ke-diya said. She then made a fierce face at Mrs. Ashby-Jones, followed by a series of threatening mimes, to show her what would happen if she tried to escape. She would chase her, catch her, and beat her mercilessly and make sure the cords never came off her feet again. "Her power lies in her writing stick and her notebook," Okwere-ke-diya added, "and she cannot write anything now."

"I wish there was a way we could find out what she has written in that notebook," Ngwanze said, reaching for the notebook.

Mrs. Ashby-Jones clutched the notebook ever more tightly to her chest and would not let it go.

Feeling challenged, Ngwanze suddenly intensified her interest in the notebook, which previously had only been passing. She snatched it with more than necessary force from Mrs. Ashby-Jones's hands and gave the White woman a long, dirty look. Then she fiercely tore some pages out of it.

Mrs. Ashby-Jones screamed, a long piercing scream that shattered the afternoon lull and sent a flock of birds in hurried flight away from the branches above them. Then followed a tirade of what the two African women took to be curses, because of their vituperative sound and the fierceness with which Mrs. Ashby-Jones's face was contorted. She lunged at Ngwanze in an effort to retrieve her notebook. Ngwanze held the notebook away with one hand and gave Mrs. Ashby-Jones a shove with the other.

Mrs. Ashby-Jones glared at Ngwanze with a rancor that pumped her breath rapidly up and down.

"Leave her alone," Okwere-ke-diya said. "There is nothing to be gained by persecuting her."

"I am not persecuting her," Ngwanze said, "but I notice that she does feel pain. I wonder what she has written on these pages, which I am now going to use to wipe myself." She tossed the notebook at Mrs. Ashby-Jones's feet, crumpled the pages in her own hand, and began walking into the bush to ease herself.

"White woman," Okwere-ke-diya said after Ngwanze had disappeared, "why did you come here? Why did you not stay in your own place? I mean *you* personally, not just the Government, because the same spirit must have driven you to come here as drove them. You said you came here to find out about us, woman to woman. Have you found out everything that needs to be found out about everything in the place where you have your home, and the only thing left to be found out about was us? Can you understand what I am asking you, even a little bit?"

Soon, Obalanze returned. The news was not good. Soldiers were headed in their direction early in the morning. The District Officer had gone to the Rest House earlier in the day and declared Mrs. Ashby-Jones missing. A search party was being organized and would set out in the morning to begin looking for her. Six court messengers carrying guns had already visited Ugbala's house.

"Are there any instructions?"

"We are supposed to move."

"Where?"

"Some distance from here. Wait for nightfall. Wait for the moon to rise. Then return to the village and eat and take shelter and get a wink of sleep. Then in the dead of night, when the roads are clear of travelers, set out for the junction where we will be met by the people of the next village that will host her. Word has been sent to them and they will meet us without fail."

"I notice you did not bring back a fire."

"I was told that it would not be a good idea for us to light a fire in the bush, as that was bound to call attention to us."

"It will be a dark night before the moon comes out."

"Yes, but I suppose we will have to grope our way around until then. I do not feel comfortable with the White woman untied. I will put back the cords on her feet while we still have some daylight."

"There is a strange feeling in the village. I did not get the full sense of it, but it is there everywhere. All the women have their faces covered with soot and indigo, and so no one is recognizable. You have to peer into the faces of people you know or recognize them through their voices. My younger daughter ran away from me when I approached."

"You were not supposed to go to your house."

"I could not restrain myself."

"How do you know you were not followed?"

"By whom?"

"By whomever. A spy. A soldier. One of the men who could be induced or coerced into revealing what he knows."

"No one followed me. I did not come here by a straight route."

"Obalanze, I have to remind you that we are at war. And we have taken an oath. Part of that oath includes not being careless or heedless."

"I am sorry, but these bushes will be full of women tonight. No one wants to stay at home and be captured by the soliders in the morning. So everyone was preparing to feed and bathe the children and maybe sleep a bit. These bushes will be full of women tomorrow."

"We will not be here tomorrow."

"Any news about your mother-in-law?"

"No. They are still holding her. No one is even talking about bail or anything like that. My husband and his brothers have met and have tried to summon an *amala* meeting of the entire village, but the men are afraid to meet. They are afraid that any meeting they conduct will be taken as preparation for rebellion, and with so many soldiers around, a detachment may be sent to shoot up any village where the men seem to be raising up a disobedient head. My husband and his brothers are not going to sleep tonight. Our children will have to sleep at neighbors' houses."

Her voice suddenly cracked and she began sobbing. Ngwanze put an arm around her shoulder. "It will be all right. Nothing will happen to your children. Or to anyone."

"I swear to God, if anything happens to my children, I will kill this White woman with my own bare hands."

"Nothing will happen to your children," Ngwanze comforted. "Do your husband and his brothers plan to resist the soldiers?"

"They do not know what to do. Or what not to do. But with their mother arrested and the war raging here and there like forest fire, they are afraid that the soldiers may try to do as they usually do, shoot up the compound and burn everything down."

"They will not do that. They did not catch your mother-in-law doing anything."

"But you know how her name is on everyone's lips whether she has done anything or not. Is she in jail now because she has done anything more or worse than anybody else?"

"I know Ugbala," Ngwanze said. "Wherever they take her, as long as she is dealing with men and women who walk on two legs, nothing will happen to her."

"Yes," Okwere-ke-diya agreed. "Ugbala is *iwi agwo*. One day in the distant future when her time comes, she will expire quietly on her own sleeping mat."

8

Ebube!

WHEN I WAS TEN YEARS OLD and in Standard Three, my teacher, Mr. Ukah, was a tall, erect-standing, and handsome young man. Usually a fullback on the teachers' soccer team, he had the reputation of being so strong that he could kick a wet, size-five ball from goal to goal. Mr. Ukah was so strong that the headmaster forbade him to kick penalty shots, after one of his shots once broke the arm of our school's goalkeeper. Anyway, as the story was later told to me (I was not in school the Friday afternoon when it happened), Mr. Ukah had a confrontation with an old man named Nwa-Agwu as our class was clearing a piece of land adjacent to our school in preparation for making a school farm. The people of Nwa-Agwu's compound often had confrontations with our school, because they claimed the school constantly encroached on their land.

"Off my land!" Mr. Nwa-Agwu said, shaking his tasseled *oti* fly whisk at the boys. The fearful students promptly complied.

"Back to your work!" Mr. Ukah shouted at the students, when he returned from getting a drink of water and learned what had happened.

And so the confrontation began between Nwa-Agwu and Mr. Ukah.

The highlight came when Mr. Ukah, who had been speaking in Igbo all the while, used the English expression, "Imagine the likeness!"

For some reason, Nwa-Agwu heard only the word *imagine*. For some reason, his mind seized on it and translated it to the Igbo word, *ima-ji-ji-ji*. Mr. Nwa-Agwu thought Mr. Ukah was commanding him to "shake and quake!"

"Nwata-kiri ogbede, isi nna gi maa ji-ji-ji? Eeh? Eeh? Lekwa-nu-ji-ji-ji!" [Young man, are you asking your father to shake and quake? Eh? Eh? Well, here's shake and quake for you!]

Nwa-Agwu, as the story was told to me by several classmates, recited some strange incantations and then flung a handful of sand at Mr. Ukah.

According to my classmates who saw it, Mr. Ukah fell down and was overtaken by chills. The headmaster and two other teachers had to come and help him up from the ground and escort him to his quarters. I know that when I returned to school on Monday, Mr. Ukah was not there and did not return to school for that whole week. His whole body, we were told, was covered with rashes, from the sand Nwa-Agwu had flung at him.

That was *ebube,* and Nwa-Agwu had it.

Koon-Tiri had *ebube.* Koon-Tiri, who *pinned* Fada Getz, the R.C.M. priest at Agalaba Uzo, as he was saying Mass, and the priest could not recite the words he was supposed to say at Consecration, but kept repeating *Hoc est enim . . . Hoc est enim . . . Hoc est enim . . .* like a scratched record.

Ebube!

Amuma-ogwu!

Man pass man!

Spirit pass spirit!

And the way Koon-Tiri died was *ebube!* A bolt of lightning tore through the roof of his house, reaching into the innermost room, where he had a shrine and was at that very moment invoking spirits. He was burned and blackened beyond recognition.

Ebube!

In the confrontation with Pharaoh, Moses threw down his staff and made a snake.

Ebube!

Pharaoh's magician threw down his staff and made a snake.

Ebube!

Moses' snake swallowed Pharaoh's snake.

Ebube pass ebube!

Ebube, the aura of power, the all-enshrouding force you feel around the shrine of a powerful juju, a force that causes your scalp to crawl and your skin to be covered with goose pimples.

The power of a curse put on you by the old clay-pot trader, whom you caused to stumble and break all her pots, a curse so powerful and unshakable that it followed you everywhere, in every incarnation, and you could not hide from it, not in an anthill nor in a rabbit hole, unless you never ever ate anything cooked in a pot. That was why your mother warned you—and pulled at her ears again and again as she warned you—never to repeat what heedless children often thought was a clever saying: *"Ogwu akpola onye ite!"* [The old pot trader has stumbled on a twig!]

A leopard in a crouch, about to leap on a prey, a python about to strike. The power to transfix and paralyze prey with a powerful stare—all power of body and spirit singularly focused on the piercing point of the eyes, while the victim stands helpless and hopeless, knowing that all thought of escape is futile.

Ebube!

Ehihi!

Ekike!

The unseen force of Eke Ngbawa and Ngwu, which seized selected people from the towns of Umu-Akpara and Ovungwu during their respective juju festivals. That force reached near and far, high and low, to seize those it had selected. It made no difference whether they were young or old, rich or poor, male or female, high on an eagle's nest or deep in a rabbit's hole. The spirit always found its people and possessed them.

In the well-known folktale, the contest between the powerful *dibia* and the wood nymph was *ebube* versus *ebube.*

Ebube was what deserted Chief Nwakpuda the day he stood on the railway track at Afara and held up his charmed cow-tail whisk in the face of an onrushing train. *"Tah!"* Nwakpuda said. "No one, not even the White man's train, can pass by my compound without paying homage and tribute!" The train blew its whistle and blew it again, but Chief Nwakpuda stood fast, with his hand aloft. The train scattered his meat along the track all the way to Ovim. *Ebube pass ebube!*

The White man had *ebube.* He was cantankerous, irascible, and inscrutable. And powerful! *Agwu* of the worst kind. Mean, ill-tempered, and apt to take offense at the slightest provocation and to inflict the most painful retribution for the smallest offense. *Gburu bara uru, gburu bara okpukpu!* [*a double-edged knife!*] *Gbakuru nwoke, gbakuru nwanyi!* [stinging centipede!] There were not many of them, and the few there were seemed personally weak and sickly, but together they now haunted the land like vindictive ghosts in khaki shorts and pith helmets, carrying guns that spat deadly fire. All types of guns, pistols, and *riva-rivas*, big repeat-fire guns, poison canisters. The White man was poison. He had captured the thunderbolts of Amadioha in metal shells and flung them here and there and everywhere, not minding whom or what he killed. Knocking down houses, uprooting trees, or just making frightful booms and digging huge holes in the ground and spreading poison fumes.

The White man made and broke laws as he went along, shook hands to treaties he had no intention of keeping, violated oaths the same day, week, or month that he swore them. He was not bound by any code or deterred by any taboo. And whatever spirit or god he swore by never seemed to take him to task for violating his oath. If you extended your hand to the White man you could never be sure whether he would shake it or put handcuffs on it.

Word was that one of the early White traders in our area, a sort of pro tem consul who explored the hinterland from the coast, had the colonial office send him several hundred treaty forms. With these he went about signing friendship treaties with all the towns he traveled through. The area was backward, he said, and there were no chiefs or natural rulers. No village or town paid homage to another, so every few miles a new town and a new treaty. Bewildered elders made their marks or pressed their thumbprints on these treaties, taking the White man's word for what he said. Later they found out that they had signed away land or autonomy or whatever the sole interpreter of the written oracle said. Yes, the White man was the only known priest to his own oracle. In fact, he was both the priest and the oracle.

"Is this not your mark here?"

"Yes."

"Is this not your thumbprint here?"

"Yes, it is."

"Well, this document says that all of this land, hereunder named and described: . . . has been affeofed and deeded over to the Crown by the assembled elders and village heads of . . . It is all here, in black and white. We have no choice but to enforce the terms of this treaty."

Boom!

Boom! Boom!

Ala hentu! Hentu!

Ikpe amagh eze!

Ogwu akpogh nkita!

Any village or town that displeased the Government was declared a "disaffected area." A disaffected area came under the Peace Preservation Ordinance. And if a disaffected area did anything that could be construed as "misbehavior," the Collective Punishment Ordinance immediately took effect. Villages were burned down, growing crops were uprooted, animals were shot, barns were destroyed—as punishment and to make a show of force and meanness, to show the people how vengeful and ruthless the Government could be.

The White man was *ihea n'adigh otu n'eme ya* [something about which nothing can be done]. The people ran to their seers and their gods, but the seers had no answers and the gods seemed powerless. The White man was immune to the vengeance of both Ihi Njoku, the farm god, and Amadioha, the god of thunder. He broke their taboos at whim, and did things that no villager could dare to do and expect to live for more than a season, but nothing happened to him.

The men fought the White man however they could—with spears, but a spear could only be hurled so far. They fought with machetes, but a machete was good only against another machete and could only be used at arm's length. The men fought with the best weapon they had, the flintlock gun, stuffed with three or four fingers of gunpowder, bits of metal, or old ball bearings from their bicycles. These guns made huge booms and big clouds of smoke but could hardly kill a rabbit or a squirrel. One shot, and then they had to be reloaded. Their powders sometimes became damp; their ignition caps sometimes failed to spark.

The White man's guns fired surely, and they fired again and again.

The men fought bravely but the White man fought with stratagems and ruses, lures and ambushes. The people of Ahiara were lured to an open marketplace for what they thought would be a peace conference, then mowed down with Lewis guns. At the coast, King Jaja was lured onboard a ship for what was supposed to be a conference. The ship lifted anchor and took him to Akra and ultimately to exile in the West Indies.

Elders and juju priests were kidnapped and held at ransom until their kin complied with whatever the Government was demanding. "You want your elder back? Then send ten able-bodied young men to work the new Government project for ten days without pay!"

Given that the White man could do all of these mean, cruel, unbelievable things and seem to get away with them, the people could only shake their heads and marvel. This was *ebube* of a type they had never seen before.

Ebube kwuru ebube!

In the popular folktale, the tortoise is supposed to have said to the spider, whom he observed pulling yards and yards of web out of his belly: "Master Spider, if after pulling all that stuff out of yourself you are still alive by next year, I promise I will try pulling stuff out of myself too!" Impressed, awed, mesmerized by what they had seen the White man do and get away with, some local men decided to join him—the daring ones, those not connected to the main branches of their respective families, ne'er-do-wells who had little to lose, those whose innate disposition to crime and evil had been kept in check by the severity of local taboos and punishment—all of these found release in the White man—eloped with him and became his servants and savants, acolytes and apprentices, houseboys and *nyash*-lickers, and chiefs. When the White man lost his way, they showed him his way. When the rest of the village chose to keep quiet, they spoke up. When the rest of their towns shook their heads in dissent, they nodded theirs in assent. Such men, attention seekers as they were, received the White man's attention. In fact they became *notables*. Middlemen. Ultimately, chiefs. Because they stood out in the silent, sullen crowds that usually confronted the White man, he considered them *outstanding*.

"Wherefore, *urupirisi, urupirisi, urupirisi* . . . ," the White man said.

"It has been decided and decreed," his interpreter, an *osu* from the tribal markings on his forehead, announced to the bewildered townspeople, "that from this day henceforth the following shall be chiefs for the town of Usotuma . . . For Ikputu-Ala, the chiefs shall be . . . For Uzemba, the chiefs are . . . And for Amapu the chiefs shall be . . . All of the said chiefs shall assemble at District Headquarters at Agalaba Uzo on the twenty-seventh *inst.* for investiture and receipt of their caps and staffs of office. As a sign of general concord and in honor of chiefs duly appointed, let us give three 'Hip-hip hurrahs!' "

"Hip! Hip! Hip!"

"Hurrah!"

"Hip! Hip! Hip!

"Hurrah!"

"Hip! Hip! Hip!"

"Hurrah!"

Villagers and townspeople, bewildered and befuddled, scratched and shook their heads in amazement, shut their eyes and opened them again to see if they were dreaming. When the nightmare did not go away, they began to decide ever so slowly that what they beheld was real. They talked to one another in low voices and in slow sentences, searched one another's faces for answers. "Have you seen what I am seeing?" became the expression with which men passed one another on the paths of various towns and villages. And the answer to that question was "What my eyes are seeing my mouth dares not utter," usually spoken with a slow shaking of the head. It was like something in a fairytale. The world as they had always known it had done a somersault.

So, chiefs and clerks and interpreters of all types came into existence, priests and oracles of the new White god. He spoke to them and they spoke to the rest of the people. If the people had anything to say to him, they said it through their chief. There was no other way. The White god was impatient with complaints. His constant admonition was "Obey before complaining." If you did not obey, if you thought the whole thing was a preposterous joke, the White man had strong-armed enforcers of all types to help you change your mind, and to remember well the lesson they had taught you.

My grandfather was one of those who learned a lesson. Someone reported him to the local court for distilling a gin, *eti-eti*, out of palm wine, something that many, many villagers did, but something that had been declared illegal on a whim by the White man. No matter. My grandfather spent a year in prison for that crime. The chief instigator of the plot against my grandfather was a kinsman, our own local Chief Orji.

Orji, how shall I describe him and be fair to him? Well, he had a type of *ebube* that made him a terror to most of the people of our town. Awesome as well as awful, Orji stood tall and huge as an iroko tree. In his youth he was an unthrowable wrestler, as well as a bully who tended to acquire things by the strong eye and the strong hand, undeferring to elders and to custom, apt to do things out of turn. If a goat or cow was slaughtered for a village festival, for example, men chose their shares of the meat by age—from the oldest to the youngest. But not Orji. He would step up and choose whatever share he wanted without regard to whoever was supposed to choose before him. And the rest of the kindred were reduced to shrugging or pouting and murmuring privately or making nervous jokes about the fact that for Orji, rules and protocol were not necessarily binding.

Orji was a nemesis to all his kin, but especially to my grandfather, who continually opposed his roguishness. At one time, all of our people lived in a common *ezi ukwu,* or big compound. In time, however, we became too numerous to be comfortably situated on one spot. Some of the kin moved to other locations nearby. Custom was that the younger men moved, and the elders stayed. However, after Orji became chief, he asked the senior man in our compound, Izhima, to move instead. He, Orji, needed more space to erect a new zinc house befitting his new status. De-Izhima refused. One of the results of De-Izhima's refusal is the big bend in the new road just past Egbelu. Because Orji was then fifth in line among the surviving sons of our great ancestor, his place in *ezi ukwu* was to the side and the back of the compound. However, after the road was bent at his behest, it passed behind rather than in front of *ezi ukwu.* Orji at once cut a new lane from his house to the new road. De-Izhima protested that it was taboo to have two opposite lanes to the same compound. Orji's answer was "Then let there be two compounds!" So our ancestral compound was divided into two by a high *mgbidi* wall with which Orji separated himself and his wives from the others. Some months later, when the old road was abandoned for the new one, *ezi ukwu* was left facing the past with its back to the new, from which it was further eclipsed by the height of Orji's wall.

Orji was the type of person who caught the White man's eye and became Chief. As Chief, he turned our Native Court into a Justice Store, where he and a Court Clerk named Enoch asked all comers: "How much justice do you want? How much justice can you afford?

We have justice for five shillings and justice for five pounds. Which one do you want?"

But then Orji, too, had one day met his own nemesis, and my heart throbs with excitement whenever I think that I helped put him and it together. It was none other than the man who has since become my father-in-law, Stella's father, A. S. P. Kamanu. Orji was then doing his worst on my grandfather, and as a young person fresh out of secondary school, I had felt duty bound to strike some kind of blow. Especially since my grandfather had no other close male relatives. My cudgel was the A.S.P., my mercenary *ototo*, who arrived with two lorry-loads of policemen at the scene where my grandfather was being tried on a trumped-up charge by my townspeople.

I shall never forget that day as long as I live: A police Land-Rover pulling to a stop at our *okasaa*, and three police officers stepping smartly out of it. Then followed the gray police Mercedes, with official crest and markings. The tall man who emerged slowly from the Mercedes with an air of deliberate authority, the kind of authority that was used to getting compliance without much physical exertion. Lean and fibrous like a bamboo cane, black as a Munchi soldier, with tufts of mixed gray hair growing out of his ears, his cap set at an angle, the creases of his khaki uniform sharper than machetes, aviator sunglasses for mystery—eyes that saw without being seen—A. S. P. Kamanu, *Afo-Ojo-o*, or Bad-Belly Kamanu as people fearfully called him, had slowly eased himself out of his car, tucked his staff under one armpit, and had begun walking forward toward the crowd.

"*Ototo!*" I remember muttering to myself as he arrived, virtually jumping out of my skin. "*Nta Muu-muu!*"

Ebube Orji, meet *ebube* Kamanu!

Orji was impressed but not cowed. Anyhow, not until the first lorry-full of policemen in brightly colored uniforms arrived and was followed immediately by a second lorry, whose engine backfired as it pulled to a stop and sent some of the people to flight.

What happened that day was *ebube kwuru ebube* in special demonstration. The A.S.P. and the policemen were on their way to a parade and drill competition with another police detachment at Agalaba Uzo. The rifles they carried were empty. Even so, their mere appearance thoroughly confounded Orji and his schemes.

Ebube!

That was in 1959.

Back in 1929, Ndom had decided that the best way to fight the seemingly invincible White man was not with guns or strong talk, but with *Ebube* Ndom, the awesomeness of the Solidarity of All Womanhood, the Mother and Nurturer of all humankind, kneaded together by Mgbara Ala, the Goddess of the Unity of All Land. Oha Ndom joined the rich woman to the poor, the prostitute to the virgin, the young girl who had just had her first monthly to the old widow who could no longer remember when she had had her last. Women in the prisons. Women on the farms and in the markets. Women on their way to the well. Women on their way to the bushes to find firewood. The aura of Womanhood rose from the earth and descended from the sky and covered everything in a convulsive swirl. Even little girl babies just beginning to crawl and grow their first teeth, if they had seen a Government agent, they would have crawled up to him and bitten him with their first pair of baby teeth. Even the madwoman Tank-Panza-Brockway-*Peccata Mundi* was heaved by its power.

Brockway-Tank-*Peccata-Mundi* led a charge of women against her old enemy, Fada Getz, pastor of the R.C.M. Church at Agalaba Uzo. This crowd swept past the priest and was about to torch the church and the rectory, were it not for the intervention of two nuns and a group of about fifty girls who attended the Holy Rosary Convent School. The girls, holding hands at the entrances of both buildings, were led in prayer by the two nuns. After watching them for a while, Brockway and her retinue turned around and left for the prisons.

On their way to the prison yard, the group led by *Peccata Mundi* came upon two warders returning with a dozen prisoners from a day of work at some Government project. The prisoners carried hoes, machetes, and axes. The warders carried only truncheons. *Ebube!* The two warders, apparently unaware of what had happened to their colleagues elsewhere, showed no concern when they saw the throng of women approaching them on the run. They were Government people protected by the Government's *ebube*. The same *ebube* as kept the prisoners from doing them physical harm or trying to escape. They had heard that women were rioting in the outlying villages, but no one was supposed to riot in town, which was Crown Territory. Or so they thought, until the women lit into them, knocked them to the ground, and proceeded to tear off their uniforms as trophy, taking time even to unwrap their lengthy woolen puttees.

"Gbaa nu nfa!" Peccata Mundi commanded the warders. "Scram! Your tail is on fire!"

The prisoners stood, mesmerized, like people confronted by two gods, unsure which one to worship. The women were on their way; when some of them looked back and saw the prisoners helping the warders off the ground, they turned back and gave the prisoners a beating, spat on them, and tore off their scanty prison uniforms.

Ndom!

Ebube!

Ndom was everywhere, because women were everywhere.

Ebube poured out of Ugbala where she was being held in prison. Seized her like *Amuma-Muo*, like a fit of delirium brought on by a high fever. Enough to overpower the warder who was guarding her. "Child," she said to the young warder, "are you going to be a woman or a dog that wags her tail for an unknown master? Haah? Haah? You do not answer me? If I ever meet your mother, I shall tell her she should have taught you better manners. What town do you come from? Are you an *osu* or a freeborn? Turn your face to the side, so I can get a better look at your tribal marks. I see, you are a freeborn. In that case, my question to you is: Why have they put you in charge of me? Did they tell you what I did to merit being brought into this hole? How much are they paying you? You still do not answer? Well, I will not ask you any more questions. You know, if my hands were free I would slap you for your cheekiness. Do you know who I am? . . ."

Some of the other prisoners chimed in. "Yes, do you know the person they have asked you to guard? This is Ugbala that you are guarding. Where could you be from that you have never heard of Ugbala? If your hometown is anywhere around here, you should have heard her name. . . ."

"Take off these things so I can go to the latrine," Ugbala said.

"You do not need to take them off to go to the latrine," the warder replied.

"And after I finish, how shall I wipe myself? Or will you wipe your mother? Take these things off, so I can go to ease myself," Ugbala commanded, her voice rising, her eyes staring fiercely.

"I cannot take them off," the warder replied.

"Then call someone who can order you to take them off."

The warder blew her whistle. Another, more senior, warder

came. The younger warder saluted and explained the request. The senior warder assented. The handcuffs were removed from Ugbala's hands. She grabbed the bunch of keys from the young warder and tossed them to the other prisoners. A scuffle ensued. The two warders grabbed Ugbala, one on each hand. The other prisoners used the keys to let themselves out of their cages. Together, the fifteen or so prisoners overpowered the two warders, but not before they could blow a few emergency blasts on their whistles.

No matter. The fifteen erstwhile prisoners were ready for war. They went from gate to gate trying keys and releasing as many other prisoners as they found. Down a narrow passageway, on their way to the men's section of the prison, they came upon two male warders—older men who had been left behind to man the prisons, while the others had been seconded to the District Officer's contingent force. The two were carrying truncheons, but so were two or three of the younger prisoners, who had picked up these weapons from the warders they overcame. The two warders blew their whistles and drew their truncheons. Clearly, they were no match for the women about to confront them, but they relied on their own aura—*ebube*—their manhood, and their weapons to keep the women at bay.

At first encounter, the narrowness of the corridor made it difficult for the women to press their numerical advantage. However, the momentum of their rush sent the two warders reeling backward, even as they were swinging their truncheons. They managed to draw a few anguished howls from the women as the truncheons found their initial marks, but that was it. The women presently overpowered them, stripped them naked, and sat on them.

Ndom!

Ebube!

Ndom was unstoppable. They were clubbed but kept coming, were whipped but kept coming, were dispersed but regrouped and kept coming, knocked down, but climbed over their fallen comrades and kept coming. Ndom became like the proverbial Munchi soldiers—*onuru vuru, anugh zia!*—they heard "Pick it up!" but never heard "Put it down!"

In front of the prison gates, *Peccata Mundi*'s group met and merged with Ugbala's group. The joint force, each of its members drawing power and resolve from all the other members, rushed to the daily market. There they asked the few women they found, "What are you doing here? Trading while Ndom is at war? Have you not heard that the earth is heaving? Or are you not women?"

Eke Oha market heaved!

Telegraph poles all along Asa and Factory roads came down. Groups of three or four women attacked them in turn, heaving each pole back and forth, back and forth, until it was loosened around its foundation and finally toppled. The main post office on the edge of the waterside caught fire.

Approaching the section of town known as The Factories, the area where the European firms had their oil and kernel depots, the group met another smaller group, carrying the corpse of a woman identified as the popular prostitute Oyoyo. Oyoyo had died in battle, run over by a car driven by Doctor Bradshaw. On his way to the hospital, the doctor had been confronted by a group of women. In panic or out of malice he had accelerated his car in the midst of the crowd that surrounded him. Oyoyo was one of the women who fell under his wheels.

Ndom saw blood. Ndom saw red. Hitherto, they had done what they could to avoid the shedding of blood. But the White man did not hesitate to shed blood. It was at the junction of Factory Road and Milverton Avenue that this large crowd confronted a detachment of soldiers from the Fourth Battalion, and it was here that the earth heaved the most. And the most blood was shed.

Ala hentu!

The soldiers—it was impossible to tell how many of them there were—were apparently arriving from somewhere and grouping themselves for battle. The dust kicked up by the open-back lorries that carried them was still swirling, and to the far right of their formation, near the chain-link fence that marked the beginning of the compound of the John Woodrow Trading Company, a monster lorry painted in diarrhea-green colors was grunting to a stop and more soldiers were leaping out of it. At the forefront of the detachment, two rows of men were kneeling or crouching in firing position. Other rows stood thickly behind the first two, their rifles palmed at an angle, at the ready.

As the crowd of about two thousand women swept into view, stomping, chanting, and kicking up a lot of dust, the White officer in the Australian bush hat of World War I vintage peered into his field glasses and then gave instructions to the native sergeant, who then translated what he had been told to an order in the vernacular and in pidgin English to his men. At about a hundred yards from the soldiers, the most forward members of Ndom stopped to allow those behind to catch up with the rest. The chanting grew louder, more spirited and more rhythmic.

Iweh! Iweh! Iweh!

Iweh nji anyi! Iweh!

Nwa Beke-e ekweh aluwah, ekweh!

Ekweh! Ekweh! Ekweh-aluwah, ekweh!

The women wielded sticks, kitchen knives, pounding pestles. Their cloths were retied in the war-readiness *isi-ngidingi*; most had wreaths of palm leaves around their head and waists; their faces were darkened with indigo and pot black.

The White officer, Malcolm Davis, stepped forward toward the women, flanked by two soldiers and an interpreter. He held a piece of paper in his right hand, ready to read the women the riot act.

"Ndom *kwenu!*" Ugbala intoned, when the White officer and his delegation were about fifty feet away.

"Yah! Yah! Yah!" the crowd answered.

"Kwenu!"

"Yah! Yah! Yah!"

"Huo-ra-nu Nwa-Beke-e ikeh! Huo-ra-ya-nu otila!" [Show the White man your backsides!]

As if on cue, all the women turned around, facing away from Mr. Davis and his soldiers, doubled over, turned up their buttocks and aimed them at the approaching White man. Then they pulled up their loincloths, so as to expose their naked bottoms. Mr. Davis did a double take, then froze in place. The soldiers with him turned away their faces, as did the formations behind them. It was a sight none of them had ever seen before and hoped never to see again. They felt insulted, assaulted, defiled, and cursed. Cursed by this field of female bottoms, fat and lean, old and young, brown and black, and at every stage of the monthly cycle. It was enough to give one recurrent nightmares and bad luck for all of a lifetime. The soldiers shut their eyes fiercely in the manner of little children learning to wink, as if thereby to squeeze the image of what they had seen out of their minds. They felt like throwing away their weapons and running. Mr. Davis was simply dumbfounded.

Then again as if on cue, the women straightened up, and with a

cry of "Shoot your mothers! Shoot your mothers!" they charged into
the soldiers.

More than one hundred of them died in the barrage that followed.

Nne-nne then returned her attention to Mrs. Ashby-Jones.

"Ajuziogu, this woman was a pitiable sight. Thornbushes and
blades of *waghiri-wah* and *achara* had scratched and slashed her in
many, many places. Flies and gnats had feasted on her delicate skin,
covering her with red welts and blotches. I suppose they had never
seen such delicious skin before. Her dress was nothing but rags just
barely hanging on her shoulders, and you could glimpse her
underthings, including her breast pouch and the strange *ogodo* with
which she covered her crotch. I had never seen breast pouches before
that day, and to think that so many of our younger women are wearing
them today. Your Sitella wears them, does she not?"

"Yes, she does."

"Anyway, I have not even told you about the worst thing of all.
Her belly was running. The first we knew of it was when she jumped
up suddenly from where she had been sitting and ran off into the
bushes, and we ran after her, thinking that she was trying to escape,
tackled her, and knocked her to the ground. It was only then that
we found out that her other end was going spit-spat. Then we had
to find a calabash of water to wash her and ourselves. We gave her a
new piece of loincloth and tried to teach her how to tie it and keep
it on. This was the only time I can remember her smiling. She looked
at herself this way and that, smoothed a rumple on the cloth with
her hand and smiled. We began laughing because it was such a relief
to see her smile. In the end, she too laughed, when Ogbodia, one of
the women, tickled her under her chin.

"I have to tell you that she was really a strange creature, like an
apparition you might encounter in a bad forest on a day of evil omen,
her white skin trying to show through the indigo, circles of white
around her eyes and mouth where the indigo did not quite reach, her
lips shining red through the black, her teeth long—she had long,
rabbit upper teeth, which her upper lip could not cover completely.
With her hair shaved off, her head was small and pointy. She had a
narrow face and pinched nose with narrow nostrils and beady glass
eyes that were very close together, squinting from a face blackened
by indigo.

"Early on the morning of the day after we got her, one of the women stepped on a viper and killed it with a stick. It was quite a big viper, and we made the mistake of showing it to the White woman. She became so frightened that she fainted. When she woke up from her faint, she was still screaming with fright and went into shivers like a child suffering from convulsions. She looked here and there, as if every shadow, every twig or rustle of leaves, was a viper.

"Later that afternoon we received a message that soldiers were coming in our direction and had already passed Ntigha and Ama-Orji and had almost reached Obikabia. We had to move the White woman somewhere else far away from the major roads, which could carry a lorry and bring the soldiers. The message also said that the soldiers traveled only by day and had no water in their bellies—that was how cruel they were. We also had to be careful about their spies, who were not wearing uniforms and who might be traveling on bicycles. Strange men with distant accents had been seen asking questions in some of the villages just ahead of the soldiers.

"That evening, we set out toward Okporo Ahaba, where we were supposed to hand over the White woman to the Ndom of that town near their big market, Eke Mgbede Ala. But we had to carry the White woman, because her feet were swollen and covered with sores. We bound them with rags and made walking pads for her soles, but still she could not step on them. So we carried her in turn astraddle on our backs or with her hands draped over the shoulders of two people, and her tiptoeing and hobbling along between them. Night overtook us near Uhum, and we decided to stop. And that was the strangest night of all.

"We were sitting and roasting corn by a small fire we had made for the night to keep us warm against the harmattan cold and to keep the wild animals away, when a great horned owl, *kowu*, found a perch on a tree branch next to us and began his moanful hooting. Women, we became afraid about what this might mean; we feared it might be the omen of something evil. We threw sticks at it, and it went away. But then a short time later it returned with a mate, and together they kept us awake and shivering most of the night. That was a night of the spirits. The sky hung low above the trees, and clouds, which looked like smears of dirt, drifted across the face of a dull and unhappy moon.

"The White woman was crying and whining and groaning all the time. And talking to herself. During the time my group had her, in every village we passed we were met by two escorts, sent by the women of that village, who showed us the way through that village by the less-traveled paths.

"We reached Mgbede Ala just before the first cockcrow. We were weary and hungry and sleepless. Not just the White woman, but the three of us who had been with her for four days and four nights were ready to collapse with fatigue. And then the delegation that was supposed to meet us by Eke Ukwu Mgbede Ala did not appear at the base of the cottonwood tree near the edge of the market clearing. We did not know what to do, and dawn was fast approaching. Soon enough it was daylight, and we had no choice but to wade into the bush a good distance from the market and stay put.

"But the bushes here were strange to us. There were no landmarks by which we could tell how far or near we might be to someone's compound. Thick bushes these were; they had not been cut down for farming in many years, so we knew we were a good distance from where anyone was living. But then we did not want any hunters or trappers to come upon us suddenly as they sneaked their way through the early morning dew to catch animals that were getting up to feed. Anyway, we moled our way into a dense *akoro* thicket, so thick that a climber on top of a nearby palm tree would not have spotted us.

"Our biggest concern was that something had gone wrong, something that prevented the delegation from Mgbede Ala from coming out to meet us. This was the first miscue we had experienced, and we were worried about the meaning of it. And then after we retreated to the bush we realized that the delegation would not know where to find us if it came looking. We put our thoughts together and selected Ahudiya to go to the *okasaa* and wait. She disheveled herself even more than we were disheveled already, borrowed everyone else's rags to hang on herself so that she looked like a madwoman. Then she went to the *okasaa* and sat on a log or wandered around muttering jibberish to herself, so that anyone who saw her would surely have concluded that she was mad.

"For that whole day no one got in touch with us. Also through the next night. We slept huddled together in the nest of *akoro* bush, cold and afraid of bush cats and hyenas and snakes. Our spirits were low. After so long a time in the bush, our enthusiasms were no longer what they were in the beginning. We were dirty and hungry, and itchy from hundreds of gnat and mosquito bites, and for three days now we had no news of how the war was going. If only we could have heard Ndom chanting and singing in the distance! One of the women, Ogbodia Nwankwo, began to say that the war was probably over and everyone but us had returned home.

" 'That cannot be,' I said. 'Ndom would have sent someone to inform us.'

" 'Maybe everyone has gone home and forgotten us,' Ogbodia said.

" 'But they know we have the White woman,' I replied. 'They cannot abandon her and us. Anyway, it was only three days ago that we were met by delegates in every village we passed through.'

" 'But when we arrived here at Mgbede Ala no one came out to meet us.'

" 'But that is only the first time,' I said, 'and there is probably a good reason for it. Anyway, are we even sure that this village where we are is Mgbede Ala? Perhaps we are in the wrong place.'

" 'It is Mgbede Ala. I have been through Mgbede Ala before on my way to the *ogwumabiri* of Umu Oba.'

" 'But you forget we arrived here at night. And another thing, there was no Pad Symbol made of rolled palm leaves hanging on any of the trees near the market. Did Ndom also forget to put up our symbol?'

"You see, Ajuziogu. Ajuziogu, are you asleep?"

"No, Nne-nne, I am not asleep. You were talking about the pad that Ndom used as a symbol."

"All right. So you were awake. Ndom used the carrying pad as a symbol. You know why? Because a woman is a carrier. A woman carries the world on her head without a carrying pad. Anyway, we decided to send Ahudiya to the market clearing to look for the pad, a wreath of palm leaves hung from a rope of *mgbalala*. Ahudiya did not find a pad, but what she brought back was a notice written on the White man's paper and gummed to one of the trees in the market clearing. Since this notice had not been there when we first arrived, that could only mean that the White man was nearby. Or maybe one of the court messengers had put it up. I even thought maybe the chief.

" 'But it is written by writing machine, not by hand.' Ahudiya observed. 'That says White man, as no chief has that machine.'

" 'The White woman can tell us what it says,' I said, but as soon as the words were out of my mouth, we looked at one another and shook our heads. If the White woman read it, only she would know what it said, and she could refuse to tell us, or even lie to us. Anyway, even if she wanted to tell us, how could she, since she did not speak our language? We did not know what to do.

" 'Let us leave her and go home.' Ogbodia said.

" 'No,' Ahudiya disagreed. 'She will surely die, and her blood will be on our heads.'

" 'Yes,' I agreed with Ahudiya. 'She is so weak she will not last a night in these bushes by herself. She cannot even move. She will die of starvation, if a hyena or some other wild animal does not get her before that.'

" 'Have we not agreed that the notice I brought back from the tree is from the White Nwa-D.C?' Ogbodia said. 'If we abandon her at the market clearing someone is bound to find her.'

" 'And then what shall we tell Ndom later about the duty we were given to guard her?' I said. 'Is that not part of our oath? Suppose the whole war is lost because of us?'

"We all agreed that it was strange that we had not heard any sounds at all from a town as big as Mgbede Ala—no people on the roads, no men going to the farms or climbing palm trees or cutting fodder for their animals, no children looking for mushrooms, wild vegetables, or firewood. That was very strange.

"We made a pad and sent Ogbodia to go and hang it on one of the trees by the market clearing, and asked her to look around while she was out there to see if she saw anything. We were waiting for her to return, when suddenly we heard the sound of shooting, two or three cracks of a White man's gun, not the big boom of a native gun. Ajuziogu, my heart dropped into my stomach, and goose pimples formed all over me when I heard those shots. My shoulders pulled up to my very ears, for I knew something bad had happened. My mind flew at once to those two owls that had been hooting over us two nights before. Ogbodia's children had become motherless children.

"Later that night, two women from Mgbede Ala explained everything to us. The town had received news that soldiers were marching toward it from three different directions, and everyone had fled. Someone had betrayed Ndom's pad Symbol. Spies had seen the pad hanging in the market. Soldiers from near the junction at Icheku were heading toward the town. Another group of soldiers was coming from Obikabia and Agbaragwu, using the new road, Ogidiala Nwatu. The iron road for the trains had been repaired and soldiers from Ugwu Awusa and Bende had come off at Umu Oba and were traveling toward Mgbede Ala. With so many soldiers coming its way, Mgbede Ala had fled.

"Ndom! *Iyi omimi!*"

As things turned out, Nne-nne and her cohorts were the last group in the relay of custodians to handle the Mrs. Ashby-Jones. The war was then at its peak, with smoke and fire everywhere: A train carrying ore and groundnuts had been derailed near Mgboko Halt. Near Achara Etu Amapu, Ndom had dug and concealed a trench across a main road, and a lorry carrying soldiers had plunged into it, killing four or five soldiers and severely injuring their White officer—some even said he had been killed. Courthouses, trading depots, and post offices had been torched. There was destruction everywhere. The women were out of control. The men were dismayed and disheartened, seeing no good outcome to this whole thing. News of the massacre at Factory Road was everywhere. Initially, it included the rumor that both Ugbala and Brockway-*Peccata Mundi* had been among the victims. Eventually, the word that filtered down to Nne-nne and her group of guardians was: "Do whatever you like to the White woman! Kill her, if you wish, because so far our people are doing all the dying!"

Later, it turned out that Ugbala had survived the barrage at Factory Road with only a bullet wound in her arm, and on the very day Nne-nne and her companions were trying to decide how to get rid of Mrs. Ashby-Jones, Ugbala and her friends, Ngwanze and Okwere-ke-diyankara, appeared where they were hiding.

I watched Nne-nne's face as she recalled the agony of the decision they had been trying to make about Mrs. Ashby-Jones, and the exhilaration with which she and her group of young guardians greeted the arrival of the older women. I could see the pain in the distant focus of her eyes, as she said, "This woman had been with us for nearly a week. She was thin and emaciated and sad. None of us had the heart to do her any harm. And then Ugbala appeared.

" 'Ugbala!' we all exclaimed on seeing her. 'You are still alive!' We had lost all caution about calling ourselves by our first names.'

" 'Only by the power of God,' Ugbala said. 'You can say that Death took me into his mouth, decided that I did not taste good, and spat me out again.'

" 'Thank God,' we all said. 'Thank God that your life was spared. Is it true that hundreds died at Factory Road?'

" 'Many died,' Ugbala said. 'Very many. So many the killers got tired of killing us. Their *ediman* told them to stop their shooting, as their bullets did not stop us. We fought hand-to-hand with them, until they piled into their lorries and drove off. We did not run. We were all ready to die. So many had died already. . . .' Ugbala continued:

" 'Ah, here is my friend with all the questions and the notebook. She does not look like her old self. Do you remember me?' she asked, slapping her chest while looking at the White woman.

" 'Ub . . . ub-la,' the White woman said, with something that may have looked like a smile on a normal, clean face.

" 'Ah, you remember me then,' Ugbala said. 'Well, we meet one more time. Tell me, why are your people killing us?' "

No answer from Mrs. Ashby-Jones, who continued to stare at her appealingly. Seeing someone she recognized seemed to lift her spirits and add a glimmer of hope to her eyes.

" 'Yes, yes,' Ugbala told her. 'You must tell me: Why are your people killing us?' "

According to Nne-nne, the light, whatever there was of it to begin with, faded from the eyes of Mrs. Ashby-Jones.

" 'Do you not wish she could speak our language,' Okwere-ke-diya asked, 'so that we could hear her answer?'

" 'She would probably lie to us,' Ugbala replied. 'So it may be better, or at least as well, that she does not speak our language. That way, she has no opportunity to lie to us.'

" 'That is true,' everyone agreed. 'That is very true.'

" 'You came just in the nick of time,' Oyiridiya, the woman of Mgbede-Ala, said. 'We were trying to decide what to do with her. You know how the saying goes.'

"Ugbala asked: 'Had you made a decision?'

" 'No,' Oyiridiya answered. 'We had not made a decision.'

" 'If you had made a decision, I would have no choice as a latecomer except to side with you.'

" 'No, we had not made a decision,' Oyiridiya said. 'We were trying to decide whether to let her go or to let her *get lost*.'

" 'H'm. If she *gets lost*, she *gets lost* on our account. If we let her go, her people may think she escaped through her own bravery or cleverness. How I wish she were not a woman!' Ugbala became suddenly serious and shook her head in a strange way. 'If she were a man,' she said, 'I would have the pleasure of splitting his head with a stick and letting his drying testicles drip fat over my cooking stand!'

" 'Keep a restraining hand over your heart,' the older women counseled Ugbala. 'In the last few weeks, you have seen more than one person ought to see in a lifetime. But you must keep a calming hand over your heart.'

" 'Yes,' Ugbala agreed. 'Anyway, she is a woman. And that tangles her around our necks, arms, and waist. We have no choice except to let her go. But we must drink the wine of union with her. We must swear with her.'

" 'It will be all one-sided,' Ngwanze said. 'She will not obligate herself to anything. She cannot even understand what we are saying as we swear.'

" 'What can we do? She is a woman, nontheless.' "

As Nne-nne told it, one of the women sneaked into the nearby village and procured a small gourd of palm wine. The women soaked their menstrual rags in the bowl of wine, and Ugbala invoked *ogus* over it:

" '*Ayi!*' she began. 'Land of our ancestors, I ask you, please notice that my hands are open and empty. I am concealing nothing. My hair is gray, but I have a child's heart, such that when I am told to bathe I know only to bathe my belly. A person who is not carrying anything, why should I stumble and fall so? Why should I die before my time? Why should I die a death that is not due me? Why should I not close my eyes quietly on my own sleeping mat, with my body intact, instead of being bored full of holes by soldiers' bullets. . . .'

" '*Iyah! Iyah!*' the other women said.

" 'This woman!'

" '*Iyah! Iyah!*'

" 'This woman, whose skin is without color, hair is like corn tassels, and eyes are like shiny glass beads!'

" '*Iyah! Iyah!*'

" 'But nevertheless a woman!'

" '*Iyah! Iyah!*'

" 'Dumb and speechless, but nevertheless a woman!'

" 'Barren, but nevertheless a woman!'
" 'Be the judge between us and her!'
" 'She came to us, not we to her!'
" 'We did not seek her out to harm her!'
" 'The war that now engulfs us has been made by her husband and her people!'
" 'Ala, make a woman of her!'
" *'Iyah! Iyah!'*
" 'Edoh, make a woman of her!'
" *'Iyah! Iyah!'*
" 'Let her feel our grief!'
" 'Let her feel Woman's Grief!'
" 'Let the burden of our grief sit before her eyes!'
" 'And sit on her tongue!'
" 'And make her fingers limp, so that she cannot pick up a writing stick and write with it!'
" 'If she writes, let her write the truth about us!'
" 'If she speaks, let her speak the truth about us!'
" 'If she should fail to speak the truth about us, if she should fail to write the truth in her writing, let this wine that we all drink together, this wine of our joint womanhood, consecrated to Ala and Edoh and to Efanim, let it intoxicate her into a state of madness that no one can cure! Let this wine, which contains the blood of our wombs, seal her womb in this incarnation and in all her future incarnations. . . .' "

Her *ogu*s over, Ugbala lifted the bowl to her face and drank from it, then held the same bowl to Mrs. Ashby-Jones's lips, until they parted and she drank some of the wine. Then the rest of the women took turns drinking the oath.

After that, as evening descended, Ngwanze and Oyiridiya, the woman of Mgbede-Ala, were selected to escort Mrs. Ashby-Jones to a place near Onu Miri. Some soldiers found her there the following day and returned her to her people.

Ala hentu!

PART
TWO

9

Stella's Wars

THAT NIGHT BEFORE I LEFT HOME, Nne-nne brought up Assistant Superintendent of Police Kamanu's name only a few times, each time only briefly. Nevertheless, he belongs fully in this story as Stella's father, the husband of Stella's mother, and especially as my ally in the ensuing Stella's Wars. A. S. P. Kamanu, Bad-Belly Kamanu as he was notoriously called, hero of Egypt and Burma, was a man whose stomach juices were supposed to be pure vinegar. He was that way with me the first day I met him. I had just begun "chasing" Stella, and had gone to his quarters more or less on a dare by my friends, on the day our School Cert results came out. The A.S.P. was about to get into his car when I rode up on my bicycle.

"Good afternoon, sir," I said.

"Good afternoon yourself. Who are you?"

"My name is Ajuzia."

"Ajuzia who? Where do you come from?"

"I work at the brewery, sir."

"Is this the road to the brewery? What are you doing on my premises?"

I can remember pausing and clearing my throat, and the A.S.P.

impatiently shouting at me. "Are you deaf? I said, What are you doing on my premises?"

"I have come to see Stella."

"You've come to see who?"

"Stella."

"Your father's Stella or your mother's Stella?"

"Stella, your daughter, sir."

The A.S.P. had become very angry at what he thought was a cheeky answer. "How did you come to know her?" he asked, walking menacingly toward me.

Before I could answer, Stella emerged from a side gate. "Do you know this person?" her father asked her.

"Yessah," Stella answered, explaining that I was supposed to help her with the science subjects she would offer for School Cert later in the year.

The A.S.P. fixed me with a long, intimidating stare before he tucked his staff under his armpit and sidled into the backseat of his car, while his driver accelerated the engine and drove off.

I had first met Stella one Sunday afternoon in late February, at the home of a co-worker named Jude, who happened to be her cousin. Jude and three friends were dancing with four girls from Saint Cecilia's when I arrived. Stella was without partner at the time, so I asked her to dance. Something close to magical happened between us.

"Stella, Stella!" I said with boyish delight as we shuffled to the music coming over the radio on the "Listeners' Choice" program.

"Ajuzia, Ajuzia!" she called back to me.

"Are you truly a star?"

"Don't you see me shining?"

"I must confess I am dazzled." I cupped a hand over my eyes as if to shade them.

She laughed. "You're a funny man," she said.

"You're a funny woman," I replied.

"You're also an echo," she said.

"You're also an echo," I replied.

"How do you like working at the brewery?"

"Okay. How do you like the sisters at Saint Cecilia's?"

"They're all witches."

"Someone will tell Mother."

"I hear you're good at Maths and Science."

"Don't believe everything you hear."

"Do you have any old School Cert reprints that I could borrow?"

"If you want them. What subjects are you offering?"

"I am not sure yet. I know they will include Maths and English Lit. Why don't you give the papers to De-Jude, and I will get them from him?"

"Why don't you come to my house and get them yourself?"

"From your house?"

"Yes."

"Where do you live?"

"New Layout. Tetlow Road."

She frowned half seriously, and rolled her eyes at me as the record we were dancing to ended. "Star! Star!" I whispered in tune with the dying song.

"If you tamper with this star," Jude said, "her father will share your meat among the vultures in the daily market."

Stella came to visit me the following Sunday, arriving at about eleven in the morning and staying until five in the afternoon. We talked. We worked physics and chemistry problems out of old School Cert reprints. We danced and we played a game of snakes and ladders. At one point I kissed her.

"Stella! Stella! "

"Ajuzia! Ajuzia!"

"Why did you come here today?"

"Because I wanted these papers, and you insisted that I had to come here to get them." Her cheeks ballooned with laughter.

"Didn't you realize you were walking into a lion's den?"

"*Hoo-sai* lion? I don't see any lion." Laughing, she looked this way and that for the lion.

"Seems like you'd like to be devoured," I said, standing behind her and laying my hands across her shoulders and neck.

"*Na* so," she continued in pidgin. "Who give squirrel roasted palm nut?"

"So your father is a terror, huh?"

"Aha."

"That's what you think."

"Wait till someday and you will find out."

"Be my girlfriend, Stella."

"Okay."

"Okay?"

"Sure."

"Look. I'm not joking." I turned her face around, holding it in both my hands.

I tried to kiss her, but she averted her face quickly and then said, "He misses!"

We staged a minor struggle, then kissed passionately. That was how Stella had come into the midst of my life. Deep in the midst of it. She visited my flat often, usually on weekends, on the way between the convent and her parents' home. As her tutor, I earned the privilege of being able to visit her occasionally at home, presumably with the A.S.P.'s tolerance.

In time I got to know not only Stella but her mother and the A.S.P. quite well. Stella, as a matter of fact, was able to persuade her father to intervene on my grandfather's behalf in a case that Nnanna had with one Chief Orji and the people of our village—the famous case during which the A.S.P. put our whole village to flight when he arrived at our *okasaa* with two lorry-loads of policemen.

Following her School Cert exams in December, Stella was relatively idle. She was half-heartedly looking for work, but as the privileged daughter of a Senior Service man, she was under no pressure to find immediate employment. As a result, we spent a lot of time together. I left work at about four, cycled the two miles to my flat, and ten or fifteen minutes after I arrived home, there she was, with a new hairdo, a new dress, or a new prank.

"I see you, Stella," I would say. "So, you might as well come out from behind that door."

"How did you know it was me and not a thief?"

"What kind of thief would cover himself with Sasorabia perfume before he went out to steal?"

"You don't know. Maybe a new kind of thief."

"I know one thing you have stolen."

"What?"

"My heart."

"You no get heart," she would say in pidgin. 'What you get inside your chest *na* big piece of stone."

"Come and feel it, and see how it is pounding because of you."

"It may be pounding but not because of me. You be like just any other young man. As soon as you see woman your heart begin to motor. And not just your heart only."

"What about you? Come here and let's see if your own heart is not pounding as well. Come here." I would move toward her and try to grab her hands.

"At ease!" she would order. "At ease!" She would push me off and hold her hands behind her back so that I could not grab them. Stella had a habit of sliding into her father's drill commands, often telling me, "Attention!" or "At ease!" or "As you were!"

We would grapple and wrestle and pursue each other around the room, and finally collapse exhausted into a chair.

"I like your dress," I might say, as we sat in the deep, soft cushions of the me-and-my-girl. "May I touch it?"

"The dress you may touch but not where you are looking."

"Please, Mister, don't touch my tomato," I would begin singing.

> Please, don't touch my tomato!
> You touch me dis, you touch me dat
> You touch me everything I got
> You touch me apples and pumpkins too
> But dis one thing you just can't do!

I found Stella intoxicating. Before I met her, my life had tended to be dour, or maybe doughy, from a natural disposition that often caused old people to say that I was a child with an old person's head. Stella was my yeast. In her company and in her friendship my heart found a perfect leaven. I laughed easily and heartily. I felt fulfilled and happy.

And then she came that evening in March and plumped right away into a chair without playing a hide-and-seek game with me at the door or engaging in any of her usual pranks. "Well," I said, retying my wrapper and standing in front of where she sat. "Who beat you?" She was dressed in a blouse and *ukpo* wrapper and her head was covered with a carelessly tied *akisi* scarf that might have belonged to her mother.

She sighed sharply, as she looked up at me, as if I had told a joke at a funeral. Sensing that something was up, I lowered myself into the chair beside her and asked, "What's the matter?"

"I don't know what's the matter but it could be terrible."

"Are you pregnant?" I asked playfully.

My question seemed to jolt her, literally to cause her to shudder, as if a charge of electricity had been passed through her. "I may be," she said. "How did you guess that?"

It was now my turn to be shocked. "I was only playing," I said. "Are you really pregnant?"

"My time is late."

"How many weeks?"

"Two or three. Maybe even a month." She sat up abruptly. "Let me see," she said, narrowing her eyes and furrowing her face as she began reckoning dates and the occasions of our encounters.

"It's probably nothing," I said. "You just miscounted the days."

"I don't think so. Not by that much."

"You are serious," I said with emphasis, narrowing my eyes at her and trying to ensure that this was not an extended joke that would have her laughing uproariously at me in the next few minutes.

"I am serious," she said.

"Oh my God," I exhaled in despair.

She stared at me, balled up her lips, lay back in the chair, thrust out her legs, and folded her hands across her chest. "What am I going to do?" she asked, closing her eyes and squeezing them in apparent pain until tears ran from them.

"Have you told anyone?"

"No. But only last week my mother was warning me about all the time I was spending over here with you." She let her head roll over and rest on my shoulder.

I slid my hand under her neck and pulled her closer to me. We sat silently for a while, her head resting on my chest. I watched her breathing and noted the outline of her breast pressing against the thin blouse. Ordinarily, this would have been an irresistible provocation to my glands, but right now my glands had been shocked into silence. It seemed that Stella was waiting for me to speak, to say the words that would put the best cap over this moment. I did not know what to say, except perhaps to express my disbelief one more time. My thoughts were all over the map, as the saying goes, but for the most part, they dwelt on my future. Hitherto, that future had had one major highway carved through it, and that highway led to a university degree overseas. After that I would return home and commence living

the "real life." What I was living now was a mere prelude, a sort
of introit to the real thing, which would only begin after I had
finished my university training. When I finished putting on my
clothes early in the morning in preparation for going to work and
looked in the mirror, or when I saw myself in my own mind's eye,
what I saw was the picture of the proverbial young man with a future,
a young man rushing to rendezvous with greatness and fame, laden
only with a single portmanteau with an airline sticker on it—BOAC
or KLM—with airline advertisements ringing in his head—"Say good-
night in Lagos—say good morning in London!" I did not see a husband, nor did I see a father.

A pregnant Stella beside me was not a mere amendment to the
picture. Rather, the picture would be entirely different. She and the
baby would not be mere passengers taken along for the ride to my
erstwhile dreams. The dreams would cease, and in their place would
emerge the nightmare of a Nigerian clerk's life—a one-bedroom flat
with linoleum carpet over a cold cement floor, belongings piled everywhere from floor to ceiling and shoved under the bed, snotty-nosed
children sleeping on roll-up mats in the living room, the monthly
pay gone by the twentieth of the month, a perennially pregnant or
nursing wife constantly carping at her *chi* and her improvident husband. "God forbid!" I must have said aloud, for Stella's head turned
on my chest, and she opened her eyes to look at me.

"What is God forbidding?" she asked.

"Nothing," I replied.

"What are you thinking?"

"Nothing," I said again.

"Think of something," she ordered, "and then let me know. This
thing, if it is true, will not go away, you know."

"Perhaps it is not true," I said.

"But what if it is? What will you do?"

I did not answer except with a sigh. Then the form of her question
struck me. She had asked what I would do, not what she would do,
or what the two of us would do together. I sensed that I was being
asked to take responsibility for her and the pregnancy, not just for
myself. The idea of such responsibility frightened me.

For me, one of the special benefits of having someone like Stella as
my girlfriend was that she was not needy. What she wanted by way
of clothes and trinkets her mother and father amply provided for her.

As a result, I got off scot free, where my friends and co-workers were always complaining that, on payday at the end of each month, their girlfriends unfailingly led them on shopping excursions through Queensway or Chandra's. Perhaps more significant than the expenditure of money was what was now symbolized by Stella's fingers clutching mine and her head resting on my chest. Heretofore, we had met and played and made love as independent entities, co-agents, yes, in the common act of love, but otherwise separate and independent. Stella was now asking to depend on me, not only to have me stand my ground firmly beside her, but to support her, if she chose to lean on me, and to carry her if she could not stand at all. I was reminded of one of my grandfather's favorite proverbs: A young man who can make love at will and for free to his mother's slave maid does not realize how expensive it can be to get a woman into bed!

"What are *you* going to do?" I asked Stella. As soon as the words broke through my mouth, I realized that my question was the same one she had asked me a short time before.

She turned to look at my face and then said, "I don't know. It all depends on what you are going to do."

"You have not told your mother?"

"No."

"Do you plan to tell her?"

"Everything depends on what you are going to do."

I became annoyed at the repetition. "Why do you keep repeating the same thing?" I asked.

"What am I repeating?"

"What I am going to do."

"That's right. Everything depends on that. I need to know how you feel. After that I'll know how to approach everyone else. I am sure that when I talk to Mama she will ask me how you feel. So, how do you feel?"

"Stella, you know you're my girl."

"But," she cut in.

"What do you mean, but?"

"I am your girl, but. There is a big but at the end of that sentence you were making. I was putting it in for you, that's all. You see, *this thing* has gone beyond me being your girl. It is now about me being your wife."

"My wife?"

"Yes, your wife."

"I am not ready for marriage, Stella!"

She bolted to her feet. "What are you ready for? Tell me, what are you ready for? I am not ready for it, either. I just took School Cert three months ago and have not yet received the results. But here I am pregnant, thanks to you. If I had come here this evening and nothing was wrong, you would have me in your bed by now."

I bit my lips to hold back my words and closed my eyes. I had never seen Stella angry—this angry—before and just sat there staring at her. At length I said, "Sit down, Stella. After all this, you may not even be pregnant."

"This is good, because I am finding out things about you that I did not know before. *Onye ji uwa gworo aju, ga evu ivu ya n'isi efu!*" [I thought I could use you as my carrying pad, but I see I have to carry my load on my bare head!]

"Sit down, Stella," I said. "Sit down. I haven't made anyone pregnant before, and goodness knows I wasn't thinking about marriage half an hour before you came here."

She stared hard at me. I stood up and gently pulled her down with me. We continued talking.

Nne-nne was the first person I told. She could not have been happier. She actually reached out for my hand, which lay idly by my side, shook it vigorously, and said, "Ajuziogu, God has answered my prayers and done us a great favor." In my presence, and seeing my distress, she was comforting and merely reasonable, but I have no doubt that after I left her that Saturday afternoon, she did a dance across her kitchen floor. Why—her only grandson, her only surviving child, the only stake she and my grandfather had in immortality, had a child on the way. She wanted to see Stella.

"Why?" I asked.

"To give her my heart and let her know that everything will be all right, that we will do whatever is necessary to keep a smile on her face, so that the time of her pregnancy is a time of gladness and eager anticipation and not a time of sorrow and worry. Ajuziogu, are you asking me why I want to see her? I want to see her because she is carrying my great grandson. Because in my time I have been pregnant nine times, and I want to tell her what to expect, what to eat, and what to avoid eating. Not that her own mother or grandmother could not tell her these things, but I want to have the pleasure of telling her myself. I want that unborn child to hear my voice from the womb. From the way you sound this afternoon, you have probably soured your Sitella's mood. Why, Ajuziogu, you could not have found a better girl from what I have heard you say about her. Or better in-laws. Everyone around here still talks about how that man brought two lorries full of policemen to our *okasaa* and caused our whole village to flee in panic. That is the man I am going to call my in-law!"

Nne-nne tempered my feelings, enlarged the perspective from which I had been looking at things, so that when I left her that afternoon, I saw possibilities I had not seen before. She did more later—much more. I returned from work one afternoon to find the familiar figure of an old woman sitting on the floor in the dark passageway of my flat. Her head was bare, for she had formed her head wrap into a tiny cushion between herself and the hard cement floor. Her torso leaned against the wall; her legs were thrust straight out in front of her and crossed at the ankles, and her hands were thrust into the folds of her wrapper between her laps—in other words, vintage Nne-nne. I would have recognized her from a mile!

"How did you get here?" I asked.

"Your mother-in-law," she replied. "She brought me here in their big motor with the police driver."

"Mama-Stella?"

"Yes," she replied, getting on her knees and then scrambling up. "So, this is where you live?"

"Yes. Have you been waiting a long time?"

"No, I just got here. I saw your Sitella too. Ajuziogu, she is a beautiful child. Your eyes were clean when you picked her."

"Yes," I said, parking my bicycle and unlocking my door. "How—" I said once, twice, and for the third time, before I could find the words to complete my question. "How did you find your way to Stella's mother?"

"By determination mostly," she replied with a chuckle. "I asked your grandfather from the time you and he went to thank your father-in-law for the favor he did us during the case with Orji."

"My father-in-law, my mother-in-law. They are not yet my in-laws, Nne-nne."

"Not yet, but they will be. I went to see them so I can begin my talking early. When you are trying to negotiate a bride price and do not have much money, you have to do a lot of talking. If we had a lot of money, we would simply go before your in-laws and their people and turn our moneybags upside down in front of them, and let their eyes drop out of their heads in wonder. Everyone would exchange compliments, and the wine would flow. But when you do not have money, your tongue has to carry much of the load, as you dispute certain customs and try to convince them to close an eye on others. In all of this, your mother-in-law is the key. She is the one who has to consent to release her daughter to you. If she says yes, it is hard for anyone else to say no.

"That is why I decided to find my way quickly to that woman's house. She received me very well too. Yes, very well indeed. I told her all the good things you have always said about their daughter and about her and her husband, and told her that we too are good people and that the only thing we lacked was money. I said that where you were concerned our corn had already been planted and promised a big harvest but was not yet ripe. I told her that we were going to marry their daughter."

"What?"

"Yes!"

"How?"

"By however a man marries a woman."

"But Nne-nne, you did not ask me."

"Ask you what?"

"If I wanted to marry Stella."

She frowned, then rolled her eyes around in her head as if searching for a focus for her thoughts. Then she chuckled and said, "Ajuziogu, what could you be thinking? Surely not about not marrying her and letting our child become a bastard or become claimed by someone else? She is such a beautiful girl. Surely you were not thinking of not marrying her?"

"I had not made up my mind."

"Well, my son, say that your grandmother made up your mind for you this one time. I know your mind has been taken up by your overseas thing, but this girl is a precious stone we cannot permit to escape through our fingers. We have to close our hand around her before she escapes. The proverb says that the first time a boy makes love to a girl he usually cannot find the hole and has to be guided to it. You need guidance. I know you want her. You just do not know how to get her and still do the other thing you want to do.

"I truly thank God that your mother-in-law is so agreeable. Her main concerns are her husband's anger when he finds out that his daughter is pregnant and that we fulfill custom for the village relatives. I told her not to worry, that we would put a smile on her face too, and even on the face of her stern-faced husband, but we would start with village customs first. As for what is due directly to her and her husband, I told her she could take me as her slave woman—I would till her farms and clean her house—until I had worked off the debt we owed to them. She laughed and said she did not need me to work for her. She truly received me well, Ajuziogu. The food she served me was full of meat and fish, and even though I saw many servants bumping around, she cooked and served it with her own hands, which was a great honor to me. Afterward, she brought me here in the big car."

Over the ensuing weeks, Nne-nne paid several other visits to Mama-Stella, and the two of them began to lay the groundwork for a marriage between Stella and me—all of this without the A.S.P.'s knowledge. In the meantime, Stella and Nne-nne discovered and fell in love with each other. Stella paid Nne-nne two or three overnight visits and began to call her Nne-nne directly instead of referring to her as my grandmother. In her turn, Nne-nne began calling her Eze-Nwanyi (Queen). As for Stella and me, we acquiesced to the arrangements that were being made on our behalf. Our feelings for each other were not diminished; they were simply drowned by the torrent of events let loose by Stella's pregnancy.

Then the A.S.P. found out all the things that had been happening behind his back. What he said and did, as reported by Stella and her mother, I cannot relate here, but one of them was to forbid me ever again to set foot on his compound. Stella was banished from the compound as a "disgrace" and went to stay with her mother's sister.

I stayed away from the A.S.P.'s compound for a time, but then one day, in a fit of boldness and with Nne-nne's encouragement, I decided to go to see the A.S.P., whether he shot flames from his mouth or blew smoke from his ears.

A. S. P. Kamanu must have stared at me for a full minute before he said a word. Then what he said was, "What are you doing here?"

"Sir, I would like to talk to you."

"About what?"

"About Stalla. And me."

"About Stella and you. Do you realize how insulting you are, standing in my gate, inside my compound, all by yourself, talking about Stella and you? After making my daughter pregnant?"

"Sir . . ."

"Go away! I don't want to catch you on these premises ever again, do you read me? Go! Disappear! Vamoose!"

I stood my ground, thinking that I had come too far now to be cowed. Not to be too defiant, I lowered my gaze to about the level of his chest. Otherwise, I stood perfectly still.

The A.S.P., his face screwed up in an unbelieving scowl, walked up to me, hoisting up his loose voluminous evening wrappers, bristling as if about to attack me. "You did not hear me say *go?*"

"Sir, I heard you, but . . ."

Stella's mother was approaching. "*Nnanyi,*" she said haltingly. "Forgive me, but . . ."

"I will never forgive you," he retorted before she could complete her sentence. "You were here day in and day out, when all this happened. What happened to your common sense?"

"Blame me all you want," Stella's mother said. "I will not try to dodge your anger or blame or to make excuses. The proverb says that whatever falls to the ground has unavoidably become dirty. So whether you bite or swallow me, no blame can be assessed against you. Stella is my daughter and was in my care when this thing happened. So you have every right to be angry. But what has happened has happened."

"Why then are you standing in my face making all these proverbs?"

"I have been talking to Ajuzia. Kill me, divorce me, do whatever you like to me, but I have been talking to him."

"Behind my back? Are you and he now on the same side?"

"*Nnanyi ukwu,* there are no sides in this thing. We are all on the same side. Ajuzia is not our enemy. He is a little boy. He and Stella were little children playing with fire without knowing what they were doing, and as usually happens in such cases, they got burned. Anyway, you know his background, and I know you like him. He has only his grandfather and grandmother, and they are both very old. Remember? You were the one who helped to rescue his grandfather from that chief of a man, I don't remember his name now. Anyway, he tells me that he and his grandfather want to come and see us. That is what he is here today to tell you . . ."

"See us for what?"

"About . . ." She restrained herself. "Tell him yourself, Ajuzia. You are a man after all, no matter how young. Tell him what you have told me."

"Sir, I want to marry Stella."

Something in that statement seemed to pour a bucket of cold water on the A.S.P. He stopped smoldering. I watched his countenance as he turned away from his wife and looked at me for several moments, then turned away from both of us and stared at nothing in particular, while expressions formed and faded on his face.

"Has she agreed to marry you?"

"No, sir. I have not asked her. Not directly. But I am sure she will consent."

"This is not custom, I know," Stella's mother put in. "A mere boy does not come by himself to ask for a girl's hand in marriage, but we are in an unusual situation. And really, today he is not asking. He only wants to know what day he can come with his people. Is that not so, Ajuzia?"

"Yes, ma'am."

"You want to marry Stella?" the A.S.P. asked.

"Yes, sir."

I was sensing a breakthrough and was about to become very happy when he dashed my joy by saying, "Go away. Get away!" He waved his hand briskly several times, as if to show how quickly and how far he wanted me to go. Then, inexplicably, he added, "I will think about it." He shook his head, pursed his lips, and released a heavy breath but said no more.

I saw a smile creeping into the face of Stella's mother, but she suppressed it.

"Next time you come," the A.S.P. said, "do not come by yourself. Do you understand me?"

"Yessir."

He looked at me squarely. "When I first met you, I thought you were a very intelligent chap—and sensible too. Perhaps I should not have allowed you into this compound. Anyway . . ." He let out another heavy breath. "Go away . . ."

"Thank you, sir," I said with heartfelt gratitude, and began walking away, past the gate to where my bicycle was parked.

"Ajuzia!" his voice called after me. This was the first time I could ever remember his addressing me by my name. Even though he had to raise it to reach me, his voice was noticeably mellower than usual, not the usual official bark with which I supposed he ordered miscreants to "Halt!" It was the softer, more distant, preoccupied tone of someone deeply lost in thought.

"Saah," I answered and turned to look at him.

"Come here," he said.

I leaned my bicycle against the lantana hedge and walked back toward him. He led the way past the back veranda into the penumbra of his smaller sitting room.

"Sit down," he said, motioning me toward a chair. "What do you drink?"

"I don't want anything, sir."

"Don't be silly. Lilly!" he called, and one of his younger wives ambled up through the veranda. "Bring me some Guinness and two bottles of Fanta."

As the A.S.P. disappeared into an adjacent room, I lowered myself into a chair. I was not quite prepared for this and could not help wondering what might be up. Whatever it was, it was pleasant, and I could feel myself smiling with relief. I had been in this sitting room once before, on the day grandfather and I had come to thank the A.S.P. for the help he had given us in vanquishing Chief Orji. That day, though, we had not been able to sit down for more than a brief moment, for the A.S.P. had several batches of visitors, who took turns at seeing him.

Anyway, it felt wonderfully comforting to see the A.S.P. out of uniform, and not even wearing a dress shirt and trousers but a sleeveless singlet and a voluminous *ukpo* wrapper around his waist. When he reentered the sitting room and began talking, I noticed with added pleasure that his voice and attitude were relaxed and mellow, and as they emerged from his mouth, his words did not stand at stiff attention beside one another.

"What exactly are you planning to do?" he asked.

"Sir, I would very much like to marry Stella. I would like to ask your permission to seek her hand. I realize this is not custom, and how I am doing things is not the way they should be done, but I also feel that time is of the essence, and if we follow all the traditions. . . ."

"You are a small boy. What do you know about custom? Most young people nowadays are neither here nor there. You are even much better than many of the others, more sensible, anyway, especially to be as intelligent as you are."

"Thank you, sir."

"Do you have any money?"

"Little to speak of."

"So, how are you going to marry my daughter without money?" He sighed, shook his head, and chuckled. "You expect me to allow her to marry you on credit?"

I smiled and could sense that my face was beaming. The weight of privilege being extended to me this afternoon was not lost to me. If when I got to work the following morning I were to announce to my fellow workers, "Guess with whom I was quaffing some Guinness and Fanta yesterday," and then gave the A.S.P.'s name, my friends would say I was hallucinating. But I was not dreaming. I was sitting with the A.S.P. in his living room, he and I alone, discussing how I would marry his daughter, making jokes about my marrying her on credit. I had always felt, even from the very beginning, that the man liked me, despite his official snappiness and the stiff starchiness that invaded his behavior from his uniforms. Stella and her mother had shared the view.

"You see, my friend," the A.S.P. was now saying, "marriage is no small *bizness*. Like alligator pepper, it is a privilege intended for grown-ups. If you eat it and your mouth is not ready for it, you will hear hot. The same thing with taking a woman to bed. The reason for that is that sometimes women become pregnant, and then you can't say, 'I didn't mean that,' because whether you meant it or not, whether you are ready for it or not, it happens.

"I blame myself for not keeping you out of this compound from the very beginning. But then, what am I saying? You did not meet Stella in this compound, and whatever the two of you did you did not do in this compound." He bit his lips and let out a heavy breath.

That, in essence, is how I made my peace with the A.S.P.

*   *   *

One day, while the customary ceremonies of marriage were in progress, I went to visit Stella where she was staying at her aunt's, and she handed me a wad of notes adding up to fifty pounds.

"What is this?" I asked her. ·

"Mama said I should give it to you. She wants you to keep it on hand in case you need it for things to take to our home people. . . . Wait! Wait! Don't say anything yet until I finish giving you her message!" I was angrily waving her hand aside and rejecting the offer. "Mama knows your pride is involved, and I know it too, but she wanted me to explain to you that her own pride is involved in this too, so far as our home people are concerned. Our people are talkers and will say many nasty things if you do not make a good show for them. Actually, I think this money belongs to Papa, and he gave it to Mama to give to you because he did not want to give it to you directly."

"I don't care whose money it is. I am not taking it."

"Why?"

"Because I'm not, that's all! If I am going to marry you, I must marry you with what I have, not money your parents have slipped to me under the table."

"Your own money nko? Where is it? If we begin to wait for you to get enough money this child I am carrying will finish school before you save enough for all the osikwagh-na-osigh, which all the palm-wine-drinking villagers will come up with. You just finished school the other day. You don't have money yet, and no one expects you to. But when we go to our village people next week, we cannot tell them that. All they want is a good feast with plenty of food and drink. If the whole thing is not lavish, they will backbite Papa until doomsday and say that he gave away his daughter for nothing. Next time they go to someone else's marriage ceremony, if that one is rich, they will say: This is wonderful, not like the ceremony of Kamanu's daughter, where we were given dried grasshoppers and stale wine."

"I still do not want to take it."

"You do not want to get married then."

"Are we back to that again?"

"No, we are not back to that again, but you are like a person who says, 'I want to go for a swim but I don't want to get wet.' This is not something that is uncommon nowadays, that the bride can slip money to the groom under the table, as you say, to help him pay the high bride price her people are demanding. Anyway, Mama thought you might reject the money because of your pride. She told me to tell you just to keep it in your pocket for the time being and return it to her if you do not use it. However, she said you should feel free to use any of it or all of it, if you want to buy a new suit, or charter a taxi, or buy some European drinks like whiskey or cognac. What is important to her is that our people, *our people*, get a good feeling about our ceremony."

I took the money from Stella and stuffed it quickly into my pocket, to keep from deliberating further on the issue. However, I still had an unresolved sense of being compromised.

"Oh, by the way," Stella continued, "Mama said I should tell you not to say anything about the money to your grandparents."

"How come?"

"Because they are so traditional and it could offend them."

"But me?"

"But you?" Stella said with a chuckle, reaching over and circling her hand around my neck. "You just want to marry me, that's all." This was a sudden flashback to earlier moments of conviviality between me and Stella, and it drowned the angers and anxieties of the present moment. "Have a seat," she said. "Don't leave yet. You know, since you came here this afternoon you haven't touched *your* belly."

Smiling, I said, "Forgive me," and ran my hand over the curvature of her pregnancy. She pulled up her blouse, so that I could feel her skin directly. In the old days, before she became pregnant, I used to lay playful claim to parts of her body, often speaking of "my lips" and "my breasts." She had now extended my ownership to the pregnancy, dubbing it "my belly."

After our official marriage Stella and I lived in my flat for a little over two months. Then, as was custom, she returned to her mother's house to await the birth of her child. The time we lived together was strange for both of us. I did not feel married at all. The common proverb says that when running water runs into a pit, its running days are over. Not so in my case. Marriage did not give me the feeling of coming to rest or of settling down. I felt instead like a marathon runner who had stretched out a hand to accept a towel or a drink from a roadside friend, but who all the while had to continue running and keep pace with himself. I continued running toward my appointed goal, which was to study overseas.

Through it all, there was a weight in my chest, like a lump of hurriedly swallowed food, which I could not quite get down. I felt bad on my own account for having hurriedly, absent-mindedly, and by side step entered into something as important as marriage and begetting a child. I felt especially bad for Stella. She deserved better. She was a beautiful girl, was well brought up, possessed a grade-one pass in School Cert, and was the daughter of a dignitary. She deserved to have entered marriage with a flourish, with a wedding ceremony that was the talk of the town, with her wedding photo in the *Express*. But I had prevented all that.

In our personal relationship, both Stella and I tried gallantly but could no longer recapture the richness and abandon that used to be characteristic of our laughs together. We still laughed together but now seemed to stop just short of yielding ourselves totally to laughter. We still dreamed aloud before each other but now stopped short of exposing our innermost dreams openly to each other. One day, I tried to express to Stella the frustration I felt about not being able to give her what I felt was a full measure of the person I was—as a friend, as a husband, as a person.

"Later," she replied. "You will give to me later everything you're supposed to give to me."

"You think so?"

"I hope so. I believe I will be able to give you more also. This isn't me you are seeing right now."

"No?"

"No. When we were just friends, before I became pregnant, was I not a pretty good girlfriend?"

"Excellent," I replied.

"Remember the first time we slept together? It was not very good. In fact, the first few times were not very good. I believe that after we get over the shock and suddenness of this whole thing, we'll do it much better."

"You're so sensible," I said, and pulled her to me and kissed her.

We reminisced for a while about what kind of boyfriend and girlfriend we had been to each other and decided that if we could be that way as husband and wife we would be doing pretty well. The problem was that—I stated it and Stella agreed—events had descended on us very suddenly. As a young man or woman one looked forward to *someday* becoming married and *someday* having children. Each of these major events would be preceded by a period of preparation and anticipation. One would count off the days. In our case, *someday* had suddenly been overtaken by *already*. We were *already* married, *already* parents.

Stella sighed.

"What?" I asked her.

"Nothing," she said.

"What?" I insisted.

She sighed again and then said, "But if you are going overseas and I am not going with you, when will we get the chance?"

"Before I go and after I return," I replied. "We have a lifetime to be with each other." I did not sound convincing and Stella did not appear convinced. As time went on, I became cautious about telling her of new developments in my plans for overseas travel.

Our daughter, W'Orima, was born in early December.

In March, I won a university scholarship to study in the United States.

"I am sure you know the A.S.P. holds you up as what a proper young man ought to be, especially to our son, Mike, who is about your age, and who, as you know, has not done so well in school. He is glad you have married Stella. That is not something you will ever hear come out of his mouth, but I know it. He is not particularly happy with the way it happened, but since the baby has come, things do not look as bad as they did while Stella was pregnant. He believes that Stella will be overseas with you in a year or two. As for Mike, it is *tanda* at home for him here in Nigeria and see if he can pass one subject or two at Advanced Level GCE.

"So, what I am really saying is that in a way the A.S.P. has adopted you. You are a son-in-law who has become the son he would have preferred to have. If he cannot say, 'My son is going overseas,' he can say 'My son-in-law is going overseas with my daughter.' In a way it is good that he can say that; in another way, it isn't. It does not make Mike happy—mark you, not because of anything you have done, but because of the way he knows his father feels about you and him. It is like Jacob has stolen Esau's blessings. As for me, I am not altogether happy either. I like you, as you well know. I think you are a promising young chap who will go places. But I am also Mike's mother. Because of that I catch some of what he feels. Also because of that I catch some of what *Oga* feels about Mike. You see, fathers have a tendency to blame mothers for the failures of their children. If a son does well, he is his father's son. If he does badly, he is his mother's son. So, when the A.S.P. scolds Mike, I feel as if he is indirectly scolding me as well."

I was seated with Stella's mother in her parlor, I in the middle of the room at a table on which formal meals were served, she in an armchair against the west wall. It was Sunday and midmorning in August. The sun was shining brightly outside and streaming indoors through the open windows, whose curtains were pulled back. Succeeding waves of frying aromas filled the air, as the women prepared their Sunday dinners. Children scampered around the dwarf coconut trees and shouted at each other across the big compound.

Stella's mother, or Janet, or Maa—I had not settled on what to call her—was looking very beautiful in the new hairdo her hairdresser had given her the day before. She had bathed, dressed, and done her face as if she were going somewhere, except for leaving her hair uncovered, which of course added to her good looks rather than subtracted from them, since it had been so skillfully plaited. In fact, when I had first seen her that morning, I had teasingly whistled and said, "Miss *ebeh?*" and smiling she had replied that she was not going anywhere.

"But everything is not about you and Mike," she was now saying. "The A.S.P. and I have been married for almost twenty-three years now. When we married he had just come out of the Army, after World War II, in which he had made the rank of *sajin-major*. He was young, tall, darkly handsome, and a war hero from the jungle campaigns in Burma—educated too, which many of the ex-service men were not. I had just passed Standard Six myself, and in those days had looks that could manage to turn a few heads. . . ."

"You still do," I said. "You are a beautiful woman. I sometimes tease Stella about not being quite as beautiful as you."

"Thank you, but I think you did better than the A.S.P. in that department. You married the more beautiful one. Anyway, we had a church wedding at the C.M.S. Church, and I thought I was going to be a real missus all of my life, richly ensconced with a husband all to myself. Then I lost my first pregnancy to a miscarriage. Then a second one. After that, the A.S.P. decided to get another wife. That was like a slap in my face. Not that it was that unusual for a man even after a church wedding to get a second or even a third wife, but because of the way this happened I felt as if I had been found inadequate because of those miscarriages. So, Patience came as the second wife. Then Lilly as the third. Then I successfully carried Mike to full term, and when he turned out to be a boy, you cannot imagine the joy I felt. As first wife, I had also become the mother of the first son. Patience had Chidiadi a few months after Mike was born. Then Stella came, meaning that I was the mother of the first daughter also, as God would have it. I felt completely vindicated. I had given my husband a son and a daughter. But from then on, for some unknown reason, my womb closed, and I have not become pregnant again.

"Patience now has five children, three boys and two girls. Lilly has four, two and two. Angelina, the youngest, has three and is pregnant with her fourth. These younger women are still bearing and may still have three or four more children each. Me, I have become a grandmother, thanks to you and Stella. But even before W'Orima, I was made to feel like a grandmother by the way my husband and these younger women treat me. Mark you, they all treat me with respect, and I cannot truthfully accuse any of them, my husband or the wives, of ever insulting or disrespecting me. But sometimes I wish they did not respect me in the particular way they do. They treat me too much like an elder, as if I were their mother or mother-in-law. They compete among the three of them for whatever they think they can get out of their husband, but they don't count me in that competition. I have been relegated—do you understand what I mean? Relegated.

"It is a very difficult thing to explain, but one way to explain it is perhaps to recall something one of the national politicians, I believe it was Akintola, said not long ago about the new House of the Senate, which they are trying to create as part of the National Assembly.

Akintola said it would be a good place for *spent forces*, a sort of dozing gallery for elder statesmen. My husband and these other women treat me like an elder statesman. I am the senior wife, the wife of his youth, the one who knows him better than anyone knows him, the wife he confides in, the wife who holds the *awufu* money people give him. When he is angry and breathing fire, I know how to approach him and quench his fire. To others he may be a porcupine, but I know where his soft spots are and how to slip my fingers into them. About such things I feel good. My position is one of respect and privilege at home, and prestige among the women of the town. Because he uses the official car so much, I believe I drive his personal car even more than he does. I am the only one of the wives who can drive. The driver usually drives the others, and if I am around and the A.S.P. isn't, he asks me before he takes them anywhere. Whenever I emerge from that car, whether I am driving myself or whether the driver is driving me, and people whisper 'Mrs. Kamanu' or 'the A.S.P.'s wife,' I know they are talking about me and not about anybody else.

"With all that, what then is my complaint? Really, I have no complaint. My bread is buttered on all sides. I still get my turn to sleep with the A.S.P. The only trouble is I no longer see any fire in his eyes or in his blood for me. I have become the wife of comfort and solace, rather than of drive and passion, the wife of relaxation and 'take it easy.' He treats me as if I am too old for certain things, but I am not too old for anything!

"You see, for example, a man can come home for lunch, with nothing but regular business on his mind, but while he is eating or working with his papers, or whatever, a wife may pass by him in all innocence, but he may just happen to catch a slight shake of some part of the body, which suddenly excites his passion and makes him want to do something that will make him late for his two o'clock appointment. Well, that wife is no longer me. One of these other women maybe, especially Lilly, but not your mother-in-law. . . ."

She chuckled, and then the shadow of a blush moved across her face. She shook her head and said, "My God, what am I telling you? What has possessed me?"

Smiling, I replied that there must be a mark on me somewhere, which was drawing confidences out of people. I recalled for her that on my arrival several days before, Nne-nne had kept me up all night telling me things that were hard to believe a grandmother would tell a grandson.

"You are a good child, Ajuzia," she said, "and I like you. I think Stella has done very well to bring you into this family. You are a welcome addition to it, and I feel proud to call you my son-in-law

244 • T. Obinkaram Echewa

and my son. A few years down the road, when you have finished your schooling and the things you are now sowing begin to ripen for you, I believe you and Stella will make me happy. And the A.S.P. too."

"I hope so," I said. "I pray to God that it is so. I am sorry we started with a bump and a lurch, but I hope things will be smoother as we go along. I am surely happy that the A.S.P. is no longer angry with me and Stella."

"He was angry, yes, but even more than that, he was afraid. He had high hopes for Stella. You see, Stella became the bearer of his hopes when it turned out that Mike wasn't carrying them well. And then you came along and Stella became pregnant. Now, he sees you as carrying Stella even higher than she may have been able to go on her own. . . . Oh, Ajuzia, don't forget to write to your Mama when you get to the United States. And I don't mean asking Stella to say hello to me or enclosing a note for me in her envelope. I want my own letter. . . . By the way, what do you call me?"

"Mama!" I replied.

We both laughed.

"I had never heard you refer to me by any particular name, so I was wondering. I will gladly have you as my son."

"Thank you," I said. "I will gladly have you as my mother."

"What is this?" Stella said, walking into the room from the veranda. "Two of you professing love for each other?"

"Yes," I said, "and you can keep on walking. We are having a private conversation."

"Is W'Orima still asleep?"

"Yes," I said.

"Anyone check her, or have you been so deeply engrossed in this conversation?"

"She's fine," I said, "and my mother-in-law and I—I mean, my mother and I—were having a deep, personal conversation, which you interrupted. What did you buy in town? What's in the bag?"

"Can't tell you," Stella replied, sticking her tongue out at me. "Continue with your deep, personal conversation. Signal me when it is over."

Stella exited, and for several moments, her mother and I were not quite sure how to resume our conversation. At length she did begin:

"Idleness," she said, "having nothing to do, that is one of the things that is really tormenting me. I wake up in the morning and eat and take a bath and I have little to do except wait for it to be night again. The other women take care of most of the A.S.P.'s needs. The two young men in the servants' quarters do most of the things that need doing in the yard. If I need someone to run an errand, I can send one of them. So, my days are empty, and as days and weeks pass, I begin to feel that my whole life is empty."

I laughed.

"Really, it is no laughing matter."

"I am reminded of the folktale in which the tortoise goes to the seer and complains that he is bored with having too much good luck and asks if anything could be done to vary his luck a little."

She chuckled, slumped lower in her chair, and crossed her legs. "Well, maybe I am suffering from too much good luck. I am thankful to God for it, but still I feel an emptiness in my spirit. My children are grown. I have a husband who makes enough money to support me well. I don't have a farm to cultivate or a shed in the market to mind. Tell me," she said, her tone becoming earnest, "what would you think of my having a shed in the market?"

"Trading in what?"

"Cloth, most likely."

"Wonderful."

"You really think so?"

"Yes. It would be clean and not too hard. And fitting."

"Fitting?"

"For someone of your stature. A senior service wife. It would not be like selling pepper or crayfish or soap and kerosene."

"Aha," she said, beaming with pleasure. "It is interesting that you should say that." She paused thoughtfully, going over what I took to be reminiscences.

"Why don't you do it?"

"The A.S.P. is not in favor."

"You have mentioned it to him and he said no?"

"No, I have not mentioned it to him explicitly, and he has not said no explicitly. I hinted it and he hinted his disapproval."

"Do you know why he might object?"

"I think I do, but it may be a difficult thing to explain. It is one of those things you come to know by living with a person a long time. There may be no exact word for it, but fear comes the closest."

"Why would he be afraid of your trading?"

"Maybe it is not so much fear as that he is not comfortable with the idea. For one thing, it would change things in this compound, and if I am suggesting that things ought to be changed, that means that something is wrong with the way they are. You see, in twenty-three years I have been nothing but the A.S.P.'s wife. He said 'Heave!' and I said 'Ho!' In spite of what you have heard me say about these younger women he is married to, I am still the *isi-ekwe* and the *mboro* of his house. If I move or shift, the house will begin to shake and lurch. These younger women may be the soup and the meat, but your old mother-in-law is the *fufu*, the foundation."

"Your trading will not change that," I said, turning in my chair to face her more squarely. I had turned one of the dining chairs around and had been sitting sideways on it, with one elbow resting on it and my head supported in the palm of my hand. I now sat squarely facing her.

"It shouldn't, but then again who knows what might happen, what offspring that situation would be pregnant with? You see, with trading I will not be at home every day to keep an eye on this compound. I will be making my own money."

"I think maybe you are exaggerating his fears a little. I cannot imagine that he is that insecure about you. I mean, you are not going anywhere or doing anything untoward."

"You see, that is the mistake you make," she said with a laugh. "That is the mistake everyone has been making, including perhaps the A.S.P., about me. I am not going anywhere, you say with assurance. It is that business of the *spent force*, which I was talking about earlier. Or as the proverb says, running ground water that has run into a pit and has nowhere else to go. Your responsible mother-in-law—Mama-Mike or Mama-Stella as everyone calls me—will not do anything untoward, or even worse, is not capable of doing any such thing. I have been written off as too old and too responsible, such that if a rich and handsome man meets me in the street and in the market and says, 'How do you, *kwanu?*' my body and mind would be so dead that my fancy would not be tickled, even a little bit. But

I am not that dead yet. I am only forty-two years old. My mother was still having children at my age."

"But the A.S.P. must know that there is plenty of good wine left in this jar. Good, potent wine, not the cheap kind. The way you look today, and you are not even dressed at your best, if you were my wife I would not let you out of my sight."

"Perhaps he does know that there is a little wine left in this jar, and that may be why he does not want me to get a shed in the market. And as I have hinted it to him and he has hinted back his answer, if I bring it up again, he will begin to wonder why and perhaps will become offended. What he does not realize, though, is that I have entered the third age of my womanhood. From a little girl standing on the bank of the river, wondering what the water is like, I have dived in and swum around in the shallow as well as in the deep water and have made back to the bank again, where I can now sit and dry. I am now prepared to risk offending the A.S.P. a little bit. That is something new. In our time, girls were trained to please their husbands no matter what. Anything you did that did not please your husband was wrong. I do not really want to disobey or displease the A.S.P., but I cannot sit here day in and day out with nothing to do. I might as well sit in a shed in the market and make money. From time to time I will go to Y.A.C. and P.T.C. or G.B. Coquillards and buy some *juj* of the best kind, and cultivate senior service customers and the wives of the rich traders. Because of the A.S.P., I have met many women at the cocktail parties whose husbands are senior service people. I am also friends with the wives of the big traders, who may not be able to read or write but have rope girdles around their waists filled with money. I will have many good customers."

"I am sure," I concurred. "There will even be plenty of people who will want to befriend you and become your customers on the chance that you may drop a kind word to the A.S.P. on their behalf."

"Yes, even those too." Her face set, and she declared resolutely: "I will do it."

"What will you do, Mama?" Stella asked, walking into the room, cradling W'Orima in her arms.

"None of your business," I said playfully.

"Thief," she called me. *"Onye ohi!"*

"Thief yourself," I retorted. "What of yours did I steal?"

"You stole my father from everybody, and now all he says is Ajuzia this and Ajuzia that. Now you are trying so hard to steal my mother. Thief-man, you!"

"You forget the first thing I stole—your heart. After that, everything else was easy."

"Yeah," she said. "That's why you are such a thief-man."

I took her finger, the only part of her accessible, because of the way she was holding W'Orima, and pulled her toward me. She dropped W'Orima into her mother's outstretched arms and stood with playful cheekiness in front of me, pushing her face a few inches from mine. If her mother had not been there, looking at us, I would have kissed her, but as it is, all I said was, "Little girl, respect your elder."

"Little boy," she said, "where is my elder?"

"The two of you are really in love, aren't you?" the mother said, lifting her eyes from tickling W'Orima's cheeks.

"He specializes in making people like him," Stella said, as I pulled her against me and put my hand across her shoulders. "After that, well, anyway, I won't say more."

"There's nothing more to say," I said, "except to sing the song you sing to me all the time."

"What song did I sing to you all the time?"

"You have stolen my heart; don't go a-away. When you hear the little birds singing, they seem to say: You have stolen my heart . . ."

Singing that song, I steered Stella through the door into the next room.

During the days I spent with her before I left for Lagos and from thence to the United States, Stella was in a bad mood. She was irritable and inconsolable, and, having taken a week off from work, she had plenty of time to be that way and to let me know about it. Much of the time she cried; the tears rolled down her cheeks at the drop of a mischosen word from me. On the day before I left for Lagos, she was standing a short distance away from me in her mother's living room, watching me as I tried to squeeze one more thing into a suitcase.

"I am sure this is more than forty-four pounds," I said, trying to break the uncomfortable silence.

"I wonder," she said sometime afterward, but did not finish her sentence. Then she backed away from where she had stood over me and the suitcase and sank into a chair.

I looked up briefly at her and said, "You wonder?"

"Yeah," she said. "Why do they give you such a low limit? Someone leaving home and traveling to a foreign place. You have to take everything you own in the world and they say, 'keep it to forty-four pounds.' Why forty-four pounds, anyway?"

"I think it's twenty kilograms."

"Don't you think you should do your final packing here and not have to repack everything all over again in Lagos?"

"I will be in Lagos for two days. I am sure I will go into the suitcase for things like toothbrush and underwear."

"When you get to Lagos and start throwing things out, what will you throw out?"

"I have no idea. I have to wait and see."

"Perhaps some of these things I spent my time and money buying. None of them will reach America with you." Her voice was so doleful that I rose from my squat, stepped across the open suitcase, and sat on the arm of her chair. Laying my hand on her shoulder and pulling her against me, I kissed the side of her face, near the hairline. She remained unresponsive. When I let go of her, she resumed her previous pose of *The Thinker,* with her left hand under her chin and her elbow dug into her lap.

"Do you really like these photos?" I asked, as I stood up and picked up two framed enlargements of photographs of her and me and her and me and W'Orima, which were leaning against my flight bag.

"They are all right."

"I think they are terrific. As one would expect, you steal the show." I tugged playfully at her cheek. "W'Orima has your eyes exactly, and your mouth too." I pushed out my lips, pretending to simulate her mouth.

"Who has a mouth like that?" she asked peevishly.

"Right now, you," I said, pushing out my lips into a more exaggerated pout. "But I still love your mouth." I reached my face across her and kissed her. She received my kiss impassively. "This child looks so much like you," I said, "next one we have, I'll make sure I make a greater contribution."

She rolled her eyes at me. "We may never have another child."

"We'll have ten more children."

"Not me and you."

"How many then?"

"I am telling you, we have already had our last one. You will be away for at least four years."

"So? Who says we cannot have another baby after four years?"

"I may be gone by the time you return."

"Just let me catch you so much as looking at another man."

"What will you do?"

"Flog you well-well."

She laughed. "You won't be there to do anything. You will be in America, perhaps even jollying with American girls."

"Seriously, Stella, don't you think these photos are terrific?"

She wiped the back of her hand across her lips.

"Are you wiping off my kiss?" I asked, backing away from her in mock indignation. I kissed her again, saying, "Here! Since you wiped off the other one, here's another one."

"Since you don't seem to need my help," she said, "I think I'll go and lie down for a while. I am sleepy."

"Don't go, Stella. Stay with me."

"Just stay here and watch you?"

"Yes, stay here and admire me. Since you won't have me after tomorrow."

"You're telling me." She slumped down again into the chair and stretched out her legs to their full length in front of her and folded her hands across her chest.

"I will start working on a chance for you to come over as soon as I set foot in the United States. I swear to you."

"How can you do that? You cannot even tell the people you are married for fear they will take away your scholarship."

"I am not talking of the donors of my scholarship. America is full of universities and rich people who are careless with money. Someone will befriend me, or I will befriend someone. You do not even have to come over as my wife, so long as you come over."

"You see? That's what I told you."

"What?"

"That you cannot even let people know that I am your wife. Whose wife will I be?"

"Nobody's, as far as outsiders are concerned. You can travel in your maiden name."

"With a baby?"

"Oh," I said, remembering W'Orima. "Maybe after a year or so I can let the donors of my scholarship know that I am married."

"And they will say, 'When did you get married?' and 'To whom?' and 'Why didn't you let us know before you left Nigeria?' What will you reply then?"

"That I became married after I had filled out the scholarship forms—which is the truth. I did not lie on the forms."

"You are not going to tell anyone that you are married. You will think it is too risky."

"Come on, Stella, give me credit for being honest and decent. Am I a liar? Are you in effect saying that you cannot trust anything I tell you?"

"Oh, I trust you, Aju, but . . ."

"But what?"

She sighed, but did not otherwise offer a response. However, I eagerly pressed the issue. "But what?" I insisted.

"But you're a man."

"What is that supposed to mean?"

"Man come and man go. As you and I sit here and now, I believe you mean everything you say, but what about tomorrow? The reason you cannot now tell your donors you are married is not going to change until they are no longer your donors. And that will be at least four years. You will still be afraid of their taking away your scholarship next year and two years from now."

"No-no, umh-umh. That's not it. If I tell them now, that's it. I don't go at all. There are dozens of people on the standby list. But after I have already spent a year there, they will not be too inclined to send me home without letting me finish my course."

"Yeah," she said, her mood lightening a bit. "That's what the tortoise said to his wife, Ofai. 'Be patient, darling. The beehive is full of honey. I will suck the first two combs all by myself, and after that you and I together will enjoy the others.' And after the first two combs, there was no more honey."

I sighed. "Help me close this thing," I said. As she stood, I circled my arms around her and kissed her. It took a lot of caressing and stroking and fomenting before she began to thaw and respond. At length, though, her hands did awaken and rise up from her sides, one to my shoulder blade and the other to the back of my neck. Her lips warmed. Then she began crying.

Her mother walked into the room with a tray and two frosty bottles of Fanta. "I thought you people were busy packing," she joked, "but you are here kissy-kissy. How's the packing going? Can you get in everything?"

"Pretty much so, but I think I am very overweight."

"So, what are you going to do?"

"I don't know. I will probably repack in Lagos. There are still some things I want to buy."

"*Na waya-o*," she said. "What would you people like for supper? Aju, since you are going away, it is your choice. And Stella, since your sweetheart is leaving, you don't have to cook it. I know you want to spend all your time with him."

"Anything you cook tastes wonderful, Mom," I said.

"Flatterer. Stella, what about you?"

"Anything," Stella replied.

"All right," the mother said. "Carry on. And stop kissing so much." She turned to leave.

"It's not me, Mom. It's Stella. Tell her to stay away from me."

Stella rolled her eyes at me.

"*Na so*," the mother said skeptically as she exited.

"Just what am I supposed to do after you leave tomorrow?" Stella said with sudden, vehement umbrage, as soon as her mother was gone.

With that question, I knew that she had finally stuck a scalpel into the abscess. I did not answer, could not answer, as I finished snapping the suitcase shut and went and sat down on the chair beside hers. Trying to lighten the mood, I assumed a slumping posture identical to hers, and matched my breathing to hers, so that we lay like two fatigued farmers staring across the room at the opposite wall. Our chairs, which were identical, had wide armrests that formed a broad platform because of the way they were pushed together. Our arms lay side by side on that platform.

"Stella, my darling," I said.

She turned to look at me. Our eyes held. Then she sniggled.

"What?" I asked.

"What is this Stella-my-darling business? When did you start that one?"

"Just now," I chuckled and took her hand and interlocked our fingers. "You don't like it?"

"It sounds strange."

"You sound strange."

"I sound strange?" She turned to look at me without lifting her head off the cushion. "Well, forgive me for not being cheerful to see you go, but that still doesn't answer my question. What will I do after you go off to Lagos tomorrow, and while you are in America during the next year or two or three or four years?"

"I'll stay one year. Definitely not more than two."

"That's what you say. But anyway, what will I do for the next year or two?"

"Stella, at some point you have to start believing something. You have to believe me. It is not as if I am going to the United States on a holiday. I am going there to study. And the course I am taking will be difficult. The winters will be cold. It is a strange place that I am traveling to, and as the proverb says, neither my father nor my mother has ever been there to pave the way for me, so I don't know what dangers or problems I will face."

"I feel sorry for you. You will have such a hard time."

I laughed. "Oh, Stella, come on. Stop being so sarcastic, as if I have done something to offend you. You don't want me to go? I can unpack my suitcase and go outside and announce to everyone that I am no longer going, write to my donors and tell them to give my scholarship to someone else. Is that what you want? Then you and I can sit here and stretch out our legs and look at the walls together, till we grow old. And our children can eat grasshoppers. Is that what you want?" I repeated the question: "Is that what you want?" and squeezed her fingers a little, then sat up in my chair so as to face her more squarely. I wanted to squeeze a concession out of her.

"No, that's not what I want," she conceded, but almost immediately she reversed herself. "That is what I want. I want to be together with you, but I am not supposed to want that. If you went out and announced that you are no longer going overseas because of your wife, people would laugh at you. You would be the talk of this whole town. And so would I. Even my own parents would not side with me. In fact, they, more than others, will think I am out of my senses."

"Most girls in your position would feel proud and excited and would go about shaking everyone's hand and announcing it around town: 'My husband is about to *sail*. I will be joining him in a year.' The situation we're in is very common among people who go overseas. No one goes with the wife at the same time. It's always the husband first, and then after he has been there for a while, the wife goes to join him."

"Sometimes," Stella said heavily. "Sometimes, I remember the case of Mrs. Ejiogu who used to teach at our school. Her husband stayed and stayed, and every year she was supposed to go over and join him, something happened and she couldn't go. And her two children were always being sick."

"Did she eventually go to join him?"

"No. He married someone else while he was over there, and had two children with this American woman before she found out anything. So while she was at home suffering and waiting, her husband was jollying in the United States with another woman."

"For your sake, Stella, I will make sure I don't enjoy my stay in the United States. I will suffer all the time."

"Silly."

"Well, that's what you want, isn't it?"

"No, that's not what I want. I just want you to promise me that you won't forget me when those American Negresses come flocking to your room. Or even the White girls. I have heard that they are all smiles from the very first time they see you, and even at the airport, if you simply say hello to them, they will be ready to follow you to your room and do anything you want. Have you not heard the same things?"

"Yes, I have heard some of the same things, but they are all travelers' tales. Mere *tori*. I am sure they are not true. And besides, look at these two photos." I stood up and retrieved them and held them up to her face. "What other girl can I find to compare with the one I already have? You are *ofe ukazi*; beside you any other girl would be tasteless *okpoko*! I will put these photographs on my desk, and more important, I will carry them in my heart everywhere I go. Don't worry. If anyone looks at me, the sign will say Occupied!"

"That is what you say now while you are in my presence. But they say those girls don't care about anything. Even if you are wearing a wedding ring, they will take it off your finger and put it in your pocket, and if you have a photo on your desk, they will turn it facedown. Anyway, you may not even take these photos with you. I notice that you have not put them in your suitcase."

"Silly. I will carry them in my flight bag. I did not want the glass broken when I start mashing on the suitcase to lock it."

"If you put them on your desk, won't your donors see them?"

I had not thought about that before. "Uuumh," I said. "Maybe I will not display the one with W'Orima."

"You see? That's what I said."

"No-no-no!" I heard myself saying. "I will not hide either of my girls. If they want to take their scholarship, they can take it! Oh, Stella," I heard myself cry desperately. "Stella, believe me at least a little bit. Give me some credit. I love you. You are a star, my Stella, or Sitella, as Nne-nne calls you, who has lit up my life recently. We have a beautiful daughter who also has the mark of a star on her forehead. Everything is wonderful—really. It may not seem that way, but it really is, if you stop to think about it. I realize that so many things have come upon us suddenly—marriage, W'Orima, and my going overseas—but we will be all right on the long run. You have heard the proverb about the itch and the fingernail . . ."

"You don't even know half the story," Stella said, when I was finished.

"Tell me," I said.

And so she began telling me about *Stella's Grief*. I could say that I had the same or similar grief, but I was a man, so how could I? Besides, whatever I felt, whatever I was capable of feeling as a man, was overcome by the excitement of my being about to go overseas. As for Stella, in a little over a year, she had sat for and passed School Cert, become pregnant, endured the wrath of an implacable father, married, and had a baby. And now, her husband was about to leave her for one or two or up to four years—maybe even forever—just as she was getting ready to enjoy the first samplings of marital bliss.

Suddenly I heard Nne-nne's voice behind my ears explaining *Woman's Grief* to me, in this case Stella's. No matter how a man and a woman got together, whether he seduced her or she him or whether they jointly seduced each other, it was the woman, not the man, who became pregnant. The snuffbox of *grief* belonged to the woman, not the man. A man could take a pinch of snuff, apply it to his nostrils, and sneeze in profound catharsis, but in the end, he returned the snuffbox and its contents to the woman. The woman stored the box. The baby at birth suckled off her breast and stayed with her. The man was always free to come and go as he chose, and nothing limited him except his own willingness to stay. A woman did not have the same choices. A woman never left. Could I imagine, for example, that she, Stella, would leave me and W'Orima while she went overseas? No, if parenthood was a funeral, then a man was only a guest mourner. He wailed a bit, maybe quite a bit, and then he wiped his eyes and went home. If grief came in a trough, a man took as much of it as would adhere to a dipstick; the woman took the whole trough.

Stella's grief was overwhelming for her, and ultimately for me. I never felt so bad, so guilty for having succeeded at something. Even as we lay in bed later that night, every argument I made, everything I said, corroborated her sentiments and made them more poignant. I was severely pained by her disconsolateness and appealed to her with every ounce of sentiment I could muster.

"Stella," I said, "we used to be friends before we became married, very good friends. You were on my side in a world that seemed against me. You were thoughtful, kind, and considerate. More than anyone else you helped me through the problems my grandfather and I were having with Chief Orji. When I was about to lose hope you encouraged me. On your own, you talked to your mother and father about me, and it was because of that, because of what your father did, that we were able to get Orji to leave us alone. That is, or was, you, Stella, as I remember you. You were my friend. You made my heart sing, whistle, and dance at the same time.

"I grant that we did not get married under the best auspices, but I think that was because we were both driven by the same love and passion for each other. I believe we can still make the best of what may now appear to be a bad situation. We are married. We have a daughter. I am going overseas and leaving you behind, that is true, but would you prefer for me to stay a clerk at the brewery for the rest of my life? That way you and I can stay together and never be separated and be like so many people you see all over this town living with six children in two rooms? I am trying to improve myself—for us—for you and me and W'Orima and all the other children we will have."

"I love you, Ajuzia," she said, tucking her head more snugly into the crook of my arm. "I am still your friend. I never had too many so-called boyfriends. You know I was a virgin until you came along. You were everything to me—brother, confidant, everything. I was drunk with feeling for you, and all that before we ever did anything. You remember I told you afterward that our going to bed left me confused and disappointed and somewhat angry. I wished I could rewind the clock and go back to the moment before it happened. It even seemed to take away from the depth of my feelings for you. And then I became pregnant. And then there was my father and mother. Passing School Cert with a good grade and aggregate. Getting my first job, receiving my first salary, and presenting it to my father— the joy of these things was overshadowed by my pregnancy. I had to resign from my job as soon as my belly began to protrude. My father banished me from this compound, and I had to go to the village to stay with my mother's sister. Even there, I isolated myself to keep from answering the questions people asked me.

"So anyway, we were married, a kind of *patch-patch* marriage, but we were married. Our daughter is beautiful and was not born a bastard. I look at her and a smile breaks out on my face. She is a miracle. Rearing her will be a joy or a burden to me—whichever it is, it is something I would have preferred to share with you, but you are leaving in the morning and I will have to bear that burden or relish that joy all by myself. What we have is a load you and I picked up together. It would have been best if you continued to hold one end while I held the other. As it is now, you are saying to me, 'Hold both ends till I come back.' Whether you are going to ease yourself or buy food and drink for both of us, the fact is that I am going to have to carry this load all by myself until you return. And anything can happen to delay your return.

"That does not mean that I am against your going overseas. It is just that I feel two ways about it. One part of me is glad that you are going. Another part is sad because I will miss you, my husband, to whom I have just begun to become attached these last few months since W'Orima was born and my father stopped being so angry. I have started to feel about you again the way I felt in the beginning, on all those Saturday and Sunday afternoons when I used to sneak out of school and visit your flat. Do you remember?"

"Yes, I remember."

"Tell me something. If I had not become pregnant, would you still have married me?"

"Yes, of course I would have married you. Maybe not right away, but definitely later."

"If you did not marry me now, you would never have married me."

"How do you know?"

"A feeling."

"Another thing that only women can feel?"

"No, it's like in *Julius Caesar*. A tide in the affairs of men."

"Nonsense. You do not believe even that I love you?"

She grunted "H'm," as if she could not automatically give me a full measure of assent, but could on further consideration concede that perhaps, just perhaps, I loved her. "You probably loved me as much as you are capable of loving, but you are a man."

"Meaning that men don't love?"

"Men love but not as deeply as women. That's what I have been trying to explain to you." She felt the vaccination scar on my arm, and chose to use it as an illustration. "It is like this here," she said, referring to the scar. "Yours is very small. Mine is large and deep."

"Did you read all of this somewhere? One of those books the hawkers sell on the edge of the market? What we are having sounds like what you hear in those boring English love films—ouch!"

She had pinched me very hard. "I am quite serious, Aju."

"In that case, you ought to talk to Nne-nne."

"Why?"

"You and she have been reading the same book about *Woman's Grief.*"

"You think it is a joke?"

"I don't know what it is but I am sure women are not the only ones with *grief.*"

"Suppose I die, or you die, how will you remember me?"

I shrank, then bolted away from her, jumped out of bed, and turned on the light. Then I stood looking down on her. "What is the matter with you?"

She did not answer. Her eyes were closed, perhaps because of the light, perhaps with grief. A large tear was making a slow track across the bridge of her nose toward the other eye. At the opposite end of the same eye, I saw the shadow of an earlier tear track going in the opposite direction toward her ear. I sat down on the edge of the bed and picked up one of her hands and then laid my other hand gently on her face. With an index finger, I began to erase the tear track from her temple. I tried to pull her up and place her head on my lap but she made no effort to help me. Instead, she curled into a tight, fetal knot.

"I thought I should have been happy to be going overseas," I said at length.

"You should."

"And all my friends, as well, should have been happy, especially my wife."

"I am."

"You are happy?"

"Yes."

"A funny way you have of showing happiness."

"Believe me, I am happy, but it's mostly when I am not with you. In your presence, all I can think of is the fact that you are going away. But believe me, I am happy." She patted my hand. "Turn the light off and lie down. You have to travel in the morning."

"I don't like your implying that I don't love you."

"I am sorry."

"But you still think it is true."

"Yes."

My prolonged silence caused her to open her eyes.

"Look at that beautiful daughter of ours," I said. "I suppose that as soon as she learns to talk she'll be telling me about *Woman's Grief* and all the other things I do not understand about women."

Stella tittered. "Probably," she said, and moved close against me as soon as I lay down. She thrust both her legs between mine, threw both arms around my neck, sighed with frustration for not being able to make the degree of *contact* with me that she seemed to crave. The tangle in which she had both of us was exceedingly uncomfortable, choking as a matter of fact. We both realized this at the same time and burst out laughing as we tried to untangle.

"You know what I am most afraid of about your going?"

"What?"

"That I will be a misfit everywhere, without you."

"You will never be a misfit anywhere."

"I want to be with you, Aju. I want to walk beside you, sit and lie down beside you, go with you to dances and films. I want to experience being a wife. Your wife. I just became a wife, but before I can really experience what it is like to be a wife, my husband is gone. If anyone asks me, 'How is married life?' I still cannot answer. And I keep asking myself: 'What will I be the day after you leave?' "

The following day I left for Lagos and from thence to the United States, where I was for the next five years. Much happened in that time.

10

Civil and Domestic Wars

"AH, AJUZIOGU, IS THIS REALLY YOU, or am I dreaming?"

"Nne-nne, it is really me."

"Ah! So you have come. I am very happy you have come. I knew you would come."

"Yes, Nne-nne, it is me. How do you feel?"

"I feel just fine. Just fine. God in heaven, I had almost started to despair. I was like a diver underwater, holding my breath and holding my breath, not knowing how much longer I would have to hold it." She was gasping now, as if in fact holding her breath. It was coming in short shallow spurts, not deep enough to sustain more than a few words at a time. "Bend over more so I can touch your face."

I had been standing beside her bed holding her hand. Stella shoved a chair under me, and I sat down. Then I lowered my face to her unsteadily reaching hand, and she grasped at it with the tips of her fingers and the heel of her hand, unable to straighten out the fingers because of her rheumatism.

"You have grown whiskers," she said. "I can feel the roughness on your face."

"I need a shave," I said. "I have been traveling now for a couple of days."

"Is that not a wonder, how far away you were and you could still come back? Did you fly in an aeroplane?"

"Yes."

"It is truly a wonder. I cannot trust my eyes anymore, but I believe your complexion is lighter. Do you not also think so, Eze-Nwanyi?" She wished to include Stella in the conversation.

"Yes," Stella agreed. "It probably comes from not spending too much time in harsh sunlight."

"I see. The sun is not strong in America?"

"Not as strong as it is here," I said.

"I am glad you are here, Ajuziogu. I am very glad." She exhaled. "You cannot imagine how happy I am." A smile broke out on her face, now pure leather, dark, pallid, and deeply furrowed. Her eyes had lost their sparkle; more than that, they had lost their earnestness, their zeal. They sat in their sockets without enthusiasm behind several folds of wrinkles. Even her teeth, which used to be as much a bragging point as her breasts, were gone.

She clasped both her hands around my right hand, squeezing my knuckle from time to time, feeling each of my fingers in turn. "You must be tired," she said after a while. "You have traveled a long way. Eze-Nwanyi, is there no food?"

"Yes, as soon as he finishes greeting you."

"He has greeted me enough for now. Give him something to eat and bathwater to wash off the dust of the road from his body. He can greet me more later. I am not going anywhere. All I wanted was just to set eyes on him one more time. *Obasi ndi n'igwe!* I thank you and I thank you. *Ndewo!*" A smile overcame her face, and as I looked at her, I was overcome by the same smile. Then she began crying. Tears appeared in the corners of her eyes and rolled down her cheeks. I shook my head to chase away my own feelings, a strange mixture of sadness and joy, which was squeezing my heart with rough, gnarled fingers.

"Nne-nne, I am glad to be home," I said.

"I am glad you are home, Ajuziogu. Have you come to stay?"

"Ah . . ." I began.

Stella kicked me in the leg before I could complete my answer.

"Ah, yes," I said, understanding Stella's signal. "Yes."

"That is good. That is very good." She exhaled heavily. "I can then breathe easy. You see, I told you I would let nothing happen to me until you returned. Have I not kept my promise?"

"You have, Nne-nne. You have. And nothing is going to happen to you anyhow. Especially now that I am here."

"Aaah. Go and wash and eat. Then come back and tell me everything that has happened to you while you were in America. Everything you have seen and done. No, you do not have to tell me all of that this evening. I can wait until tomorrow. You have a wife and child who have not seen you in years. How many years has it been now?"

"Five."

"God in heaven, that is a long time. So, talk to them tonight. Let tonight be their night. You and I can talk in the morning when the light is bright and I can really feast my eyes on you. Give him his food now, Eze-Nwanyi. What have you prepared for him?" As Stella drew in her breath and did not answer promptly, Nne-nne said, "Something special, I am sure. You are a good girl. Ajuziogu, I want you to know that she is of the best kind. You could not have married better. And her father and mother are the kindest people in the world. I never knew that rich people could have such kind hearts. Now the two of you go on and greet each other. If you let me, I could go on talking until the cock crows. Go on, and I will talk to you later."

"I am pregnant," Stella said, without preamble. It was a statement she seemed to want to make and be done with.

"So I see," I said, plumping down on a dusty chair beside a table. From the first time I had seen her as I stepped out of the taxi, I had wondered about the roundness of her waist and her seeming lack of enthusiasm for me.

Stella drew the other chair away from the table, as if symbolically to put some distance between us, pushed it roughly against the wall, and then sat down on it with the squarish composure of a young schoolgirl who had been recently admonished to sit like a lady. She even took care to pull the hem of her jumper dress over her knees.

I took slow measure of her: Her hair was in long thin plaits tied with black thread and swept to the side of her face so that it hung over her brow like the brim of a hat. The hairdo was elegant but some weeks old; the plaits were no longer smooth; their ends were

tufted. She had not done anything special to beautify herself in anticipation of my return. No makeup. Her eyes were sad, her gaze distant,
her face tired and distressed. Pregnant women usually go through
stages of beauty and ugliness, beginning with beauty in the early
months when their bodies respond to a tide of new hormones and
their glowing skins inform knowledgeable people of their new state,
and then a later stage of ugliness at about four or five months,
when their faces become pudgy and pimpled and their bellies begin
to curve outward, their legs look thinner, their buttocks sucked
up, and their posture tilted. Stella was in the early phases of the
latter stage.

"Is that all you are going to say?" she asked after a long period of
silence. She seemed to be smarting for a fight, as if I had somehow
offended her and she wanted to have it out with me.

"What is there to say? You said you're pregnant, and I said 'I
see.' "

"Aren't you going to ask me anything about it?"

"No, I am not interested in anything about it right now."

She breathed out heavily, stared at me for several moments, then
said, changing gear, "Would you like to eat first or take a bath first?"

I sighed. "Right now, I just want to rest and collect my thoughts.
Whichever I do it would have to be later. How is W'Orima?"

"She was at school when I left home this morning. I thought of
keeping her out for the day, but then I decided against it. I'll have
her stay home tomorrow. . . . Did you have a good flight?"

"Yes. Long, but otherwise okay. I have been traveling for thirty-
six hours."

"You must be tired."

"Yes."

"I have made some *uha* soup as well as some rice stew with chicken.
Which would you prefer?"

"Right now neither. I thought I told you already that I am not
hungry." I noticed the edge in my voice.

"You ate on the plane?"

"Nibbling at this and that. Perhaps I will eat something later."

"As long as you are here and can stay through the night with your
grandmother, I think I will return tonight to Agalaba Uzo."

I thought I detected some tentativeness in her voice, perhaps an
invitation for me to argue her decision and persuade her to change

her mind, but I had no desire to do anything about her right then. I wished simply that she would go away, just disappear for a while so I could think and make up my mind about things.

"You have been staying here?" I asked, looking over at the cot in the corner, which was covered with bedding that belonged to her.

"Off and on. I have tried to be here every other day after work. Sometimes I stayed overnight."

I sighed and felt a wave of anger wash over me. Then another wave. Then another. I wanted to be elsewhere, anywhere else, far away from this scene. I wanted to turn back the clock, erase the reality before me and reorder it. Most of all, I wanted to scream at Stella—not in anger but in frustration. I wanted to shout: Stella! Why have you done this? Why? Why? Why? Why have you spoiled everything? Why couldn't I find you in a state such that I could reach out to you as I am dying to do now, and embrace you and hold you tight, and pour myself out to you and meld with you?

Sitting in the plane, I had been washed over by two alternating waves, one of fear that Nne-nne would be dead before I reached home and the other an anticipation of being reunited with Stella.

Stella sighed, stood up, and took a couple of steps toward me, then lost her nerve and just stood there awkwardly looking at me. I felt the warmth of tears sliding down my cheeks and was surprised and stood up and went to the door, turning my back on her, ashamed that I was not handling the situation adroitly. I could not bear to touch Stella—in fact, I felt repulsed by the very idea. I could not touch her *at all* because I could not touch her as deeply as I would have wanted to touch her, that is, to the innermost depths of her being. I could not embrace her *at all* because I wanted to be able to embrace her totally, as it were, to absorb her totally into myself, even as I yielded myself totally to her. No half measures. This was not altogether a sexual longing, for at this moment sex was the farthest thing from my mind. What I felt was deeper, older, and more primordial. Staring into the darkening yard, at the birds in the *ube* trees, I imagined myself embracing her, and then unable to abide the image, I shoved it forcefully away, though not before I had noticed that even if I should be willing, the curvature of that pregnancy would have prevented me from hugging her as tightly as I would have wanted. How could I throw my hands around another man's pregnancy? Anger washed over me as I recalled feeling the solid bulge of her belly against mine when on first seeing her I had thrown out my hands and hugged her tightly. Yet, she looked so desirable! A mature and settled beauty! Or as the old women said, a young woman who had come into control of her body and her beauty. When I had last seen her five years before, she had been luxuriant but mostly budding. Now, she was a settled beauty, despite her pimply face and pudgy skin.

"How could you do this, Stella?" I screamed, whirling around to confront her. "You have spoiled everything! Everything! My God, what a homecoming! What am I supposed to do?" Despite my outcry, my chest was exploding from emotions I could not fully articulate. I was being cheated. This could have been one of the happiest occasions of my life, and I was being denied it!

Wiping her eyes, Stella walked off to the next room to attend to something Nne-nne wanted. Just then I picked up the sounds of an approaching car. Headlight beams slashed through the ensuing darkness at the front gate of the compound. A horn beeped to announce an arrival. Stella came out of Nne-nne's bedroom, and I turned to look at her. "Are you expecting someone?"

"It's probably Mama," she replied.

Just then, I heard the voice of a little girl, and my heart jumped. "W'Orima!"

"*Kpaa! Kpaa! Kpaa!*" Mama-Stella said, mimicking the sound of a door clapper. I ran out to meet them and swept W'Orima into my arms.

"Hey, Aju, my traveling man," Mama-Stella hailed joyfully.

I switched W'Orima to one hand and offered Mama-Stella my free hand for a shake.

"You and who go shake hand?" she said in mock annoyance, brushing aside my hand. I put W'Orima down and offered Mama-Stella an embrace. She made it deep, full, and long. "Welcome home, my dear man. We missed you. You look well cared for."

"Thank you. You look well cared for too."

"A little lumpy here and there," she said, patting herself on the hips, "but that is the result of the easy life. Otherwise I have been trying to care for these old bones before old age catch me for well-well."

"You look terrific."

"So do you. Even with your beard-beard. Everyone has been missing you so. Talk to this little girl here because she has been worrying me night and day. Everytime a plane passes by, she points to the sky and says: 'That's my daddy coming home!' Or, 'That is the aeroplane I am flying to America to be with my daddy!' No other child is allowed to own an aeroplane. They all belong to W'Orima, and she is going to fly them to America to see her daddy. W'Orima, here is the daddy!"

W'Orima grinned and put a finger to her mouth and began to stare upward into my face. I picked her up again to get a better look at her and give her a chance to observe me from closer quarters. "How are you, W'Orima? How are you?"

"I am fine," she said with great propriety.

"Do you know who I am?"

"Yes."

"Who am I?"

She felt my nose and my cheeks and other parts of my face and beard. "You are my daddy," she then said.

"Yes," I said, filled with a kind of pleasure I had never known before, and filled so full of it that it seemed to well up in my stomach and chest, all the way up to the back of my throat. "You are my girl."

"You have a beard now," she said. "In your photo that I saw, then you did not have a beard."

"That's right. I grew a beard since that photograph was taken."

"I am not afraid of your beard."

"No, you should not be."

"One of the A.S.P.'s friends, Mr. Onwukwe, has a big beard-beard," Mama-Stella said. "She used to run away and hide every time Mr. Onwukwe came to visit."

"I am not afraid of my own daddy," W'Orima said, grabbing a handful of hair on my chin.

"Stella, how *kwanu?*" the mother called out, attempting to include her in the camaraderie.

"Why don't you all come inside," Stella responded, standing in the doorway with the kerosene lantern she had just lit, "instead of standing out there as food for the mosquitoes."

Her mother chuckled. "Where you see mosquitoes in the middle of the harmattan?"

"They are out there," Stella retorted. "You closed shop early?"

"Yes. I was eager to see Aju, and of course you-know-who kept asking me if it wasn't time to go yet." She eyed W'Orima.

"New car," I commented.

"Yes. I treated myself to that last Christmas."

"Congrats. It is very nice. Talk of people who have arrived."

"Arrived my eye. *Okpara n'ereh-ereh, asi na ona'ha nmanu!*" [While the cricket is burning, people are talking of the delectable juice coming from it!]

"But business is good in the shop, not so?"

"Pretty good, but patch-patch is all we do. Prices keep going higher and higher, but still we manage as we can."

"*Na waya-o!* You look like a million. How's the A.S.P.?"

"He's fine. He doesn't like retirement, but he's fine. He says hello."

As we sat down, visitors began to arrive, the first of them De-Odemelam, my grandfather's ageless, ancient friend. Mama-Stella had a case of Heineken in the trunk of her car, as well as a bottle of White Horse whiskey. After offering his initial greetings, De-Odemelam returned to his compound, and soon afterward pots of food and jars of palm wine began arriving from his sons and his son's wives. Word circulated that I was home, and, late as it was, the entire village came out to greet me. A log fire was built in front of my grandmother's house, and chairs were set around it. Palm wine, *eti-eti,* and of course the beer that Mama-Stella had brought began to flow.

I was ill at ease, overwhelmed, confused, and out of touch. Tired. The fatigue of several days' travel lay on my neck and shoulders like a sack of gravel. I had received Mama-Stella's cablegram on the twenty-first, used the twenty-second to prepare, and then set out on the twenty-third. Reaching London on the twenty-fourth, I found that my flight to Lagos had been canceled. The crew of the British airline, I was told, did not wish to spend Christmas in Nigeria. As a result, I spent Christmas at Heathrow Airport.

In addition to my physical fatigue, Stella's pregnancy sat on my chest like a block of stone. Luckily, she had arranged with her mother to stay out of sight, her mother explaining to all who inquired that she wasn't feeling too well and was lying down. I had a sense of enduring the visitors who had come to make me welcome—their long

speeches, their petulant insistence that I greet each of them individu-
ally with a little story or tailor-made reminiscence. And then there
were all the things I had left behind in the States, most notably my
Ph.D. qualifying examinations, which I had been scheduled to take
in mid-January, and which would now have to be postponed. To
compound these, I was plagued by a sense of personal inadequacy. I
did not feel at home or at ease. I was out of my element, a stranger
among these people who were supposed to be my people. I needed to
be told how things were in the village and country and where things
were in the compound and in the kitchen. This was supposed to be
my compound, since I was now the last surviving male in my line of
people. To all of these people, who were making me welcome and
treating me with the type of kindness and hospitality reserved for
strangers, I should have been a host and not a guest. But in truth, I
was a guest and a visitor, with my most important belongings packed
in two unopened suitcases tagged for travel. And if I was out of my
element here, if I felt as if I did not belong here, it was because I
was out of my element everywhere and really belonged nowhere. What
was left of me back in the United States was very disposable—furniture and utensils I had acquired from thrift stores, my books, and a
framed diploma on a wall. That was all.

My heart flushed suddenly as I stumbled over the thought that
there was no absolutely compelling reason why I had to return to the
United States. When my blood simmered down and I took cold measure of this thought, I was struck by its cogency: Indeed, if something
happened to make it impossible for me to return, there was really
nothing, really no reason why I had to. I began to wonder why I was
so frightened by this thought, why I was so reluctant to grapple with
it, as if I wanted to hide the ultimate conclusion from myself. I knew
that people would ask me that question over the next several days:
"Are you going back?" I knew also what my answer would be and
how unsatisfactory my interrogators would find it—my books, my
diploma, my continuing Ph.D. studies in faraway Philadelphia against
everything else that now stood physically and mentally around me.
Returning to America would be like flight, an abdication. On the
other hand, the thought of staying permanently at home at this junc-
ture of my life filled me with dread. I was still preparing for life. I
wasn't yet ready to start living.

Most of the village people who came that evening did not tarry. *Izodu ukwu* is what they called this first visit. They all promised to return the following day for a fuller and more proper visit.

"I better be going," Mama-Stella said sometime after the others had gone. "I will see *all of you* tomorrow."

"Bye-bye, Mama-*ukwu*," W'Orima said. "Bye-bye."

"I'll be going with you," Stella said.

"Oh," Mama-Stella said, as if her daughter's statement had taken away her breath. Her gaze turned from Stella to me, as if she wanted me to contradict or appeal the statement.

"I am very tired," I said.

"I want to stay with Daddy," W'Orima said, slipping into the gap between my knees as I sat on the edge of my chair. I linked my arms around her.

"If you get hungry," Stella said, gathering her things from the bed, "the food I mentioned earlier is in the pots. You want me to warm it for you before we leave?"

"No, I'm sure I can manage."

"When was the last time you made a fire?" Mama-Stella interjected with a chuckle. "You realize it is not just a matter of lighting a gas or electric cooker?"

"Pour a little kerosene on wood and light a match," I said. "I have not forgotten."

"There is water in the drum outside," Stella instructed. "This area still has no water. You have to buy it in tins."

"I will bring some in the boot of my car when I come tomorrow," Mama-Stella said. "Is there an empty can I can take with me?"

"No, I don't think so," Stella replied firmly.

"I'll buy one in the market then," Mama-Stella said. She turned sharply and stared at her daughter. "Stella, I think you should stay."

"No," Stella replied.

"Aju?" Mama-Stella said, facing me squarely, inviting me to express a wish.

"Maybe not," I said.

"All right," she said conclusively. "*Oya* we go then. We'll see you tomorrow. You have no transportation and no supplies. I'll come for you tomorrow, so we can go shopping together. Besides, I want to show you off to my friends in the market to whom I have been bragging about you." She stopped to take stock of her thoughts. "I was going to suggest that maybe we could all go back to Agalaba Uzo tomorrow, including your grandmother, but I realize she will not agree. You don't know what a time we had with her before she would consent to leave this compound and go to the hospital. And you are not too eager to go with us either."

"Not right now," I said. "Let's talk tomorrow, okay?"

"Okey-doke. Stella, are you ready?"

"Yes."

"I want to stay with my daddy," W'Orima said, looking appealingly at Stella.

"Not tonight," Stella replied. "You have to go to school tomorrow."

I saw W'Orima's face fall, as I rose to verify that the faint voice I had heard was my grandmother calling me. I went to her room and asked her how she felt.

"I feel fine," she replied. "I just want to let you know that your Sitella is still your Sitella, no matter what. Do you hear what I say?"

"I hear you, Nne-nne."

As I returned to the room, W'Orima stretched out her hands to me, and I picked her up. "I will see you in the morning, okay?" I comforted her, kissing her on the forehead.

"Okay," she said reluctantly. "I am going to America with you."

All of us walked to the car. Stella and her mother got into the front, W'Orima by herself in the back. The car started noisily, as Mama-Stella mashed down heavily on the accelerator. "Ntufuru driver!" I called out jokingly to lighten the heavy atmosphere. The lights came on. Mama-Stella reversed, peering into the darkness and making a joke about knocking down some trees. Everyone waved, and then I watched the red taillights until she turned the corner.

As I turned around to return to the house, I noticed the dimness of the hurricane lamp I was carrying and the enormousness of the surrounding darkness. This was darkness as I had not seen it in years, for such did not exist in America. America had little mystery. Everything in it was brightly illumined, even the ghettos of North and West Philadelphia.

"Ajuziogu," Nne-nne called, as soon as I entered the outer room. I walked into her room and sat down on the chair beside her bed.

"I am very happy you have returned," she said. "Very happy."

"I am happy to be home, Nne-nne," I said. "I wish you were not ill."

"At my age, a person keeps daily company with illness."

"Do you hurt anywhere?"

"Everywhere and nowhere. Now it is here. Then it is at another place. One moment the pain is not too sharp. Another moment it is unbearably sharp. But you should not mind me, even if you should happen to hear me grunting. Seeing you makes me forget all of my pains. Are you really happy to be home?"

"Yes, Nne-nne."

"*Ogom nwanyi* sent you a wire message, did she not?"

"Yes."

"That is what I thought, even though she denied it to me and tried to tell me that you were coming home on your own. Well, anyway, she meant well, and you are home. She is a good woman. They are a good family that you married into, even the father. His face is not very welcoming but his heart is kind. All of them have come here many, many times to see me. About two weeks ago, they took me to the hospital. I was not sure I would make it then, and I was crying because I thought I would not be able to see you again or keep my promise to you. And then I did not want to leave the compound empty while I was in the hospital, until I realized that if I died, it would be empty anyhow. That is really when I began crying. Eze-nwanyi stayed here with me that night. All night, she stayed up watching over me. I do not believe she slept even one wink.

"Did your studies and other things go well while you were in America?"

"Yes."

"You did well in your bookwork?"

"Yes."

"That is good. You always did well in your bookwork, though. I prayed for you every day, asking God to be with you and to protect you and guide you. You were a motherless, fatherless child in a foreign land, many, many miles away from where you were born. Only God could protect you. I am sorry you had to leave in the middle of the things you were doing to rush home. But you are going back after a short while, so it should not be too difficult to rejoin things where you left them."

"I am not sure, Nne-nne, when I am going back, or even whether I am going back at all."

"Uummmh," she grunted deeply, and then attempted to smile. "You do not have to lie to me, Ajuziogu. You came so quickly after you were sent for that I am sure you did not have time to say a proper good-bye to the people with whom you were staying. If you have lived in a place for five years, you do not leave it in one day in response to a *gbata-gbata* message, and not expect to go back and say proper good-bye to your friends. I know you are trying to make me feel better, but I can assure you that I feel very good already just to see you, just to know that that time five years ago when I said good-bye to you would not be the last time. I did not want to die surrounded by strangers. Apart from that, I had no anxieties about meeting death. I have no anxieties now, in case you are thinking that I am worried about what you will do after I am dead. No. That now is up to you. You are now a man and have grown into adulthood. There is only one thing that troubles me, and it has to do with Eze-Nwanyi, about her condition. You have noticed?"

"Yes, I noticed, and she has also told me."

"Why did you not ask her to stay here with you tonight, so that you and she and W'Orima could be all here tonight? That really would have pleased me."

"She did not want to stay, Nne-nne."

"Did you ask her?"

"No. Her mother asked her, and she refused."

"But you did not ask her. Her mother asking her is not the same."

"How could I, Nne-nne?"

"Because you have a large heart. How long were you away?"

"Five years."

"That is a long time. A very long time."

"Nne-nne, she is pregnant with another man's child."

"That is true. That is very true. But you were away, Ajuziogu, for five years. A very long time for a young woman, beautiful and full of the juices of young womanhood, to be left unattended. Even if she had been her mother's age, that would still be a very long time. I am not saying that you are not justified to be angry, only that she is a good woman, even though pregnant."

"How could she be all that good and pregnant? I mean, what am I supposed to do? I came home thinking that I had only your illness to worry about, but now this. And everyone can see that she is pregnant."

"Would you have preferred that she hid herself? Or kept away from coming to welcome you home today? Or from attending to me, as I have been sick? I tell you, that child could not have been more attentive if she had been a child of my own womb. Every time I coughed, she was beside me. Every time I yawned, she wanted to know what I needed. Together we all wondered what had become of you, why you did not make a way for her to join you, as you had promised, why you did not come home after you received your first paper but instead decided to go after another one? Did you forget her? Did you forget all of us? After a while, your letters were not coming as frequently as they did in the beginning."

"Nne-nne, I did not forget you or her or anyone. It's just that things did not turn out the way I imagined they would. When you are at home, you imagine many false things about a foreign country, but after you get there and collide with reality, you realize things are very different from what you imagined. There are many, many things, Nne-nne, about America, that no one will ever understand who has not been there."

"I am sure it is as you say, but still you were gone for five years, and for five years a young woman like her endured life without a husband. The child she was nursing when you left home became weaned. Why, W'Orima has reached an age when she should have two other children behind her. Even three, the way young women are not spacing out their babies nowadays. I think she did well to have held out for so long. That she still wants to be married to you should prove to you the depth of her love. If her affection for you was not deep, she would have been long gone by now."

"Perhaps it would have been better if she had married someone else, whoever it was that made her pregnant."

"Would you really have preferred that, Ajuziogu? Would you?"

"Yes."

"Mmmh. I do not believe you. You are saying that out of anger and wounded pride. It is not coming from the bottom of your heart."

"It would have been over and done with, and I would not have had to deal with it."

"Mmmh," Nne-nne said, shaking her head slightly. "You would

let pride cause you to throw away a good woman." Then she became silent.

I joined her in the silence, took off my shoes and my shirt and unbuttoned my trousers, leaned back in my chair, and withdrew my hand from her clasp. The sounds of the night invaded the silence from outside, birds and crickets, and bush babies leaping between the fronds of the raffia palm trees. This was a reprise of the night we had spent five years before, the night before I set out on my outward trip, lit by the same brown light from the same hurricane lantern, except that everything was now refracted through eyes that during the intervening five years had become accustomed to the relative gigantism of American objects.

"You did not eat anything at all?"

"I was not hungry."

"You are so much like your father and grandfather. All of you men of this kindred, the slightest trouble and your appetites go sour. Anyway, it is not good to eat so late at night, especially a person who is tired and has been traveling. You will have a good appetite in the morning. When is your Sitella coming back?"

"I do not know."

"When she comes tomorrow, I want you to take her hand and pull her to you. Will you do that for me?"

"Nne-nne, please do not put it that way. I know that she has been very good to you. She and her whole family. For that I am very grateful. If I look back over the years to what the father did for us in our troubles with Orji, I feel nothing but gratitude to all of them, the father, the mother, Stella herself."

"I am not talking about the father and mother, and I am not talking about what all of them have done for us. I am talking about you and your wife."

"No, Nne-nne. I do not see how I can still call her my wife."

"If you had lived together for the past five years, you would have learned how to forgive her. You would have had more than one thing to forgive. So, will you divorce her then?"

"Yes. I have no choice. If she found another man to get her pregnant, then she should marry that person."

"What about W'Orima?"

"W'Orima is mine."

"That is true, but what will you do with her? How will you care for her? You do not have another wife or mother or sister to care for her while you are gone. I am now too old and too sick for you to leave her with me. Can you take her with you to America?"

"Not really." I had not thought of that.

"What will you do with her then?"

"I do not know. I will have to think about it."

"Sometimes things come upon us and do not permit us time to think, like the urge to vomit or use the cesspit. If in the morning Eze-Nwanyi comes here and tells you that she has decided to bestow her virtues on another man, what will you do? Would you not say that a man who has got her has got a good woman, pregnant or not? I say, when a large, juicy piece of meal falls out of a plate onto the ground, you do not throw it away because it is too valuable. After you wash it off, it is still edible. It may be a little gritty from having fallen on the ground, but it may be more valuable than other lumps of meat that are not so big or so good."

"I am sorry, Nne-nne, but I do not like the way this is sounding. Stella is the one who has been unfaithful to me and who is now pregnant. Somehow, I feel that this burden is being shifted to my shoulders."

"Taking another woman does not count against a man, even though in your generation, some men are now marrying only one wife. Still, five years is a long time for a young woman to be alone. After you received your paper at the end of your fourth year, we all thought you were on your way home, or at least that you would come home and see how everything and everyone was before you embarked on something new. You did not come then but instead began a new study that was supposed to last another three or four years. Was she supposed to wait for you for nine years? And spend all of her youth waiting? And then your letters stopped coming for three or four months. We all wondered what was happening and did what we could to console each other. Did you marry another woman there? Do you have another wife?"

"No, I do not have another wife over there."

"She thought maybe you had married someone else, and I had to keep reassuring her. She asked me for the letters you wrote to me, so she could reread them and see if they contained any hints about your being married to another woman over there. I advised her to be patient with you and promised her many things on your behalf, telling her that her cup would be large and brimming full when at last you handed it to her. I said to her that with your bookwork, you were probably like a person in an *anara* garden: though you already had a full basket, you kept seeing more and more *anara* that you wanted to pluck. At some point you should have realized what you left at home and come back to tend to it. If you leave a pot on the fire unattended, what you are cooking will burn or boil over."

She sighed, and I sat up to help her. "Would you like me to turn you over?"

"No, I am fine," she said. "Just let me hold your hand and pull against it to rearrange these bones a little bit. . . . There. That is much better. Aaah. I have a sore spot on my hip from lying so long on it."

"What kinds of medicine has the doctor given you?"

"If all the medicines I have taken in the last three or four months did what they were supposed to do, I would live forever. Your in-laws have taken me to all kinds of doctors. They have all put their listening thing on my heart and felt and squeezed and looked and listened. And they would not tell me what they saw or heard, except that I was sick. Yes, Ajuziogu, my son. I am sorry about what has happened, and it pains my heart that your heart was heavy when you left five years ago, and now your homecoming is not a feast. But be patient. Your feast day is coming and will soon arrive. You will give it to yourself, if no one else gives it to you. I am sorry I will not be there for it, but my spirit will be there. Where we all are in the spirit world, all of us, your ancestors and relatives, will rise together and rejoice with you and accept the four kolas, pod of pepper, and wine libations you offer in our memory. Anytime you pour a libation to me, do it with Gordon gin, not with stale palm wine. Let that be what I get because my grandson spent so many years in the White man's country. In the spirit world, I want to be known as a woman who drinks expensive drinks.

"But what I have told you about Eze-Nwanyi is true. The fact that she is pregnant by another man does not make her a bad woman, just a woman who went astray once. Once. You should forgive her. You left your soil fallow for too long and someone else planted on it. It happens that way all the time. She bared her soul to me, asked me if I thought she should abort the pregnancy. I said no as often and

278 • T. Obinkaram Echewa

as loudly as I could. And then she asked me how I thought you would take it, and I told her you would be angry at first but in the end would take her back. She said I did not know about your temper. I told her you had been my grandson longer than you had been her husband. Ajuziogu, I promised her that you would take her back. That is part of what gave her the courage to be here today. As you noticed, it was her mother who sent the wire message to you. She did not want to see you, or rather let you see her in her condition. I made her promises on your behalf. That, Ajuziogu, is something I have done a lot since you went off five years ago. When something came up that would have been up to you to do, I said, 'Hold it until he comes back.' I told that to your Sitella so many times that it almost became a song. Now, you cannot disappoint me and her and others. You cannot act as if to say that I was wrong to vouch for you. I have trusted you. Now I am asking you to show that you trusted me by doing what I promised others that you would do. I promise it will be my last request to you, the last big one. I know you will give me a decent funeral when my time comes, so I do not have to ask you for that. But this one I do ask you. Will you do it for me?"

I exhaled, then sighed.

"Do not answer me now," Nne-nne interjected. "Answer me in the morning after you have rested and have thought about it. Life is full of strange turns, I tell you. Did you know . . . I hesitate to tell you this, but if I do not, this secret will be buried with me. Besides, it may be the type of thing that nudges you to do the right thing about your wife. You remember that your grandfather often used to talk about the time he was sent to prison for boiling *eti-eti?* Do you remember?"

"Yes."

"Mmmh. He was gone for about a year, and in that time three of us, his wives, young as we were and burdened with children, we had to learn to fend for ourselves and get along without a husband. For that year we were like widows. And you know widowhood is the worst lot that can befall a woman. You know that it was his relatives who betrayed your grandfather to the police, in spite of the fact that everyone in this village drank or distilled *eti-eti.* Those same relatives were on us like vultures the year your grandfather was in prison. I never confessed this to your grandfather but, as I said, I am telling it to you now to help you understand and perhaps forgive your wife.

Yes, Ajuziogu, even your dear grandmother once breached faith with her own absent husband. I crossed legs with another man, while your grandfather was in prison. How and why it happened, I cannot now tell you, but it happened. Yet at the time I had no intention of leaving. Of his three wives I was the only one who stayed. The other two left. The day he was released from prison, I went to meet him at Agalaba Uzo. That night, as he touched me, a chill covered my body because of what had happened. That is the way life is. It is not always tidy, like a head of *ukazi* leaves neatly piled up and tied together. A child is born in a glob of mucus and blood and urine and sometimes even shit, but still we take it out and wash it clean. Every life has knots and wrinkles. None is seamless."

"Whose child would this be, if I took Stella back?"

"Yours."

"How can it be mine? It is someone else's bastard child. How can it be mine?"

"It is still yours. The other man cannot claim a child from another man's wife. . . . You are tired, Ajuziogu. Let me not weary you anymore tonight. Come here and give me a hearty embrace. I wish I could get up and really give you a hug. Ah, son of my son, my heart is glad that I have set eyes on you once again." She patted me on the back as I bent down to rub cheeks with her. "Sleep well," she said. "Everything will be all right in the end. God in heaven is watching over us."

I breathed heavily as I withdrew from her and felt so leaden with fatigue that I seemed to have forgotten how to place one foot in front of the other. I stumbled into the bed in the other room. Stella's perfume was in the sheets and on the pillow. I drifted off to sleep uncertain whether to be pleased or annoyed at the nearness of her essence. I opted for anger. I wanted to scream at her as I had done earlier. "Why, Stella, did you go and spoil everything? Why? Why?"

The day was far advanced when I opened my eyes. I could tell because the room was flooded with light, not with the dull penumbra of dawn but with the strong glow of an ascended sun. Someone was knocking on the door outside. That, I realized, was what had awakened me. I scrambled out of bed, buttoned my trousers, and went to the door. De-Odemelam was there and with him several other men and some women. They said good morning and made a few jokes about how we African White men sleep long past dawn, long past the hour when they, village farmers, would have hoed an acre of yams. I offered them chairs, then went looking for water to wash my face. It was then that I passed by where Nne-nne lay. She lay so still that I was drawn to look more closely at her. "Nne-nne," I called, touching her, then shaking her. "Nne-nne!" I repeated, shaking her vigorously. I felt her face, chest, and hands. She was cold all over. She was dead.

11

Modern Women and Modern Wars

"SHE WAITED FOR YOU TO GET here," many of the women mourners said to me. "Her spirit probably left two weeks ago when she went to the hospital. That was when she really died."

"Yes, I saw her then," another woman concurred, "and I knew she was gone."

"Yes, indeed," still another woman said. "It was fortunate that she got to see you and you to see her. That means she died peacefully."

"What did she say last night when she first saw you?" one woman asked.

"Just that she was glad to see me."

"I am sure that is not all. I am sure that if you recall correctly all that she said to you, you could tell that she knew she would not be here this morning."

"Did she not talk in a way that you found strange at the time? No? Did she not say things that are only now beginning to make sense to you?"

As news of Nne-nne's death spread through the town, people came running from everywhere to pay their traditional calls and join in the mourning. Because word also spread that I was home, more people came to welcome me home from several years abroad. Our compound, shrunken over the years by death to just three houses (my grandmother's house, my grandfather's house, and the *ovu*), teemed with people all day long. Because Nne-nne had no surviving daughter, her best friend's daughter played the role of chief female mourner. I, on the other hand, took what would have been my father's place as chief male mourner.

Ndom Alu-alu inaugurated their traditional mourning ceremonies with songs, dances, and mimes of ancient feats. With whispers, winks, and head nods, they assigned themselves all the tasks necessary to complete the funeral—dispatching emissaries to *dibia* houses to ensure that everything was all right with the ancestors and the spirit world, buying a coffin, washing and dressing the corpse, buying a cow for the people of Umu-Awah, my grandmother's maiden village, hiring the *ukom* drummers who would play for the four days of mourning, buying the gunpowder that would be used for the four days of cannonading. Nne-nne had been a member of several title and honor societies—First Wives, First Daughters, *Nkpu-Edeh*—and had of course been warrior in the Women's War. For each of these there were ceremonies and rituals.

By midafternoon, the *ukom* drummers were drumming spiritedly, and volleys of ear-splitting flintlock fire were being let off by the five or six guns present. Several fires had been built on various corners of the compound, each with a large pot of cooking meat. In the midst of all this, I had little opportunity to be alone with my thoughts, yet I could feel the tug of two opposite sensations: one of pain because of Stella, the other of joy because I had been able to see my grandmother alive.

Much of the day, I had kept expecting Stella or her mother to appear, but around three o'clock it was the A.S.P. who drove up. I perked up as I heard the sinuous whine of the diesel engine of the Benz. He greeted me heartily, pumping my hand and clasping me in a warm embrace. "*Ndo,*" he said. "*Ndo. O-o-nya!* I am sorry. *Ndo!* And welcome back in the country. When did this happen?"

"During the night sometime. I don't know exactly when. I woke up to find her cold. She and I were talking deep into the night."

"It is a proper wonder. Good thing you at least got to see her. Janet and your wife do not know this has happened."

"No. When they were here yesterday, Nne-nne seemed fine."

"Ndo. And welcome back." We shook hands again, and several men rose from their seats and came forward to shake his hand.

The A.S.P. was given an honor seat in the men's circle. Or rather, as soon as he was seated, people who had been seated in other alignments rearranged themselves in such a way as to make him the center of attention. He had become legend in our town from that day when, at my behest, he had landed on our *okasaa* with two lorry-loads of policemen and had proceeded to arrest our chief, Chief Orji, and to put the rest of the town in flight. When later I had married his daughter, Stella, my prestige with them had soared, and so had theirs with their neighbors, for the legendary Assistant Superintendent of Police, *Afo-Ojo-o* (Bad-Belly) Kamanu, had also become their in-law. Nearly everyone in the crowds, perhaps everyone who was not cowed into shyness, came forward to shake his hand and indulge the familiarity of calling him "in-law." For his part, he did not disappoint them. Beckoning to two boys, he walked with them to his car and presently returned with two cases of beer and a bottle of cognac. He made a short speech to introduce the drinks, saying that he had come to welcome me, his son-in-law, home from my overseas travels, but sadly had come upon the death of my grandmother. "Joy and sorrow were always mixed together in life," he said. Fortune often traveled in the company of his daughter Miss Fortune.

While the ceremonies continued, I had no opportunity to speak privately with the A.S.P., until he was about to leave and I walked with him to his car. We stood beside the car talking.

"I am sorry about your grandmother," he said.

"Thank you, sir. I am thankful that I managed to get here in the nick of time and see her."

"She waited for you. Old people are supposed to be able to do that. There is plenty you and I have to talk about, but it cannot be now— with all of these things that are happening."

I could not help noticing his distance and absentmindedness. "Yes," I agreed, inferring from the way he said "all of these things" that he included Stella's situation. "I am very grateful," I said, "for all the help and care you gave to Nne-nne. Last night, as I talked with her, she would not stop saying what a kind and wonderful family I married into. Those were practically the last words on her lips before I left her to go to sleep last night."

"H'm," the A.S.P. grunted, then relapsed once more into silent thoughtfulness. When his hands came out of his pockets, he handed me a wad of notes.

"No, sir," I said. "I am thanking you for what you have done already, but I do not need the money. I have money. It is in travelers' checks, and I need to get into town to change it, but I do have it."

"Don't be silly, my friend. I am just fulfilling custom, and besides, how much money do you have anyway? It is custom to place some money beside a jar of wine. The case of beer is my jug of wine. This is what goes with it. I did not want to give it to you in front of all the people. And what I am sure you do not realize is that all these people are not going to leave until they see the clean bottom of every pot and plate in your house, plus the bottom of your pockets."

"Thank you, sir."

"You saw Stella yesterday?"

"Yes, sir. I saw her."

"I am sorry," he said, shaking his head in disbelief. "I was coming out here this afternoon to talk to you about her and then only to find out about the death of your grandmother." He flattened his lips against his teeth, and he continued to shake his head. "All the things a man can *jam* on the road in one day," he then said. "Janet told me last night that you had returned. I said I would drive up today and greet you. You know I am now retired from the Force. Early this morning Armageddon breaks out. I hear that Stella is in the hospital, on the critical list! . . ."

"What!"

"That's right. I rushed to the hospital . . ."

"What's wrong with Stella?"

"My brother, this is the kind of *eshishi* I cannot understand. They said she tried to kill herself."

"What!" I cried out in alarm.

"Yes," the A.S.P. confirmed. "No one knows what she swallowed."

"How is she?" I don't know if I merely felt faint or actually fainted, but I know that I wished I could opt out of consciousness for a while. My mind was overloaded and about to go into *fag*.

"They say she was critical at first, but she improved after they pumped her stomach. She had just regained consciousness by the time I reached the hospital, but then she saw me and became unconscious again. The doctor told me she will probably pull through, but no one can be sure of these things even now as we speak. I may get there and the story may be different." He focused an earnest gaze on my face. "Did you know she was pregnant?"

"Yes, I saw it last night, and she told me."

"Well, you knew before I knew. I only found out this morning at the hospital. Imagine the likeness. You live with a woman like Janet for all these years and still you do not know what is going on in your own house, until the pot boils over and drowns the fire. I had been wondering why I had not seen Stella in the last month or two, especially in the last month—she moved to her own flat about a year ago—but it seems whenever I asked about her I was told she had just come and gone while I was out." The A.S.P. wagged his head in unbelief. "Not long ago, in the old days, a son or daughter would see it as duty to go before his father or mother and greet him or her. Even if it meant traveling ten miles just to say, 'Father, I have come to greet you. . . .' Anyway let me go back and see how she is. We will talk at another time."

"Wait for me. I will go with you."

"No, you cannot leave your guests. Your grandmother is lying unburied, and you have no one to take over for you."

"No, I will go with you nevertheless. These people can carry on with the ceremonies until I return. All I can do for Nne-nne now is bury her, and that will not be until tomorrow. I want to see Stella."

I put the ceremonies in the hands of De-Odemelam and one of my granduncles from Nne-nne's maiden village, and, without explaining what emergency prompted my sudden departure, went off in the car with the A.S.P.

Our trip was silent for the most part. Once or twice the A.S.P. asked me about things in the United States, but I could not muster the interest or the mental energy for a full-fledged discussion. For my part, I asked him about retirement, and he was similarly disinclined to talk about it, except to say that independence had *not* ushered in the best of times for dedicated and professionally minded civil servants like himself. Beyond these short questions and answers, each of us seemed filled with his own thoughts. For my part, I was terrified about Stella—angry and sad and anxious about her well-being, selfishly distressed about how sad I would really be if she died. In response to America, where daily life was saturated with unending discussions of "love," I had come to regard that particular emotion as a form of weakness and faintheartedness, the exaltation of sensations caused by hormones into a form of spirituality. Nevertheless, I could not deny that Stella aroused in me a kind of craving and hunger that could not be accounted for by a mere surge of sexual hormones, and that when I had her in my embrace, I felt a sense of satiation, completion, and wholeness that only she could give me. In five years, I had almost forgotten, but the sensations now returned to me. If love existed, then I loved Stella. I met her and had union or communion with her in an alcove deep in my heart to which no other woman had ever found entrance (not Melva nor anyone else). She was my perfect other half, the silent echo of my spirit returning to embrace me, thereby creating an explosive resonance in me because everything between us was in phase. In one of the letters Nne-nne had written to me (with Stella as her scribe), she had said that W'Orima was probably an *nne-nna* (father's mother), a reincarnation of my mother, and as such would show an unusual affinity for me, because we were doubly related. Stella was like that from the very first time I met her.

"What did Stella take? Did the doctors know?" I asked the A.S.P.

"APC or Resorchin. They were not sure, but they were hoping it was not Resorchin. It is more powerful and can cause a lot of bleeding. How do you feel about Stella being pregnant?"

"Speechless," I answered, and heard myself exhale one more time. I looked out of the side window into the forest through which the road was slashed. "I suppose angry, too," I added. "And sad." I paused to weigh what I had said, out of a sense that it did not give accurate expression to my feelings. "I am more sad than angry," I added. "Right now, I am just afraid and praying that nothing happens to her." All my statements were tentative, each a trial balloon lofted to see if it fit the feeling. But nothing seemed to fit the feelings that swirled within me. Among other things, I felt weighed down by a sense of my own guilt.

Everyone, it seemed, had weighed my conduct and found it wanting. Only their love and their pity of me as a hapless, recent returnee kept them from dumping the full weight of my negligence on my shoulders. I felt sorry and remorseful at this unfortunate confluence of sad events, and I felt sorry for the A.S.P., imagining the way he had to be feeling at that very moment, realizing that his darling daughter, made pregnant by me before marriage, had become pregnant again by another man while I was away. And to top it all off, she had attempted suicide and at this very moment could be lying dead in a hospital bed.

When we walked into the hospital, I could sense not only my own apprehension but the A.S.P.'s, as we monitored the faces of the nurses for any sign that the unspeakable had occurred. At the nurses' station, the A.S.P. asked, "How's my daughter?"

"Much better," the charge nurse said, much to our relief.

Our breaths became more relaxed as one of the nurses led us down a long corridor to a small ward with only four beds. Stella occupied the one farthest away from the door and next to a window, and as we entered, Mama-Stella, who was seated aslant on the side of the bed, was using a small, dainty handkerchief to wipe the sweat off Stella's face. She acknowledged us with a slight smile and slightly lifted brows. Stella opened her eyes, noticed who we were, closed them again and turned her face to the side, away from us. I could not help wondering whether the response was to me, to her father, or perhaps to both of us.

I stepped forward and took her hand—her mother surrendering it to me as if it were a gift—and put my other hand across her brow, as if checking her for a fever. The A.S.P. and Mama-Stella stepped out of the room into the corridor. The nurse pulled a divider between us and the next patient and then left. I was alone with Stella and sat down on the side of the bed still holding her hand.

"Stella," I called. "Can you hear me?"

No answer.

"Can you hear me, Stella, or do I have to tickle you?" I tried not to look at her midsection.

"It's me, Aju," I said. "How are you feeling?"

Still no answer.

"Open your eyes and look at me."

"I'm sorry," she said, suddenly breaking into a sob. Tears began cascading out of her shut eyes.

I used my fingers to dab them away. "Don't cry, Stella," I said. "Everything will be all right."

She shook her head. "Nothing will ever be all right again. As you said, I have spoiled everything."

A loud moan came from out on the corridor. "Is that Mama?" Stella asked. "What is wrong?"

"Let me see," I said, and began walking out to investigate. I did not want to upset Stella with the news that Nne-nne was dead.

Just then, the A.S.P. and his wife were returning to the room, with Mama-Stella walking very fast to get to me. She reached out eagerly and embraced me. I led her away from the door, while the A.S.P. returned to the ward alone.

"I am very sorry," Mama-Stella said. "*Ndo. Ndo!* Boy, when it rains, it really pours. Sorry *kwanu.*"

"As they say, that is life."

"It is too much at once."

"What does the doctor say about Stella's condition?"

"She's lucky to be alive."

"Thank God. Is she out of danger?"

"Here comes her doctor right now."

The doctor waved at us but then turned to enter the big ward without seeing Mama-Stella beckoning him.

"I am sorry about all this," Mama-Stella said, sighing and beginning to cry.

I put my arm around her shoulders and tried to comfort her.

"Here, take this," she said, opening her handbag and extracting a handful of currency. "Consider this *nmayi orio-rio*, a jug of wine for your grandmother who has died."

"I cannot take it," I said. "The A.S.P. has already given me twenty-five pounds. That is enough wine from one family."

"That is the A.S.P.," she said. "This is from me, your mother-in-law, your mother. You do not realize how fond I became of your grandmother while you were away. Everyone loved that woman. She became like a mother to me."

"Thank you," I said, still trying to return the notes to her. "But this is too much. I may take a jug of wine—that is tradition—but fifty pounds is too much."

"Take it and stop arguing and making a scene."

"Thank you, Mama." I squeezed her shoulders.

"The A.S.P. will take you back? Who is in charge of things back in the village?"

"My grandfather's friend, Odemelam. Tell me, exactly what happened to Stella? When did it happen?"

"My brother, talk of God being awake and preventing the evil thing, this is the best example I know. Last night, after we left your place, I took Stella back to her flat. She was crying all the way back and did not say a word to me for the whole long drive. That did not bother me too much, as I knew how she was feeling about your return and all that. When we reached her place, she asked me whether I would take W'Orima and let her sleep at my house. I said, 'Sure,' as that was something she had done many times before. But somehow I had a bad feeling about the whole situation as I drove away with W'Orima still sleeping in the backseat. Stella's behavior was queer. Then after I reached home and carried W'Orima into bed, it occurred to me that Stella had not said anything about taking the child to school in the morning, whether I would do it or she would do it. And of course you know I go to the market first thing in the morning every day. Something said to me: Go back to Stella's flat and check about her. I am so glad that I followed that voice, because when I got there she opened the door for me and then fell down on the floor. If I had not gone back, we would not have any Stella by now."

"Amazing. Did the doctor say anything about her baby?"

"He doesn't know. She has been bleeding a lot. The doctor says the situation is wait-and-see."

"H'm."

We returned to the ward to rejoin Stella and the A.S.P.

Nne-nne was appropriately buried.

Stella lost her pregnancy and stayed in the hospital for nearly a month.

During the time Stella was in the hospital, I stayed alone in our compound and underwent experiences that left me dumbfounded— days full of wild hallucinations, when I was all by myself, and nights terrorized by phantasmagoric nightmares. Everything I knew, everything I had ever experienced, everything I had ever said or had heard someone else say, everything I had ever read, imagined, or written was chopped into pieces and thrown into a giant mixing machine.

At night I was terrified of being alone and of the darkness, of the noises made by strange animals, of the relative ineffectualness of the hurricane lamp that lit my way around the compound and the house. Above everything else, I was alone, all alone, in a compound surrounded by memories and graves of my ancestors, my ears filled with the echoes of their voices, their spirits tiptoeing into reality just off the edge of my vision. Often I sat awake with the lamp burning low, as I was afraid to go to sleep in total darkness. When I finally went to sleep, it was usually after cockcrow.

This was a time for recapitulations, for taking stock of my life. I thought about the United States and all the things I had left in midscene on that stage—my professors and fellow students, Melva, and the people in the building where I lived—how they were all getting on with the daily routines of their lives without me, while here at home I was active on another stage, with a different set of co-actors. Day by day I watched the fresh earth around Nne-nne's grave turn into dry clumps of sod, and then slowly begin to crumble. Memories of her, though, did not crumble. I especially thought a lot of her confession of having lain with another man while Nna-nna was in jail. I dredged my memory for who it could have been, living or recently dead, but could come up with no one. She had sat on her secret most of her life, until the very end. I wondered what Nna-nna might have done if he had found out. Could he possibly have found out? Did he guess? If Stella had sworn to me that during the five years of our being apart she had not looked at another man, would I believe her?

As I thought more and more about her, Nne-nne began to amaze me. First of all, of all my relatives, most of whom were now dead, she was the most substantial in my memory. Perhaps this was because she was the one with whom I had interacted the most in my adult life. Others, including my father and mother, lived in my memory as passing glimpses. My grandfather I remembered, but not as sharply. I had to press my mind to squeeze pictures of our interactions into focus. Nne-nne, on the other hand, was a clear picture, and a clear, loud voice, slowly decanting its words and punctuating them with dry chuckles. "Ndom!" I heard her saying. "Another name for a woman is . . . Men brag about their sorrows, but the things that lie buried in a woman's heart . . . Do not worry about me, Ajuziogu. I may be sleeping, but I am not yet dead . . ." I imagined that if she and I were to have an actual conversation now, she would probably say, "I may be dead, but I will not be forgotten!" Indeed, she was the least forgettable of my relatives, and I wondered again and again what *else* lay buried in her heart, what other wars and secrets had existed in her storehouse of *grief* that she had carried with her into the grave.

Despite my present preoccupation with Stella, Nne-nne brought joy—a big smile that broke out spontaneously on my face—to my thoughts. She had mastered her *griefs*, whatever they were, and defied them. I recalled the determination that vulcanized her voice as she said, *"Kama ji sii, nku gwuu!"* I recalled her head shake and chuckle as she had told the story of how several thousand women turned their naked backsides into the faces of a battalion of soldiers. I broke out in an unrestrainable guffaw when I remembered how Nne-nne had once made the same gesture to the men who were trying my grandfather on a trumped-up charge before our village's *amala* assembly.

Nne-nne was a good woman. Her having lain with another man while my grandfather was away did not make her less so or change what I thought about her. That was true enough, but I was not prepared to apply the same grace to Stella. No, Stella was another matter. Stella was *my* wife.

Mama-Stella took me by surprise. I suppose I had become so used to her gentle, jovial, and easygoing manner that her vehemence on this particular evening surprised me. Our conversation began innocently enough. She had come to our compound on a Sunday afternoon to pick up W'Orima, who had spent the weekend with me, and then I had allowed her to persuade me to return to Agalaba Uzo with her. At the time, Stella had been home from the hospital for about a week, and I had not yet visited her at home.

"What are you going to do?" Mama-Stella asked. "What are your plans?"

This was a question I had turned over in my mind many times, only to lay it aside again because I could not make up my mind. On one hand, I felt a deep sense of debt to Stella and her family for all they had done for me personally and for Nne-nne during my absence. Even after Nne-nne's death, their gifts had enabled me to "bury" her without stinting over money. Still, I did not feel that the way to pay this debt was to erase Stella's pregnancy from all reckoning. Her miscarriage, to a degree, had reduced the problem—the memory of an aborted pregnancy was easier to deal with than the tangible reality of an ongoing one, or the crying, suckling presence of another man's infant.

"I had been scheduled to take the prelims for my Ph.D. this very week," I said to Mama-Stella, "but I petitioned my dean for a deferment after I received your cablegram, although it was very difficult persuading him that my grandmother's health was reason enough to come home at this time. If it had been a mother or father or some other first-degree relative, they could understand it, but in Ph.D. studies, one of the things you have to show is a singleminded earnestness. . . ."

"Look," Mama-Stella said, cutting me off. "I am not really asking you about the States—what you are doing or will do or should have done there, et cetera. My only question is about here and now. What are you going to do here?"

I swallowed. I have a weakness for people I consider my friends and an extreme reluctance to start or join a quarrel with them. What Mama-Stella said was like a fist in my face. Her tone was especially severe and combative. I swallowed back the rush of feeling that welled up in my throat and bit my lips.

She turned to glance at me. I kept looking straight ahead, as the gray tarmac disappeared rapidly under the car. W'Orima, who was lying in the backseat, snorted in her sleep.

After a while, Mama-Stella said, "Ajuzia, I believe I asked you a question. Don't you realize it is an insult not to answer?"

"I was trying not to offend you even more with my answer," I said.

"What is your answer, anyhow? Let us hear it. Offensive or not, go ahead and offend me."

"I have not said very much to Stella since I have been back and so much has happened."

"So?"

"I am trying to give her time to finish recovering."

"And then?"

I sighed, irritated by the prosecutorial tone of her retorts. "And then I will talk to her," I said.

"Just talk?"

"Yes, just talk. To me that would be quite a lot right now."

"Well, I think you ought to act instead of talking."

"Well, that is what you think!"

"Ajuzia, whom are you insulting?" She slapped me on the thigh, the nearest part of my body that she could reach without taking her eye off her driving. "If I did not have my hands on this steering wheel, I would slap your face for you. Look at you, snotty-nose child like you." She scowled at me and sighed. "You are a child, finish. Everything that has happened is because of you."

"Madam," I said, "what we are talking about is your daughter who became pregnant while I was gone."

"But I am here to tell you that it was all your fault."

"How could it be my fault? Did I get her pregnant all the way from the United States?"

"No! You should have been here at home to get her pregnant. Or you should have had her with you wherever you were, if you were interested in being a husband. Instead you went to America and got lost. Why didn't you work a chance for her to come and join you, as you promised? After you finished your first degree, why didn't you come home for her before you started on your so-called doctorate? In the beginning, when you started running *kpuru-kpuru* around our quarters, the A.S.P. was for throwing you out as he had done so many others, but I said no. You would be Stella's chance for getting overseas quickly. Now, more than five years later, where is she? Where is overseas? Many of her classmates have gone over. You hurried up and made her pregnant, and then promised to send for her, *and then who give squirrel roasted palm nut?*"

I shook my head in disbelief. "Let me understand this," I said. "Are you saying that it is my fault that Stella became pregnant by another man? I have heard of instances of blaming the victim, but this has to be the worst."

"Blaming the victim, my *nyash!* Who victimized you? Tell me, how have you been victimized? I am trying to show you how you have made a mess of everything, and you are telling me about being a victim."

I closed my eyes to squelch my anger. Mama-Stella also became quiet for the rest of the drive, until we were in the A.S.P.'s yard. I could tell that she was still agitated by the way she bumped into the yard, swerved into the garage, and pulled the key out of the ignition. We gave the A.S.P., who was sitting in the veranda, a cursory greeting and marched immediately into Mama-Stella's living room.

"You are such a small boy, Ajuzia," she started off, even before we sat down. When I lowered myself into a chair, she continued to stand, her handbag slung over her arm, car keys in hand, head tie pushed up and askance to reveal the outlines of a freshly plaited hairdo. "Or at least you act like one. But you shouldn't. How old are you now?"

"Twenty-five."

"You are a man, whether you like it or not, and not a small boy. What surprises me is that intelligent as you are, you do not see your responsibility in this whole situation."

"Since you see it so clearly, why don't you tell me?"

"I am getting ready to. First, answer this question for me: Are you married?"

"What kind of question is that?"

"Just answer. Are you married?"

"For now, yes, but one of the things I am considering is divorcing my wife."

"You no fit divorce Stella! No way! You don't have the courage. Besides, you know which side your bread is buttered on. Go ahead and divorce her. Or how do you know she has not divorced you already! I want you to know that about a year ago, when you stopped even writing to her, I asked her to consider finding herself another husband, but she was still confused about her so-called love for you. You see, me I am from the old school, and don't understand some of this love business that some of the young people talk about nowadays." She slipped into pidgin English. "I believe wetin the book *Money Hard* say: when poverty come in for door, love fly out of window. Our people have another way of saying the same thing in proverb: *nga oku nyuru, achisa owa!* I cannot be bothered by a bundle of sticks that cannot hold a fire! Tell me, if your grandmother had not become sick, would you be here now talking to me about how you have been victimized? Or would you still be gallivanting around America? Tell me, am I lying? Is that not true? Now, after your grandmother has been buried, what is foremost on your mind? Is it not returning to America, so you can continue with your studies? If you go back there now, how many more years before you come home again? In the meantime, let me hear how you judge yourself. Perhaps I am judging you too harshly. What kind of husband have you been in your own eyesight? If somebody were to say now: those who be good husband, raise their hands, you get courage to even lift up one finger? *Ojare,* you are a living example of what the proverb say: Someone else marry for you, buy sleeping mat for you, and then raise the woman's leg for you too! No, that last one no apply to you; you did the leg-raising part all by yourself. But that has been your only contribution to this whole business—one erect penis, that's all! Ajuzia, you should not have annoyed me, because you could not take all the things I could tell you. Tell me, the time you leff Nigeria five years ago, you left anything for your wife and child? What kind of arrangement you make for boff of them, hah? Wetin make you Stella's husband? You giv'am chop? You buy cloth for'am?"

"I married her the way a man is supposed to marry a woman, didn't I? I may not have paid *puku-ndi* for her bride price, but I fulfilled custom, and she said yes to me, and you and the A.S.P. gave your consent. Are there degrees and levels of marriage, the more you pay the more married you are?"

"As a matter of fact, there are! I am sure that sometime in your life you have heard of *utu gbara* and *tukwuo lia*." She sighed, then sank into a chair, chuckling. "Yes, indeed, there are degrees and levels of marriage. When the A.S.P. married me, I cost him some sweat. It is was not a matter of him saying, 'Be my wife,' and I followed him home. Afterward, he did me all right too. Just imagine, Ajuzia, have you ever bought your wife a dress? A mere scarf? Ring or necklace? I realize you had to come home suddenly after you received the cablegram about your grandmother, but what did you bring her that will make her the envy of other women that her husband is in America?" Switching gears suddenly, she said, "You care for something to drink?"

"No, thank you."

"How much bride price would you say you paid for Stella?"

I looked up at her and could feel the tightness of the furrows on my face. "Why?" I asked.

"Would you say fifty or maybe a hundred pounds?"

I stayed silent.

She opened her handbag, pulled out a wad of notes and began counting them. "Here's one hundred pounds. That's your money back to you. So now take it and go, Ajuzia. You and Stella done finish. Come on and take it."

I stood up. "I'm leaving," I said. "I will talk to you another time. You and your husband have been kind to me in the past, and for that I will always be grateful. But let me go before I say things that I will later regret."

Mama-Stella stood up beside me and draped her hand across my shoulders. Then she burst out laughing. "Sit down, my friend," she said endearingly. "Sit down and let me find something for us to drink." She stuffed the notes back into her handbag. "I love you too much to let you go. Besides, it is late, and I cannot drive you back now. Sit down."

"I can go to the motor park and catch a lorry."

"Oh, sit down." She exited toward the kitchen and returned shortly with a tray, glasses, and cold drinks.

"The trouble I am having with you," she said, "is that you are behaving like some kind of apprentice husband."

I gagged on my drink.

"*Ndo,*" she said but without losing breath continued. "Young people like you nowadays are so thoughtless. You *sabi* book but you *sabi* nothing else. You see, Stella didn't become your wife just because she consented to marry you or because you got her pregnant or because you paid a bride price to her parents. Yes, you did all those things, but real marriage is a daily thing. It is not a touch-and-go thing. You have to be near enough to your wife for long enough for her to feel and see and hear your presence, so that when she stubs her toe against a tree root, your name is on her lips. *Di'm ezeh! Di'm omah! Di'm oga eweta!*"

I could not restrain a chuckle.

"In the daytime," she continued, "you go and get. At night, when you lie down beside your wife, she calls you by those fond names. When a husband stops going or getting or when he goes and stays and stays and does not come back, what does his wife do? Who will she call all those sweet names? Seriously, Ajuzia, do you realize that because of you I nearly lost my daughter? That she became pregnant is one thing, but that was not the worst of it, because she is not the first woman ever to become pregnant with a man other than her husband. But suicide? That is taboo. The A.S.P., strong as he is, nearly pissed in his trouser. I never saw him so angry and frightened. As for Stella, I know that if you were anywhere within five hundred miles she would never even look at another man. But you abandoned her, and there was a period of time when you would not even write a common letter. We kept hearing stories about people who went overseas and left a wife and child behind, then married someone else over there."

"Let me understand you correctly. Do you think Stella is justified in becoming pregnant?"

"No, I did not say that. But what she did is not the only wrong thing that has been done. I cannot sit here and indulge your wounded innocence or discuss with you how much Stella has offended you and therefore how angry you have a right to be. No. What I have to tell Stella, I have already told her, many, many times."

"What do you think I should do? Advise me."

"To start with, open your eyes wider and see the bigger picture."

This evening with Mama-Stella was weird. She continued to damn me in one breath and then laud my virtues in the next. She fed me supper, plied me with fruit and soft drinks, but then topped it all off with severe remonstrations. We sat in her living room late into the night in a scene that reminded me of one of my long confabs with Nne-nne, except that Mama-Stella's house was lit by harsh, naked electric bulbs, her chairs were softer, and her floors were linoleum over cement.

She said, "You know how when you give a child a bucket of water to bathe himself, the only thing he knows to bathe is his belly. That's you. The only thing you know to think about is your book. It is as the Bible says, 'Where a man's treasure is, there his heart is also.' It may surprise you, but I don't care if you *never* go back to America. You already have your first degree. Other degrees can wait. There are more important things."

"Mama-Stella," I called out.

"Mama," she corrected.

"After all has been said and done, what I have to resolve in my own mind is the issue you are refusing to address."

"That one issue I have addressed fourteen different times this one evening alone. But you are not satisfied with what I have to say about it. So, that's your own palaver now. Do as you like. I can say, since you were gone for so long and behaved as you did, you had no right to expect anything. You have heard of the old folktale in which the young *osu-agwu* had to stay up all night to stoke a fire for his old *dibia* master during a cold harmattan night. Night after night he had to keep the fire going. Then one night he did something he felt he had to do. Because he had no wood and the old man kept moaning and complaining, he stuck some of the wooden idols into the fire. The old man enjoyed a wonderful, warm night. The following morning, when the *dibia* said, 'Some clients have come for a divining. Bring out the idols,' the *osu-agwu* said, 'For all the warmth you enjoyed last night, do you remember fetching any wood?' My question to you is like that: for all the warmth you are demanding, do you remember fetching any wood? Stella is your wife and your responsibility. Did you ask me to watch her for you while you were gone? She became yours after you married her. You should have kept her. Before you married her, I was supposed to watch her. You remember, though, that I could not keep her from you. You got to her in spite of my vigilance. Maybe that is where all this started. This is adult talk, Ajuzia. The children's lullaby says:

"Aluta nwanyi oho-o [When a wife is newly married]
Enye ya okpuru-kpu anu [She's fed big pieces of meat]
Izu n'abu k'ato [After she's been married for a while]
Enye ya okpuru-kpu ukah! [She receives big pieces of talk!]

What I am giving you now is the *okpuru-kpu ukah* which comes after the *okpuru-kpu anu."*

"The man who made Stella pregnant, do you know him?"

"No."

"So far, there has been no mention of him by Stella or by you and he has not stepped forward on his own. Who is he? Where is he?"

"What do you want with him? You want to fight a duel with him? If you ask me, I would say that is what is between you and Stella. If you still want to be married to Stella, then let's get on with that program. If you don't, then make up your mind and declare your wishes. But tell me, have you really talked with Stella since you returned? I mean, really talked with her?"

"Not really. That first day of my return, we talked very briefly, but I was too shocked to say anything, in addition to being concerned about Nne-nne. After that first day, of course, she went into the hospital."

"In that case, I think the two of you ought to talk. Whatever comes out of it comes out, but you ought to talk." She looked toward the passage door and called out: "Stella! Stella!" She then rose from her chair and inserted her feet into her slippers, and saying "Wait a minute," she flopped out of the room. A couple of minutes later, she returned with sleepy-eyed Stella in tow. "Sit down," she ordered.

"No-no, over here beside your husband," she corrected, steering Stella into the seat beside me. "That's better. Now," she enunciated with great formality, "Stella, I have been talking with your husband, and I believe there are some things he feels you and he should talk about. I am sure there are things on your own heart that you would like to talk to him about. So the two of you talk! You may remember," she said with a smirk, "that when the two of you first got together, I wasn't there. So I won't be here to hear what you will say to each other. If you don't know what to do with your hands, feel free to put them on each other. I am just going to leave the two of you alone for a while. Talk! I don't care what you talk about. Just talk! Fight, if you like. Bite each other, if you like, but when I come back here, all I want to hear is that the whole thing is settled one way or another."

She paused like a schoolmistress and said, "Have I made myself clear?"

I said, "Yes."

Stella said nothing at first. However, as soon as her mother was gone, she said, "I am sorry, Aju." She reached over and touched my arm lightly.

I felt a quiver run through my whole body at her touch, and then an impulse to pull away. "Why?" I asked, standing up.

"For everything. Everything!"

I could sense that she was fighting back tears, a gallant but unsuccessful effort. After a while her fingers traveled to the corner of her eyes and then the tears began falling from her face to her lap. Her hair was in fresh plaits, her face bore the freshness of sleep and recent washing. She wore a green blouse over one of her mother's expensive juj wrappers, blue-green in color with fringed edges. Her feet were bare, and her toenails painted red. She looked very beautiful.

"I'm sorry for all the trouble I have caused you."

"Stella, I don't want to be mean or cruel to you. You have been an excellent friend. You still are. For the way you took care of my grandmother, I shall forever be grateful to you. But then there is this other thing. All the kindness in the world does not wipe it away. Can you understand?"

"Yes, I understand. As you said that first day, I spoiled everything. I have been thinking of that expression ever since I first heard it. It is the only thing you said that first night when you got home. It is true. I spoiled things. If I waited for you all the time I did, why didn't I continue waiting? But I don't know what else to say except that I am sorry. You came home expecting to see a wife who had saved herself for you, not one who was pregnant with another man's child. I can't blame you. I can't say you shouldn't feel the way you feel. I should have written to inform you as soon as I found out that I was pregnant. That way you would have come home knowing what to expect. But I was afraid, too shocked really, to put it down on paper. Even when your grandmother became very ill and you had to be informed, I was so afraid I could not write the cablegram. That's why Mama sent it."

"You were shocked when you became pregnant?"

"Yes. Even more shocked than when I was pregnant with W'Orima. At least that time I knew you were in my corner, in spite of how angry I knew Papa would be."

"And your boyfriend . . ."

"He was not my boyfriend."

"Lover, whatever you call him, he was not in your corner?"

"No."

"What is his name?"

"I will not tell you."

"Why not?"

"I just will not."

"What was he to you? How long were two of you involved with each other."

"I am sorry. I just do not want to talk about that. I cannot."

"I *want* to talk about it. This thing is like a boil, an abscess. It will never heal unless you stick a scalpel into it and squeeze out the pus."

"Maybe another time, but I just do not want to talk about him now."

"There may be no other time."

"In that case, so be it. As I said before, there is nothing you do for which I will blame you. I have even reminded myself that I would not be very understanding or forgiving if I had, let's say, arrived in your flat in the United States and found another woman living there with you. But even at that, it is different for a man to have a woman on the side than it is for a woman to have a man. For one thing, a woman gets pregnant, whereas a man can simply walk away. A woman who has been unfaithful to her husband carries the mark of her infidelity. I was a virgin when we first got together. You were not. Even if you had said you were, I had no way of proving you right or wrong. Besides, it was not expected of you, while it was expected of me. You just don't know, Aju, you cannot even imagine what I have gone through in the last four or five months. All my friends know. I am the talk of the town. That is part of the reason why I wanted to end it all, so I would not be around to listen to the gossip. I can only imagine what the gossip is now, all over. And whether or not you and I continue to marry or divorce, it will continue. Every *asiri* in town will have you and me on his or her lips."

I was struck by Stella's maturing disposition, even her vocabulary. She sounded so grown-up and reasonable, her mother with a better English vocabulary. This was the lengthiest conversation we had had since my return—our years apart had turned her from a bouncy, spirited girl into a sedate young woman in full possession of herself.

"Why don't you sit down," she suggested with consumate reasonableness. "If not here beside me"—she patted the me-and-my-girl cushion beside her—"over there."

"Do you want a divorce? Would you like to marry—what's his name—this person who got you pregnant?"

"No."

"No? You sound so definite."

"I am definite."

"Who is he, anyway? What's his name?" I sat down on a chair opposite her.

"I don't think his name is important."

"Is he in town? What does he do? What would you have done if I had not come home at this time?"

"I don't know. All I know is that I would not have tried to abort the baby."

"You would not have married this person?"

"No."

"Why not? Is he married?"

"No, he is not married."

"Why then wouldn't you have married him?"

"Because I have never thought of myself as anything else but your wife."

"Even while you were carrying this other man's baby?"

"Yes, even then."

I sighed in disgust. "I suppose you will next tell me that even while you were in bed with this person, I was foremost on your mind."

"You were!"

"Rubbish!" I sighed sharply. "Whom are you kidding? I was foremost on your mind, but you went ahead and had intercourse with him anyhow." I said the word *intercourse* with intentional vehemence. "Next you will tell me you were careful not to enjoy it—all for my sake."

She turned her face to the side, toward the wall, and closed her eyes. Tears began running down her cheeks. For some reason, at this point, Melva's face assailed me, her face the first night I ever made love to her. I recalled my nervousness and maladroitness that night, the second thoughts and regrets that kept oozing up in my consciousness, so strong were they that I did not much enjoy the act. No, I did not enjoy it at all, being greatly distracted by my thoughts, and afterward I had a great sense of loss—no guilt, but loss—a sense that I had crossed a threshold and lost something precious. I remember feeling that night the way I felt on the earlier occasion when I lost my virginity—very disappointed that the woman to whom I had lost it didn't at all deserve it! On the latter occasion, not that Melva was bad at all, but rather that between her and Stella there was no contest. None.

I wondered whether Stella might have felt the same way toward her consort. Suddenly I became angry with myself as I realized that my feelings were undermining my resolve and my thinking. I continued to gaze at Stella's tear-streaked face, at her bosom rising and falling with her breathing movements, her hands interlocked and resting on her belly. I remembered the night I left home for the States five years before, when we lay tangled in each other's arms, unable to make love because she was on her time. I was filled with longing for her.

"How long was this affair going on?"

"Why? You want to calculate how much you lost?"

"Please answer me," I said severely.

Her throat moved up and down as she swallowed. "It was not really an affair, and it only happened in the last six months."

"Is it over?"

"Yes."

"Are you sure?"

"Yes."

We both became quiet, until Stella asked, "Did you have a girl-friend in the States?" She still had not opened her eyes.

"Why?"

"Just wondering."

"Stop wondering."

She sighed, and made as if to open her eyes. "Anyway," she said, "if you want a divorce, you can have one. I will get out of your life, and you can return to the States, and finish what you have started. As for the things I did for your grandmother, you should not let those deter you from doing what you want to do. You married me for yourself, not for your grandmother. Besides, she is W'Orima's great grandmother, so you can say what I did for her I did for W'Orima."

I barely heard her, for my feelings had welled up in me like water backed up in a dam. I was drowning in things I wanted to share with her, thoughts, feelings, fears from the last five years, things I had seen and done and imagined or read. There was no one else in the world with whom I could share them, no one else with whom I desired to share them. I wondered if she too felt the same way.

"Stella," I called out.

She opened her eyes and turned her head to face me. I was now standing in front of my chair.

"Come here," I said, beckoning her up.

She did not move but only continued to stare at me with the doleful eyes of a lost sheep.

I repeated the gesture, but still she did not rise. I reached down and picked up her hands and pulled her up. Her wrapper fell off, exposing her slip. She calmly picked it up and rewound it around her waist. Then she stood obediently in front of me, looking straight at me but without discernible expression, with her hands folded across her chest. I pried the hands apart and pulled her against me. She yielded but remained free of feeling, her hands hanging limply at her sides. I noticed, though, that despite her seeming reluctance, her head hung limply on my shoulder.

"I am sorry, Stella," I said.

"What about?" she asked. "I am the one who ought to be sorry."

"I am sorry that I have made you sad. That we are both sad."

"Yes, you cannot imagine how sad I am." I felt her hands rising to clutch me around the waist. "Once, when we first met, I made you happy, I think. It made me very happy to notice how happy I seemed to make you. Now, I am just as sad when I notice how sad this homecoming has been for you. I have to beg your pardon for it. I am truly sorry."

"This is very difficult to explain, Stella, and it may not even make sense to you as I try to put it into words. When I found out you were pregnant, I wasn't filled with rage or jealousy or any of those emotions. What I felt was sadness and disappointment, that my Sitella, as Nne-nne used to call you, had become sullied. I could no longer idealize you. You were no longer perfect."

"I am human. I was never perfect."

"I know. Still I could pick you up in my mind and think of you as such. You were for me all the adulation names the young girls in the dance circle nickname themselves:

Osi nji ghara uri! [So darkly beautiful, needs no further adornment!]
Anya nlecha-a ohara nyo! [So beautiful, leaves an imprint on the mirror!]
Aria ogugu enwegh igba!" [Seamlessly smooth, like a raffia frond!]

"How do you think I feel about you?"

"I don't know."

"You don't, huh?" I could hear the old, teasing Stella. "I'm sure you do," she added in a more somber tone.

"Do you want to continue to be my wife?"

She smiled, and then could not stop smiling. "Even though I am no longer perfect?"

"Yes, even though you are no longer perfect."

"Do you want to continue to be my husband?"

"The only reason I would consider reconciling with you—mark you, I only said consider, not that I would actually do it—is that I need someone to talk to," I said.

We both laughed, then sat down.

"Same here," Stella replied. "There is so much that has piled up in my mind for more than five years. Jokes and stories I have been saving to tell you. I used to tell you some of them in my letters, but there are so many more I could not have written down. If I let you go now, what will I do with them? To whom will I tell all those stories?"

"Did I hear two people laughing?" Mama-Stella said, reentering the room.

"Mama, I think you are beginning to hear things," I said jovially.

"Yes, I know I heard you, Ajuzia. I can tell that teeh-teeh-teeh laugh of yours anywhere."

"Not me. I have not laughed in eons. Maybe you heard Stella. She is the one who began rejoicing."

"I don't care who I heard. I am happy I heard someone laugh. There hasn't been any laughter in this house for ages, and between the two of you for at least five years. . . . Are those tears of joy you are shedding, my dear?" She sat down on the arm of Stella's chair and reached over and began to wipe her eyes. Then she said, "Why am I doing this? Ajuzia, you are the one who should be wiping your wife's tears."

"Okay," I said, "but it is only because you forced me."

"Forced you, my eye."

I pulled Stella up again and hugged her. Then I began wiping her eyes. That, however, made her cry even more. "Look at this," I said, pointing out the fact to her mother. I wiped, and then both of us watched as large teardrops reformed at the corners of Stella's eyes.

Mama-Stella exhaled heavily, shook her head, and said, "Thank God. Thank God Almighty."

Later that night, Mama-Stella suggested that Stella and I go away together. "Go on a honeymoon," she said. "Get away from the commotion for a few days and be by yourselves. I will send you anywhere you want to go."

We accepted part of Mama-Stella's suggestion, the part about being together, but we did not go anywhere far. Instead we returned together to my compound—yes, it was now my compound—to take stock of Nne-nne's things, and my grandfather's things and things that had belonged to other members of my family, all now dead. It was very strange living in our compound all alone with Stella—I thought of us as a young couple, as in an American movie, in a sort of back-to-Nature foray, cavorting amid the ancient ruins and trees and tall grasses, indulging in a form of rarefied sensibility that seemed alien to the sensual immediacy and substantiality of Africa, observing flowers and insects and hearing the music of the spheres at midday or midnight in the leaves and grasses.

Nne-nne had sorted out everything very nicely, her own belongings and those of Nna-nna. In fact, she had even laid out the clothes with which she wished to be buried and hidden away twenty pounds for her funeral. It was only now that I found these.

"Do you know what this is?" Stella asked, handing me an old faded piece of fabric tied into a knot. I recognized it at once as the fabric Nne-nne had shown me five years before as having once come from the dress of Mrs. Ashby-Jones. "She told me to give it to you. What is it?"

"A memento from the Women's War," I said, untying the knot and showing Stella the pearl and the strand of hair. "You can have it for a keepsake," I said, and noticing that she was squeamish about touching it, I added, "Or you can save it for W'Orima. A remembrance of her great grandmother."

12

Woman Wins

"I FEEL LIKE A FROG WITH a string tied around its waist," Mama-Stella said one day. I knew the figure well, because as a child I was an expert at snaring frogs from our pond and tying ropes around their waists to keep them from escaping. The frogs had room to jump to the limit of the rope's length, but they could never get away. Where Mama-Stella wanted to go, with respect to the A.S.P. or her marriage, I did not know, but she felt the restraint of a rope around her waist.

I disputed her conclusion, pointing out that the A.S.P. had never forbidden her to begin her cloth trade, or to do anything else she wanted. He had cherished and protected and husbanded her. "For most of your married life," I said, "you have been a woman of leisure."

"True," she replied, "but I can feel his eyes at my back, and I can sense disapproval in his voice. No, he has never said to me, 'You can't do this' or 'You can't do that.' He is too gallant for that. For him to raise his voice with me would be to admit failure, to admit that he could not control me without raising his voice. A lion should not have to roar all the time to show his strength or to have his wishes met. All he has to do is growl deeply in his throat. That is the way the A.S.P. is with his officers. He is not enthusiastic about what I am doing, just tolerant."

"At least he has not broken your arms and legs," I said, and we both laughed. "As the old song says,

"*Nluta nwanyi zuora ya igwe*
Ya akara'm agba
Gbajia ya ukwu, gbajia ya aka
Kpolara ya nne ya!"

[If I marry a wife and buy a bicycle for her, and she dares to become a better rider than I am, I'll break her arms and break her legs and send her back to her mother!]

"Men," she said, drawing a deep breath and holding it for several moments before letting it out slowly.

"Men?" I said, when I had tired of waiting for her to continue.

She shook her head at some private understanding, but would not share it. I had a feeling she was filtering her thoughts, perhaps considering what would be appropriate to divulge to me about her relationship with her husband. "The A.S.P. probably thinks I no longer act like a married woman." She chuckled. "You know how as a child you are taught not to stare back at adults, never to match eyes with them. If you do, you are considered starry-eyed and ill-mannered, and all sorts of unwholesome futures are predicted for you. A woman is supposed to do likewise. I respect my husband and my elders but I look the world in the face and do not aim my gaze at half-mast. There is too much *ntche* in my palm wine; that is the trouble I am having with the A.S.P. The sweet palm wine, *goro-goro*, is supposed to be a woman's wine, whereas the sour, overnight *ugara* is for the men. They shake their heads and grit their teeth as they force it down and they say, 'No woman could possibly drink this down.' " Again, she switched gears and, narrowing and cocking her eyes, she said, "Has the A.S.P. said anything to you about my trading in the conversations you have had with him?"

I took stock of my memories and said, "No."

"It is not so much that I act like an unmarried woman as I am like an *unhusbanded* woman," she continued. "I do nothing to dishonor my husband or my marriage but I am not as fully husbanded now as I used to be. I have been married to him for more than twenty-eight

years, have given him two grown children. Whatever he invested in
me, he has made a nice profit from it. Besides, he has three younger
women to do for him whatever he needs to have done. So it is all
right for me to move out from under his shade and meet the sunshine,
the rain, and the wind of life on my own.

"The car that I now drive is *my* car, not the A.S.P.'s. It is not as
good as his Benz, which I used to drive before, but it is mine. That
makes it different for me as well as for him. I can remember that he
was not very happy the day I bought it. He could not understand
why I needed a car, when, according to him, I had a car. I made
sure, though, that he went with me, and I was careful not to say
much during the haggling and to let the people at the shop believe
that he was buying a car for his wife. Nevertheless, throughout the
whole transaction, his face looked as if someone had rubbed raw cocoyams on it.

"When I go beep! beep! on this little red car and raise a little dust
as I pass, people still call me Mrs. Kamanu, but they know my face.
I am in the driver's seat, controlling the steering wheel, not sitting
in the back like some decorated and fat Mami-Wota doll. When I go
to Y.A.C. and Oliver's and sign for a consignment, I sign my own
name. I can slap my chest and say, 'You know who I am?' not 'You
know who my husband is?' "

I was reminded of more things that Nne-nne had said during that
long night before I left for the States. A woman, she had said at one
point, is like the *mgbalala* runner. It blooms late in the season, when
other plants are beginning to wither and die. Where it finds space,
it runs merrily around and around on the ground, covering the whole
patch with a flourish of large pink and purple flowers. If *mgbalala*
found a bush, it usually became a climber and wound itself around
that bush, covering its wilting head with glorious flowers. A woman
had three ages, Nne-nne had said. At first, she was her father's daughter, then her husband's wife, and then finally—if she was lucky—her
own person, either as a widow or as an emancipated wife living
outside her husband's shadow. I can distinctly remember Nne-nne's
chuckle as she said: "A woman becomes her *own man* after her monthly
bleeding stops." If such a woman was fortunate enough to have married a husband who had done well, she came into a new bloom, the
spiritual and emotional counterpart of her early physical bloom as a
young woman. Her children were grown, her life had been established

and she could stretch out her legs in leisure and laugh heartily or smile slowly, switch her chewing stick slowly from one side of her mouth to the other, spit thoughtfully into the dust and rest in the assurance that no ill wind would blow her away, that she had seen most of whatever there was to see in life, and in fact that her life, like a river which had begun its career high up in the mountains, cutting deep gorges through rocks, running swiftly and giddily, its current fractured often by boulders, had at long last entered the wide channels of the plains, where the flow was slow and easy.

Mama-Stella was obviously in the third stage of the life Nne-nne had described. She had married a man who not only had lifted her vine off the ground but had nourished and cultivated her. In my view, she had no reason for complaints, but she insisted that she had them. Her two children gave her cause, she said, and so did her husband's quiet resentment of her success as a cloth merchant.

"That is fine," I said, referring to her Mami-Wota doll image. "That is wonderful. What I don't understand is who is arguing the contrary? Who is saying that you should not sign your own name or slap your own chest?"

"Really, no one—explicitly. And that is the source of the frustration I feel. When things are stated openly you have a chance to argue against them—explicitly. If the A.S.P. would say to me, 'I don't want you, my wife, sitting in the market trading,' I would at least have the chance to ask him politely to explain to me why not. Or to persuade him. Or even to beg him. But if the argument is conducted in silence, with the sullen face and the question that is really a rebuke, how do I defend myself or my point of view against this unstated opposition?"

"The opposition may be something you are imagining," I said.

"Spoken like a man," she said jauntily. "That is exactly what men say. Because they have not stated an opposition, they are able to deny it. A man can say to a woman, 'I never said you shouldn't. I never told you you couldn't do this or that. You limited your own self.' Most of our traditions are like that, unwritten like the British constitution, and just as powerful. Parents train their children mostly with silent looks and facial expressions, not necessarily with words and hands. . . ."

I saw in this statement far more meaning than Mama-Stella realized or perhaps intended. It explained the Women's War. Perhaps it explained women in general, especially their tendency to accumulate their frustrations and then heave or erupt. Women were like earthquakes. When I left the States in December, there was a lot of talk in the papers and on television about a possible earthquake in California. Geologists talked of the earth's plates rubbing up against one another and building up immense pressures along the San Andreas Fault. Someday soon, they were saying, the earth in California would heave forcefully, in order to relieve this pressure.

In 1929, both the men and the British colonial administration had marveled at the depth of the women's agitation. Both had acted as if to say, "We didn't realize you were so upset! We had no idea you felt so aggrieved!"

In 1776, Thomas Jefferson and company had produced a long-winded Declaration of Independence, and had followed that eleven years later with an elaborately written Constitution. The result was a loquacious and verbose culture and legions of lawyers who made a living grinding America's founding documents into mincemeat for legal hamburger franchises. Even the common frustrations of everyday life were the subject matter of endless discussion around coffee and cocktail tables and on radio and television panels. Perhaps unarticulated truth remained true much longer; by being diffuse and almost impalpable, it defied both familiarity and falsification.

Mama-Stella's statement also brought to my mind some of the statements written by Mrs. Ashby-Jones in her journal about the diffuseness and intractableness of native culture and of her efforts to find structure in it and to extract, identify, and perhaps crystallize its essence. If the natives had been sensible enough to govern themselves through some easily identifiable administrative structures, then any foreigner who wanted to colonize and govern them would have had an easier time of it, and a consul would not have had to send home to the Colonial Office for more than 400 treaty forms with which to enter into understandings with uncountable and confusing village groups.

The statement also explained what had recently occurred between Stella and me. Just as the native men and the colonial administrators said to the warring women, "We didn't realize you were so profoundly aggrieved!" I, in effect, said to Stella, "I didn't realize that my long absence meant so much to you!" That, too, might have been the basis of the "trick" Mama-Stella pulled on me when she insisted that Stella and I talk. So long as my anger about Stella's pregnancy had remained unarticulated, there was no basis for attacking and dissipating it, but once I began talking, first to Mama-Stella, then to Stella herself, I gave them an opportunity to argue it down and away.

That also could be what had happened to the men in their responses to colonization. They talked. They reasoned. They rationalized away their angers and their frustrations, and ultimately they learned to adapt to everything.

"I have decided to say nothing," Mama-Stella said, returning to the discussion of her relationship with her husband. "So, we both play the silent game. I do what I am doing without announcing my intentions or plans. The A.S.P. has his silent objections. We have a drawn game. He is the husband. I am the wife. After all, when we are in bed, we do not announce to each other what we would like to do. He makes his silent signal, and I respond without words."

Stella, to the contrary, was not always willing to let me proceed silently being her husband, but instead wanted to know my intentions and plans, especially after a letter arrived from the States informing me that my dean demanded to hear from me. The letter was written by Melva.

"Who is Melva?" Stella asked.

"Department secretary."

"Is she your girlfriend?"

"Yeah, sure! She is my girlfriend."

She punched me on the arm. "You think you are very clever, and if you say she is your girlfriend that will put me off her trail. She's probably your girlfriend for true-true. How did she get this address? Did you write to her since you have been home?"

"I had to leave an address with the department."

"*Na so.* Anyway, when you reply, inform her that Stella is coming back with you, and she had better disappear."

"Yes, ma'am."

"Stop being silly. I am quite serious."

"I'm serious too."

Later that evening, Mama-Stella said, "You ought to begin making plans. Travel to Lagos and begin working on a passport for Stella and W'Orima."

The following day, the A.S.P. said the same thing.

About a week later, Stella and I set off for Lagos.

In about two weeks, we were able to bribe our way to a passport for her.

About a week later, we obtained visas from the American consulate.

In the middle of the preparations for returning to the United States, Stella and I one day made a trip to my compound, to spend a night there and make love for the first time since my return.

"Aju," Stella called out in the middle of night as we lay side by side.

"Yes?"

"Are you asleep?"

"Not now."

"I cannot go back with you to the States."

"What?"

"I said I cannot go back with you to the United States."

I wanted to look at her face, but where we lay there were no light switches and no electricity. I would have to grope for the matchbox on the bedside table and then grope for the hurricane lamp on the floor. What I felt impulsively like doing was to flick a switch and flood the scene with light. I had to settle for imagining Stella's face in the dark.

"H'm," I said. "Are you serious?"

"Yes, I am serious."

"Why did you wait till now to let me know?"

"I have been thinking about it, but I just now made up my mind."

"Do you have a reason?"

"Huh!" she said in a derisive chuckle. "Do I have a reason? Yes, I have a reason."

I waited for her to state whatever her reason was, but for a long time she did not. "What is your reason?" I asked her when I became tired of waiting.

"I have more than one, but the first one is a promise I made to Nne-nne. I promised her that I would do whatever I could to persuade you not to abandon this compound and let it go to ruin."

"This compound?"

"Yes. Did she not also talk to you about it?"

"What she said the night I returned was that she knew I would be going back to the States."

"That's what she feared. During all the years you were gone, that woman had only two prayers—to see you again one day, and to be able to hold this compound open until you returned. When she became very sick, she even made me promise her that if she died before you came back I would do everything I could to keep it open until you came back. Now that you have come back, are you just going to abandon it and leave again?"

"What am I supposed to do? Live here for the rest of my life?" This question embarrassed me, even as I uttered it—the implication that Stella saw merit in preserving my ancestral compound and I was arguing that merit.

"Do you not see it as your responsibility?" Stella continued. "If you do, then how you fulfill that responsibility is another question, whether you live here or find some other way to keep it open."

"What other way to keep it open?"

"I don't know," she said. Then, chuckling in the darkness, she added, "I am only a woman, and the child I have is a woman. So the responsibility does not fall on her or on me. But just think of what this place will look like by the end of this coming rainy season, how much of the roof the termites will have eaten and how high the weeds will be. How many months will it be before the fences collapse and the houses fall down? Is that what you want? All your people are buried here—Nne-nne as well as your grandfather and others. . . ."

"When did Nne-nne reincarnate into you?" I asked. "You sound exactly like her."

"Nne-nne and I spent a lot of time together. As I told you before, she taught me many things and showed me many things. She told me about your great-great-great grandmother, the one who fought tooth and nail to keep the compound open for her only son, and how the place has since been called Ama Nwanyi by the members of your kindred. I would keep it open if I could, but I don't know how it can be up to me when you are around. Anyway, you and me are a question mark right now."

"What do you mean? What you said earlier, did you really mean it?"

"Yes, I said I am not going back to the States with you at this time."

"At this time? Does that mean you will come later?"

"I do not know, but I rather doubt it."

"What are you really telling me, Stella?" I scrambled up from bed, struck a match and lit the lamp.

Stella closed her eyes against the glare of the light and turned her face away from me toward the wall.

"Now, Stella," I said, sitting on the side of the bed and staring hard at her. "What is this you are telling me?"

"I will use one of Nne-nne's proverbs to tell it to you again. Nne-nne used to say, 'If you are giving medicine to a very sick man, a man who is almost at the point of death, and all the while his penis keeps getting up, the best thing is to leave him alone, as he probably already has a girlfriend in the other world.' Your mind is completely in America. You came back, your grandmother died, you buried her, and now all you want to do is hurry up and get back to America. That is where all of your mind is. Let me ask you this: Are your studies more important than everything else in life? More important than life and death? Than your daughter, W'Orima? Than me? If it is your studies on one side versus everything else in the World on the other, I believe your studies will win. Even going back to the States with W'Orima and me is something you have been forced to do, especially by Mama. It is not something that came out of your heart to do. Who is to say that when we reach America you will not abandon W'Orima and me in a cold flat while you are pursuing your studies?"

"Stella, do you now hate me?"

She turned her head and opened her eyes slowly against the glare of the light and looked squint-eyed at me. "What kind of question is that?" she asked.

"A question I want you to answer. So answer it. Do you now hate me?"

"What did I tell you a while ago while you were making love to me?"

"Whatever it was, I had to wring it out of you. And you refused to sing to me."

"I told you I did not know any songs to sing."

"I didn't want *just any* songs. I wanted you to make up your own songs for me."

"And I told you I did not feel like making up a song."

"Why not?"

"Just did not feel like it, that's all!"

"You now despise me, do you? You didn't think I deserved a song?"

"I said I didn't feel like singing a song. Why are you so concerned about a love song now? You never seemed to mind before whether I sang to you or not."

I was struck by her question. The answer that crept into my mind as I sat on the edge of the bed was not at all to my liking. The reason it had not been important to me before that Stella sing to me was that I had never before felt a need for her submission, her loyalty, her admiration, or her love. I had always felt that I had those without a need to ask for them. The encounter between Ahunze and Old Man Aja-Egbu, as Nne-nne related it, flashed across my mind. Old Man Aja-Egbu demanding that Ahunze sing to him. Ahunze refusing because Aja-Egbu had not fulfilled a necessary precondition. I became hot with anger and turned sharply to stare at Stella. Her face was again turned toward the wall, and I could see only the back of her neck, the rest of her body being under her wrapper, which she was using as a blanket.

"Stella, why don't I deserve your song?"

"I don't want to talk about that anymore."

"I *want* to talk about it!"

"Go ahead and talk then. I will listen."

In a fit of anger, I picked up a pillow and blanket and went into the other room with the lamp, planning to spend the rest of the night in Nne-nne's bed. As I sat down, I found that bed to reek more of Nne-nne's aura than I could abide for a whole night. That was the bed Nne-nne had died in, the bed on which she had endured several months of illness. I sighed and picked up my pillow and blanket again and returned to the bed where Stella lay. She had not turned to see me go or return, but she was awake and spoke up presently.

"Aju," she said in a voice which sounded like a disembodied oracle.

"Yes," I answered reluctantly, turning to look at her.

"What have you ever given up for me?"

"Nothing," I said, trying to be sarcastic.

"That's right," she agreed. "If you have given up anything, remind me of it. I know that this sounds like something Mama has said to you, but she is not the source of it. If anyone is the source, it is Nne-nne. As I already told you many times, I am truly sorry for what happened on my part, that I became pregnant. The fact is that for four long years I preserved myself for you. You have no idea at all the type of *nkotosi* I endured from all sorts of people. But they were all outsiders. At the end of the day, I left outsiders outside and locked my door between myself and them. My real hellfire started when I was alone. That is when I began asking myself what I was suffering for. I asked myself: Am I married or not? Do I have a husband or not? What is he doing right now at this very moment? What time is it where he is in America? Is he alone in his bed and missing me as much as I miss him, or does he have another woman in his arms? You do not have to answer this question, if you don't want to, but how long was it after you reached the States before you went to bed with another woman? Do you remember? Was it one year? Two years? If you do not want to tell me, at least bear the date in mind and compare it to the more than four years that I lasted. From the beginning, I gave myself to you freely. I liked you—that was all. I did not hesitate or hold back. But now, I cannot just jump on the plane and follow you without an explanation from you about what you have been doing during the last five years, without a promise of what I can expect after we reach America. I just do not feel confident enough to say, 'Aju is going, and I am going with him. And that is enough for me.' Suppose we get there and you have another wife?"

"Which of these things you are saying is the one that is really bothering you?"

"All of them."

"Which one do you want me to address?"

"That is up to you. I'm just telling you why I cannot follow you back to the States. . . . While you were gone, I waited for you, whereas everyone was asking me to forget you and get married again. You know how people talk, not only in the village but in the township. They were saying: 'If this husband of hers has become lost in America, why doesn't she find another one? Why isn't she in America with him? When is she going to join him there?' Some even said that what you had given me was just a so-to-speak marriage, because you had given me a 'belly' and were afraid of Papa. But once you were out of sight, you vamoosed completely.

"I wondered about that myself. I wondered many times. If you read my letters carefully, you would have noticed my tone. To tell you the truth, if it wasn't for Nne-nne, I would not be here now. In a way, it was like I was married to her and to your whole family. She would send a message asking me to come because she hungered for me. I would spend weekends with her and she would give me and

W'Orima all the things she had been saving for us since the last time
we had seen her. Like us, she was neglected too, an old woman with
no one to care for her, but always cheerful and more determined than
anyone I had ever seen. She died in the flesh two or three years ago,
but her spirit refused to die. It was her spirit that kept her alive until
you came back. Notice that the night you returned is the same night
she died. There is great meaning in that.

"As I lie here now, my heart is filled with things she told me about
you and your family during those five years. About how you were
born, how your father and mother died, all the troubles you have had
with other members of your kindred, including the one with that
Chief Orji, which Papa helped you to settle. I feel that I have been
married to your family but not to you. I feel a part of the history of
your family because Nne-nne filled me full of it, and made me a
member of it, and showed me where W'Orima and I were joined to
it. You and I are joined at the roots but not at the top. If you want
us to be joined at the top, and complete the circle, then you must
reach out and grasp my hands and hold me. In case you are wondering
about all this, it is what Nne-nne told me to tell you. I cannot simply
stumble along behind you, and, forgetting everything else, get lost
in the excitement that I am traveling to the United States with you.
If America is so important to you that you must return there now at
all costs, then that is your choice. So far as I am concerned, America
can wait. Or America can stay right where it is, if I never get there!"

I listened to Stella, feeling as if she had indeed become an oracle,
as if the spirit of Nne-nne had invaded her and was using her as a
mouthpiece. The scene reminded me of the one with Nne-nne on the
night I left home—the brown light from this same hurricane lamp,
the gaunt, bent shadows of me and articles of furniture shimmering
against the wall, a gecko half concealed in a crack, muffled night
noises filtering in from outside. My chest and belly suddenly felt full
to the point of bursting, and I had no idea how to give vent to
whatever they were full of. I exhaled and exhaled again, lowered my
head into the palm of one hand, and pillared my elbow against my
knee. Nne-nne's aura seemed to rise from the earthen floor and overwhelm my senses. The chanted eulogies of her *Ndom Ibe,* her fellow
women, on the day of her funeral filled my ears:

"She had a slight build, but she was a giant of a woman!"

"*Zhem!*"

"She walked lightly, but her footsteps made the earth tremble!"

"*Zhem!*"

"If Ndom were being counted upon to do something important, is she not one that could always be counted upon?"

"*Zhem!*"

"In the War which Ndom fought, was she not a hero?"

"*Zhem!*"

"Was she not ready to bite a steel blade into two with her bare teeth?"

"*Zhem!*"

"Would she not step into a fire and dare it to burn her feet?"

"*Zhem!*"

"Would she not stick her head into a rope noose and defy it to choke her neck?"

"*Zhem!*"

"Did she not go nine times to the back of the house and each time deliver a live baby?"

"*Zhem!*"

"That death has taken all of them, is that her fault?"

"No!"

"Is that not instead a tribute that even though death could take her children it could not take her smile?"

"*Zhem!*"

"Is she not the only one among us whose son has gone to America?"

"*Zhem!*"

"Is she not a member of *Ekwu Ato?*"

"*Zhem!*"

"Is she not a member of *Nkpu Edeh?*"

"*Zhem!*"

"Has she not earned all her titles?"

"*Zhem!*"

"Was she not well born?"

"*Zhem!*"

"Has she not lived well?"

"*Zhem!*"

"Did she not die gracefully on her own sleeping mat?"

"*Zhem!*"

"*Zhem!*"

"*Zhem!*"

Nne-nne's eulogies had been so spirited that some of the men had begun murmuring that the women were carrying on as if the funeral were for a man. As a matter of fact, De-Odemelam, my grandfather's lifelong friend, had at one point pulled me aside to remark that my grandfather had died before my grandmother, and that he, the man, seemed to have received the less illustrious funeral. It behooved me, De-Odemelam cautioned, to be careful not to cause anger or jealousies in the spirit world.

Straightening up from my thinking pose, I took a glance at Stella and then blew out the lamp. Then I keeled over into bed beside her. What my chest had been full of from an earlier moment was a thought, which had now taken recognizable shape in my mind: If this is going to be my wife, I need to reach deep, deep down inside me and find the wherewithal to marry her, because she would take a lot of marrying! Just then, I could feel myself smiling as one of Nne-nne's sayings drifted across my mind. *"Awtu aligh-li!* No limp or half-erect penis will ever find its way into me!"

I reached toward Stella, found her hands, and slowly turned her over, so that we were face to face. Then I put my hands around her. She, in turn, circled her hands around my neck and drew me into the tightest embrace we had ever exchanged.

"America can wait," I told her.

"That is good," she whispered, beginning to sob. "That is very good."

Ndom!

Mgbara-Ala!

Ndom!

Heaven-and-Earth in one body!

Ndom!

Iyi Omimi!

Ndom!

Deep, deep, water!

Pronunciation Guide

In the Igbo language, an 'M' or 'N' at the beginning of a word followed by a consonant is pronounced as in "mmmh.' *Ndom*, for instance, is pronounced *mmmh-dom*. Double consonants, not commonly found in English, such as 'gw,' 'ng,' 'kw,' 'nw,' and 'ny,' are best pronounced by splitting the consonant pair into two syllables. Thus, *'aqwu'* would be pronounced *"aaq-woo."* 'Kw' is pronounced as if it were a "Q."

GLOSSARY

Afiri-kpoto—a fruit containing immature or sterile seeds

Akatiko—Wily resourcefulness

Akisi—A colorful scarf

Ala Hentu!—Let the earth heave! Let there be earthquakes!

Ama nwanyi—a compound headed by a woman

Anya nlech-a nwa ite, ya foro kuwa!—All you can do to the defiant, little, boiling clay pot is stare at it. You dare not pick it up and smash it!

Awtu-aligh-li—an organ that makes a mockery of a man's virility

Diala—a true, native son

Di'm ezeh! Di'm omah! Di'm oga eweta!—My husband, the chief! My good husband! My husband, the go-getter!

Emegh-eme—an impossibility; that which ought not to happen

Enwegh isi nwegh odu—that which has neither head nor tail; something which cannot be comprehended or tackled

Etere—A broad, glossy leaf used for wrapping

Ewere-ewe—the practice of unauthorized "borrowing" from the community chest

Gadaga—a sliding gate

Garri—a starchy staple

Gbaa nu nfa!—Run helter skelter!

Huo-ra-nu Nwa-Beke-e otila!—Bend over and show the White man your bottoms!

Ihe n'adigh otu n'eme ya—An insurmountable problem

Ihie-ede—A ceremony celebrating a woman's farming success, admitting her to a title society

Ikwe maa'm onu ikpu, ma avora-gi ya nvuvo—(a line from one of the bawdy songs sung by women during a childbirth ceremony)—If you give me a good price for my thing, I will even comb the hair for you

Isi-ngidingi—the normally loose loincloth retied in a way that makes a person ready for a fight

Ivu anyigh ndanda—no load is ever too heavy for a horde of ants

Iweh, iweh, iweh nji anya iweh!—Anger! Anger! We're angry, angry!

Iwi agwo—a grand snake

Kama ji si, nku gwuu!—A resolve to use up every available resource rather than not accomplish an objective

Kilaki—Clerk

Kpuru-kpuru—Round and round, the sound of scurrying mice

Mara suru—a woman's outfit which includes a blouse

Mbara ezi—The common space usually enclosed by the houses on a compound

Mbichiri-ezi—head (usually the oldest man) of a compound

Ndom-misisi—A modern type of wife, of the type called Missus

Nki—Tattooed decorations

Nkotosi—Severe back-biting

Nnu-kwuru-nnu—Thousand-upon-thousand

Ntche—the bark of a tree used to make palm wine stronger

Nwa eleghe-le—something claimed and protected by the gods because it is otherwise helpless

Nwanyi ibem—My fellow woman—a name which betokens female solidarity

Nwa ohiri—a "phantom" child

Nyash—backside

Obasi ndi n'igwe—God in heaven

Ogbakwasa—a bonus or supernumerary reward

Okoro otu nkpuru amu, ke muna gi k'oleke?—Worthless man with only one nut in his testicle sac, what do I have to do with you?

Okpoko (ngbugbu)—a thick, dark vegetable soup without meat, fish, or condiments

Okpokoro futa, na nri eghela—a man whose sole function in life is to make sure that no food is left over in the bowls

Okpo-onuma—a big boil or abscess

Omugwo—pertaining to the period around childbirth

Onunu—A magical powder

Onuru vuru, anugh zia—(literally) someone who hears only "Pick it up!" but never hears "Put it down!"

Osu—a ritual slave

Ototo-o, nta muu-muu—a monster or bogey

Pagha-pagha-yeghe-yeghe—an impossible load which cannot be pushed, pulled, hefted or rolled

Sisi, toro—sixpence, threepence

Tukwuo-lia, utu-gbara—A woman who goes to live with a man when all the marriage customs have not been fulfilled is enslaved or mortgaged to a penis

Ukazi—A highly prized and delectable wild vegetable